W9-DAE-954

Praise for Michael J. Martinez and the Daedalus Series

The Daedalus Incident

"A true genre-bender. It mixes alchemy, quantum physics, and historical figures in ways you haven't seen before . . . adventurous, original, and a blast to read."

—*Tor.com*

"Genre bending often comes at great peril, but Martinez pulls it off with an assurance that makes all the pieces slot together perfectly."

—*BuzzFeed*, selected as one of "The 14 Greatest Science Fiction Books of the Year"

"A thoroughly enjoyable, swashbuckling romp through worlds in which I would happily spend more time."

—*Fantasy Faction*

"Martinez's debut is a triumph of genre-blending, as steampunk adventure merges with modern space opera. With a cast of superbly drawn characters, Martinez's title is a mesmerizing tale of two universes that briefly cross paths, leaving both worlds forever changed."

—*Library Journal* (starred review), included in "BestBooks 2013: SF/Fantasy" year-end wrap-up

The Enceladus Crisis

"Continues the first novel's mix of alchemy, intrigue, mystery, science fiction and high adventure . . . A follow up that manages to improve on the first in significant ways."

—*SF Signal*

"Blends 18th-century alchemy and 22nd-century interstellar travel, makes it all seem natural, and gives us a great adventure story to boot."

—Django Wexler, author of *The Thousand Names*

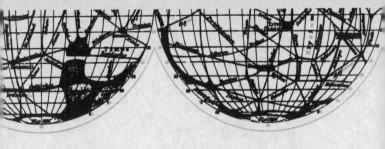

THE VENUSIAN
GAMBIT

Books by Michael J. Martinez

The Daedalus Incident
The Enceladus Crisis
The Venusian Gambit
The Gravity of the Affair (novella)

MJ-12: Inception (coming soon)

THE VENUSIAN
GAMBIT

BOOK THREE OF THE DAEDALUS SERIES

Michael J. Martinez

NIGHT SHADE BOOKS
NEW YORK

Night Shade books may be purchased in bulk at special discounts for sales promotion, corporate gifts, fund-raising, or educational purposes. Special editions can also be created to specifications. For details, contact the Special Sales Department, Night Shade Books, 307 West 36th Street, 11th Floor, New York, NY 10018 or info@skyhorse-publishing.com.

Night Shade Books® is a registered trademark of Skyhorse Publishing, Inc.®, a Delaware corporation.

Visit our website at www.nightshadebooks.com.

10 9 8 7 6 5 4 3 2 1

Library of Congress Cataloging-in-Publication Data is available on file.

Print ISBN: 978-1-59780-860-6
Ebook ISBN: 978-1-59780-825-5

Cover illustration by Lauren Saint-Onge
Cover art and design by Victoria Maderna and Federico Piatti
Interior layout and design by Amy Popovich

Printed in Canada

In memory of my mom.

PROLOGUE

4,122 B.C.

Mars will rise once more.

That is what the Martian told himself as he looked out over the cities of the Xan, laid before him in splendor, spread across the rings of mighty Xanath and trailing off into the distance of the Void, a riot of light and color circling the planet.

It was terrible beauty, a reminder of his failure, and the last view of this universe he would likely ever see.

The Martian—no longer a warlord, now a mere prisoner—turned away from the window in disgust. His accommodations now as a captive of the Xan were far more luxurious than the ones he'd chosen for himself as leader of the Martian people. His cell—for it *was* a cell despite its trappings—included a cushioned bed, a chair, books, even a device that would allow him to listen to the mewlings these Xan called "music." He did not use any of these. He did not wear the robes given to him. He sat and slept on the floor. He meditated. He was allowed two servants—those reptilian savages from the wilds of Venus—but he did not use them. The trappings remained untouched. Despite it all—the loss of his armies, his weapons, his very homeworld—Althotas of Mars remained singularly fixated on victory. No matter how long it took.

A soft melodic chime—damn these Xan and their soft sounds!—drew his attention to the door. It opened to reveal four Xan, hooded and armed, with the two little Venusian servants flanking them. In the seven Mars-years since Althotas had been imprisoned, he had seen the Xan transform before his very eyes. When he first arrived, his guards were true soldiers, armored and armed with projectile weapons capable of killing any creature on impact. Now, those who dared call themselves guards and soldiers wore voluminous layers of cloth. The weapons were now staves, tipped with a canny device that would shock and stun their targets, rendering them ineffective but alive.

It was laughable, this softness. Yet, Althotas knew, these creatures had beaten him. As much derision as he had for the Xan's newfound pacificity, he constantly reminded himself that somehow—*somehow*—they had beaten him. And perhaps it was his own people's martial ways that awakened the rage and determination necessary for the Xan to rise. Perhaps the Xan simply needed a suitable target before they unleashed their hidden barbarity—for barbarity it was. They had little sense of true honor in the throes of battle, and he expected none from them now.

"Althotas, the council has reached a determination," the lead Xan sang, its two mouths creating harmonies that sounded somber and excited all at once. "You are required to accompany us."

Althotas looked down at his clawed green hands and saw them clenching involuntarily. His very essence was that of a warrior. His first instinct was to rip these "guards" apart with his bare hands, to flee captivity, to rage through their cities and gather an army to him.

But there was no army. The Martians were as dead as their planet. And the Xan would not follow him. Not these Xan, at least. He could see from his perch the battles upon the rings, both near and far. As ironic as it seemed, in the aftermath of the great Martian-Xan war it was the Xan's pacifist political party that emerged victorious to lead the Xan into the future. The warrior caste was being hunted. The pacifists were now in charge.

Wordlessly, his body trembling with disciplined rage, Althotas walked through the door and down the carpeted hallway, his guards scurrying to keep up. Althotas knew the way to the Xan's so-called Temple of Justice. He had been going back and forth between his cell and the temple for many long days.

It was about time the damnable council had reached a determination. Althotas was a warrior of Mars, first and foremost, and a leader of his people. Sitting and waiting in captivity was anathema, much as a fish slowly, inexorably expired upon dry land. He would still watch closely to see if these soft Xan would provide him even a sliver of opportunity. But he knew, deep down, that they would take no chances. All he could hope for was death, honorable and painful, one that would allow him to show these creatures true greatness in the end.

Down stairways and through halls and salons, past gossiping clusters of Xan whispering harmonically amongst themselves, Althotas walked toward his fate. The smooth stone and glass of the Xan buildings were in stark contrast to the rough-hewn fortresses of Mars. The Xan reveled in their aesthetics, with ornamentation meant to show beauty and peace on nearly every surface. And yet there was no virtue in the looks he received from the Xan as he passed them, only fear and loathing. He returned these stares with a smile that showed his razor teeth, and reveled in the double standard of these people. Beauty and peace only lasted so long as he was not there to remind them of their own crimes.

Finally, he stormed toward the massive double-doors leading into the Temple of Justice's inner sanctum, pushing through them impatiently and striding into the chamber. The guards behind him immediately rushed forward, flanking him on either side, staves at the ready. He proceeded to the circle where all inquiry subjects stood, lit brightly while the rest of the temple was shrouded in complete blackness. There, around the area in which he had stood nigh daily for such long years, were a series of devices. Small boxes, connected by a cord, reeking of ozone…Althotas could practically taste the occult and alchemical power flowing through them.

The Xan had, apparently, come up with something new. Perhaps there would be new agonies, ones that would not shed blood. Would the pacifist Xan find the same pleasure in torturing their enemies that their war-obsessed brethren had? He did not break stride as he strode toward the circle. Without being prompted, he stepped over the ring of devices and into the circle. It was the same place where he stood and was tried for so many months. He could see the scratches in the floor where his foot-talons rested as he listened to the Xan's intolerable singing of justice and peace.

"Althotas," a voice boomed.

"I am here," the one-time warlord shouted, his voice a raspy buzz compared to the melodic Xan that had addressed him from the darkness. The cowards never showed themselves, not for all this time. It was, he was told, to show the unity of the Xan people in the face of injustice. Althotas knew it for what it was, however. They were trying to place themselves at a remove from their vengeance. They were afraid of what they had done to Phaeton, to Mars itself. They had wielded such immense force in the last days of the war—such destructive power indeed! They had razed verdant Mars into a red desert, and proud Phaeton, one-time colony of Mars, was now a million boulders, scattered around the Sun between Mars and Jupiter.

Of course they would distance themselves from that. Because they were as children. The Martians knew that life *was* conflict. And pain. And power.

Even if you lose.

"It is the finding of this council that you are indeed guilty of numerous war crimes. You have broken the laws governing conflict between individuals, conflict between nations and conflict between worlds," the disembodied Xan voice sang.

"These are your laws, not mine," Althotas hissed. "the conduct of our war was done in accordance with the highest honor of my people. So pass your sentence and be done with it."

"There is more," the Xan continued. "Recent inquiries have shown that you are also guilty of violating the laws governing alchemical practice, occult practice and scientific inquiry."

A second spotlight flared to life from above, shining down upon a stone altar in the center of the room. There, Althotas saw two very familiar items—a green stone slab and a black-covered book.

"You have used these items to draw the souls from your people and place them in the bodies of others. This plague has been placed upon the lizard creatures of the second world and the ape creatures of the third world, but also upon the Xan themselves," the voice said. "Dozens of souls. Hundreds."

"It is well that you have figured this out, for you know full well there is nothing to be done about it," Althotas hissed. "These souls will travel from life to life, down through the centuries, until such time as you are forgotten, and the spirit of my people will rise again in new form."

"No," the voice sang with notes of sadness, tempered with an undercurrent of steel. "We have harvested these souls. We have tracked them down and captured them, bringing them back to our Pool of Souls, so that they may learn peace amongst others of our kind."

Althotas hung his head, but smiled inwardly. The ritual was massive—more massive than they had suspected. It would be impossible for them to capture every soul. There would be enough for them to one day rally, when the time was right.

"You have the blood of the lizard and ape people upon your hands, then, along with your own kind," Althotas said. "So much for your peace."

"Peace is larger than any one life, Althotas," the voice said, tiredly.

"So is vengeance."

"Vengeance is not our way," the voice replied. "The lives taken to free the souls trapped in other forms was a mercy. We will hide these cursed objects you used for your working, so that they may not be used again. The apes and lizards will not be polluted with your ways. They shall grow independently, and we have agreed to remove ourselves from them as well.

"And for your crimes," the voice continued, sounding notes of triumph and determination, "*you* will be removed from all of us."

Althotas smiled once more. "Then kill me and be done with it. I tire of your vapid songs."

The boxes at the Martian's feet began to hum, and lights began to glow upon them.

"You will not be slain."

It took several moments for these song-words to sink into Althotas' mind. "So how, then, do you propose to 'remove me,' Xan?" he spat. "You know that I will struggle to escape from any prison you place upon me. Or I shall simply take my own life to be rid of you."

"You will do neither. We have created a special prison to remove you not from society, or from the sight of other creatures, but from this very dimension."

As the hum increased in pitch and intensity, Althotas noticed a spot of darkness starting to form before him. It seemed as there was a rip in the very air of the chamber itself, a swirling eddy in reality itself that sucked all light and life from around itself. As it grew, the warlord thought he saw the blackness move within the fissure. In that moment, with all his occult and alchemical knowledge, Althotas came to a conclusion that shook him to his core—he would be removed from reality itself, and placed in a prison where no light, no sound, no sense of *being* would be permitted. It would be no less than his own personal hell. Althotas could sense the very fabric of reality fraying as the blackness grew. "You have no idea the powers you tamper with!" Althotas shouted. "Complete your working, you cowards, and be damned for it! You fools would tear apart your world to be rid of me, so do it! You are like children with fire, and you will burn for it someday. Know that you should have simply spilled my blood and be done with it, for so long as I live, in whatever place you send me—*I will find a way out.*"

The boxes began to glow with a bright, white light and the rift before Althotas grew wider…blacker…as if it were about to swallow everything and extinguish all joy and happiness from the universe.

But Althotas had not known joy or happiness for many years.

With a scream, he leapt into the rift.

And the universe shuddered.

June 20, 1803

"Stop tugging at it, Tom, or I swear I shall hang you by it!"

Sir Thomas Weatherby, Knight of the Bath, former captain of HMS *Fortitude* and newly promoted Rear Admiral of the Blue in His Majesty's Royal Navy, clenched his fists at his side while his longtime friend, Dr. Andrew Finch, adjusted his cravat. There was, in Weatherby's opinion, nothing more useless than a cravat, and should he rise to such a rank in the service where he might effectively do so, he planned to order them out of existence.

Yet even Finch's clumsy efforts at sartorial improvement were not enough to dent Weatherby's overall excellent mood. "Have you seen her yet today?" Weatherby asked.

Finch smiled, finally giving up on Weatherby's cravat for the moment. "She looks quite lovely, as you very well know," he replied quietly. "One does not become a legendary alchemist without using a bit of working on one's appearance, you know."

"She does not need it," Weatherby said. "She never has."

"Well, you could use a bit, old man," Finch said. "I keep offering, as I know she has, but you refuse it."

Weatherby smiled back at this old jibe. He knew of the gray in his brown hair, the lines upon his face drawn by wind and weather, Sun-motes and Void-storm. The scar upon his face more than two decades old, and other, fresher, nicks and cuts. Yet his eyes shone clear, as sharp as the day he became a midshipman, and he remained strong and healthy by whatever grace he had earned in the service of His Majesty's Navy.

Of course, he wouldn't be surprised if his love had been slipping some alchemical concoctions in his tea to keep him hale. But not his looks.

"She has never offered, Doctor. Perhaps she enjoys my countenance perfectly well as it is. Besides," he added, casting a weather eye upon his old friend, "you're looking a bit haggard yourself. Your researches of late are all too consuming. It took my very wedding to pry you from your labs!" And indeed, Finch looked altogether wan and pale, though still strong and quick of step. His sandy blond hair was receding and graying as well, and there had been ever-present circles under his eyes of late.

Finch favored his old friend with a wink. "I dare say your wedding, old man, is perhaps the finest miracle anyone might have wrought, so of course I had to see it. And it's about bloody time."

A few steps away, Brownlow North, Bishop of Winchester, cleared his throat, drawing their attention. "I do believe we are ready, Sir Thomas. Shall we?"

Weatherby grinned, shot a look at Finch, and exhaled. "Most certainly, my Lord Bishop. Thank you."

The bishop nodded toward the back of Portsmouth's Church of St. Thomas of Canterbury. And the dowager Countess St. Germain began her walk, smiling radiantly.

Finch's indiscreet comments to whether the former Anne Baker used alchemical means to provide her with the bloom of youth, as many women with means had begun to do as alchemy became more prevalent, may certainly have been true. Yet Weatherby did not care one way or the other, for he knew he would always see her through the eyes of a nervous 18-year-old second lieutenant who had fallen hard for the brilliant, determined young woman with a knack for alchemy.

"You know, Tom," Finch whispered, "first love rarely gets a second chance. Do try not to foul it up."

Weatherby turned quickly toward his friend, only to see the impish smile he'd come to know well over the years, and the sparkle in his eye despite his wan countenance. "I think I can manage, Finch. I'll simply avoid repeating your mistakes in affairs of the heart."

Lady Anne reached the altar in quick time despite the peach-colored dress that seemed to envelop her. She was flanked by her son, Philip the Count St. Germain, and Weatherby's daughter Elizabeth. Both Weatherby and Anne had married after they drifted apart, and they were both widowed. Second chances indeed.

Weatherby took a moment to marvel at both children, now all but grown. Philip had recently been accepted to read alchemy at Trinity College, Oxford, while the young Elizabeth hoped to follow in a few short years, as her intensive readings and studies of the Xan and Venus had already impressed some of the foremost academics of the day. Even for a bookish girl like Elizabeth, reading at Oxford would've been impossible but a few short years ago. But when your future stepmother was one of the foremost alchemists in the Known Worlds—and a woman possessing of a formidable personality besides—doors could open. If there was a way for Elizabeth to study at a university such as Oxford, Weatherby had no doubt that his soon-to-be wife would find it.

Then Weatherby's gaze fell back upon Anne, and all other thoughts were lost. Amazing how she could still do that to him.

Weatherby took Anne's hand and kissed it, receiving a brilliant smile in return. Her blonde hair shimmered in the morning light streaming through the church's windows, accented by the sparkling motes she had created and placed into her tresses that morning. She looked utterly ethereal.

Another cough from Bishop North brought their attention to the matter at hand. "Dearly beloved," he began, "we are gathered together here in the sight of God, and in the face of this congregation, to join together this Man and this Woman in holy Matrimony; which is an honorable estate, instituted of God in the time of man's innocency, signifying unto us the mystical union that is betwixt Christ and his Church; which holy estate Christ adorned..."

Weatherby let the good bishop speak on, not heeding the words, instead holding the hands of the woman he loved for so long. Finch was quite right; there were rarely second chances at first love. To think that she had harbored such feelings for him as well was a revelation. Had the circumstances been different upon their second meeting, Weatherby would've married her sooner.

As it was, four years seemed appropriate, given the nature of their reunion, which involved the need to hunt down and kill her then-husband, the Count St. Germain, who'd been trying to unleash a new alien hell upon the Known Worlds. Even in the most thorough works of etiquette, such circumstances were wholly unheard of.

"Therefore if any man can show any just cause why they may not lawfully be joined together, let him now speak, or else hereafter forever hold his peace."

The following silence drew Weatherby and Anne away from each other, turning and smiling toward the small congregation invited to this most intimate affair. A handful of senior officers and their wives, notable alchemists, some of London's more scandalously intelligent women—it was an eclectic mix of sailors and society, academics and rebels. And they were friends, most importantly. Even Sir James Morrow, well and truly retired for the first time in his life, came down from Cambridgeshire for the festivities.

Suddenly, from outside the church doors, they heard a faint scream.

Weatherby looked to Anne, who looked back at him with equal measures of bewilderment, annoyance and amusement. Surely it was a bit early in the day for revelries, but Portsmouth was indeed a major port for the Royal Navy, and revelries for men long at sea knew no clocks.

It was upon the second scream, and the third, that the murmuring of the crowd began.

At this juncture, the doors at the rear of the church burst open, and a young man wearing the uniform of a midshipman ran through, racing up the aisle to the gasps of all in attendance.

Weatherby's first thought was the sword at his side. Shedding blood in a church was bad form, of course, but one does what one must.

"Admiral!" the boy panted. "Urgent message from the Admiralty, sir! Portsmouth is under attack! You must…" The boy slowed to a walk, his face turning the color of beets, as realization of the ceremony he'd burst into dawned upon him.

"Under attack?" Weatherby asked, motioning the young midshipman forward so that he might deliver the message upon the paper clutched in his hand. "Surely not! Would not our pickets have detected an incoming fleet early on?"

The boy once again found his feet and ran up to the admiral, surrendering his papers. Weatherby snatched it up and began scanning it quickly. He quickly ran pale. "Under the channel…dear God."

He looked up at the crowd assembled for what was to be a joyous day. "I am afraid it is true. Portsmouth is currently under attack by a French invasion. Please take your carriages and flee immediately. Head north, either for Oxford or Bristol. Midshipman, escort these people to their carriages and horses, if you please, and get them on their way with all due haste."

The boy ran back down the aisle, but the crowd simply gaped at Weatherby, stunned and uncomprehending.

"Damn you all, go!" Weatherby roared. "The French are upon our very shores!"

Weatherby's outburst brought the crowd to its feet and immediately they made for the doors in a perfect rush and panic. Elizabeth and Philip stood close by their parents, unsure as to what else they might do, while Finch stood resolutely by Weatherby's side.

And Sir James Morrow remained as well, third bench upon the right side, his weathered hands pulling him upright. "I suggest you get on with it, Tom," he said gently. "We haven't much time."

Weatherby shook his head sadly before turning back to the bishop with eyes wide and visage most grim. "My

Lord Bishop, we will have to delay our ceremony under the circumstances."

The clergyman, a wiry and spry man in his early sixties, was understandably taken aback. "Excuse me, my Lord Admiral?" And when Weatherby looked upon Anne, her face bore great surprise—and restrained fury.

Weatherby squeezed Anne's hand. "I am afraid, my love, we must away before it is too late."

To Weatherby's very great surprise, Anne pulled him back as he made to leave. "I have waited far too long for this, and will not wait a moment longer. My Lord Bishop, how quickly can you marry us?"

Bishop North was, by this point, completely at a loss. "I suppose but a minute or two, my lord."

"Very well," Weatherby said. "Pronounce it quickly, then! Finch, keep watch."

The good bishop began quickly flipping through his prayer book, reciting the words necessary to join the couple before him in matrimony, even as the tumult outside began to increase. Finch stood in the rear of the church, his head poked through the door, joined by a half dozen officers, armed with naught but swords, who had stayed to protect the couple during the now abbreviated ceremony.

"Do you, Thomas, take this woman, Anne, to be your lawfully wedded wife, to have…" The bishop trailed off as Weatherby arched an eyebrow. "Do you, sir?" the bishop stammered.

He turned and gave Anne a soft, sad smile. "I most certainly do."

"And do you, Anne, take this man, Thomas, to be your lawfully wedded husband?"

Tears flowed gently down her cheeks as Anne squeezed Weatherby's hand. "I do indeed."

Suddenly, Finch slammed the door of the church shut and began shoving one of the nearby wooden benches in front of it. "They're coming!" he shouted.

Weatherby turned back to the ashen-faced bishop. "Now, if you please, my Lord."

The bishop slammed his book shut. "I now pronounce you man and wife. You may kiss the bride." And with that, the clergyman dashed toward the church's sacristy.

Weatherby and Anne looked to one another. "We really have horrible timing," she said. "But we are married."

"Not yet," Weatherby said—just before he leaned down and gave her the kiss that was more than two decades late.

Then the doors burst open.

Anne gasped as a squadron of French soldiers marched into the church, bayonets at the ready. The fact that their blue and red uniforms were completely soaked was quite secondary to the fact that the soldiers themselves were... dead.

The soldiers' skin was stretched thin across their skeletons, so much so that there were tiny tears that exposed white bone to open air. Their lips were peeled back from their teeth, their noses were shrunken, and their eyes were gray and filmy. Under their bicorn hats, the revenants' hair was limp and stringy. And even from the altar, they could all smell something of the charnel house when the troops entered.

Yet they marched effectively—indeed, almost as if they were connected by invisible clockworks. And their bayonets certainly looked sharp and ready.

"Finch!" Weatherby shouted as he drew his sword. "Are these...?"

"Revenants! Just as we feared!" the alchemist replied as he rushed back to the altar, his blade already drawn. Finch was one of the very few at the Admiralty who thought it possible the French may have gleaned enough alchemical knowledge from Napoleon's adventures in Egypt five years prior to create mindless but effective soldiers from the corpses of the dead.

The officers who remained engaged the French squadron with zeal, blocking the center aisle of the church in order to allow the admiral and his bride to escape. Anne quickly gathered Philip and Elizabeth to her and made for the back of the church, following in the footsteps of the bishop.

Weatherby and Finch followed, swords at the ready, even as the cries and clashes of steel rang through the hallowed building.

And that's when Weatherby saw his old captain and mentor, Morrow, amongst the blue-coated officers, a blade drawn from the old man's walking stick.

"James!" Weatherby shouted. "There are too many!"

The old captain turned and favored Weatherby with a sad smile. "When has that stopped us, Tom? Go! I will take command here." He then turned to the officers, one of whom had already fallen to the French bayonets. "Men of the Navy! Defend your admiral!"

And with that, Morrow dove in to the fray, while the others gave a rallying cry and redoubled their efforts.

"No!" Weatherby cried.

He moved to join his friend and mentor, but Finch grabbed his arm and pulled him back. "Tom, no," Finch said quietly, but urgently. "We must fly. Allow James his choice."

Choking back tears, Weatherby watched as Morrow deftly parried the first attacker and stabbed the revenant in the heart. Yet while the revenant staggered, the creature nonetheless took the butt of its rifle and smashed it into the side of Morrow's head.

The old man fell wordlessly. The other officers continued to fight, but only one managed to fell his opponent, cutting the revenant's head clean from its shoulders.

Weatherby quickly slammed the door of the sacristy shut, then fled with his wife and family out the back of the church, and into a world he could never have imagined.

CHAPTER 1

December 9, 2134

The man behind the antique wooden desk looked exhausted and overwhelmed. His gray hair, normally coiffed to perfection, was slightly shaggy looking now. The bags under his eyes weighed on his usually clear, dark, lean face, and the blood-shot eyes themselves spoke of a lack of sleep and the anticipation of more sleepless nights to come. His shirt was rumpled, his tie hanging loosely. The holomonitor in front of him was strewn with folders and documents, videos and messages. His inbox was full of somber condolences, sober good wishes. He scanned the holograms blankly, eyes darting, not seeming to know which specks of data should come first.

Maj. Gen. Maria Diaz felt bad for him. Historically, there weren't that many vice presidents called upon to succeed their running mates—certainly none so abruptly as Jackson Weathers. But Diaz figured President Linda Fernandez hadn't really planned on the cardiac arrest that killed her five hours ago.

And now President Weathers was sitting at the desk in the Oval Office—a desk made from the timbers of the 19th century Arctic explorer HMS *Resolute*, and a gift from Queen Victoria some 250 years past. Given what she was about to disclose, she found the desk oddly fitting.

"General...Diaz, isn't it?" Weathers said, running a hand over his face. "Didn't expect to see you here. You still with JSC?"

Diaz stood at attention and gave Weathers a salute. "Yes, Mr. President. Executive director of Project DAEDALUS."

She could see the new president search his memories for a moment while his eyes gave Diaz the once-over. He lingered a bit too long over the curves of her uniform—for a woman pushing sixty, Diaz was still in excellent shape. And

Weathers' reputation for the wandering eye, something of a throwback to late 20th century presidents, was apparently well deserved. Diaz smiled slightly. Let him try. Her wife was a sculptural welder and, if anything, was in better shape than the general. President or not, he'd be pummeled to paste.

Weathers finally shrugged. "I don't remember that project. What is it?"

"You weren't cleared for it until today, Mr. President. DAEDALUS is the Dimensional And Extraterrestrial Defense, Analysis & Logistical Unified Services," Diaz said. She started counting the seconds until Weathers' mind parsed the legalese of the acronym. To his credit, she only got to five.

"Bullshit," he said, his tone one of both trepidation and resignation. "Can't be."

"Sorry, sir. It's true. I've put all the background files, reports and videos on your secure server. We need your approval for something that's pretty critical right now, so if it's all right with you, I'm going to give you the five-minute version before we get to the latest," Diaz said.

Weathers nodded, and off she went, having given the same précis at least two dozen times to other top military and civilian leaders in the U.S. and the European Union, the two governmental partners in JSC's efforts to explore space. She felt her spiel was good at getting her audiences through anger and denial pretty quickly, though nobody seemed to have a perfect handle on acceptance. Hell, she still needed work on that now and then.

"In 2132, there was an extradimensional incursion on the planet Mars," Diaz began. "This other dimension, the one that peeked through, is a mirror of our world in the year 1779, with a few key differences. Over there, folks use a process they believe to be 'alchemy' to sail between worlds in wooden sailing ships, and to colonize said worlds, which apparently are quite different from those in our own Solar System in terms of survivability. Yes, there are aliens there too—inhabitants of their very different versions of Venus and Saturn. The dimensional overlap was brought about by an alien in that dimension who had been imprisoned for past crimes against the race of aliens living on Saturn. It took the combined efforts of some of their people—the crew of the English frigate HMS *Daedalus*—and my team at McAuliffe Base to seal the dimensional rift, which we did."

Weathers leaned back in his seat, eyes wide, and didn't speak for a while as he flipped between reports and images Diaz had sent to his holoprojector. He lingered on the images and vids in particular—a frigate crashed on Mars, a massive alien beast tearing into a bunch of 18th century sailors. Finally, he cleared the images and turned back to Diaz with a haunted look on his face. "There's a lot more to this story, isn't there, General?"

"Yes, sir. The complete files are on your server, sir."

"And since you're just skirting past all that, I assume we have something even *more* pressing?" the President said. "God help me. Skip to that part."

Diaz nodded. At least he wasn't staring at her uniform anymore. "Little less than six months ago, as you'll recall, the JSC ship *Armstrong* reached the Saturn system, the first manned expedition there. You'll also recall the Chinese got there at the same time."

"I remember," Weathers said. "The Chinese played chicken with our ship, then ended up conducting some kind of mining experiment that ended up destroying one of Saturn's moons, right? What was that moon's name again?"

"Enceladus," Diaz said. "And the Chinese didn't blow it up. One of ours did."

"And I suppose I wasn't cleared for *that* tidbit because… aliens?"

"Yes, Mr. President. We have reason to believe that two of the *Armstrong* crew, along with the lone Chinese survivor, were somehow infected by an extradimensional alien intelligence related to the incursion on Mars. We also believe that there were primitive lifeforms in the oceans under Enceladus' ice which served as the infection vector, and that the moon's destruction freed those lifeforms. Subsequently, the Chinese ship flew through the moon's debris field, then turned and headed back for Earth. Our concern is that they picked up several of these alien entities."

"How primitive are they?" Weathers asked.

"Nothing more complex than viruses, but you know what happens when you catch a virus," Diaz said. "Sir, we currently theorize that these primitive lifeforms may possess extradimensional properties, allowing them to serve as carriers for cross-dimensional infection and personality displacement— possession, if you will. We think that's what happened to our people, and we're obviously concerned that the Chinese ship, the *Tienlong*, is bringing more of those bugs back to Earth."

"And why not just blow it to hell and back?" Weathers said, sounding a bit irked. "If it's an alien invasion force, even if it is goddamn microbes, I think we're justified, don't you?"

That's exactly what President Hernandez said four months ago, Diaz thought. "I appreciate the direct approach, sir, but our people believe that if the lifeforms could survive for thousands of years under the ice on Enceladus, blowing them up could very well just spread them around the rest of the Solar System. The Earth, Moon, even Mars could end up getting showered with them. All it seems to take is one of them to make contact, and we're concerned they might serve as a vector to bring in others once infection and personality displacement takes effect. The possession of the Chinese, in particular, we believe may have occurred prior to their departure for Saturn via a different source."

Weathers' face wrinkled at this. "Another vector?"

"There's been at least one recorded instance of a cross-dimensional rift being re-opened here on Earth, by a former corporate sponsor of McAuliffe Base on Mars. That rift nearly brought other things, stranger things, into our world. That project used a pre-existing artifact that, we believe, had an extra-dimensional counterpart that allowed for infection of the Chinese officer to take place prior to his departure for Saturn. Long story short, we need to study every aspect of this mess in order to figure out how best to defeat the next incursion."

Weathers flipped through the reader embedded into the ancient wood of his desk, marveling at the images and details before him. Images of a sailing ship in a canal on Mars. A journal that wrote itself. Carvings found in a cave on Saturn's moon Titan. The video of Enceladus dissolving into a massive cloud of ice crystals and leaving a small rocky core behind. And schematics of a particle collider buried in the sands of Egypt, which created a second rift between worlds.

"How long until *Tienlong* arrives?" the president asked finally.

"Five weeks. We're already working on contingency plans. You have write-ups in there already. We'll need your approval for a few of them in the next few days, sir. The biggest one, though, would be to make an official request to the Chinese government, directly, that we be allowed to board *Tienlong* before she makes Earth orbit. We need to capture that ship."

Weathers frowned. "Why do you need me to do it? Surely there are processes in place for salvage or something like that."

"There are, sir, but we would prefer this request be made off the record, and at the highest level, to impress upon the Chinese the need to cooperate," Diaz said.

"So you need me to be the heavy and strong-arm the premier."

Diaz smiled. "Exactly, sir."

"Fine," Weathers said absently as he moved the folders on his holomonitor to a list labeled TOP PRIORITY. "So what happened to *Armstrong* in all this?"

Diaz sighed quietly. "She's coming in hot, right behind *Tienlong*. I know her acting skipper. She's…very motivated to see this through, sir, whatever happens."

Stars surrounded Shaila Jain, shining upon her from every direction. The Milky Way stretched across the blackness of space, a bold highway of light leading off beyond vision itself. It was gorgeous.

She never felt more alone in her life.

Lt. Cmdr. Shaila Jain, RN, JSC, acting captain of the JSCS *Armstrong*, sat in the cockpit of her state-of-the-art ship, the room around her transformed via virtual-reality glasses into the starscape before her. Occasionally, the view would be interrupted by a graphic or text and accompanied by a subtle chime, alerting her to some routine shift in the ship's functioning, or to the presence of yet another message from Earth, wondering if and when she would talk to anyone ever again.

She wasn't sure she ever would.

Five months ago, she had been on top of the world—a new world, in fact. The first person to set foot upon Enceladus, the mysterious ice moon of Saturn. They were there to search for life—evidence of life beyond Earth itself. There wasn't any on Mars. The Jovian moon Europa was being stubborn. Enceladus, with its under-ice lake, warmed by the push-pull of Saturn's gravity, was humanity's best, last hope for finding neighbors.

The neighbors found them instead.

Shaila wasn't supposed to be the first person on Enceladus. She led the landing team, but they had drawn straws, and the honor had gone to Stephane Durand, a French planetologist and her boyfriend and lover of two years. They had been together at McAuliffe Base on Mars. They fought to save two dimensions from an inexplicable, ancient evil. They had become inseparable. And when it came time for Stephane to make history, he had physically picked her up off the landing craft and, in Enceladus' extremely low gravity, tossed her over the side in his place.

How many men have given the woman they loved an entire world?

She smiled sadly at the thought. Smiling was ever-so-slightly easier now, after five months. She would occasionally think of seeing her family on Earth, or the simple delights of a blue sky or a beach. She would smile. And then the guilt and anger over what happened would erase that smile quickly, and she would lock it all down inside and focus on the work again.

She reminded herself daily that Stephane wasn't there anymore. Something had gotten to him on Enceladus, and she worked hard to figure out how and why. She reviewed all the videos and records, and tracked down the source. On their first landing, they had been in the path of a cry-ovolcanic ejection– a cold-water geyser. They got wet. And the microbial lifeforms believed to be in the water must've gotten on them. She remembered Stephane in the lander after their historic mission, heading back to *Armstrong*. He took off his helmet and, reflexively, wiped his gauntleted hand across his face.

Then he complained of the taste of the water covering him.

That's how it got him. That's why he wasn't there—both physically on the ship, and present in his own mind. Something had taken possession. And Shaila knew—without more than circumstance and conjecture, she nonetheless *knew*—that it was tied to what happened on Mars two and a half years ago.

Back then, they defeated that alien—some horrible, monstrous thing calling itself Althotas. And she was hell-bound and determined to defeat whatever possessed Stephane, whatever made him board the Chinese ship, whatever made him kill *Armstrong*'s captain, U.S. Marine Col. Mark Nilssen.

Whatever made him plant the explosive charges that reduced Enceladus to its tiny, rocky core, freeing thousands—maybe millions—of similar little lifeforms, just like the one that possessed him.

Another chime sounded in her ear, and a small window popped up to her right, next to the constellation Taurus. "DAILY REMINDER: VIDEO TO STEPHANE."

Shaila chased the text away with a wave of her hand. She wasn't in the mood. There were a lot of days where she wasn't. But…

"Jain to Archie, come in," she called over the ship's comm.

A few moments went by before the response came. "You really need to let me relieve you up there for a while," Dean

Archibald replied in his maddeningly paternal old-man drawl. "And you really should eat something today, young lady."

How long have I been in here? she wondered. She idly called up the holocam to catch an image of herself, and was mildly surprised at the result. She didn't look too bad—her military training prompted her to stick to a decent exercise and hygiene regiment. Yet the dark circles under her eyes were impressive, reminding her of the black stuff American football players used to cut down glare and intimidate opponents. Shaila's skin, usually the color of café au lait, seemed sallow and wan. "Roger that. You can relieve me at next watch," she said. "Going to swing the dish to target *Tienlong* and send a packet. You have yours ready?"

"It's on my server, the usual place. Recorded it a while ago," the old engineer replied. "And I'll see you in three hours to kick your ass out of there. Out."

Shaila and Archie were the only surviving in-place members of the *Armstrong* crew. Nilssen was killed when he went to investigate a distress call from *Tienlong*, the rival Chinese ship that drove them off course from Titan, prompting their landing on Enceladus instead. The ship's biologist and medic, Maria Conti, was on board *Tienlong* now, also possessed. The mission's corporate sponsor, Elizabeth Hall, died on Titan.

The Chinese had been less fortunate. The DAEDALUS task force investigators believed that one of the Chinese may have been infected prior to leaving Earth, thanks to a minute space-time rift in Egypt, in the ruins of an ancient temple in the Libyan desert town of Siwa. The guy had gone to play tourist there prior to leaving. He may have infected others en route to Saturn. They didn't know the details yet. But in the end, of the six Chinese crewmen aboard *Tienlong*, only one remained alive, and he was aiding Stephane and Conti. Four were brutally murdered by their fellow crewmen, and Shaila watched in horror as the fifth took his own life by putting a laser drill to his head on the surface of Titan.

The image of that suicide still haunted her, when she wasn't thinking of Stephane.

"Locate *Tienlong*," Shaila told the ship's computer. A moment later, a red dot appeared in front of her, along-side a window showing as much of that ship's status as the computer had handy, mostly course and speed. *Armstrong* was gaining on her. They'd enter Earth orbit mere minutes apart, even though Shaila's ship had been delayed more than a week due to engine problems. They had burned salt-laden Enceladan water in order to respond to the *Tienlong*'s original distress call, and Archie had needed the time to clean up the mess the solids had made inside the engines.

Shaila locked *Armstrong*'s communications array on Tienlong. There was no way of knowing whether a laser comm would work, so Shaila had to rely on old-fashioned radio for these little exercises. That was fine. She could still focus the call somewhat, and hope that she wasn't appearing on every holovision set in eastern Europe or something.

"Record vidmail message and stream to target," Shaila said. The computer obliged within microseconds.

She cleared her throat, straightened up, and forced a smile as she began.

"Hello again, Stephane. I'm still on your tail, of course, and we're still gaining on you. I know Archie's trying to find a way to get us over the hump so we can intercept you before you make Earth orbit. If anyone can do it, he can. He says hi, by the way. He told me to say that. Funny, isn't it.

"I'm going to keep this short today, because I'm really tired and really fucking pissed at you, and at the world, and at the strange things that are doing this to you and to us. You know, I liked being an 'us.' For the first time ever, I actually wanted to be part of another person's life like that. I…yeah. Anyway, I'm still here. I'm coming to get you. Keep fighting. I love you."

Shaila stopped and waved the recording closed as she fought back tears. *Every goddamn time.* She plucked Archie's vidmail from his folder and sent it along as well.

Shaila had ordered him to send vidmails to Conti, just as she'd been sending them to Stephane.

Every day. Without fail.

For the past 159 days. It was the only thing she could do to prevent herself from going crazy sitting around waiting.

There had been no response.

"What do you mean there's been no response?" Harry Yu asked crossly, running a hand through his otherwise immaculate black hair. "You've been setting this up for months now, and there's been nothing from *Tienlong* at all?"

Harry paced inside a small office inside a nondescript office park on the outskirts of Kabul, Afghanistan. A century ago, the country emerged from civil war and sectarian strife to become a high-quality corporate safe haven; in exchange for regular "taxes" and outright bribes, businesses could do whatever they wanted in Kabul, no questions asked, no regulations enforced. A lot of financials and biotechs had outposts here, in very similar, un-logoed office parks.

But Harry Yu wasn't working for the congloms anymore. The former Total Suez and Billiton MinMetals executive, once a rising star in the corporate world, was on the lam, wanted for questioning by Interpol, the Egyptian police force and—most importantly—Project DAEDALUS.

Harry didn't let it show; at least, that's what he tried telling himself. He still wore the finest clothes he could afford, and with the terras he'd stashed in various accounts around the world, he could still look good. Today was a grey suit and white shirt, the only nod to the weather and location was the lack of necktie. He always felt clothes helped project authority.

Whether or not he had any authority left was an open question. Most days, his "team" seemed to be humoring him.

"Your conventional signaling won't work, Harry," Evan Greene replied with the hint of a smile. "That's why we've been working on the dimensional phase communications here, which is why we replicated Yuna Hiyashi's Mars experiment in the desert outside town. That's the only way we've been able to reach them before."

Them. The folks from the other side. Extradimensional aliens. Martians, to be specific.

Harry saw Greene trade a very pointed look with his companion, former U.S. Marine Capt. Margaret Huntington. Both Greene and Huntington had been part of Maria Diaz' DAEDALUS team over the summer when they turned up and ruined Harry's attempt to replicate the rift created on Mars two years prior.

Discovering a whole new universe of worlds was a monumental moment in human history, and Harry Yu would have done anything to be the man to capitalize on it. And he'd gotten so close.

Yet Harry's experiment in the Egyptian desert was—well, it wasn't a failure, was it? A portal was opened. How could he have known that there were some seriously fucked-up creatures on the other side? If Maria had just given him more time, he could've replicated the rift, brought in some heavy artillery from G48 or Unity-Halliburton, taken care of things. He didn't want to go in shooting, of course, but there were worlds full of resources—and alchemy!—that were going unexploited.

But the portal wasn't stable. He didn't have enough time.

After that, Diaz shut him down and took over his worksite, his company disowned him, and he was busy getting drunk-as-fuck under the radar in Dubai when Greene—who had secretly been on Harry's payroll—and Huntington walked up clear as day and convinced him to try again. The thing was, he thought Greene and Huntington were buried under the rubble after his particle collider blew the hell up. And Greene never told him he'd recruited Huntington.

But since then…well, it had been a weird trip.

First off, Harry didn't know this Huntington woman in the slightest, but he knew Greene—and there were days Harry felt that the guy wearing Greene's face wasn't Greene.

Greene was funny, for one, and cocky as hell and downright charismatic; the scientist used to host educational holovision shows before going to work for Diaz and, later, Harry. But lately, Greene was none of those things. Sure, he still had his trade mark mane of silvery hair, his bright teeth and holovision-ready looks. But he had some nervous tics to him, drumming fingers and the occasional twitch, and a near omnipresent thin sheen of sweat on his forehead, even in the air-conditioned offices. To Harry, Greene seemed… stretched. Thinned out, somehow.

And from what Harry knew of U.S. Marines, the woman before him now was far less disciplined, cool and detached. There was a feral fervor about her that made "unnerving" seem like a garden party in comparison. The fact that she was physically ripped and nominally pretty was even more disconcerting.

When Harry finally confronted Greene about his survival, the scientist said he'd been in contact with the aliens from the other side—just as Martian scientist/astronaut Yuna Hiyashi had been two years ago on Mars. Greene said he and Huntington had managed to avoid the worst of the building collapse in Siwa and, armed with new knowledge, were working to reestablish contact with the other side to re-open the portal that had flared wide and slammed shut in the temple below the Siwa oasis.

But they seemed to be keeping Harry very much in the dark. And that wouldn't do.

"And you've been in contact?" Harry pressed.

Greene and Huntington kept working away on their rented holostations. "That's right, Harry," Greene said coolly. "Not often, not every day, but enough. Soon, we'll have enough resources available to us to rebuild what you did in Egypt, but better. Bigger. In the meantime, the dimensional phase communicators will help both *Tienlong* and ourselves better manage the entities aboard that ship so that they can be put to use in opening a new portal when they arrive."

Huntington smiled as she worked, a predatory expression that sent a shiver down Harry's spine and, for the thousandth time, made him question just what the hell he was doing with these two.

But there were no alternatives. Wanted by the authorities and running low on even his extensive lines of untraceable credit, he'd hitched his wagon to the notion that Greene and Huntington could reopen the portal between worlds, stabilize it and make it so that resources and people could be safely transported from one to the other.

In business, the only way to correct a mistake is to achieve an exponentially bigger gain. And opening up an entire universe worth of new markets certainly qualified.

"All right," Harry said. "But we only have a few months left before my lines of credit run out. After that, all this gets shut down."

"It won't get shut down," Huntington said quietly. It was the first time she had spoken within earshot of Harry in a month.

"See that it doesn't," Harry snapped, grabbing his coat. "I have to go see about making another tax payment to the local governor. Hoping I can get the price down. No-questions-asked is harder to do these days."

Greene and Huntington didn't bother to respond. And in that moment, not for the first time, Harry wondered just who was working for whom.

He left the little office and headed out into the cool Afghan afternoon. He didn't really care how it played out now, he reminded himself.

It only mattered who was in charge at the end.

He was distracted by a text, which conveniently popped up on the inside of his sunglasses. It came via an unlisted account on a black corporate network—one that even government stooges couldn't hack.

The message read simply: "I know what you're up to. You can do better than Kabul. I can help. I want in."

Harry raised an eyebrow as he got into his car, which dutifully transferred the message onto the windshield. These sorts of messages, while not an everyday thing, were part and parcel of modern corporate life. Some people made a living being anonymous angel investors for questionable yet potentially profitable enterprises. Heck, Harry had dabbled himself, back in the day.

Now he was on the other end. And he was getting pretty damn tired of uncertainty.

But…

"Send reply as follows," he told the car as he drove off. "I'm interested. Set up a secure link and we'll talk."

CHAPTER 2

March 27, 1809

Capt. Patrick O'Brian, commander of HMS *Thunderer*, looked at his young officers and midshipmen with a practiced eye as they filed into the great cabin of his 74-gun ship. *So young. How could I have ever looked this young?*

Yet they were the best England could provide—or, rather, the best the North of England could provide, along with Scotland, half of Ireland and a bit of Wales. Perhaps that's why the frigate captains looked like green lieutenants, the lieutenants appeared to be naught but midshipmen, and the mids…dear God in Heaven, the mids looked barely weaned from their mothers' bosoms.

They were the newest addition to the fleet protecting Elizabeth Mercuris, the floating outpost above the blasted cinder that was the planet Mercury. They would have to do, for the outpost was critical to keeping the French from taking control of the Void itself.

O'Brian looked out his aft windows at the outpost. It had grown immensely in the thirty years since he first laid eyes upon it. It had started as a commercial trading post for the miners who worked in the caves and caverns of Mercury below, then blossomed—if such a term might be used for such an unsavory place—into a major Sunward Trading Company port. Through alchemy, plenty of sails and no small amount of genius born of desperation, the floating outpost consisted of old ships and hulks lashed together with rope, joined by wooden walkways and bridges, weighed by alchemical lodestones designed to keep gravity and air in place. It was tucked directly behind Mercury so as to keep the heat and light of the Sun from becoming too intense.

And today, it was England's last hope.

There was a rapping upon O'Brian's door. "Come," he said over the low murmur of his wardroom officers.

When the admiral walked in, O'Brian smiled as he stood. *Only Thomas Weatherby would knock before entering a subordinate's cabin.*

The officers and mids scrambled to their feet, eyes wide with shock as they saluted Admiral Lord Weatherby, and O'Brian registered a slight shock of his own. It had been nearly six years since he last saw his old commander and friend—the man's wedding day, in actuality—and the years seemed to weigh upon Weatherby like an old cloak.

Weatherby, it seemed, saw something similar in O'Brian as he came across the room and clenched the captain in a warm embrace. "For God's sake, Paddy, why the hell aren't you eating?" Weatherby said quietly, his concern broken with a warm smile that, for a moment, banished the lines of worry upon his face and lifted the air of palpable gloom around him.

"Likely the same reason you aren't sleeping, my Lord," he replied. "There is plenty to go around, I fear. Thank you for coming to speak to the lads."

"It's good they know what they're fighting for here, Captain. Shall I?"

O'Brian nodded, and Weatherby turned in the cramped cabin to address the wide-eyed youngsters present, thinking much the same as O'Brian with regards to their youthfulness. Those eager eyes, those unblemished faces…it was a sin to think how quickly they would be replaced by glassy dullness and hard lines. And Weatherby felt acutely that his own appearance would be an object lesson on the results of a life in service. His hair was grayed, his face lined with worry and wind, the two-inch scar on his cheek, gained 'round Mars some thirty years past, a white ghostly line on leathery skin. Yet he could stand tall, walk briskly and hold fast, and his voice could still raise an entire ship to action with one bellow. He might have looked worried—and he was, for England was on the very brink of war—but he was, by no means, ready to bend.

"Gentlemen," O'Brian said, quieting the room immediately. "May I present Thomas, Baron Weatherby, Vice-Admiral of the White, Knight of the Bath, and commander of all Sunward forces of His Majesty's Navy."

Weatherby shot O'Brian a look for that overly formal introduction, though he knew that listing his various titles and honors might lend additional weight to his words. Still, it seemed that if those in this cabin needed the additional weighting, there was little Weatherby could say that would move them from whatever strange mind-set they possessed.

"Officers of HMS *Thunderer*," Weatherby began. "I should like to come to know each of you as well as I know your captain here, but I fear time and tide shall not allow it in these dark days. But I tell you this: You have in command of your ship one of the finest men with whom I have ever sailed sea and Void. I trust him with my very life. Follow his commands in both spirit and letter, and you will find naught but success, I promise you.

"Now, your captain asked me to address you briefly, for many of you have had little word of England, or how our war fares with the damnable French. I should wish to report better news than I have...Napoleon has control of much of the Continent, and has recently taken Spain almost entirely unopposed.

"I am happy to report that Wellesley and the army are holding fast to Yorkshire, and have even begun an effort to take Derbyshire and advance into northern Nottinghamshire. The French have sent reinforcements, of course, and the battles are hard fought. Their invasion force has dwindled—due in large part to the limited life-spans of their revenant soldiers. Apparently, these abominations can only be animated for three or four years before finally collapsing, allowing their poor souls at last the rest God intended. And with the rest of the Continent pacified, Napoleon's alchemists have a lack of new...material...from which to create new troops.

"Meanwhile, the victory at Trafalgar—may God rest Nelson's soul!—has allowed our fleet to continue dominance of both sea and Void. We have kept the plague that is Napoleon's army from spreading beyond the Continent. Elizabeth Mercuris is absolutely critical to this effort."

There was a whispering and a few chuckles from a corner of the room that caught Weatherby's ear, and he spied a sandy-haired young lieutenant smiling from that direction. "You there," Weatherby said, pointing. "Repeat what was just said, if you please."

At this the young man's grin turned into a visage of abject panic, but he immediately stood ramrod straight and spoke clearly. "An opinion was stated, my Lord Admiral, as to the critical nature of Elizabeth Mercuris as anything other than…a whorehouse."

Weatherby could not help but smile slightly, as there were indeed several such establishments within the outpost. "Indeed, Lieutenant. But can you tell me why that opinion is entirely incorrect and the truth as to why it is critical to our efforts?"

The lieutenant—barely past his midshipman years—could only shake his head no. And those around him looked upon him with a mix of terror and pity.

"Lieutenant, the alchemists here use the ores mined below to create the solution known as Mercurium. This allows our ships greater freedom of movement; with the proper application of Mercurium to the ships' sails, they may launch for the Void from any point, upon any sea, on any world. Without Mercurium, ships must sail—sometimes for weeks—until they reach a world's aurorae at the poles, and only there can they catch the Solar wind and be off into the Void. But of course, you knew this already, did you not, Lieutenant?"

The young man nodded vigorously, and seemed quite apt to have a nervous episode at any moment.

"France has very little Mercurium at hand," Weatherby continued. "So little, in fact, that they've found it easier to simply build ships from their holdings on Venus, then send them into the Void and keep them there. These Void-squadrons are growing, I'm sorry to report. And with Venus so close, our critical holding here upon Mercury—one of the keys to our dominance of the Void—has been sorely tested, and will likely be tested many times again. It is Mercurium, produced here, that allows our ships to quickly make the Void from wherever our ships may be, while France and her allies must ascend at the poles of any given world—effectively hampering their imperial ambitions considerably. This outpost is thus critical to our efforts."

Weatherby looked closely at his audience. He told them nothing new, really, but he had them well in hand, the benefits of rank and legend manifest. "I know you would like nothing more than to make sail for England and expel the French from our homes. And I should be quite glad to give the order. But we face a canny, cunning, well-armed enemy. We must fight intelligently, attacking at points of weakness. England *will* be liberated, I can promise you. Napoleon will answer for the crimes he's committed against our King, our Country and against God Himself. And your actions here, aboard this fine ship, under this most excellent commander, will help bring us to that fine day.

"Mind your stations, heed your orders and excel in all that you do, and the French shall hear *Thunderer* in their ears before long! God save the King!"

The young men in the room stood as one and cried out, "God save the King!"

With a nod, Weatherby moved toward the door, shaking the officers' extended hands. It both amused and saddened him to think that these young men would one day say, "I once shook Lord Weatherby's hand!" He overheard a young midshipman say exactly that upon a frigate he inspected last year, and felt both embarrassed and morose afterward. Weatherby had done much since the invasion of England... but Napoleon still held their homeland. All the accolades and titles would mean little until he could see the King return to Buckingham and Windsor once more.

Then he could finally rest.

O'Brian escorted Weatherby out onto the main deck and toward the gangplank that would take him back upon

Elizabeth Mercuris. "I must apologize for Lt. Stiles, my Lord. I shall see to his further education, of course," O'Brian said.

Weatherby smirked as he stepped onto the "ground" of the outpost –more wooden planking, slapdash paths made of old timbers that linked Elizabeth Mercuris' buildings together. Below the planking was nothing but the Void. "Of course, though do remember we were much like him back in the day."

"We were, and we were whipped for it," O'Brian retorted as he escorted Weatherby toward the outpost's Admiralty headquarters—a former second-rate ship, long stripped of sail and mast, with windows where its gunports once were and a surprisingly ornate door cut into the lower hull. "Anyway, I shall do what needs be done. How fares the Lady Anne, sir?" O'Brian asked.

Weatherby smirked, his mind rushing back thirty years to an impromptu fencing lesson—and Anne being the one to teach a very young Midshipman O'Brian a few things. "She is well, Paddy. Already trying to come up with ways to increase efficiency here and produce more Mercurium. T'was never a problem she didn't enjoy solving, even if there was none to solve at first!"

The two men laughed as they walked along the wooden path, the hustle and bustle of portside activity all around them. The stars shone clear, and the Sun's corona was visible around Mercury's dark sphere below. Above, alchemically-treated sails fluttered in the solar winds, helping to keep the outpost in place, rather than plummeting toward the dark, cold desert of Mercury's night side. "It was good of you to mention Nelson in there," O'Brian said. "I know you didn't get on with him, but since Trafalgar, the men—the officers in particular—see him as a martyr. And we, of course, served with him at the Nile."

"Actually, we *interrupted* him at the Nile," Weatherby said. "Displaced his favorite captain and put a decisive end to an otherwise long battle. I'm sure he was quite put out. But yes, we need our heroes in these days. If Nelson can continue his service from beyond, then we must use his memory well."

Just then, bells began to toll across Elizabeth Mercuris. Old church bells, ship bells, even strings of carriage bells. The entire outpost erupted in a nerve-wrenching jangle.

It was the general alarm. Something—someone—was coming for the outpost.

Weatherby turned to O'Brian. "You're in the van. Take two frigates and make sail at once. See what's coming and report back as quickly as you can. Do not engage if outnumbered. I'll be along shortly."

O'Brian turned and yelled toward the quarterdeck. "Beat to quarters! Prepare to make sail! Clear lines and moorings!" A moment later, *Thunderer*'s bell joined the cacophony of others, and her captain turned and extended a hand to Weatherby. "An honor to be sailing with you again, sir."

"The honor is mine, Captain O'Brian," he replied with a small smile, taking his friend's hand firmly. "But don't stand on ceremony. I'll get out of your way. Go be my eyes, Paddy."

Weatherby turned and quickly made for the gangplank, clambering across onto the wooden pier of the outpost. He quickly hurried along, ignoring the salutes of fellow sailors when they came—and they were few and far between, with Elizabeth Mercuris erupting into chaos. He ventured a glance off toward the Void, but saw nothing. He could only hope that the brigs and sloops on picket duty had been able to signal the outpost well in advance. If not, they would be hard pressed to sail quickly.

"Tom!" a voice called from behind. "What is it?"

Weatherby turned and saw Anne, half-covered in silver-black soot, her gown a perfect wreck, her hair a tangle absently drawn back. She looked worried, and rightly so—she had not been upon Elizabeth Mercuris for many, many years, and likely had dismal memories of what such an alarm might bring. Then again, her memories of the place were dismal no matter the condition.

"I cannot say, my lady," he replied quickly, not breaking stride, though Anne quickly took her place beside him and matched his pace neatly. "How goes your Mercurium refinements?"

"We are close, very close, but then your fleet's alchemists rushed to their ships, leaving things in a complete state of arrest. I should wish them back post-haste."

Weatherby smiled slightly; she knew the request to be absurd, and a glance at her showed as much in her smirk. "I shall, of course, send the lot of them back to you as soon as I'm able. But there is the slight matter of their duty to their ship, first and foremost."

"Very well. I shall carry on until you've taken care of this terrible business," Anne said with an airy breeze, but then quickly reached over and gripped Weatherby's arm slightly. "Do be careful," she added with evident concern.

"As always, my love," he smiled. "Now go secure your stores. I shan't be long."

Anne turned quickly for her makeshift laboratory, stored in the hold of a decrepit merchantman lashed to the outpost, and made for where his flagship was moored.

And he was quite pleased to see that HMS *Victory* was well and ready to make sail, waiting solely upon her admiral. She was truly a magnificent ship—three decks and 104 guns, one of the largest in His Majesty's service—and informally considered to be the flagship of England itself, though this was due in no small part to Nelson's heroic passing upon her quarterdeck nearly three years ago.

And *Victory* had been extensively refurbished since Trafalgar, so much so that it was hard to believe her keel was laid in 1759. She was old, certainly, but a fierce lioness if there ever was one.

Her captain, John Clarke Searle, waited for Weatherby on the maindeck as he boarded. "We are prepared to set sail, my Lord Admiral," Searle said. "Shall I give the order?"

Weatherby nodded curtly as he took up his hat and handed his satchel of papers to his long-serving, long-suffering valet Gar'uk; the three-foot tall Venusian lizard-creature had been with him for nearly 15 years. Nobody knew for certain what the life-span of the Venusian people might be, but Weatherby could attest that Gar'uk did not seem to allow advancing age to slow him overmuch, despite a noticeably leathery look upon the scales around his beak, a droop under his eyes and a touch of hobble in his step. Of course, Weatherby could say the same of himself—except for the scales, of course.

"Any word on the cause of the alarm, Captain?" Weatherby said as he and Searle made for the quarterdeck.

"No, sir," the captain replied. "All we know is the lookouts caught a signal rocket from one of our pickets. The governor sounded the general alarm at once."

Weatherby frowned slightly; the governor of Elizabeth Mercuris was one Roger Worthington, a man who achieved his role and title simply by being the son of his late predecessor, and was wholly unlikely to rise to even his father's meager level of competence. "At least there was a signal, then, and the governor wasn't simply suffering under a case of nervous delusion," he quipped. "Make sail for the direction of the signal rocket. Signal the fleet to form up behind us."

"No need for signals, Admiral Weatherby!"

Weatherby wheeled about to find his fleet alchemist, Dr. Andrew Finch, rushing up toward him. And it was hard to determine what surprised the admiral more—the sudden, loud and undisciplined approach, or the general look of unkempt exhaustion and wide-eyed fervor upon his old friend's face.

"My God, Finch, do try to be a better example for the men," Weatherby chided softly. "You look like a perfect wreck."

Finch smiled, and his eyes grew wider. "What if, Tom... what if you could communicate with Paddy O'Brian right now, with but a thought, rather than use signal flags and telescopes to try to divine his messages?" he asked. "What if you could quickly, clearly express your commands to your captains as if they were standing right next to you?"

Weatherby saw two seamen walk up behind Finch. One carried a small table, while the other held a oval mirror ringed with occult and alchemical etchings. "Finch...I must ask, have you returned to your old habits of late? Are you addled even now?"

The alchemist looked confused a moment, but then waved the question away with his hand. "Tom, I'm being quite serious here. I've come across a method by which we may be able to allow you to communicate and coordinate all the ships under your command simply through the power of thought and speech! Think of what a boon that would be! A strategic advantage like none other!"

Weatherby turned and walked slowly up the stairs toward the quarterdeck, knowing Finch would follow. "Has this been tested at all, Dr. Finch?" Weatherby asked.

"We've been able to engage in some limited tests, yes," Finch said. "We've managed to cast our thoughts from one end of the ship to the other."

"One end to the other? Do you know how far our ships sail in the Void? We may be ten miles away, maybe more!" Weatherby said.

"And what of the side effects?" asked Searle, who had little love and a great deal of mistrust when it came to matters of alchemy.

Finch suddenly looked away, as if he were distracted. "What are you doing here?" he muttered.

"Excuse me?" Searle said, with some force behind it.

"Oh, quite sorry," Finch said, snapping back. "Something...just occurred to me. Anyway, there have been some cases of headaches, a bit of nausea, one very isolated case of vertigo and unconsciousness, but, I promise you. Admiral, these issues have been addressed. The days of signal flags and fog-of-war are over!"

It was very clear to Weatherby that Finch was intensely passionate about his discovery, and that he likely had spent many sleepless nights perfecting it, as was his wont when creativity struck. "I'm sorry, Finch," Weatherby said gently. "We shall test your innovation at our very next opportunity—just one that does not involve actual combat. We cannot afford to have myself or my captains incapacitated."

Finch nodded sullenly. "Of course, sir." He then brightened up slightly. "I shall discuss this with Captain Searle when we return to the outpost, then?"

"As soon as we return," Weatherby agreed, giving Searle a slightly apologetic look. For his part, the captain of *Victory* smiled tightly, and excused himself to see to Weatherby's orders.

"It'll work," Finch said quietly.

"I know, old friend," Weatherby said, equally *sotto voce*. "But the captains need to focus on the task at hand. It is not your working, but their lack of preparation for it, that has me worried."

It was something of a fib for Finch's benefit, and Weatherby felt badly for it, but it seemed to assuage him greatly, and the alchemist soon made his way below decks to begin preparing for battle. Not only was Finch responsible for all the alchemists aboard Weatherby's ships, but in times of battle, Finch would use his knowledge of the Great Work to help treat wounded, repair the ship and fire back with the deadliest weapons alchemy could empower.

As the crew of *Victory* unfurled her sails and prepared to make for the Void, Weatherby paced slowly on the quarterdeck, his mind already among the stars, mentally reviewing where each of his ships would be. There were, of course, standing orders as to the positioning of the ships in the fleet, depending on what *Thunderer* and her squadron found as they scouted ahead. There were six other major warships at Weatherby's disposal—all third-rate, 74-gun vessels—along with a host of smaller ships taking up picket positions around the outpost. The pickets would be the last line of defense—aside, of course, from the hundreds of guns on the outpost itself. These guns had never fired upon a French vessel while Weatherby was in command, and he would do much indeed to further such a record.

Weatherby started slightly as *Victory* pulled away from the outpost and sailed out toward the unknown. When he was a mere captain, his mind captured every small detail of his ship's operation and could identify a slack line or misplaced ammunition with but a glance. But he'd been an admiral now far too long, it seemed. His mind was on every ship, not just the one upon which he personally sailed. Taking out his glass, Weatherby saw the other ships in his fleet form up, creating a kind of chevron in the void, with *Victory* herself at the point. Over years of engagements, Weatherby felt such a formation was ideal for most circumstances, allowing the ships to scatter and engage or form up into a single line with equal facility.

Returning his attention to where he stood, *Victory* herself seemed in fine form. He had never been her captain, and thus did not know every inch of plank and sail as Searle would, but Weatherby knew well enough her rhythms and ways. There were two sets of planesails upon each side of the massive, three-decked warship—a first rate, and England's largest—and plenty more sailcloth upon her three masts. For such a large ship, she handled in the Void like one that was much smaller, though certainly not as fast as any would like. Thankfully, her guns were effective compensation for the lack of speed.

"Signal from *Thunderer!*" came the call from the lookouts above, more than 150 feet above the maindeck. "Enemy sighted! Ten ships!"

Weatherby nodded at this, though Searle seemed less pleased. "Ten! That's a full fleet, then. Orders, sir?"

"Another signal to the fleet, then. We shall scatter and engage as soon as *Victory* fires. Let's hope they're as hidebound as the last ones," Weatherby said.

"You'd think they'd learn," Searle commented after passing Weatherby's commands to his officers. "Nelson's tactic at Trafalgar should've been a clear enough warning."

Weatherby simply shrugged. "Understand, Captain, that so many of their finest sailors, their career officers, were purged during the revolution. And then again in the Terror. And again after Napoleon came to power. They may build ships well enough, and they can sail, but tactics...that's experience. That's why we've maintained supremacy at sea and Void, and I'm quite unwilling to give it up today. Now, let's run out. Where's *Thunderer*?"

As *Victory* ran out dozens of guns from her flanks, the lookouts spotted *Thunderer* heading back toward Weatherby's fleet in something of a chaotic trajectory—likely because she was being followed. O'Brian did not wish to provide a clean shot upon his stern, the least defensible portion of any ship, and the wide, swooping turns and spirals in the Void allowed him to fire upon the two ships following.

One of which, as the ships came into clearer view, was a Xan ovoid.

"Damn it!" Weatherby cursed, snapping his glass shut. "We keep telling Vellusk there are partisans aiding the French, and yet he does nothing!"

The Xan, natives of the rings of Saturn, were nominally a pacifist race, but for the better part of the past decade, a small but growing faction had sought more warlike ways—and allied themselves with the French, no less. England had, of course, sought alliance with the main body of Xan, led by Representative Vellusk, but these worthies remained committed to their precepts of peace, unlike their fellows, and would offer naught but verbal support against the partisans, and the aforementioned promises of attention to their increasingly strident faction.

And yet there was an ovoid—the queer, egg-shaped vessels half the size of a frigate and three times the speed of the fastest brig—and it was quite a problem. Their strange electrical-alchemical armaments could cripple a 74-gun ship with but four or five well-placed shots.

Searle paled. "Change in orders, sir?"

"Aye. Signal *Swiftsure* to come up alongside, and *Thunderer* to come sail toward us. Let us see if we may crack this egg before it hatches."

As the signal flags flew, Weatherby spied ahead with his glass. The ovoid was among the ships counted by the lookout, which was good news. The rest were closing fast and, aside from *Thunderer*'s pursuers, were hewing to older naval tactics by forming a column of ships, bow to stern. At sea, this would be most prudent, as battles were fought in two dimensions. Out in the Void, however, vessels could take advantage of the third dimension through canny use of their planesails. Likewise, the speeds at which engagements took place were significantly faster, thanks to the alchemical working upon ships' sails that harnessed the very Solar Wind itself.

"*Swiftsure* is in position, my Lord Admiral," Searle reported. "*Thunderer* acknowledges her orders as well, though she's taken some damage amidships."

"Then let us be on our way, Captain," Weatherby responded. "Off toward the ovoid. The rest of the fleet may engage at will."

Weatherby watched as, one by one, the ships in his fleet peeled off and, with royals and studding sails unfurled, swooped toward the French line in a hodge-podge of directions. The French could continue to hew to old tactics if they wished, but Weatherby would not oblige them such a stodgy battle.

Meanwhile, *Thunderer* grew ever closer as *Victory* and *Swiftsure*, the latter a "74" of fine lines and good form, spread out further apart on either side of the incoming ships in their fleet. For a moment, Weatherby wondered just how effective Finch's working might be in communicating with O'Brian and his other captains. It hadn't occurred to the admiral that the system of lookouts and signal flags might be improved, yet in this moment, and despite his extensive experience in battle, Weatherby wondered whether they should test Finch's innovation sooner rather than later.

Men raced across the deck of *Victory* as she raced toward the battle. Marines climbed to the tops, rifles slung across their backs, so they might take aim at the French officers upon the quarterdecks of their ships—just as the French sharpshooters would take aim at Weatherby and Searle. It was Weatherby's duty to stand tall in the midst of this, showing courage and heart for the men aboard—indeed, while Weatherby could coordinate the battle from the safety of his cabin by using runners to convey his orders, he well knew that he served as a symbol to the men of *Victory*, and by extension his entire fleet, by being seen.

Searle, of course, was busy with the efficient handling of the grand old ship, conveying his orders to his first lieutenant, whose shouts pierced the bustle aboard. Young men, barely out of their teens, hauled powder and shot across the decks to arm the guns, while the larger, stronger seamen loaded shot into their guns and ran them out. The men swarming through the rigging prepared to adjust sails according to whatever Searle—and Weatherby—wished in the moment. All 800 souls aboard were part of a well-trained, well-oiled mechanism designed to bring raw destruction forth as quickly and efficiently as possible.

And Weatherby, as the fleet admiral, was responsible for all of it—and none of it, as it was not, strictly speaking, *his* ship he stood upon.

The admiral watched *Thunderer* quickly grow larger as it neared, with the Xan ovoid racing after it, arcs of electric wrath firing into the Void toward the English ship. She was out of reach for now, but at those speeds, she would feel the power of those infernal workings in seconds. It would be up to the men of *Victory* and *Swiftsure* to ensure the ovoid would not get a clean shot upon their comrades aboard *Thunderer*, for if it did, the grand 74-gun ship would surely see the aft third of its hull ravaged.

In a flash, *Thunderer* passed between *Victory* and *Swiftsure*, with O'Brian suddenly tacking downward in a course-correction that would likely wrench every man aboard his ship and stress the gravitational lodestones to a great degree. And just as suddenly, *Thunderer* reversed course yet again, shooting straight upward and well behind her sister ships.

"Two points down starboard-side plane! Two points up larboard-side plane!" Searle shouted, his timing very close to perfect. Through his glass, Weatherby saw *Swiftsure* making the same adjustment.

The Xan ovoid was doing its level best to follow *Thunderer* and—as O'Brian planned and Weatherby had hoped—placed itself slightly below and in between *Victory* and *Swiftsure*.

"FIRE!" Searle shouted, just as Weatherby's mouth had opened to give the order himself.

Streaks of alchemical fire rained down upon the Xan ship, with several shots striking the egg. Soon, several more shots came from above as well; O'Brian had turned back around, rotated his ship, and contributed a broadside to the effort. Yet even as a strange orange-and-black smoke began to pour forth from several rents in the Xan hull, bolts of bluish lightning erupted from the ship, lancing the sides of both *Victory* and *Swiftsure*. Weatherby watched as the powder inside four guns aboard *Swiftsure* exploded in flame, and the tremors he felt underfoot told him a similar effect had occurred on *Victory*'s gundecks below.

"Fire crews, to your stations!" Searle yelled, and immediately a score of men raced for the hatches leading belowdecks, buckets in hand. They were not at sea, of course, so the usual seawater was replaced by an alchemical powder that would smother flame in an instant—if they were fast enough to keep it from spreading.

And yet, despite the damage—and the likely deaths of a dozen or more men below—the Xan had only gotten off weakened shots at best. Weatherby watched as the ovoid, wobbled off into the distance, spinning uncontrollably now.

"Shall we take her, sir?" Searle asked, a gleam in his eye. No English vessel had ever successfully captured a Xan ovoid. And Weatherby had given strict orders not to try, but Searle was an ambitious man, and likely wanted some recompense—or revenge—for the damage to his vessel.

Weatherby shook his head sadly, for he understood perfectly well the man's motivation. "The Xan will not allow it, Captain. Engage the nearest enemy ship still standing."

A moment later, as *Victory* moved off, the Xan ship exploded in a puff of orange flame, leaving a glittering cloud of shards drifting toward Mercury. The warlike Xan partisans would never allow themselves to be captured. Certainly not by a race of people they considered patently inferior.

Victory came up upon a large triple-decked French vessel—Weatherby could not make her name nor recognize her lines—and began opening fire, joining the 60-gun *Agamemnon* in pouring shot into her. Only half of *Victory*'s larboard-side guns fired, for it was a standing order in Weatherby's fleet to alternate fire from target-to-target whilst in the Void; opportunities flashed by quickly, and the divisions below decks needed to have at least some guns ready to engage at a moment's notice, while the others reloaded as quickly as possible.

The French ship shuddered under the assault, and quickly dove toward the Sun and away from both English ships, maneuvering toward the ribbon of glowing specks emanating from the star itself—the Solar current, a powerful flow of motes and lights that could whisk ships away toward the other planets at immense speeds.

"Permission to pursue, Admiral?" Searle asked. In actuality, it was more of a statement, and it was quite evident he wanted the French triple-decker as a prize.

Weatherby supposed that's why there were admirals aboard ships after all—to rein in talented but ambitious captains.

"Permission denied. I'm sorry, John, but we must assist the rest of the fleet, and we've not the space nor manpower to keep hundreds of French prisoners secured upon Elizabeth Mercuris," Weatherby said gently and quietly. Even though he was in overall command, Weatherby knew to not loudly countermand his captains whilst upon their very quarterdecks.

"As you wish, my Lord," Searle said, with the very ghost of a smile upon his face, for he likely knew Weatherby's answer before he gave it, but thought to chance it regardless.

As it happened, there was little more *Victory* could do. Weatherby's fleet of swarming ships had scattered and flayed the French fleet quite nicely. One French ship was adrift in the Void, fully engulfed in flames, while two others had lost their masts and had struck their colors; Weatherby would later allow one to be sailed to England as a prize. The other would be disarmed, her cannon added to the defenses of Elizabeth Mercuris, and given over to the two French crews to sail wherever they pleased, so long as they left Mercury and swore never to return. Much goodwill had been engendered by these tactics, as the bulk of the French crews—and even some of their junior officers—had been pressed into service. Many had set sail for Ganymede, where the ships would become merchantmen or be sold to the upstart United States.

The rest of the French had followed the French flagship into the current, allowing themselves to be whisked away in defeat. As was his practice, Weatherby went below decks to congratulate the men—and to survey the damage. It was upon the middle gundeck that Weatherby saw the carnage the Xan weapon had wrought, for there was a massive gash in the ship's hull, some forty to fifty feet long and four feet wide. No fewer than seven guns had been hit, disintegrating under the alchemical onslaught and sending thousands of bits of metal shrapnel careening through the entire deck. The decks were slick with the blood of brave Englishmen, and even though he had seen such horrors many times before, it was all Weatherby could do to maintain his composure and put on a brave face for the men, many of whom looked at him with any number of emotions: pride, sorrow, horror, recrimination.

There were scores wounded, and junior officers and alchemists were quickly administering curatives to any who could be saved. Finch was there as well, still looking wan, but moving deftly to save the life of some poor soul whose name he likely did not know, nor would ever learn. The fleet alchemist's arms were covered in blood up to his elbows, and it was left to one of his assistants to procure the necessary curatives from his stores, for the glass vials and cloth satchels would be tainted with blood were he to handle them personally.

"How bad?" Weatherby murmured as he drew close enough to speak quietly.

Finch poured a silver liquid into the abdominal wound of a sailor who could be no more than fifteen years of age, and the young man screamed in utter agony. "Sixty, perhaps. I cannot say yet for certain. Now if you please, Tom…"

Weatherby straightened up and left Finch to his workings, slowly making his way forward once more, shaking hands with the survivors, consoling the injured with a kind word and a hand upon brow or shoulder. He knew full well his legendry, and knew that the merest touch could be a salve to a dying man, giving those lost souls a measure of purpose and grace, even as they breathed their last.

It was appalling. It always was, it always would be. But it was the duty of an admiral to the men he used as a weapon against his enemies.

After a half-hour of this, and with his fleet turned about to return to Elizabeth Mercuris, Weatherby returned to the ship's great cabin, where Gar'uk had poured a glass of claret for him. Weatherby struggled to turn his attention to the battle's conduct, rather than its aftermath. The French still hewed to their old tactics, but the admiral knew that even their inexperienced officers may learn from this engagement. So Weatherby took pen and paper in hand and began to make sketches of the engagement, so that he could review the battle with his captains later. They could not become complacent, and so they would alter their approach next time so as to keep the French upon their heels.

His sketch complete and other notes compiled, Weatherby allowed himself a generous portion of wine before turning to his logbook to write his report on the engagement. But upon the once-blank page, a message awaited him.

By order of His Royal Highness, George, Prince Regent and Prince of Wales, acting on behalf of His Majesty, George the Third, by the Grace of God, of the United Kingdom of Great Britain and Ireland King, Defender of the Faith, Etc.,

The message was, in fact, in the midst of being inscribed back on Earth, likely at Edinburgh, where the Prince of

Wales had retreated after the French took London, and King George III along with the city. Weatherby sighed a second time, for this would likely be a message of some importance and great inconvenience.

A rap upon the cabin door was followed by the rapid entrance of Finch, who rarely waited for acknowledgement before entering. "You might be pleased to know that my original estimate was too high by at least ten or more, Tom. We managed to save more than I first thought. I—" Finch stopped as Weatherby's face grew drawn and tense as he read the message as it was written, with the power of the Great Work of Alchemy spanning the distance between worlds.

"Your damnable message papers will be the end of me, Finch," Weatherby growled as he finished the message and slammed his logbook shut.

Finch smirked as took the chair opposite Weatherby. "What now, then?" he asked as he accepted a glass of wine from the ever-mindful Gar'uk.. "I...oh…"

"What?" Weatherby demanded.

Finch looked away again, as if focusing on something else, then whispered quietly to himself.

"Finch?"

Looking even a bit more pale than before, Finch returned his attention to his commander and friend. "So sorry," he replied, a bit of forced charm coming through. "Thought I forgot something below decks. What about my message papers?"

"We're to return to Edinburgh for 'consultations,'" Weatherby said, his dismay and disgust evident. "And we're to take three-fourths of our ships with us."

"Well…at least you received your orders *after* the French were defeated," Finch allowed.

Weatherby leaned back in his chair and took a prodigious swig of wine. "Let's bloody well hope they don't try again until Elizabeth Mercuris is reinforced. Damn these consultations! I cannot help but wonder what scheme Prince George has in mind to rescue England this time."

CHAPTER 3

January 3, 2135

Maria Diaz was all smiles as she propelled herself down the corridor of her latest command, the JSCS *Hadfield*. They had launched from Ride Station, JSC's interplanetary launch hub, located at the second Earth-Sun Lagrange point. The DAEDALUS team had set up shop on Ride for the past two weeks, dumping a boatload of scientists back on Earth with very little notice. She knew the scientists had left important work behind, and probably a few experiments were shot to hell because of it, but her team needed time to prepare. There was, after all, a goddamn for-real alien invasion coming. Not exactly *War of the Worlds*, perhaps, but potentially far more insidious.

Diaz was in her element. She wore the black jumpsuit that had been a second skin for most of her career, she was floating in zero-g, she was heading off into space to do something foolish and dangerous. Life was good.

Mostly.

She entered the *Hadfield*'s control and information center, or CIC—a kind of situation room just aft of the cockpit where all the piloting was done. Spacecraft needed far less actual piloting than atmospheric vessels; just point and go. But in this case, she wanted a warm body up there, because their quarry could suddenly get ideas.

The *Hadfield*'s crew—all of whom were DAEDALUS team members—snapped to attention when she entered, giving her a little surge of pride. *It never gets old*. Even the civilians stopped what they were doing to hear the news.

"Jimmy, secure the ship," Diaz ordered.

Capt. James Coogan of the U.K. Royal Air Force nodded and flipped on enough electronic countermeasures to ensure they could not be overheard—an extremely minute but non-zero chance. The fact that these would disrupt comms to and from the ship was sadly necessary. "Ship secured, ma'am."

Diaz shot the young officer a small smile. Jimmy's red hair and round face made him look like an uppity, priggish teenager, but damn if he wasn't a fine officer. He also happened to be frighteningly adept at obtaining information, getting shit organized and generally doing anything and everything Diaz asked. She got him promoted after Egypt, and she'd consider another bump up the ladder if he'd just stop calling her "ma'am" in that British way that sounded like "mum."

"All right, listen up," Diaz said. "Just got off the horn with President Weathers. The Chinese finally signed off with us boarding *Tienlong* as a humanitarian mission. Creative way of saving face. That means Operation Bear Trap is a go. We're up in 30 minutes, unless *Tienlong* gets some ideas. Jimmy, status report."

The room darkened and the dozen souls inside turned toward the holoprojection in the center. Earth hovered off to one side, with the Moon close by. Ride Station was 1.5 million kilometers away from Earth. There were three other dots as well. The first was *Hadfield*, heading off toward Mars' orbit. The second was *Tienlong*, coming in fast from Saturn. And the third was *Armstrong*, and it looked to Diaz that Shaila Jain was hitting the gas at just the right time.

"*Tienlong* has yet to alter speed or course," Coogan said. "She's slated to make Earth orbit in about 15 hours, but we're hoping we can do something about that. *Armstrong* has reported a couple of very small burns in the last hour, which ought to position her right alongside *Tienlong* in approximately 25 minutes."

Diaz frowned; it wasn't as though she begrudged Shaila the chance to rescue Stephane—if he *could* be rescued. But there were two others on that ship, and in addition to being outnumbered, Diaz knew that Shaila was stressed, physically and mentally, by the loss of Stephane. Shaila was a thorough professional, no doubt about it, but Diaz knew that if it were *her* wife aboard that ship, she'd tear through that ship with a chainsaw to save her.

"Can we get there first, Baines?"

From the cockpit, U.S. Air Force Capt. Elliot Baines—fully rigged in VR hologear—chimed in. "Calculating new burn now. And…yes, General. We'll need a full burn in… four seconds."

"Do it."

The *Hadfield*'s engines roared to life, pushing the little ship a little faster into space—and closer to *Tienlong*. "ETA now 21 minutes, General," Baines reported after the engines died down.

"And that pushes up our timing, Gerald. How we doing?" Diaz asked the African man sitting at an impressive array of controls and holodisplays. Before him, a series of dots ringed the Earth-Moon system, and a number of lines proceeded from these dots toward *Tienlong*.

Dr. Gerald Ayim, former scientist for the Total-Suez conglom and one of a bare handful of people who understood the quantum physics behind the extradimensional incursions over the past few years, moved his fingers across his virtual control panel, and a number of lights began to glow. "BlueNet is responding. We have full control of the satellite array. Ready to release the energy at your command, General."

Diaz gave him a nod, which he returned with an absent-minded smile as he further adjusted and attuned the BlueNet array of satellites. BlueNet was originally designed to detect Cherenkov radiation—a specific and harmless type of light that served as a tell-tale sign of extradimensional incursion on Mars. Six months ago, when Ayim was working for Harry Yu and their experiment went to shit, Ayim and his late colleague Evan Greene managed to stem the runaway interdimensional energies by using the BlueNet array to redirect them.

The hope here was that BlueNet could do it again. *Armstrong* had reported hundreds of thousands of minute Cherenkov readings in the icy rubble that had been Enceladus—rubble that *Tienlong* then drifted through. By all appearances, *Tienlong* had collected whatever was giving off the Cherenkov radiation and was bringing it—or *them*—to Earth.

"All right, so we fire up BlueNet to draw off the energy from whatever's on board *Tienlong*. Next up, we get our team aboard. Baines handles the maneuvering and docking. And then we let Major Parrish take over. Report, Major."

To Diaz' right, a wiry, androgynous looking man gave her a wolfish smile. "Boarding team is ready," Canadian Marine Maj. Geoff Parrish said. "Point-focused microwaves to start, and if that doesn't slow them down, we have soft rounds."

Diaz nodded, though she couldn't bring herself to return the smile; she liked Stephane Durand too much for that. The point-focused microwave emitters could drop a horse for well over a minute, and the average human was stunned unconscious for a good fifteen to twenty minutes. But Diaz wasn't taking chances; the soft rounds would definitely penetrate human flesh, but wouldn't breach *Tienlong*'s hull. "I want prisoners, Major. Target soft rounds accordingly. Lethal force only as a last resort."

The smile dropped under Diaz' gaze, as did the gung-ho attitude. "Yes, General," Parrish replied.

"All right, places everybody, this is not a drill," Diaz said loudly. "Alert stations in ten minutes. I'll be in my quarters. Jimmy, you have the conn."

Diaz spun around and propelled herself out of the CIC. Her quarters were less than a meter into the corridor, and they were a Spartan affair if there ever was one. But she had secure comms, and privacy. On a shuttle like *Hadfield*, that would have to do.

She slid into a chair, put on her lap belt, and fired up the comm on her tiny desk, aiming it at *Armstrong*. "Jain, this is Diaz. Come in, over."

A moment later, Shaila's face came to holographic life over the desktop. In all honesty, Diaz was pleasantly surprised at how the acting captain of *Armstrong* looked. Sure, there were some bags under her eyes, a few new worry lines on her dusky-skinned face. But her black hair was regulation, her uniform spotless. And there was some steel in her eyes that came across even through the hologram.

"Jain here, General. Go ahead…." Shaila's voice drifted off. "Edinburgh?" she whispered.

"Come again, Commander?" Diaz frowned.

Shaila shook her head and straightened up. "Sorry, General. Stray thought there. Go ahead."

Diaz relented and gave her a small smile. "Trying to beat us there, kid?"

Shaila shook her head. "No, ma'am. I simply wanted to be sure we had adequate time for docking before arrival. We're a lot bigger than *Hadfield*, ma'am."

It was, of course, a valid point. Except for the fact that Shaila literally played chicken with *Tienlong* when the two ships first arrived at the Saturn system, then manually piloted the ship through the goddamn rings in order to avoid collision. Docking with a ship at the same course and speed was child's play in comparison. And to Diaz, the response seemed a little too canned, the kind of quick reply a teenager gives when they came up with the perfect excuse for staying out late.

"Well, sorry, but we'll end up there first. I'll be sure to take the ventral airlock so you can have the starboard-side lock," Diaz said. "I'll have two members of the boarding team greet you there. You'll form up with them as Fire Team Two under Parrish. Clear?"

"Yes, ma'am," Shaila said, sounding slightly disappointed.

Diaz knew why. "Once you're off your boat, you're not in command anymore. Parrish is the boarding team officer, and you'll report to him. Mess with that, and even though I love you dearly, girl, I will bust your ass down to ensign, fourth class."

Shaila smiled. "There's no fourth class in the Royal Navy, General."

"There will be when I'm done," Diaz replied. "Don't worry, Shay. We're going to get him out alive. And we're going to figure out how to help him."

Shaila gave a curt nod and swallowed hard. "Thank you, ma'am. Appreciate that."

"Good. When we give the signal, keep your comms open. Remember, full pressure suits until we're damn sure that ship's decontaminated. Get a move on, skipper."

"Roger that. *Armstrong* out."

Shaila's face winked out, and Diaz leaned back in her chair a bit. They'd chatted on and off during the *Armstrong*'s trip home; Shaila had refused all comms with anyone remotely attached to psych or medical, but Diaz had been able to get through to her on and off—with the help of psych off-camera, of course. It wasn't in her portfolio, per se, but Shaila was as much a friend as a subordinate, and they had shared something utterly amazing and historic on Mars. Few people could really relate to each other as they could.

"CIC to Diaz, two minutes to BlueNet range," Coogan reported over the intercom.

Diaz unbuckled from her chair and floated back out, around the corner and into the CIC. "All right then," she said. "Let's get this party started. Gerald, ramp it up."

"Yes, General," Ayim replied. "Initializing energy transfer sequence. I—"

Coogan interrupted loudly. "*Tienlong*'s changing course! Heading now 180 mark 6, pulling away—and into *Armstrong*'s path!"

Diaz vaulted across the room to Coogan's holodisplay. "Shit. Open a comm to *Armstrong*."

"She's already calling, ma'am," Coogan replied. "Go ahead, *Armstrong*."

"*Tienlong* is now 17 minutes from us, *Hadfield*," Shaila reported. "Permission to proceed with boarding, over."

"Hold on, *Armstrong*," Diaz said, turning toward the *Hadfield*'s cockpit. "Baines, intercept course, now, and burn hard. Gimme an ETA."

Everyone aboard *Hadfield* felt the slight pull of gravity as the engines fired once more. "Looks like…22 minutes now, General. Best we got if we're going to ease up on her," Baines reported.

"Gerald?"

"Recalculating," the scientist said. "Now coming into BlueNet range in....25 minutes."

"What?" Diaz thundered. "How the fuck is that possible?"

Ayim looked at Diaz, petrified at the outburst. "I'm sorry, General! There is one satellite in the array that has been malfunctioning for weeks. They seemed to know exactly where to go. Now I have to maneuver to compensate."

Diaz wheeled around to Coogan. "Jimmy?"

The young officer grokked her meaning instantly. "We're not detecting sensors from them, ma'am. There's a fair amount of transmissions out here, so we'll need to check their comm logs to see if they somehow got warning."

That was, of course, the biggest fear Diaz and her DAEDALUS team had. It appeared the Chinese were infected—or possessed, depending—while still on Earth. Did *Tienlong* have any Earthbound allies left? Would they try to help? And how? Guiding the ship away from BlueNet was a good start.

"Are they still on a course for Earth?"

Coogan's eyes darted over his holographic data again. "Barely. And I don't think they have any more fuel. This was their last play, I think, ma'am."

"All right. *Armstrong*, you still there?" Diaz asked.

"Roger, *Hadfield*."

"Jain, you're docking first. I want you to secure your docking port, but do not go further until we arrive and send a fire team to you. Are we clear?" *Tell me we're fucking clear, kid.*

"Yes, General," Jain replied. "We'll secure our port and await your arrival."

Diaz looked into the holomonitor, watching the beads of light representing *Armstrong, Tienlong* and *Hadfield* converge. "Roger. Keep the line open."

All she could do now was pray that those aboard *Tienlong*—whomever they were now, and whatever their plans were, didn't have too many more surprises in store.

May 3, 1809

There were a scant few souls walking along Broad Street, despite the delightful spring weather and the late-afternoon hour, when there were few courses scheduled among Oxford's scattered colleges. The march of philosophical inquiry and the education of young men were of paramount importance, of course, but principals and tutors desired their afternoon tea just as much as any other Englishmen.

Yet despite the possibilities of the day, the hour and the weather, there was a decided lack of actual tea in Oxford these days, for it was that the Royal Navy found itself blockading the very nation it served—now occupied by Napoleon's forces.

And that, more than the lack of tea, and certainly more than the educational ambitions of the students remaining at Oxford, was the reason few were upon the streets. The patrols of French soldiers garrisoned throughout Oxfordshire were headquartered here, and those patrols primarily consisted of Napoleon's *Corps Éternel*—those soldiers alchemically reanimated after their untimely passing to serve the *nouveau régime*.

So it was, then, that one young tutor walked purposefully through the near-abandoned streets, passing only a spare few students and a carriage or two. A column of blue-coated soldiers marched down Catte Street, but he paid them no mind, for it was a common enough shortcut between Broad and High Street. However, he turned to watch them go on past Hertford College, where he taught, for it would not be meet for them to become overly curious as to goings on there.

Especially when the goings on at the Bodleian Library—conveniently enough, across Catte Street from his very lodging—were far more interesting of late.

Satisfied that Hertford held no interest for the French this day, the young man continued on, entering the King's Arms public house. He smiled to the tavern keeper, who gave a broad wave in return—and a short, curt nod. There was no one to worry about within. All was well, and his compatriots awaited him down the stairs.

The tutor smiled slightly and took the glass of wine left for him upon the countertop, then proceeded to the back of the room, opening the door leading downward to the cellars. A faint glow from a small room therein gave him light enough, and he entered to find he was the very last to arrive.

Again.

"So kind of you to join us, my lord Count," a young woman said with a smile and no little sarcasm. She wore the clothing of a servant girl, one of many who attended to the needs of students and tutors alike. She did not, however, wear the bearing of such a woman. Intelligence shone from her eyes, and her face, framed by dark brown hair, bore determination upon it.

"I apologize to all," said Philip, the second Count St. Germain, returning the smile. "I had a most promising student come to me with the potential for an alchemical experiment in the *mentis* school, and I felt it wise to dissuade him from undertaking it without revision, lest his brains ooze from his ears."

Another young man, dressed in the more colorful robes of Trinity College, frowned at Philip. "If he were a Frenchman, then let his brains melt, I say."

"He was not, Mr. Lloyd, I assure you," Philip replied tersely. Alfred Lloyd was the scion of a prominent London banking family, and as such conducted himself with a great sense of ownership of all about him. He was also studying Classics, which to Philip's mind, was a profound waste of time and energy. However, Philip found Lloyd to be a true English patriot, despite whatever other shortcomings he possessed, and they were among the few members of Oxford's secret resistance—a group of students and townsfolk dedicated to harassing the French as best they could. Philip knew there were other such groups spread throughout England, engaged in clandestine efforts to thwart England's invaders.

"Gunn and Mathers will be along in a few hours," the woman said. "I can help Toby upstairs for a time, then inform them of the latest when they arrive. So shall we begin?"

"Of course, Lady Elizabeth," Philip said. It was, of course, due to the presence of Lloyd they referred to each other so formally, for they had known one another for a decade, since Philip was a teenager who had just lost his father, and Elizabeth Weatherby was but an eight-year-old who, to her great delight, was on her way to regaining a mother. "What have you heard out of Trinity, Mr. Lloyd?"

The young scholar stretched and put his feet up upon the table, sipping his wine before responding. "The principal is quite up in arms. Apparently, he has been told by his superiors that there are some very important people coming from London, and they wish to consult with many of the principals, and use the library. All upon short notice as well."

Philip looked over to Elizabeth, who nodded in agreement. "Many of the staff have been told to make ready for 'distinguished visitors' as well, and to find the best rooms for them," she said. "Apparently, they shall be here at any moment. The preparations are all underway."

Frowning, Philip took up a seat at the table as well. "Their purpose here?"

"Consultations, apparently," Lloyd replied. "I should've thought they'd seek you out, or at least your college. Hertford is known for its alchemists, and the French bastards are all quite enamored of it. That such a 'Great Work' could create such sacrilegious monstrosities upon our very streets!"

Philip slumped slightly; this was a very old argument between he and Lloyd, who enjoyed an absolutist view of the world that seemed reserved for the comfortable and privileged. "There has been no such word within my college, nor among the tutors and professors in my field," Philip said. "So it stands to reason that these visitors wish to consult upon other matters. But what?"

"Trinity is best known for its Classics work," Lloyd said, with evident pride.

"But it is also known for its work in history among the Known Worlds," Elizabeth replied. "If you'll remember, I had been accepted to read on the topic before the town of Oxfordshire was overrun. We must assume that the knowledge they seek is rare enough to warrant travelling here, and experts on other worlds are few and far between—and usually already upon other worlds."

"And your father, Lady Elizabeth, is doing a fine job of keeping the French confined to Europe, let alone Earth," Philip offered with a smile, which was returned with a nod. "This makes the most sense. Do we have anyone with ties to those tutors, or even readers?"

"Gunn might," Lloyd said. "I believe he may have mentioned it."

"I'll ask them both when I see them," Elizabeth offered.

Philip finished his glass and stood. "Very well. And I shall spend some extra time within the library, because as we know, all academic inquiries will lead there eventually. And with that, I had best get back. Lady Weatherby, a word if I may?"

Lloyd rose and, with a curt nod, stalked out of the room before they themselves could leave. Lloyd had once fancied Elizabeth, but in the way the gentleman-commoner fancied servant girls everywhere rather than in a way appropriate to the eldest daughter of a Baron. His advances earned him a broken nose at Elizabeth's hand, and a dire warning of permanent alchemical malevolency from Philip, even as the son of the famed Count St. Germain healed his nose with little more than an elixir created in the space of minutes.

"How are you faring, Elizabeth?" Philip asked when Lloyd's footsteps receded up the stairwell.

She shrugged and smiled. "I make their beds, bring them tea, and read all their books when they're not looking. I dare say I've made a finer education for myself than they've bothered to receive here."

Philip bestowed a small smile upon her. It had been her fervent desire, fully supported and encouraged by Philip's mother, to study the histories of the Known Worlds at the university. However, when they found themselves behind enemy lines, it seemed far more prudent for the children of such English luminaries to disguise themselves—Philip as an anonymous tutor, and Elizabeth as a servant. Only Lloyd and a handful of others knew their true identities. Indeed, they had hoped to keep their true names secret to all, but knowing that the son of St. Germain and the daughter of Weatherby were leading the resistance was a fine tool for recruitment.

"The students are preoccupied, many of them," Philip said. "If they are here, then their parents have collaborated with the French occupiers, or else they are as much prisoner here as if they were in prison, for their parents are outside England and of no help to them."

"And no few are preoccupied with drinking and whoring," she replied bluntly.

"Elizabeth!"

She smiled sweetly back at Philip, having received the indignation she sought. "If I am to be engaged in the manly work of *espionnage*, then should I not be able to talk like a man when with my stepbrother?"

"I remain surprised Lord Weatherby allowed you to stay here at all," Philip scowled. "But…I do think he was wise to do so. I shall report in this evening. Do you have a message you wish to pass on to him and Mother?"

Elizabeth grabbed Philip's empty glass and made for the doorway. "Send them my love, of course, and tell them whatever falsities you feel will assuage them as to my activities here. Tell them I have steered well clear of trouble, such things as that."

Shaking his head, Philip followed Elizabeth out of the cellar room. They embraced briefly in the manner of siblings, and she allowed him to mount the stairs first so he could leave quickly; it would do neither of them any good to be seen together overmuch. While both had assumed different identities, they nonetheless proceeded separately whenever possible.

It was a walk of but a few minutes that took Philip back to Hertford, a drab presence upon Catte Street, across from the finely wrought Bodleian Library. While the library was of superlative construction, Hertford was known as the "paper building," for it was in such disrepair it seemed it might be torn asunder by a simple breeze. Entering his hall, he stopped to chat briefly with his students—it would be noted if he did not—before ascending to his room. His quarters were Spartan at best, with but a bed, bureau, desk and washbasin as his companions, and guttering candles his only light. There were better rooms within even such a building as Hertford, but this particular room faced the library—and made it ideal to see the comings and goings of all, especially the French, and especially as darkness drew near.

This night would not disappoint.

As Philip planned his lessons for the following day, he heard the clatter of hooves and wheels upon the cobblestones outside his window. Extinguishing the sole candle in the room with his fingers, he rose from his desk to look. There was a carriage, of course, by one of the less conspicuous entrances to the library. This was itself notable, given the hour, but more so due to the dozen *Corps Éternel* soldiers flanking the carriage, staring ahead blankly as they waited for their living officer's commands.

Two men emerged from inside the carriage. One was an older gentleman, rotund but seemingly in fine form, while the other required assistance from the footman to simply disembark, and appeared quite ancient and frail indeed. The gentleman possessed of stronger health waited with seeming impatience for his companion, looking around for want of anything better to do.

And that's when Philip saw his face. While he had never met the man personally, he knew those who had. And furthermore, the man was considered the foremost alchemist the French Empire had produced, and had graced both the Royal Academy and the newspapers prior to the invasion.

Philip continued to watch as the two men made their way—slowly, due to the older fellow—into the library. He considered rushing out to follow, but knew that he would need time to prepare for further action. Given the hour and the importance of the library's visitors, this would not be a simple visit. They likely had business in Oxford that would keep them on for several days, at least.

Business that Philip was determined to discover.

Once the French party was well inside, Philip returned to his desk, re-lighting his candle with a match—an alchemical invention of Andrew Finch's, it should be noted—and opened the bottom drawer of the desk. Philip quickly emptied the books and papers from the drawer, then tapped thrice at the back edge of the bottom, which dutifully popped open to reveal a hidden compartment.

Philip withdrew the small sheaf of papers hidden therein, dipped his pen in ink, and proceeded to write upon the topmost.

Father and Mother,

I trust both of you remain well and in the care and grace of the Almighty. I do hope you this letter reaches you soon, for I know you will be curious as to how I spend my days here at Oxford. I think you will be proud.

Please give my regards to my dear uncle when next you see him. I believe I have seen an acquaintance of his this very evening, in fact. I remember the most amusing details of his researches back in '98, and I believe Uncle may have mentioned him prominently in a few of his stories. I hope to introduce myself to this worthy gentleman at the earliest convenience.

I miss you both very much, and I hope you are able to visit soon, for I would very much like to show you our Bodleian Library. It is a wonder, a vast repository of knowledge. They say the secrets of the Known Worlds are there inside, though I cannot say for sure. It is very large, though, and would take days to search for the most obscure things.

And before I forget, I have seen E. lately, and all is well. You have our love.

-Philip

Philip smiled slightly as the ink settled upon the page, then changed from black to a dark blue before his eyes. The message was sent. Within mere moments, Lord Weatherby and the dowager Countess St. Germain would see the message appear on a similar page in their possession.

And through the subtle code only families can truly understand, they would know that Andrew Finch's old nemesis, the alchemist Claude-Louis Berthollet, was in Oxford, and was seeking something within the library.

CHAPTER 4

January 3, 2135

Shaila and Archie sat side by side in *Armstrong*'s cockpit as the ship approached *Tienlong*. The Chinese ship looked unremarkable from the outside—a bit blocky, perhaps, as was the current Chinese aesthetic, but certainly not as though it carried an invasion force.

Yet as *Armstrong* approached further, inching relatively closer despite the ships' speed of 25 kilometers per second, Shaila could see some of the results of *Tienlong*'s drift through Enceladus' debris field. Nearly every square meter of the ship bore the marks of micrometeor impacts; it looked as if it had been clawed by thousands of angry cats.

"Look at the windows," Archie said, pointing through their shared virtual imagery.

But Shaila wasn't looking. Instead, she whispered quietly, "…by the Grace of God of the United Kingdom…"

She then sat up straight and immediately focused, ignoring the look of bemused confusion on her colleague's face. With a glance, she saw what he was talking about. The windows were all fogged up. "What the hell did they do to the environmental controls?"

"They had their external locks open when they sailed through Enceladus," Archie said. "They probably took on a lot of ice crystals along with whatever damn critters they brought aboard. Probably humid as hell in there." The old engineer shook his head sadly, his bushy white hair and mustache seemingly moving on their own. He hated whenever machines were unduly abused, it seemed.

"All right. Going in for manual docking," Shaila said. "Let me know if those fuckers try anything." She stretched her limbs inside the bulky pressure suit she wore. Diaz had ordered them both to wear full pressure suits for docking, though Shaila would've taken that precaution anyway. They were treating the parasitical alien life forms as an "infection," which was a nice, sanitized word that, in Shaila's opinion, really failed to capture anything useful at all. But she was sure that "possession by alien intelligence" was pretty much a non-starter for the higher-ups.

Archie smiled. "They don't have the fuel. Just worry about the dock."

There was little need to worry. Shaila expertly worked *Armstrong*'s chemical thrusters to align the two ships' airlocks. The computer could've lined things up just as efficiently, but Shaila wanted the stick, trusting in her reflexes and reactions in case *Tienlong*—she still couldn't think in terms of Stephane in command there—decided to make the docking difficult.

Yet there was no apparent reaction from *Tienlong* as the universal docking tube extended from *Armstrong* and latched onto *Tienlong*'s hull. *Armstrong* shuddered slightly, and then all was silent.

Shaila sat staring at the readouts for a few moments longer.

"You OK?" Archie asked.

She turned and smiled at him slightly. He cared deeply about her after what happened, she knew. He was a good guy, the grandfather she needed on the long voyage home, and she sometimes felt she gave him short shrift in return. "I'm fine. I'm going to see if anybody's home over there and secure the lock. Put your helmet on and stay here. Lock the cockpit door behind me."

She unbuckled from the seat and double-checked to see that her sidearm—another microwave emitter—was secured at her hip, then floated out of the cockpit into the rest of the sterile, deserted ship. It had been so full of life and promise on the trip out to Saturn, so utterly devoid of hope and joy on the way back. She was pretty damn sure she never wanted to set foot on this ship again when they finally got back to Earth.

Shaila shunted her thoughts aside as she reached the airlock, putting on her own suit helmet and activating the holographic heads-up display. Data scrolled across her field of visions, followed by a variety of alerts—her suit seal was good, she had several hours of oxygen and power remaining, and the ship's network reported the airlock link between *Armstrong* and *Tienlong* was secure. There was no link between the two ships' computers, however, which didn't come as a complete surprise. *Tienlong*—Stephane— wouldn't make this easy, and it wouldn't be surprising if someone aboard the Chinese ship might try to hack *Armstrong*.

"Going in," she said over her comm. She knew both Archie and the folks on *Hadfield* would be listening in. "I'll secure the other side of the docking tube."

With a few keystrokes on the control panel next to the airlock, she overrode normal docking procedures so that the tube itself wouldn't be flooded with atmosphere from either ship; she wanted a vacuum between the two ships in case something tried to get across. Shaila then stepped into the airlock, closing it behind her, and felt the familiar whoosh of air as the atmosphere around her retreated back inside *Armstrong*. Red lights shifted to green, and the door in front of her opened into the tube now linking the two ships. She floated down the insulated, plastic corridor until she reached the outer airlock hatch on *Tienlong*'s hull.

Like the rest of the ship, the hatch was scored with mete- orite impacts, black streaks upon the grey metal. Nothing appeared damaged, however, and the controls were help- fully labeled in both Mandarin and English—the Chinese took plenty of corporate exploitation missions, and English remained the *de facto* language of business around the world. Sadly, there was no window on the hatch through which she could see inside the ship.

"All right. Archie, send me the entry codes we got from the Chinese," Shaila said. A moment later, a series of numbers and Chinese characters appeared on her HUD. She flipped open a panel on the right side of the airlock hatch, exposing the keyboard she needed, and plugged in the codes, hoping the Chinese weren't suddenly feeling bad about JSC taking the lead on this particular humanitarian mission.

A red light began blinking above the hatch; the depressurization process was beginning inside *Tienlong*'s airlock, as per usual. She waited until the light turned a steady green and, with a deep breath, turned the hatch's locking mechanism. With her other hand, she grabbed her weapon and pointed.

Nothing.

The inside of the airlock was as expected. Her suit sensors helpfully ran a diagnostic on the visible ships systems, and all seemed in order. There was a small window that opened into the rest of the ship, but from her vantage point outside, all Shaila could see was dim lighting and, blessedly, no movement.

"*Hadfield*, this is Jain. All clear here. I'm going to enter the airlock and close it behind me. Over."

"Roger that, Jain," Diaz replied over the comm. "We're about four minutes out. We'll be joining you shortly. Do not pressurize and enter the ship until I give word. Over."

"Roger, *Hadfield*. Over."

Shaila couldn't help but smile slightly; Diaz seemed to think she was going to go in, guns blazing. Of course, she *wanted* to. She wanted to charge in and make her way to the cockpit, where she was sure she'd find Stephane. But dammit, she was a Royal Navy officer and JSC astronaut. She had orders, and she was going to follow them.

Shaila entered the airlock and closed the outer door behind her. More codes appeared on her HUD—activation codes that would allow her to repressurize the lock and enter *Tienlong*. She wouldn't use them, though. The outer door was easy enough to re-open, and if need be, she'd tell Archie to do an emergency "drop" of the docking tube—allowing it to release from both ships and drift off into space—rather than have someone charge through. The inner door remained secure, and she could now see through the window that the corridor in front of her was empty, with only emergency lights on.

Shaila tried to access *Tienlong*'s wireless network—using a special encrypted sandbox to keep *Armstrong*'s systems secure—but kept coming up with no response, even with the override codes the Chinese provided. She could theoretically jack in physically, but the nearest computer screen was on the other side of the airlock door...

...where someone was now floating.

Shaila gasped slightly at the sight; she'd been distracted by the technology in front of her, and the data on her HUD, to pay much attention to the darkened corridor beyond the hatch. But there, outside the airlock, a person watched her from the shadows, grasping handholds on the wall and floating silently less than four meters away.

The person—she couldn't tell if it was a man or woman—didn't even show up on sensors. She just...showed up.

"*Hadfield*, Jain. Contact made. Single unidentified target. Over." A small part of her was surprised at the calm in her voice.

"We see the feed from your helmet cam, Jain," Diaz said, equally calm. "Stay in the airlock and do not engage until backup arrives. If the target advances, retreat into the tube. Confirm."

"Confirmed," Jain replied. "I will not engage. Over."

Shaila peered into the darkness. As her eyes adjusted, she could see that the figure was female, and that meant it was Maria Conti, *Armstrong*'s biologist and medical officer. She had accompanied Col. Mark Nilsson over to *Tienlong* when it was in orbit over Titan. Nilsson was later ejected from an airlock—the very same airlock Shaila stood in—without his helmet. A transmission from *Tienlong* later showed Conti standing behind Stephane. Shaila and the DAEDALUS team concurred that she, like Stephane, was likely possessed as well.

"She's not doing anything," Archie said over the comm. "Wonder why."

"I think she's keeping me in place," Shaila replied. "She probably doesn't want me getting in. Which means...

Hadfield, they have a plan for us. That burn they did wasn't just evasion."

"Agreed," Diaz replied from *Hadfield*. "Stay glued on her and prepare to move. Three minutes."

Shaila waited, her weapon out of view but firmly in hand. For her part, Conti remained in the corridor, in the shadows between the emergency lighting. Shaila raised her hand and waved to Conti, but she remained motionless. In fact, she was so still that Shaila found herself checking to see if Conti was still breathing, but at least her chest rose and fell in rhythm. Still, it was unnerving as hell.

Shaila looked around the airlock, with her HUD giving her information on what she was seeing: outer hatch lock, emergency evac…communication relay. Not a full jack-in to the ship's computers, but a simple patch to put her in speakers.

Shaila plugged a thin cord from her suit gauntlet into the relay, then flipped the comm switch. "*Tienlong*, this is acting Captain Shaila Jain of the JSC Ship *Armstrong*. You are in violation of the U.N. Space Charter and will be boarded. You are directed to gather in the ship's common room, where you will surrender and be taken into custody. Acknowledge."

Conti didn't move.

"I demand to speak with the current commander of this vessel. Where is Stephane Durand?" she asked, her voice cracking ever-so-slightly at the mention of his name.

Again, no movement.

Shaila was tempted to talk further, but found she had little else to say. She kept her suit plugged into the comm relay, but muted the link. If they wanted to talk to her, they'd know where to find her.

"Archie, any movements you can see in the windows?" Shaila asked.

"Negative, still too damn foggy," he replied. "Got eyes on *Hadfield*, though. She came in like a bat outta hell, and lined up damn perfectly. You would've liked it."

Shaila smiled despite herself. "Can't wait to meet the pilot. Is he—wait."

Conti was moving.

Without warning, she turned her head away from the airlock toward the rest of the ship. She then pushed off back down the corridor; Shaila assumed she was headed for the ventral airlock where *Hadfield* was docking.

"Looks like I'm all clear here," Shaila said. "*Hadfield*, you're probably getting company at your airlock. Do you wish me to pursue? Over."

"Negative," Diaz replied. "Stay put until the team comes to get you. Acknowledge."

Shaila grimaced at that, but kept her cool. "Roger that, *Hadfield*. I—whoa!"

A face suddenly appeared right in front of the window.

"Fuck! *Hadfield*, are you seeing this?" Shaila said, a little too loudly.

"We have visual," Diaz said coolly. "Identify."

Overcoming her surprise, Shaila looked at the Chinese man now staring back at her. "I…yeah. Chinese officer, I think it's Shen Jie," Shaila said, pulling the man's face from her memory. She had studied the crew files regularly in transit from Saturn, though any resemblance between the holoimage of a smiling People's Army major and the man before her now was superficial at best. Shen's black hair was matted with sweat, sticking to his scalp. His eyes were dilated and bloodshot, and the bags and dark circles under them were incredibly, almost sickeningly pronounced. His mouth was slightly opened, and Shaila could see his teeth were a putrid, neon yellow.

"Confirming Major Shen Jie," Diaz replied. "Stay put. I've informed the fire team. They'll pull him off you."

Suddenly, Shen pushed off the hatch and floated back into the corridor—toward a control panel about five meters from the airlock door.

Shen pressed a few buttons, and a red light began flashing insistently inside the airlock. "Negative, *Hadfield*,"

Shaila said. "He's going to open the lock. Repeat, Shen is opening the airlock."

"Brace!" Diaz shouted.

Shaila grabbed a handhold and pressed her feet against the outer hatch. The inner door swept open, and a split second later, all the pressurized atmosphere from *Tienlong* rushed into the airlock. Despite her best efforts, Shaila's grip was torn from her handhold and she was slammed into the outer hatch by the onslaught of air blowing into the little chamber.

When she opened her eyes again, Shen was sailing toward her fast…with a knife in his hand and an inhuman look of rage on his face.

Shaila's training took over just as the air pressure subsided and she felt herself floating free again. Pushing up with her feet, she grabbed a handhold on the ceiling of the airlock and then kicked outward—catching Shen in the face with a boot. The astronaut twirled around with the force of the blow, blood spraying from his mouth in all directions, creating tiny crimson droplets floating through the lock. Meanwhile, Shaila allowed her momentum to carry her out of the airlock, effectively trading places with Shen. A few seconds later, Shaila was able to grab the control panel for the lock, arresting her movement just as Shen was shaking off the effects of the kick.

"Shit, which button?" Shaila muttered. Unlike the outer lock, all the buttons were in Chinese. Helpfully, her suit computer immediately projected translations onto her HUD. She pressed what she hoped would be the right sequence….

…and turned to find Shen wedged within the closing door, halfway between the airlock and the corridor. He was stuck, and angry.

Shaila floated over and, keeping her distance, gave the Chinese astronaut a closer look. He certainly *looked* like he was battling an infection. His skin was incredibly pale, and coated with a thin sheen of sweat. There were dark stains under the arms of his uniform and around his collar. He looked as though he'd been bedridden and hadn't been able to keep up with his personal hygiene—his teeth, now bared, were purple in spots and probably rotting inside his mouth.

But it was the eyes that hit Shaila the most. They were wide and feral. There were streaks of blood around Shen's mouth in every direction, and he was...growling, it seemed, though the sound was blessedly muffled by Shaila's suit.

"Report, Jain," Diaz said over the comm.

"You seeing this, ma'am?"

"Roger that. Neutralize him and head to the ventral hatch to support Parrish. Acknowledge."

In other words, stop staring and get your ass in gear, Shaila thought. Good idea. "Roger that, *Hadfield.*"

Shaila drew her zapper and hit Shen with it at a range of about half a meter. Surprisingly, it only seemed to disorient him, and Shaila needed two more shots until Shen's eyes closed. Shaila then shoved him back through the door and into the airlock, allowing the doors to close on him. A few keystrokes on the control panel locked the astronaut in for good; Archie would send Shen out into space before allowing him into the tunnel between *Tienlong* and *Armstrong,* let alone into the JSCS ship itself.

"Parrish, this is Jain, over," she said as she floated into the bowels of the darkened *Tienlong.*

"Parrish here, Jain. We're about ready to enter. I got Conti eying us pretty good. She's got some sort of laser drill with her."

Shaila pushed off the walls a little faster, a map on her HUD guiding her to the *Hadfield* team's location. "Don't let her get a shot off. She's probably rewired it to punch a hole through you. Concentrate all zappers on her at once. It's going to take a few shots to take her down."

"Copy that. We'll wait until you're in position. I—shit, she's opening the airlock."

The comm went silent and Shaila cursed as she barreled down the corridor, diving into an access tube. There was a flash of light before her, then a muffled scream. Then silence.

"Report, Parrish," Diaz said, opening the comm channel to everyone.

"Lost Riggs, ma'am," the marine replied. "Conti knew she was outgunned, decided to take one of us with her."

Shaila turned to see Parrish and another spacesuited marine hovering over a third. The latter man's helmet had a hole burned through it. What was inside the helmet was… unrecognizable. Between Shaila and the marines was the unconscious body of the former *Armstrong* officer.

"She's going to be awake soon," Shaila said, grabbing Conti's hair unceremoniously as she floated past, pulling her toward the airlock. "Lock her in."

Parrish manned the control panel to lock the woman in between *Hadfield* and *Tienlong*—Diaz would, no doubt, manage her capture quite nicely. The other marine—Shaila saw his name, BECKER, on his suit—tethered his fallen comrade to a handhold. There would be time to retrieve him, and mourn, later.

"*Hadfield* to Parrish, Jain. Are you guys fucking with the comms on *Tienlong*?" Diaz barked.

"Negative, ma'am," Jain responded. "We just put Conti in the airlock between you and us, that's it."

"Shit," Diaz replied. "We're reading a power surge here of incredible proportions, like every goddamn system on *Tienlong* is now powering their comms. And the dish is swinging toward Earth."

A tactical map popped up on Shaila's HUD—the power surge, and the communications room, was deep inside the ship, well away from their location. "We'll get there. Single three-man fire team. Let's go," Parrish replied. "How long we got until BlueNet is ready?"

"Four minutes," Diaz said. "Hurry your asses up."

The three officers took off down the corridor, weapons drawn, their HUDs leading them toward the source. There was an odd clanking around them as they drew nearer, and they felt the ship vibrating wildly every time they touched a handhold to vault themselves forward. What few lights were left aboard were flickering, going out, leaving only their suit lights to help them see their way; their suits compensated by layering night-vision sensors over their HUDs.

Up ahead, a bright white light flashed—and faded to blue.

"Oh, shit," Shaila said, even as her HUD confirmed her fear—a massive surge of Cherenkov radiation ahead. "*Hadfield*, Cherenkov spike!"

Diaz didn't respond as Shaila, Parrish and Becker vaulted forward. The comm room was just ahead, and already they could see something was amiss—there were extra power conduits and wiring strung down the corridor, leading into the room. "They've been doing a hack," Parrish said. "Third guy is likely in there now."

Shaila nodded and tried to keep her voice professional. "He's probably busy with this comm stuff. Suggest we concentrate fire on him—three at once."

"Hold off, fire team," Diaz said over the comm. "Power surge is falling. BlueNet is in position. Preparing to fire in ten seconds."

Parrish motioned for Shaila and Becker to move to either side of the door. Shaila watched her suit HUD count down the last ten seconds. After which…her screen flickered. And that was it. No flash, nothing.

"*Hadfield*, this is Jain. Status?"

A moment later, Diaz came on the line. "If we're reading this right, we netted…two entities."

What the hell? "Come again?" Shaila asked.

"Hang on. We're working on it. Stand by," Diaz said curtly.

As Diaz's voice faded, Shaila heard the muffled sound of laughter. From inside *Tienlong*.

From the comm room.

And it sounded a little like Stephane.

"Parrish, Becker," Shaila said. Both nodded in return, pointing to the doorway. They heard. They were ready.

"On my mark," Parrish said. "Three…two…one…MARK."

Shaila pushed off the wall and around the doorway, her weapon before her.

What she saw she would never forget.

There were two large tanks in the room, seemingly cobbled together from other parts of the ship. Wires protruded all around them and into the comm consoles around the room. In between the two tanks, an emerald stone slab, roughly a half-meter across and a meter high, rested in a cobbled-together electronic cradle, surrounded by lights and more wires. It gave off an eerie green light.

Shaila recognized it as the tablet Stephane and the Chinese had uncovered on Titan, in a forgotten ruin that, by all that was sane and logical, should not have been there.

The rest of the room was a jury-rigged mess, with equipment taped to every surface. Small bits of tech floated lazily around. There was a palpable hum of electrical energy there. Nothing looked like it should be working, but it was.

And in the middle of it all, floating in zero-g, was Stephane.

But it wasn't him. She knew that horrible, stomach-sinking truth with just a simple, half-second glance.

It wasn't his appearance that tipped her off, though he looked wretched. His hair was long, matted, greasy. He wore a beard, similarly unkempt. He was filthy, with patches of grease and food stains on his skin and uniform. Pale, sweaty, wide-eyed…he looked sick and infected. His teeth were yellowed, stained, disgusting. His body was emaciated.

But there was more to it than that. He looked like he might burst from the inside out, bloated with whatever insanity was running through him. His eyes carried sights that ought not to have been seen, reflected only in his twitchy movements, his rictus grin, his constantly moving hands that grasped only thin air.

Stephane faced them and opened his arms wide. "They're gone!" he shouted through a smile that was both beatific and utterly terrifying. "And there's nothing you can do about it!"

Shaila fired, and Stephane's eyes grew glassy. She fired again, and his body twitched, his eyes rolling in the back of his head. She fired again. And again. She fired until Parrish grabbed her weapon from her.

And still, even unconscious, Stephane still wore someone else's horrific smile on his face.

CHAPTER 5

May 6, 1809

Weatherby paced the wooden floors of the reception hall, impatient with just about everything in the Known Worlds. Sitting by a roaring fire in a beautiful marble fireplace, Anne chatted amiably with one of the Crown Prince's lady courtiers, likely regarding some trivia that would elude him. Anne was certainly the more gregarious and socially adept of the pair, and Weatherby would typically accept this with good grace and humor.

But now he waited upon a prince, the prince, it seemed, who liked to keep Weatherby waiting despite his having traveled millions of miles at the Crown's behest. Hence, the admiral's mood was foul and he was highly disinclined toward idle chatter.

Victory had made port in Leith two days prior, and Weatherby immediately made for Edinburgh Castle with all haste, Anne right by his side. Once arrived, he was told the Prince Regent was falconing, and that he should await a summons. Having been summoned across the very Void already by His Royal Highness, Weatherby was quite aggrieved at this, with only Anne's soothing words keeping him from tearing the courtier's head clean off his body.

And now, having actually been summoned that very morning, they waited yet again. Assuredly, the Royal Palace of Edinburgh Castle was a fine place to wait for anyone, with wood-paneled walls, comfortable furniture, a warm fire and wine to soothe the soul. But Weatherby was not impressed in the least. His place was at sea and Void, bringing battle to the French and ultimately evicting Napoleon's accursed forces from England once and for all.

Instead, he was waiting.

"You're going to pace a rut in His Royal Highness' floors," came a voice from the other end of the room.

Weatherby turned to find Viscount Castlereagh, His Majesty's Secretary of State for War and the Colonies, walking toward him with a broad smile and extended hand, which Weatherby returned in kind, clasping Castlereagh's hand. "I trust you're well, my Lord Minster," Weatherby said with a smile, for Castlereagh was the best sort of politician—a blunt speaker, and one who appreciated advice from the military instead of dismissing it.

"I am indeed, Lord Admiral, and I trust you are as well," said Castlereagh, fit and hale for a man nearing 40, and charismatic as one might expect from a nobleman and politician both. "You remember General Wellesley, yes?"

Weatherby had not seen the other man, but he did indeed remember, as Castlereagh well knew. The Navy admiral shook the Army general's hand perfunctorily, and with a tight smile. Sir Arthur Wellesley was singularly devoted to the goal of retaking England—of course, as they all were. But Wellesley's fervor approached manic on many occasions. He personally led sorties south of Hadrian's Wall, had taken and lost Yorkshire no fewer than three times in two years, and continued to run through men and matériel at a most alarming rate. Wellesley was a decisive military genius, something even Weatherby would readily admit. But whereas Weatherby believed in a strong Navy to keep Napoleon's forces from gaining reinforcements from the Continent, Wellesley often advocated a total assault from all sides. The year prior, the two men had nearly come to blows right in front of Castlereagh and the Prince Regent when Wellesley insisted on conscripting every sailor in the Royal Navy for a massive southern assault on Portsmouth. It took physical intervention on the part of Prince George himself to separate the two.

"My Lord Admiral," Wellesley said quietly, a tight grin upon his thin face, his dark eyes alight with what could only be described as keen assessment.

"Sir Arthur," Weatherby said, equally reserved and likewise taking the measure of the other.

Anne came over and likewise shook hands—they were all, in fact, familiar with one another, having spent varying amounts of time at Edinburgh Castle, and Anne herself was a *de facto* alchemical adviser to the court—until finally, an uncomfortable silence reigned for several long moments. Castlereagh coughed, then said: "I am told, Lord Weatherby, there is some intelligence from Oxford you wish to share with us?"

"Should we await His Highness, my Lord?" Weatherby asked.

"I am to understand the Crown Prince Regent may not be in attendance after all," Castlereagh said with a smirk. "Obviously, as Prince Regent, and with His Majesty the King still in French hands, there is much that weighs upon him."

In other words, the bloody prince doesn't give a damn. "Well, then, perhaps we best begin," Weatherby said as he walked toward the room's main table, whereupon his satchel of papers lay. He opened it and withdrew a page, laying it upon the table. "Minister, General, this is an alchemical message paper, linked to a journal kept by Philip, the Count St. Germain—Anne's son."

"Yes, I understand he and your daughter are both in Oxford," Wellesley said quietly, and with apparent earnestness. "You both should be proud of them. They are true English patriots."

"You are most kind, Sir Arthur," Anne said before Weatherby could reply. "We are, of course, both proud and greatly worried for their safety. This message requires a bit of translation, but we can safely say that the Frenchman Claude-Louis Berthollet—the very creator of the *Corps Éternel*, and France's greatest alchemist—is in Oxford right at this moment, along with another man, likely an alchemist as well. And they are seeking something in the depths of Oxford's archives."

"Do we know what?" Castlereagh asked.

"We cannot say, Lord Minister," Weatherby replied. "But Oxford remains the greatest repository of alchemical and otherworldly knowledge in all the kingdom, and the finest outside Paris or the Vatican—all of which are in French hands, of course."

"One of Oxford's foremost specialties, aside from the Great Work itself, is in lore from beyond Earth—the Xan, the Venusians, the ancient Martians," Anne added. "Our concern is that they may be seeking the key to some new working or weapon of which we are not aware, one that may lay within their grasp. They have free rein upon Venus, after all, and they remain allied with the Xan partisans."

Castlereagh and Wellesley took this information in for several long moments. "This is alarming indeed, my Lord and Lady," Wellesley said finally. "But what action might we take? Oxford is 350 miles from here if it's an inch. And there are legions of French troops, and their damnable *Corps Éternel* between."

"Little, certainly, other than to be prepared," Weatherby said. "We have given them instruction to discover as much as they are able without being discovered themselves, and—"

"And I'm sure they will perform admirably," came another voice from the head of the room. The group turned and saw His Royal Highness, George, Prince of Wales and Prince Regent, enter the room. He was tall, stout and broad-chested, possessed of a florid face and dark hair, with eyes that could hold joy and menace in equal measure—and occasionally both at once. At times Weatherby wondered whether he was King Henry VIII come back to life; certainly the prince's once-profligate spending, estranged marriage, and long-time mistress helped the comparison.

Yet Weatherby saw there was something far more interesting afoot than the mere attendance of England's ruler, for the Prince Regent was accompanied by a Xan.

All in the room bowed deeply toward Prince George, but their eyes remained locked on the looming hooded figure to his right. This worthy was ten feet tall, and its taloned hands were clasped in front of it, obscured by the folds of its robe. Likewise, the Xan's hood covered its face, as was common amongst those Saturnian folk who visited Earth-men.

Prince George, for his part, smiled wickedly at his subjects in the room. "And here I imagine you thought me off on some wastrel adventure or another," the Prince Regent chided. "In fact, I have been deep in negotiations with the ambassador here."

Weatherby and Castlereagh shared a quick look, and it became quite evident to Weatherby that this was a surprise to the minister, and thus likely a surprise to the rest of His Majesty's Government as well. Since retreating north, the Prince Regent had taken a far more active role in government than King George, especially given the latter man's enfeeblements of both body and mind. An active monarch was, in the eyes of some, a worrisome development, especially when he might act without the advice and consent of Parliament—a Parliament that continued to have difficulty meeting with more than half its elected members behind enemy lines.

George, meanwhile, smiled up at the hooded figure, which made a non-committal, melodic sound. The Xan had two mouths, one upon each side of their long faces, and their language relied on musical harmonies to add nuance and deeper meaning to their words.

At this sound, Anne's face grew brighter. "I dare say I know that melody," she said. "Is that not Vellusk under there?"

"Indeed it is, Lady Anne," the Xan sang, its body quivering slightly. "And I find it most agreeable to be in your company once more, along with our good Lord Weatherby. I hope you are both well, and your children besides."

"Yes, we overheard," Prince George said, cutting him off; His Royal Highness was never one for niceties in private settings. "In fact, that is why we interrupted. This good fellow here suddenly took a keen interest in your children, Lord Weatherby. Or rather, what they might find."

Weatherby turned toward the hooded alien. "Have you any notion as to what the French might seek in Oxford, Ambassador?" Weatherby asked.

"I cannot say for certain," the Xan sang, with uneasy harmonies lending a tension to his reply. "We remain troubled that *The Book of the Dead* was unaccounted for during the Egyptian crisis these many years past, and have always been concerned that the French may have taken possession of it."

"Dr. Finch says the book was destroyed," Anne replied, putting a smile in front of the steel of her words. "I see no reason to distrust him."

Vellusk appeared to…ripple…under his voluminous robes. "I find Dr. Finch a wholly admirable person, and one of the finest alchemists Earth has produced, my dear Lady Anne. I mean no disrespect. But the presence of these French abominations—those un-dead soldiers upon your very lands—leads me to believe that at least parts of the *Book* remain in the hands of Berthollet. So we must consider all options, including, I'm afraid, the very worst of possibilities."

Prince George stepped forward, interjecting himself into the conversation. "When might we know something from these children of yours?" he demanded.

Weatherby saw Anne bristle, and reached out subtly to place a hand upon her arm before words were exchanged. "Philip is the Count St. Germain now, sire, and my daughter Elizabeth is among the most intelligent people I have the privilege to know. Between them, we expect word any day. They have Dr. Finch's message papers, and we will know what they have learned quite quickly."

The Prince Regent looked to Castlereagh and Wellesley. "Their presence in Oxford shall not affect our plans. The invasion must be conducted on schedule, especially if we are to ask the Xan for their assistance."

Weatherby's jaw dropped as he looked to Castlereagh, and back to George. "Your Highness?"

George smirked, which in any other man would've been unkind, but was largely a part of the prince's mercurial and occasionally melancholic nature. "This is why we need your ships, Weatherby. We have found what may be a gap in France's defenses of England and Wales, and we mean to take full advantage. And Vellusk here has agreed to assist."

Both Weatherby and Anne looked to the Xan, whose robes rippled again—surely a sign of anxiousness. "We are aware that there are partisans from amongst our people who have taken up arms against you and in support of the French. We, of course, condemn these outcasts, but we recognize our condemnation is not enough. We must assist. However, our assistance must be limited," Vellusk sang sadly. "We cannot risk open warfare, nor shall we allow ourselves to battle our wayward fellows upon the Earth itself, for the consequences would be most dire. But yes, the time has come. We shall render some small technologies to you that may help you neutralize the threat the partisans pose, and may further keep the French monstrosities at bay."

"And we shall retake England!" Wellesley exclaimed quietly. "Surely, this is the hour!"

Weatherby looked down upon the prince's table, whereupon was laid a map of Great Britain. There, a number of lines were drawn: it was to be an invasion from Caernarfon, in northern Wales, sweeping through to London via Shrewsbury, Birmingham, Worcester…and Oxford. It was, perhaps, the best plan he had seen in many long months.

He looked to Anne, who took his hand in hers and held it tightly, then back to Wellesley, Castlereagh and the Prince Regent. "What do you need from me? And more importantly, what technologies can we rely upon from the Xan?"

Later that evening, Philip St. Germain looked upon the mirror in his room, and was quite pleased to find nothing there to be seen.

The elixir used to make a person invisible was not made up of rarities, but was rather difficult to create nonetheless, requiring exactitude in ingredients, heat, timing and cooling. Tales were told in the alchemical labs in Oxford of students who would turn the most curious colors thanks to improper admixtures, or would disappear for days on end. There are those who claimed a single hapless student— the time of his attendance at Oxford being uncertain, of course—disappeared entirely and completely, and was left to haunt the halls for decades.

Philip sought but a single night's haunting, and hoped his elixir would give him enough time to complete his task. He glanced out his window, and found the French revenants were once again at their posts by the side door, with the well-appointed carriage nearby. Berthollet and his compatriot were inside once more.

He opened his door slightly and, seeing no one, quickly exited his room and closed the door behind him, then made his way down the hall. A pair of his students wandered past in the hallway, discussing the merits of one of the girls in the village—he hoped it was not Elizabeth—before they moved past, unheeding. Philip merely had to step aside deftly as they walked past, then walked down the stairs to the front door of Hertford College. Another group of students entered, and he took advantage of their passing to slip outside.

The trick to invisibility, as he understood it from the accompanying texts describing the formulae, was not to disturb one's environment overmuch. People would not see him, but they would see a door opening seemingly of its own accord, and they would certainly hear footfalls, a cough, a sneeze. Philip had thought to augment his working with a means to dampen sound—a most common addition—but had not the time to prepare it. There was no way of knowing when the French might complete their business, and so he would have to make do. He left his shoes in his room to compensate, requiring him to gingerly walk across the cobblestone street, lest he stub his toe or trip.

Then there were the *Corps Éternel*, which had given Philip pause before he executed his plan to infiltrate the Bodleian Library. Precious few English alchemists had been able to study these resurrected soldiers in any great detail, for those who fell in battle seemed to quickly revert to whatever state of decomposition they might normally have experienced since their actual death. The alchemical energies quickly left once their corpses were rendered inert once more, and all too few had been successfully captured.

And so it was that there was a divergence of opinion as to these revenants' sensory capabilities. If they were limited to their normal, pre-deceased senses, then Philip would have no issue with moving past them. But if the fell means of their new life had given them preternatural senses, as some suspected, then Philip would have to face the savagery of the un-dead guardians—and tales of their prowess in combat was far more widespread than that of their sensory abilities.

Philip approached the door to the Bodleian cautiously, looking intently at the guards there for any sign of movement. He, like so many others, was fascinated and unnerved by the *Corps Éternel* soldiers' faraway gaze and their utterly still stance. It was as though they hoarded what little spark of life left to them, only to use it when called upon by their French masters—or when someone approached.

Another step, then…and another. Philip crept closer, and yet the guards remained motionless. At this distance, no more than six feet away, Philip could see their eyes shifting dully. They were assigned to guard duty, after all, and it would not be meet for a guard to be caught unawares. But even in this, they were unnatural. Philip could see their eyes look left, then before them, to the right, then centered, then left again. Over and over, as if a clockwork had been set behind their eyes.

And so he waited until one of the guards cast its unholy gaze upon him, holding his breath. The cold, dead eyes seemingly fixed upon him…then looked away.

They could not see him.

Philip almost exhaled in relief, but caught himself, forcing the breath he had held to escape slowly and quietly. He then picked his way across the cobblestones to the door, which remained closed.

He waited.

Several minutes went by, and to his utmost frustration, no one entered or left the library. The hour grew late, and he grew increasingly anxious that his quarry would leave before he might discover their intent.

Philip turned back to the guards. They stood stock still, their backs to him. And he wondered if these *Corps Éternel* soldiers were indeed as listless and aimless as they appeared.

It would be a gamble, and a failed ploy could result in a bayonet through him.

Philip slowly pressed down upon the door latch with his thumb. With a click—all too audible—it gave way.

He turned to the guards once more. They remained motionless.

Quickly, Philip opened the door just enough for him to slip inside, then closed it behind him with immense care. Another sound escaped as the latch caught once more, and he stood in the corner of the hallway, wide-eyed and sweating, to see if anyone, living or dead, would react.

All was silent.

Trembling with unspent tension, Philip slowly made his way down the corridor, listening for sounds echoing in the otherwise empty library. Thankfully, he knew the library as well as any tutor might, and some sections were as familiar to him as the contents of his own alchemical laboratory. And so he moved silently toward the stairs leading upward, to where the tomes on alchemy and other sciences were kept.

It took altogether too long, Philip felt, to make his way there, but caution remained a watchword. And yet there were no lamps lit in any of the rooms. Nothing was unduly disturbed. There were no signs of the French.

Philip thought a moment. The only other collection that might be of interest was two floors down, in the basement of the library—the collection of books and artifacts from the rest of the Known Worlds.

That, in and of itself, might warrant a report to his mother and stepfather. But he had to know for certain. And so he crept down the stairs once more, keeping close to the railings to minimize the creaking of the boards, until his stocking feet met the cold stone of the basement.

A light shone from one of the rooms further down the hallway. Philip could hear murmurs, but little else. It would not be enough.

A sound off to his right made him start, and he nearly tripped over his feet as he turned toward the source. At the other end of the hall, he could make out the form of a woman, holding a single candle. There was a basket under her arm, and he could see the outlines of a broom in the darkness. One of the cleaning women, most likely finishing her duties for the evening. Philip allowed himself breath once more, but nonetheless watched carefully as the woman walked away toward another part of the building. It would do no good to be caught by a simple worker when he was so close to his goal.

Philip proceeded closer, and closer still, and the murmurs began to grow louder. He could not make out the words, but he knew them, at this point, to be French. Another positive sign. Grinning slightly now, having gained confidence in the efficacy of his alchemical disguise, Philip made his way to the open door.

He was already familiar with the room, of course. Like so many others, it was lined floor to ceiling with books. These were organized by planet, starting with Mercury to his immediate left, and ending with Saturn to his right. As one might guess, the sections on Venus, Mars and Saturn were the most extensive, being the homes of the three intelligent races other than Man that called the Known Worlds home. Nearly half the room was given over to the study of the Xan, and there were a number of small artifacts in glass cases near the books. None of these, Philip knew, would be of great import or insight, for the Xan still guarded their secrets jealously from mere humans.

There were more artifacts from Mars, of course, including an extensive array of reddish stone carvings taken in 1779, one of the results of the HMS *Daedalus* affair, of which his stepfather and mother were most notably involved, along with the late Baron Morrow, captain of the *Daedalus* and a man Philip had grown to know and love as much as any blood relation in the time since the Emerald Tablet affair some eleven years ago.

Venus had an extensive collection of tomes and items as well, including many plant samples kept in vials and tubes—leftovers, Philip knew, from the alchemical labs, for the efficacy of Venusian flora in alchemical workings was extraordinarily well known. It was a shame that, given the English blockade of the French occupiers, such stores of Venusian extracts and leaves were hard to come by in Oxford these days.

And it was there amongst the Venusian lore, in the furthest corner of the room, that Philip laid eyes upon Claude-Louis Berthollet, seated in a comfortable chair, reading by candlelight. His compatriot sat across from him, his back to Philip, with but a tuft of white, disheveled hair protruding above the back of his chair to give him away.

With them were two more members of the *Corps Éternel*, standing watch over the door from the center of the room.

Philip took a moment to study Berthollet, a man he knew only from etchings and the stories Finch would regale them with at parties. He was a stout man, and one of a frowning countenance in his florid face. Like the rest of the French, he eschewed the use of powdered wigs, allowing his gray-and-white hair to grow more freely. Philip knew him to be the creator of the *Corps Éternel*, but remembered that Berthollet also was the vice-president of the French Senate and one of Emperor Napoleon's foremost advisors.

Philip cursed himself for not obtaining a pistol, for a well-placed shot might cripple France's alchemical ambitions for years.

As it was, his task was one of espionage, rather than assassination, and he knew himself well enough to recognize his own incapacity for murder in cold blood. So Philip carefully walked into the room, past the un-dead sentinels, and toward the seated Berthollet.

He started slightly when Berthollet spoke.

"Alessandro, what do you make of this?" Berthollet asked his companion, offering the other man the book he was reading. Berthollet's French had a deep timbre. "On the right, the second column."

The older man reached out a trembling, gnarled hand to take the book, drawing it to his own candlelight. A few moments passed, during which Philip quietly drew closer. "I think you may have something there, *monsieur*," the other man said with a light accent; Philip assumed it to be Italian, given the man's name.

"We cannot be certain, but there are enough elements to the architecture to suggest that the Venusians had guidance in building it, likely from the Xan," Berthollet said, accepting the book back once more. "They build so damnably few buildings, it would seem a logical place to start."

"Which tribe holds it?" the other man asked.

Berthollet picked up a map from the table beside him. "Let us see…it appears this is some sort of neutral ground, administered by the Va'hak'ri." The Frenchman grinned. "I do believe you have some experience with that tribe, do you not?"

Philip could see the older man shift in his chair. "Not nearly enough. I have many regrets, Berthollet. The Va'hak'ri are one of them," he said, with a weariness in his voice.

Berthollet gave the older man a kind of understanding smile, though his face looked wholly unsuited to such displays of commiseration, and it came off as quite awkward to Philip's eye. "It is unfortunately necessary to the continued success of the Revolution, and the Emperor's vision of liberty, that we press forward, old friend. Otherwise, the evil that plagued you so many years ago may once again rise."

Recognizing it as perhaps naivety, Philip nonetheless was surprised to hear such words from the French. Of course, those who commit evil often consider themselves working toward their own noble ends. But this seemed all too genuine, for there was no other audience for Berthollet's ears. Well, none that he might discern.

Philip walked around where the two men were sitting so that he might have a better look at the books and maps upon

Berthollet's table. He also got a look at the other man, the one called Alessandro. This man was wizened indeed, looking to be well past eighty years of age, with a bald pate ringed in a fringe of unruly, snow-white hair. His clothes were fine but unremarkable. He also bore no jewelry upon him, compared to the rings and adornments worn by Berthollet. Philip knew that there were those alchemists, particularly the French, who used jewelry as a focus of workings. Students of the Great Work were often warned against such overt displays of power, but some saw the opportunity to wear rings and bracelets adorned with sigils of mystic science as a kind of calling card.

So was this Alessandro an alchemist? Philip's mind went back to a story his stepfather once told of meeting the esteemed Ganymedean alchemist Benjamin Franklin, who had immediately identified Finch as an alchemist by the stains of elixirs and powders upon his hands. Philip could see Berthollet bore a few upon his, but the other fellow's hands were unblemished.

And yet Berthollet addressed him as someone worthy of respect, if not an equal, and both seemed to be engaged in whatever quest for knowledge they were upon. An expert on Venus, perhaps?

Philip moved closer to attempt to read over Berthollet's shoulder…

…and knocked over the ink bottle and quill upon the man's table.

Stupid idiot! he chided himself, even as he quickly drew back. But unfortunately, he moved so fast that he forgot where he was, and bumped into the bookcase behind him.

A second later, Berthollet was on his feet, casting his eyes about the room. "Guards! Close the door! Let no one enter or exit!"

Philip watched as the two guards stiffly but quickly moved to the door, shutting it, and turned back to watch the room carefully. Berthollet began rummaging through a small case he had secured next to the table, while the older man slowly worked his way to his feet with the aid of a cane.

Don't move. Don't move.

Philip stood as still as possible, breathing as quietly as he might. Surely he might find a place in the room to hide, rather than keeping his back pressed to a stack of books and papers all night.

The papers...he felt them on his back as he shifted ever so slightly. Motion. Movement. *Oh, no.*

Suddenly, he looked up to see Berthollet before him, blowing a powder toward his face. And in that moment, Philip knew the game would be up. He tried to spring forward, but Berthollet slammed a hand into his chest and, with surprising strength, likely enhanced by alchemy, he shoved Philip back into the wall, even as Philip saw himself regain visibility in the dim light of the candles.

"Well then, young man," Berthollet said in French. "You are a canny alchemist, though a fool and a clumsy oaf as well."

Philip struggled against Berthollet's grip, but the Frenchman was too strong; it was as though the man's arms were made of steel. Perhaps they even were. "I was...curious, merely curious, *monsieur*," Philip replied in passable French. "Surely a great alchemist as yourself would be working on something extraordinary if it were to bring you to Oxford, would it not?"

Berthollet backhanded Philip across the face, sending him to the floor. A kick from the man's shoe cracked something in Philip's ribcage, sending shooting pain throughout his body and causing him to cry out. "Do you think, boy, I am so stupid as this? You are working for those damn fool rebels in Scotland, who think they can countermand the alliance King George has made with our emperor!"

Philip heard a woman's voice from across the room. "An alliance at the end of a bayonet is hardly one at all!" she cried.

Elizabeth. Dear God, what are you doing?

Philip struggled to his feet, even as he heard the guards making for Elizabeth. There were the sounds of a scuffle, and a pistol shot besides. Overcoming the pain of his broken ribs, Philip stood and began to move forward....

....only to see Elizabeth moving across the room with a pistol pointed at Berthollet's head, a shining sword in her other hand. The guards behind her lay upon the ground moaning. They were cut in two at the waist.

"That's a fine sword, young lady," Berthollet remarked coolly. "Alchemical, I take it?"

Elizabeth gave the Frenchman a surprisingly wolfish smile. "Quite so. Made by the hand of one of the finest alchemists in the Known Worlds, and wielded by one of England's finest heroes. You may have heard of him."

Before she could say anything more, the older man reached out with his stick, knocking the sword from her hand and, with surprisingly deftness, cracking her across the head with it. To Philip's horror, Elizabeth fell to the floor, the pistol slipping from her hand.

"I know who carried that sword, young lady," the old man said, looking down at her with something akin to sorrow. "I believe I shot him once, though I was aiming for someone else."

Berthollet turned on the old man. "You know this woman?"

"No, but I know the blade," the man replied with a shrug. "Surely you've heard of Thomas Weatherby, have you not?"

Philip started to grow dizzy, whether it was from the pain in his side or the sight of his stepsister half-conscious upon the floor, he could not say. "What do you have planned?" Philip demanded, trying to sound hale. "Surely, it cannot countenance striking a woman in such a way."

The old man shuffled over toward Philip, looking him squarely in the eye. "I don't know this one either, but... but...hmmm." He drew close and examined Philip's face as though it was but a bust carved from stone in the galleries above. "I know those eyes, that nose. I dare say I knew your father, did I not?"

Philip stared blankly for several moments until a thunderbolt of recognition hit him. "It cannot be," he replied quietly. "You were said to have died in a dungeon in Italy!"

The old man favored him with a wink and a smile. "Even without the power your father stripped from me, I am a most resourceful man. And of course, I am fortunate to have friends in need of my services," he added, nodding toward Berthollet.

Philip was about to reply when Berthollet approached and blew more powder into his face. A moment later, all went black.

CHAPTER 6

January 14, 2135

Shaila gazed out her window at the small full Earth, floating in space some 1.5 million kilometers away—a bit smaller than the full moon as seen from the ground. So close, closer than she'd been in a year. And yet she wasn't going there any time soon.

She was supposed to be in her rest cycle but sleep wasn't happening, despite the long hours she and Diaz' team were putting in. There was too much to do, too much to figure out. Lives were at stake, somehow, though nobody could really pinpoint *how* quite yet.

And there was Stephane. That would've been more than enough to keep her up.

The last week and a half had been a whirlwind. The assault on *Tienlong* was a success, but not without cost. Parrish's team took the loss of one of their own very hard, and Shaila mourned with them. And yet Stephane, Conti and Shen were subdued and captured. The ship was halted well beyond Earth orbit for inspection and decontamination.

The problem was…there was nothing to decontaminate.

Deciding to give up on sleep altogether, Shaila took a quick run through the shower and threw on a fresh jumpsuit. Compared to the quarters on *Armstrong*, her new digs were outright luxurious. After a few days parked well away from anything, the powers-that-be allowed the ships to dock at Ride Station. What was once a bustling little waystation—"spaceport" seemed a bit ambitious yet—with more than sixty people aboard was now the spacefarer's equivalent of a ghost town. No extraplanetary missions, governmental or corporate, were allowed to use it. The staff was sent home. Shaila had scored the station XO's quarters as a result, a little present from Diaz.

When Shaila was finally allowed into Ride—after a gauntlet of medical tests that left her feeling like a pincushion, Diaz hugged her like a long-lost sister and Shaila couldn't help but lose it, breaking down right there at the airlock door. Someone—probably that hyper-efficient Coogan guy—cleared the room for them. All Diaz said was, "Good job, kid. Good job," over and over. Shaila couldn't find words to speak for hours after that.

That was the last time she cried. There was too much work to do.

Snapping back to the moment, Shaila left her quarters and walked down the hallway. Ride Station was a rotating spoke-and-wheel affair—the classic designs seemed to work best after all these years—which provided nearly full Earth gravity to most of the living quarters and workspaces. Only the six docking linkups and the cargo areas were kept in the station's axis. And right now, only *Armstrong* and *Tienlong* were there.

She passed through one of the common rec areas, where a couple of DAEDALUS teammates were spending their off-duty time. A few looked up, their faces brightening, but she gave them a curt nod and quickly walked past. She was something of a celebrity to many of the techs, warfighters and officers Diaz brought along, but Shaila was in no mood to make new friends. And she wasn't about to talk about what they really wanted to know—what went down on Titan and Enceladus. She'd already had two days of debriefing since arriving at Ride. It would be a good long while—if ever—before she was ready to talk about it with anyone else.

Not even Stephane.

Shaila strode through the corridor until arriving at a door labeled "ASTRONOMY." Most of the time, academics were allowed to rotate through the station to further whatever research they had going—a perk funded, at JSC's insistence, by the station's corporate customers. Since Diaz and DAEDALUS arrived, however, the room was converted into a giant containment facility. She opened the door and entered, just as she'd done at least three times a day since her debrief had finished.

Inside, the room had been split in half. To her right, a bank of computer equipment and monitors kept constant watch over the left part of the room, sealed off from the rest of the station by every means imaginable. It had its own airlock, environmental controls, bathroom facilities—even the fresh oxygen was fed in through a tank latched to the outside of the station, rather than Ride's usual atmosphere.

On a small cot in the corner, Stephane sat, looking at Shaila intently. Just as he did every day for over a week.

They had zapped him to hell and back again when they brought him aboard Ride, and someone had taken the opportunity to clean him up and put a fresh uniform on him. The hair and beard were still a mess, but at least they weren't greasy anymore. The med techs told Shaila that he'd been living on just 1,000 calories a day, tops. His body showed signs of extreme exhaustion, as if he'd been going with just two or three hours a sleep per night for the last several months. He was emaciated, his muscles atrophied; it seemed he'd spent most of *Tienlong*'s transit to Earth in zero-g, in the ship's labs rather than its living quarters. And yet, much to the med techs' confusion and consternation, his energy levels were off the charts. By rights, he should be utterly exhausted, and yet there he sat, wide awake.

Watching.

She walked over and pressed the comm button on the door of the containment cell. "Hey."

Stephane's body twitched slightly—was it a sign of recognition?—but otherwise he simply continued to stare at her, slightly glassy-eyed, regarding her as one might watch a goldfish in a bowl. It almost seemed disdainful.

No response, as usual. Shaila turned to the monitors. Accelerated heartbeat, signs of physical stress, exhaustion, exceedingly odd brain-wave patterns—and trace signs of Cherenkov radiation emanating from his cerebral cortex.

The diagnostic computers settled on "UNKNOWN INFECTION," which was an odd echo of the official line regarding whatever he picked up on Enceladus. But deep down, Shaila knew that it was more than a mere pathogen. He was under the influence of an alien intelligence, and as much as she wanted to reach inside him, rip it the hell out and stomp on it, there was nothing she could do.

Except talk. Every day, several times a day.

"I talked to your mom today," she said, returning to the comm. "I couldn't tell her what happened, of course. But I told her you're alive, and we're doing everything we can to make you well again," she said. "Of course, she doesn't have to know that we have no clue what we're doing, or how to get that fucker out of you. But we're trying. We're working on it. And we *will* get that thing out of you. No matter how long it takes."

Another twitch.

Shaila turned and saw his already elevated heart rate start to climb, pushing 120 beats per minute. His brain-wave patterns likewise started getting weird. That hadn't happened before. She had no clue what it meant, but she knew something was going on.

"You hear me, Stephane? I know you're there. I bet that's you, isn't it. Fighting. I know you. You're a cocky little joker, this laid-back guy with your sweet talk and your pretty smile, but deep down, you're a fighter. That's how you got me. That's why I fell for you."

He twitched again, quite visibly. His whole body shuddered. His hand fluttered.

Shaila's heart started to race. "You're the guy who pulled off a miracle back on Mars. You risked your life, sneaking into a weird temple to free us and stop Althotas. You climbed to the top of a fucking pyramid to cut a rope to stop that insane alien bastard from opening a rift between dimensions. If you hadn't done that, none of us would be here. That was you, Stephane. All you. I wouldn't be here now if it weren't for you. Maybe none of us would.

"And if it weren't for that, we wouldn't have…"

Stephane's entire body was fluttering now, subtly but uncontrollably. It was if he was shivering in brutally cold weather. Or had a colony of ants in his jumpsuit. And he had, finally, broken eye contact with her. He was now staring at his twitching hands.

"If it weren't for that," she continued, whispering, "we wouldn't have fallen in love, now would we? I love you, Stephane. I really do. Which is why you've got to fight this thing."

As if suddenly struck by lightning, Stephane jumped to his feet, his eyes bugging out of his skull. He staggered a moment, hands grasping his head. His mouth was moving, but Shaila couldn't hear. Then, finally, his body froze for a long, agonizing moment.

"Stephane?" Shaila said.

With a guttural shout, he picked up the cot and, with surprising strength and speed, threw it at the comm speaker.

Sparks flew. Plastic cracked. Pieces fell to the floor.

Shaila had ducked reflexively, and when she once again turned to face Stephane, he had already sat back down in the space where his cot used to be. He was once again completely still, and fixed Shaila with that terrible, distant gaze.

But she knew, in that moment, that she was right all along.

"I got you," she said, even though she knew Stephane couldn't hear her. "I got you, you fucker. He's in there."

At that moment, a tech rushed in, looking as though she had just been rudely awakened. Which she had. "What the hell happened? I got an alarm and…oh." She paused to look at the wreckage inside the containment cell.

"I pissed him off," Shaila said, grinning despite herself.

The tech, a young Chinese woman with an Australian accent, returned the smile. "That's brilliant! We've been trying to get a rise out of him ever since he got here!" She scurried over to the computers to check the readings. "Look at this! I haven't seen brain-wave activity like this… ever. And the irregular heartbeat….wow, the Cherenkov readings dipped too. This is incredible!"

"Thanks," Shaila said, turning to leave.

"Wait! You can't go!"

Shaila turned around with a surprised look on her face; she was pretty sure she outranked most folks on the station, and definitely sure about this particular tech. "Excuse me?"

"Um, well…will you come back? Try again? I mean, this is really something here."

In all honesty, Shaila had no intention of repeating it right then. But she did want to repeat it soon. "Go over all the data, match it to the holovid recording, and write up a report. Figure out exactly what worked and didn't. Then we'll go another round. Yes?"

"Yes, ma'am," the tech said, nodding vigorously before turning back to her instruments, hands fluttering across the controls. Shaila used that moment to escape quickly, shutting the door behind her and leaning against the hallway bulkhead to compose herself. She was trembling, her heart beating fast. She was oddly elated and frustrated at the same time, and utterly terrified at what she saw. Was that Stephane or Rathemas? Was Stephane winning or losing? Did she help him or hurt him?

She had no idea.

"Aren't you supposed to be on your rest cycle, Jain?"

Shaila opened her eyes—she had no idea they'd been closed—and saw Diaz standing before her, hands on her hips, a slight smile on her face. "Sorry, ma'am," Shaila said, drawing herself straight. "Couldn't sleep. Decided to visit Stephane. It was…interesting."

"Yeah, I got pinged on it. Come with me," Diaz said. "Dr. Ayim says he's ready to give me a full report on that jury-rigged piece-of-shit we found hooked up to the comm system on *Tienlong*. Tell me about Stephane on the way."

Shaila fell in beside Diaz and gave a brief description of her encounter, along with a heavily redacted version of her own feelings about it. "It's bound to be something positive. Better than him just staring, I suppose," Shaila concluded.

"Let's hope. The President's not too thrilled we got three alien-possessed people on the station and managed to lose whatever others they might've gathered. I'm hoping Stephane can get it together enough to give us some useful intel on these bastards," Diaz said, then looked over at Shaila. "No offense, Commander."

"None taken, General," Shaila said neutrally, trying her best not to sound hurt. "I hope he can get it together too."

The two walked for a few moments of silence until they arrived at another lab, where Ayim had set up shop with the contraption Stephane was found with on *Tienlong*. The door was open, and they found Ayim himself doing last minute checks of the device, which was within yet another containment cell.

"Ah, there you are, General. And Commander. Come in, come in! I think we finally figured out what happened here. Very interesting, very exciting!" Ayim said.

Shaila gave Diaz a sidelong glance, which was returned with a smirk. Gerald Ayim was very much a stereotypical academic, with a head for quantum physics and not, sadly, for social interaction. "So, Gerry, did you find our little critters?" Diaz asked, closing the door behind her.

Ayim looked slightly panicked. "Umm…no. No, we haven't, but we do have an idea or two on that. Shall I take it from the beginning?" Without waiting for an answer, he walked up to the glass of the containment unit. "So let's start with this green stone. Previously unknown geologic composition, odd green glow, bursting with Cherenkov radiation and, most likely, linked to—if not existing partially within—another dimension."

"The Emerald Tablet," Shaila said.

Ayim gave her a brilliantly white smile. "If you want to call it that, by all means. But I cannot say. All I know is that this stone has exceptional quantum properties that will take years for us to figure out. Years! I don't even know where to begin. But, that's not why you're here is it?" Again, he surged forward without waiting for a reply. "So you see this sort of electronic cradle around the device, very makeshift, this thing. Yet it somehow harnessed a bit of the energy this stone is giving off, and connected it to the two tanks you see here on either side. Now, these tanks—"

"—were used to gather up the water *Tienlong* took on from Enceladus. And the critters in the water that were throwing off the Cherenkov radiation pings, yes?" Diaz said. Shaila got the impression it wasn't the first time Diaz interrupted the scientist.

"Exactly, General! And we found enough tubing, and a homemade vacuum pump, to come to the conclusion that the *Tienlong* crew vacuumed up as much of the water as they could. Now, there was still extensive water damage aboard *Tienlong*, as you saw from the state of the lighting systems there, but they got most of it. More importantly, after several sensor sweeps, tuned to the molecular level no less, we found zero traces of any alien proteins. They seemed to be able to find and gather them all—a 100% success rate."

Shaila thought on this a moment. "Between the Chinese guy infected in Egypt, and Stephane on Enceladus, it seems like the possessed people can coordinate without comms, from any distance," she said. "Makes me wonder if Stephane and the others could pretty much sense where the proteins were on the ship, and vacuum them up accordingly."

"Exactly our thought as well, Commander," Ayim said. "Now, these tanks should be full of living alien proteins, correct? We thought we might find them in there, with this stone somehow giving them the power to maintain themselves. But they're all dead and decomposing."

Diaz stood taller. "Come again, Doctor?"

"The proteins. They may have been stored in these tanks, but when we examined them, we found they were no longer intact. They've decomposed at the molecular level. The amino acids are, right now, in the midst of dissolving. There are very few chains intact. Mostly, all we have are sodium and carbon atoms, along with nitrogen, hydrogen and oxygen isotopes. And water, of course."

"So it didn't work," Shaila said. "They're dead."

"They are dead, but that is not the really interesting part!" Ayim said, almost joyfully. "As we were investigating these tanks, we thought, why would you put this device in the communications room, of all places? *Tienlong* has labs for this sort of thing. Much better spaces for this. And we figured out why when we followed the wiring. Because this device was hooked up to their main relay dish."

Both women were still for a moment as they wrapped their heads around this. Diaz got there first. "There was a transmission burst aboard *Tienlong* right after the teams boarded. We assumed it was a distress call, and we couldn't intercept the packets, and Stephane or someone else wiped the computer memories clean. So how are these proteins related?"

Ayim clapped his hands and laughed. "That is the big question! Now, as we saw from the destruction of Enceladus and the minute traces of Cherenkov radiation immediately after, I think we can safely assume, for the sake of theory, that these proteins at one point had interdimensional qualities—that they perhaps existed in more than one place, if you will. Now, it would take years to even figure out how such simple proteins could be placed in a quantum state between two parallel dimensions, but the fact remains they were! And that, I think, is the key as to why they were hooked up to this machine, and to the communications relay."

Ayim stopped there, grinning, leaving Shaila and Diaz staring for a moment before looking at each other, confused. "You may want to keep going, Doctor," Shaila said. "We aren't following."

The physicist furrowed his brow a moment, then plowed forward again. "All right. If you are going to hook up series of proteins to a data transmitter, then can we not assume that there was something having to do with these proteins that could be translated into data? I think we can. And the fact that they are in a quantum superposition between parallel dimensions, the amount of data potentially 'stored' on each protein could be immense."

"So these proteins were glorified flash drives?" Diaz asked.

"It's possible! Yes, a crude analogy, but we believe that this device here somehow read the chemical makeup of these proteins, translated the quantum superpositioning, and then took the resulting data and downloaded it into a file to be transmitted to Earth."

"But we have no idea what that data was," Shaila said.

Ayim nodded. "We have perhaps a half-dozen decaying protein chains we're studying right now, to see if we might come up with a pattern. But there are several hundred trillion potential combinations among the remnants we have. I do not hold out hope. But that data went somewhere, so it likely still exists. From the position the ship was in, we can pinpoint the receiver to somewhere in Afghanistan or Pakistan."

"You and I have very different definitions of 'pinpoint,' Doctor," Diaz frowned. "What would the receiver look like? And what would the guys on the ground need to translate the data into something useful and/or deadly?"

The physicist shrugged. "I have no idea how they would manage to reconstitute that data, General, because I don't know what it was in the first place. But as for receiving it, it's hard to say. Would they need equipment to similarly provide some kind of quantum superpositioning in order to use this information to access a different dimensional state? If so, I cannot say what that would even look like. But if not, then all they would need is a standard data receiver. A converted satellite holovision dish would do, frankly."

"I was afraid you'd say that," Diaz said. "Looks like we need to send someone to Afghanistan."

"We need to leave Afghanistan," Harry Yu said.

"I agree, Harry," Greene replied.

Harry was surprised enough to actually show it, a rarity for him. He'd expected Greene and Huntington to really dig their heels in about relocation, especially after they'd been working hard on their new particle accelerator in the desert outside of Kabul. But here they were, simply sitting and nodding and agreeing with him as he stood, dumbfounded, in their shitty little office.

"Don't you even want to know why?" Harry asked.

"Sure," Huntington said, giving him one of her scary smiles.

"So for one, we're running out of money fast. I've maybe got two weeks' worth of bribe money left, and then we're out of luck. In fact, we should've been out of luck weeks ago, but I ended up getting a ForEx account and doing some day trading while you two were off in the desert. Wasn't much, but it helped."

Harry expected some recognition of this from his teammates, but none was forthcoming. On second thought, he was an idiot to think they'd care.

"So anyway, one way or another, we're going to have to leave. And as it turns out, I have a contact, someone I used to work with, who can give us some space and freedom and divert us some resources to get things to the point where we can successfully cross over to the other side again," Harry said. "Now, of course, she'll want a big cut."

"Where's the new location?" Huntington asked.

"Russia. Yekaterinburg. Most of the oligarchs and congloms are headquartered in Moscow, but they use Yekaterinburg for a lot of their R&D. And the Russians are almost as good as the Afghans when it comes to regulatory stuff. So. How long will it take for you to wrap things up here?" Harry asked.

Greene just grinned. "We brought in our prototypes from the desert this morning. As it so happens, we got all the data we need. We just need to pack up here and we're good."

Harry sat stunned for several moments before finally jumping to his feet. "How the fuck did you know to do that?" he shouted. "This is creeping me the fuck out! What the fuck is going on?"

Greene stood slowly and raised his hands in mock surrender. "Harry, we didn't know you were already making plans to move us. We've been playing with the data we received from *Tienlong* out in the desert for over a week now, and just today we ended up with the quantum phasing we needed to figure it all out. So we brought our gear in. Problem is, of course, that JSC and DAEDALUS will probably figure out what happened soon, and then they'll track us here."

Harry, of course, knew about the transmission from *Tienlong*, but he thought it was merely sensitive material from something they found on Titan. The fact that it took a week to decode—even with off-the-rack, second-hand quantum computers—was news. And what the hell did *Tienlong* send that they needed particle accelerators and quantum phasing—whatever the fuck *that* was—to figure it out?

Harry would find out soon, and with his new backing, he'd be in a position to take charge of this fucked-up operation once again. Harry knew he was being used, and he was looking forward to the leverage he needed to straighten that out.

"Then I guess we better get packing," Harry said, heading for the door. "I'll arrange the transport. Don't leave anything behind. I don't want anyone to track us down."

Harry went out to his car again and sent another secure e-mail to his new benefactor, asking about the security in Yekaterinburg—and advising her to get more.

CHAPTER 7

May 7, 1809

When in pitch darkness, the mind is often unclear as to whether the body is fully awake or not. Hence it was that Philip, the Count St. Germain, a brilliant alchemist and tutor, spent several precious minutes determining that, yes, indeed, he had regained consciousness.

It was the smell that gave away the game, for he could not recall ever experiencing smells in any dream-like state. Yet his nose detected notes of pine and sharp citrus quite near his head—indeed, upon the very surface he reclined against, a surface that was rough yet pliable on his skin. He was slumped up against...burlap. Yes, a burlap bag, confirmed by his fingertips.

Next, he determined that his arse was cold.

It was a most annoying sensation, of course, and he quickly realized that he was shivering as well. But as his mind continued to swim through the murk of receding alchemical sleep, he began to piece things together quickly enough.

A cold floor, one made of stone, would place him in a cellar.

A burlap bag full of something smelling of pine and citrus would be hops, the vine-fruits used in the seasoning and preservation of beer.

A brewery, then, was his most likely location. And the powder Berthollet used was, to Philip's nose, a simple enough formulation. He was likely unconscious for but an hour at most, making it quite likely he remained in Oxford Town, if not upon the university grounds. In fact, given the fact that Berthollet and Cagliostro seemed to be staying within the university halls, Philip gave it better than even odds that he was being held in the cellar of one of the college halls—likely Brasenose College, quite well known for its brewing.

Philip smiled in the darkness, congratulating himself for his deductions, until he realized he remained in darkness and, far more importantly, could not in fact deduce the location of Elizabeth without some form of light. This quickly replaced self-satisfaction with a heart-pounding fear for his stepsister, and Philip quickly hauled himself to his feet—and bumped his head on the low boards above him.

Definitely Brasenose. He had once accompanied a Brasenose tutor down into the cellars to sample the college's ales, and remembered the ceilings were quite low indeed. Shaking his head in an attempt to throw off the last of Berthollet's alchemically induced sleep, Philip sought to remember the layout of the rooms. If the hops were stored here, then this would be a very dry room, not the one where the barrels of finished beer were kept, nor the room where fermenting beer was laid in. So it would be a room he had not visited before, but one close to the rest of the college's small brewery. And it would be…

…quite near the foundation. And possibly a cellar window.

Philip walked hunched over, with his hands waving wildly in front of him, until he indeed found a wall. Like the floor, it was cold to the touch, and so it would be foundational. He then walked around the room. He encountered a door first, and naturally found it to be both stout and locked; it would make for a poor prison indeed if it were neither. But finally, just as he was about to finish his circumnavigation, he came upon a quite small window, no bigger than two feet wide, barely 10 inches tall. Not large enough for escape. However, it would be quite easy enough to break. Removing his coat and wrapping it around his hand, Philip successfully smashed the window upon his third try, which allowed a small bit of light into the room, even though it was still quite dark outside in the town. A quick glance at his pocketwatch confirmed it was but a few minutes after two o'clock in the morning.

And in the dim light of the room—which seemed more than bright enough after laboring in darkness for several minutes—Philip could see Elizabeth there upon the floor, not four feet from the bag of hops upon which he had awakened. He rushed over to her and found her breathing normal, her heartbeat steady. She would likely take several more minutes to awaken.

Perhaps, he considered, that would be enough time in which to formulate an escape plan.

It was not.

A few minutes later, just as Elizabeth began murmuring and emerging from her own sleep, the door to the room opened. A French officer, accompanied by two *Corps Éternel* soldiers, entered with a lantern raised, causing both captives to blink and raise their hands against the light. The officer—certainly no older than Philip, and likely younger—looked around the room and saw the broken window, then smirked. "There is no people outside now," the man said in quite faulty English. "You not get help there."

"I do not need the help of others to contend with the likes of you and your unholy creatures," Philip replied in his best French, which caused the officer to frown deeply. "Now bring us to whomever sent you, and let us be done with it."

Philip helped Elizabeth to her feet, though she quickly rejected his arm and walked toward the door upon her own power; it was not the first time, of course, for her to insist upon her own ability. Elizabeth was indeed an apt pupil of her stepmother in matters of independence, if not alchemy. For his part, Philip followed close behind, leaving the French officer to scurry ahead in order to actually guide the captives to the appropriate locale.

Said locale was one of the smaller reading rooms within Brasenose College, one which Philip had not visited. Therein, both Berthollet and Cagliostro sat in overstuffed chairs, with a small table between them stacked with a handful of books. They both had a glass of wine in hand, and two empty glasses were placed upon a low table before them. Philip and Elizabeth were led to a couch upon the other side of the table, and the French officer filled their glasses– whilst frowning at the duty, it should be said. Both step-siblings declined with a dismissive wave and a scowl toward the two alchemists.

Berthollet seemed quite amused. "Patriots, then, I take it," he said in English. "Shan't drink with the French, even though we have come to liberate England from its enslavement to the rich merchants who had pulled upon the strings of your beloved King George and his unfaithful Parliament."

Elizabeth smiled wickedly in return. "I am but a simple woman, *monsieur*, so I cannot speak overmuch on the matter of politics, especially when such a bald-faced misappropriation of all truth and reason, combined with your use of dark alchemy and these perverse abominations you call soldiers, would lead me to reject your wine, let alone your occupation of our land. And I should add," she said sweetly, "you offer us quite a poor vintage indeed, sir. The '97 was a terrible year for this particular Bordeaux, which is of itself from a lesser estate."

Berthollet and Cagliostro traded a look, and the older alchemist burst out laughing, a staccato bark that seemed to shake the very books upon the table. "I told you she was Weatherby's child, Berthollet! 'Tis the same arrogance and fervor! Though she does seem to better him in intellect, does she not?"

That was when Philip noticed the label upon the bottle and smiled, for the wine had come from Berthollet's own estate—a fact Elizabeth had quickly noticed. Her mind was agile and sharp to a degree Philip had never seen in others, not even his own mother. It was a shame Elizabeth had not shown facility with the Great Work, for she would've made a most formidable alchemist.

For his part, Berthollet's humor had evaporated under Elizabeth's words and insult. "I have never met Lord Weatherby, though he is but a minor thorn in our side, along with Wellesley and those other fools in Scotland," Berthollet said. "And since you do not wish to engage in civilized conversation, I will simply demand that you tell us of what you heard, and all else regarding your time in Oxford, so we may decide whether you are worth saving or must be condemned as traitors to King George and Emperor Napoleon."

"Condemn us and be done with it," Philip said, hoping a confident tone would mask his nerves. "And perhaps furnish us with better drink before we meet Madame Guillotine, if you'd be so kind. For we are highly disinclined to disclose anything, not even upon pain of death or poor wine."

Cagliostro snorted again in delight. "You make me wish I were fifty years younger, you two. Or perhaps that your father, young man, had not seen fit to strip me of my talent. Either way, it should be a grand thing to be of your age in these times. Of course, you know full well your value to the French, do you not? The children of Lord Weatherby and the dowager Countess St. Germain are fine hostages indeed. Not quite at the level of King George, but certainly valuable nonetheless. That makes it highly unlikely Dr. Berthollet here will execute you forthwith."

"Though I am sorely tempted," Berthollet scowled. "Perhaps, then, an admixture of a truth-telling serum may deliver what bonhomie or threat will not."

Philip assumed Berthollet would resort to such measures, and indeed was surprised he had not done so earlier. "And how is it that you have come to recognize us so readily as these children you speak of?" Philip asked, attempting to sow confusion.

"I know your face, for it's your father's more than you know," Cagliostro said, smiling but with a hint of wistfulness. "And I briefly encountered your mother as well, when she was alongside a very young Thomas Weatherby, oh… what was it, thirty years ago now? On Callisto. So you were quite easy, Philip, the new Count St. Germain. As for the girl here, deductive reasoning, of course, along with her father's blade, of which I remain familiar as well, having seen its potency on Mars, as well as within the library but an hour or two ago."

Cagliostro motioned toward the side of his chair, where Weatherby's sword was now leaning, well within the old puffer's reach. Given his surprising dexterity within the library, Philip was quite willing to believe Cagliostro might make good use of the blade, even if such a supposition was generous. The blade, he knew, was treated in such a way as to cut through iron with ease, and was made by his mother's hand.

"So," Berthollet interrupted, "you will now tell us of your activities here. Or shall I be forced to use the serum upon you? I cannot say how long the side effects will last, or how debilitating they might be."

Philip was about to answer, but Elizabeth spoke first. "We have given you little reason to do anything to us, and we shan't confirm, one way or another, our identities to those who keep us captive illegally. We may be in your power, sir, and we cannot stop you from committing cowardly acts such as these. But we shall not be compliant, I assure you!"

Berthollet was about to speak when the door behind Philip opened. By the time he turned around, the two *Corps Éternel* guards had fallen lifelessly to the ground, and a black-cloaked figure stood in the doorway, pistol drawn and pointed at the French alchemists.

"I really can't add much more to what the girl said," the cloaked man stated. "Stand down, *messieurs*."

Philip knew that voice, and a quick glance at Elizabeth confirmed it. "What took you so long, dear Uncle?" he said.

The man reached up to pull his hood back. "I had no idea you were in such a predicament, Philip," Andrew Finch said. "I dare say your stepfather and mother will want a word with you on it."

Before they could proceed further, both Cagliostro and Berthollet produced pistols—from where, only the Lord Himself could say—and were pointing them at Finch and Elizabeth. "So good to see you again, Andrew. I had hoped

I might shoot you one day," Berthollet said, and then fired at Finch from no more than fifteen feet away.

Philip shouted in anguished surprise, vaulting over the back of the sofa toward Finch. Yet the man he considered an uncle remained standing tall, with his weapon outstretched—this time at Cagliostro. "Do you wish to try me as well, Count Cagliostro?" Finch said. "I doubt you'll have better luck."

Cagliostro looked stricken, and slowly lowered his weapon. "Oh, you sad fool, what have you done?" he quietly asked Finch.

Finch, however, paid him no heed, focused as he was on Berthollet. "Why are you in Oxford, *monsieur*? Surely, your master Napoleon has plundered enough knowledge from the Continent to fuel your work, has he not?"

Berthollet slowly put down the pistol. His eyes were wide, and his hand trembled slightly. "Dr. Finch, it is clear now you have the upper hand, but I promise you, just as your young friends here bravely stood up to your questions, you will find Count Cagliostro and myself to be just as unhelpful to you."

Philip regarded Cagliostro and Berthollet closely. Their demeanors had changed quite abruptly, though he knew not why; there were many alchemical workings that might stop or minimize the impact of a pistol shot. What had they seen? Philip was about to ask when the trampling of footsteps echoed through the hallway outside the room, and movement could be seen outside the windows as well.

The pistol shot. Of course the French would come running.

"We need to go, Uncle," Philip said. "Now."

Finch turned to Elizabeth, who nodded in agreement, then darted forward to recover her father's sword from Cagliostro's side. "Damn. All right then," Finch said, then turned to Berthollet. "You're fortunate I've still the vestiges of a gentleman in my character, *monsieur*, or you'd be dead. Another time, then."

With that, Finch grabbed the hands of Philip and Elizabeth, placing them atop his left. In his right, he crushed

some sort of clay figure and spoke rapid words in the Eno-
chian tongue.

Then the world went black again, and an intense wave of
dizziness assaulted Philip's senses. He tried to open his eyes,
but could only see shades of blackness whirling about him,
as though he were in motion against an unknowable abyss.

A moment later, he could feel his feet upon the ground
again, though he did not quite remember them leaving the
ground in the first place. He opened his eyes…and stared,
uncomprehending, at a well-lit, ancient castle off in the
distance.

Elizabeth recognized it first. "Dear God, Uncle. Is that
Edinburgh Castle?"

Finch smiled, though it was forced through great fatigue.
It seemed the working had taken its toll on Finch, leaving
him pale and sweating. "It is, my dear Elizabeth. And there
your parents await you both."

Elizabeth smiled at this, but a moment later, seemed
quite dismayed as something occurred to her. "Uncle! We
must go back to Oxford!"

Finch looked over at the young woman with concern and
frustration. "Why the hell would we do that?" he panted.

"Philip's message papers! They are in his room, are they
not, Philip? Surely the French will search, and discover
their secrets! We cannot let such a means of communication be discovered!"

Philip agreed, but Finch merely smiled again through
gritted teeth as he straightened up and tried to shake off
whatever malady his working wrought. "Give this old
puffer a little credit, will you not? I stopped by Philip's
room first. When I saw the remnants of your invisibility
working, I figured you had gone forth to determine what
Berthollet was doing. I tried to find the message papers,
but was unable to do so. They were hidden in your room,
yes?"

"Yes, in a hidden compartment in my desk drawer," Philip
said. "Surely they will tear the room apart. They might well
be found."

"Don't worry, Philip," Finch said. "Since I could not find the message papers in a timely manner, I set fire to everything in your room. It'll be fine."

Elizabeth smiled, though Philip was taken aback. "There were some personal effects there I had hoped to keep, Uncle."

Having finally caught his breath, Finch began walking unevenly toward Edinburgh. "It's war, Philip. These things happen."

Unimpressed, Philip followed Finch and Elizabeth into the town, which was quite dark given the hour. Nonetheless, they were allowed through the gate and escorted to the Royal Palace itself, whereupon they were taken in, given refreshment and assigned simple but comfortable rooms.

But sleep was difficult to come by, for there were questions swimming through the young alchemist's head. And not all of them were about the French and their researches.

Thus it was that the valet entered Philip's room in the morning to find him awake, staring out the window into the castle's courtyard. The worthy brought tea and bread, as well as a fresh suit of clothes as befitting a Count—self-titled or otherwise. Philip had sometimes thought it ludicrous to have inherited a title that was adopted by his father on a whim and not, in fact, granted by any outside authority. But there were times when being a Count was a worthwhile thing, especially if it meant getting his first cup of real tea in many long months.

Once he had eaten, attended to his morning toilet and changed into his new clothes, Philip allowed his valet to escort him down toward the Great Hall. No doubt he would be called upon to give his testimony as to the French and their activities.

But first, of course, there was a reunion.

Elizabeth had found their parents first, just outside the Hall, and Lord Weatherby looked most satisfied at seeing his daughter again. Indeed, it seemed an errant tear had somehow escaped the Admiral's weather eye as he alternated between gently scolding his daughter for the risks she had undertaken, and holding her stiflingly close.

Anne rushed to greet Philip upon spotting him, giving him a ferocious hug of surprising strength. He then submitted to an embarrassingly thorough examination, both physical and otherwise, as his mother looked him over head to toe and quizzed him as to his health, eating habits, alcohol intake and his most recent workings. Only when she was satisfied did she then hug him once more, and allow Lord Weatherby to approach.

"I might thank you for keeping my daughter safe, Philip, but from what I'm told, it seems the reverse was the case at times," Weatherby said with a slight grin.

"We took turns until Uncle Andrew finally arrived," Philip said, taking Weatherby's offered hand. "It's good to see you again, my Lord."

Weatherby waved his hand. "For the millionth time, there's no need for formality, Philip. Now, speaking of your dear 'uncle,' where did that scoundrel fly to now?"

"And more importantly, *how* does he fly?" Anne said pointedly. "I want to know exactly how he managed to get from Edinburgh to Oxford and back within a single night, because I had not thought such a thing possible."

Weatherby looked at his wife in confusion. "Surely, it is but a variant of the Great Work recently discovered, is it not? He is a fine alchemist, Anne. How else might it be done?"

Anne merely scowled and, for a moment, the matronly side of her character showed through her still-youthful face. "I should wish to find out just that, Tom. Because there are but a handful of alchemists approaching his level of skill, and being one of them, I am surprised to be at a loss."

At this timely juncture, Finch joined their party from a side room, and Weatherby noted once more that his pallor had not improved, though his mood had.

"What are we talking about?" Finch said, eschewing formality as usual.

Anne gave him a concerned, cross look. "Your workings, in point of fact. I should like to learn more of this method you used in traveling to Oxford and back within but a single evening."

Finch easily detected the hint of challenge and worry in her voice. "I assure you, my dearest lady, that I shall be publishing forthwith, and would be happy to discuss with you at any time," he said, attempting to be serious and mostly succeeding.

Before they could speak further, the doors to the Great Hall were opened, and Weatherby's family was announced and allowed to proceed for their audience with the Prince Regent, who was present along with Castlereagh and, to Weatherby's surprise, Vellusk once more.

"I had not thought to see you here, Representative Vellusk," Weatherby said once the formalities were done.

Before the Xan could reply, Prince George spoke up. "We are finalizing the details of our alliance, Lord Weatherby, which I believe will allow us to drive the French from our green England once and for all. But, the worthy Representative found himself curious as to your son and daughter's experiences in Oxford, so I allowed him to stay."

Weatherby smiled slightly at this; George needed Vellusk far more than Vellusk needed George—or England, for that matter. Thankfully, Vellusk was a diplomat, both by nature and vocation, and simply took the prince's words for the bombast they were. "We have been concerned about the French and their activities since the crisis on Xanath's rings, as you know, Lord Weatherby," Vellusk sang. "The Emerald Tablet was destroyed, and *The Book of the Dead* missing. So we are naturally curious to find both Berthollet and Cagliostro together, and working on behalf of France."

Weatherby turned to Philip. "My Lord Count St. Germain, and my daughter, the Lady Weatherby—would you be so kind as to give a report on your experiences? It seems they are of great interest to many people upon many worlds."

And so Philip did, with frequent elucidation and interjection from Elizabeth. Of course, their findings could only be summarized to a certain point. The French had an interest in Venus, where they already had both army and naval forces, and that interest likely had to do with some "vault," which seemed to be a building or artifact of, or at least cared for by, the Venusians—the Va'hak'ri tribe, in particular.

Upon hearing the full tale, Representative Vellusk sat stoically, but the rippling of his body under his robes indicated a degree of intensity about him—if not outright distress. "I had wondered if this was something the French might attempt," he sang finally, with notes of worry and an undertone of malice.

"Attempt what?" the Prince Regent demanded. "Do you know what this vault is about?"

Vellusk nodded, his hooded cloak bobbing. "It is a repository of the history of the Venusian people, drawn from their very memories. If a Venusian witnessed something, and was able to return to the vault prior to death, that creature's memories would be preserved for all time. And through their primitive ritual practices, the Venusians would be able to tap into those memories, and learn much about the past. It is, really, how their primitive version of alchemy has lasted to this day—and likely the reason their growth has stagnated, as such a system does not allow for a great deal of innovation."

They all thought on this for several moments, until Weatherby finally spoke. "I believe this is something I saw, long ago on Venus, after Count Cagliostro's attack on the Va'hak'ri. Finch was there as well. It was as though they drew the memories out of the dying and dead."

Anne nodded. "The Venusians would often take their sick to places such as this vault when I was unable to treat them, back when the late Count and I took up residence on Venus and we served as physicians. Now, if the French were able to find this vault and access the memories therein, they may find something useful within them."

"Yes, they're focusing on Venus," Finch said quietly, looking inwardly for a moment before turning to the group again. "We're forgetting something. Cagliostro was there."

Weatherby shrugged. "And? He had interactions with the Va'hak'ri back in '79. He did quite a lot of research on Venus. Surely he's still useful in that regard, even stripped of his alchemical power."

But Finch shook his head. "No, there's more to it. Venus has been surveyed by our own Royal Society several times, and the French colonies there have many experts. Cagliostro, meanwhile, was tied up with the 'affair of the necklace,' then imprisoned in the Vatican, and likely just released by Berthollet not long ago. His information is surely out of date."

"So what then?" said George, crossing his arms and growing impatient.

"Cagliostro remains the Known Worlds' foremost expert in one thing—the processes he used to open up a portal between worlds. The means by which he sought to free Althotas of ancient Mars," Finch said. "Any other use of him would be a waste."

Anne gasped. "They want to try again?"

"Perhaps," Finch said.

Before he could elucidate further, the doors to the room burst open and a red-coated Army officer—looking no older than sixteen years—came rushing in. "Lord Weatherby! Pickets reporting several French ships making for the Firth of Forth! At least a half dozen, maybe more!"

Weatherby wheeled about and stood tall before Prince George. "Sire, I recommend preparing the city's defenses as quickly as possible, and sending forth messages to the coastlines within a hundred leagues of here. By your leave, I shall make sail and engage the enemy at sea."

The Prince Regent, looking a touch ashen, nodded somberly. "Go, Lord Weatherby. May God be with you. I shall see to the defenses."

Weatherby bowed, then paused to kiss Anne tenderly, and placed a kiss upon Elizabeth's brow as well, before grabbing Finch's arm and walking for the door. "Come, Doctor. The French seek to invade. Let us endeavor to disappoint them."

CHAPTER 8

January 16, 2135

The old Vysotsky building in Yekaterinburg was once the tallest building in Russia outside of Moscow, but now it was but one of many skyscrapers, with every day of 120 years' weathering seemingly worn on its glass-and-steel façade. The windows' coating was visibly peeling, the steel was pitted in places by acidic rain and dusty wind, and the neon lights that traced its outline at night were almost charmingly antiquated compared to the latest LED window-screens that turned most 22nd century buildings into nighttime works of commercial excess or, on occasion, art.

Harry wasn't surprised that his benefactor would set them up in the Vysotsky. When conglom execs took on these "personal projects," creature comforts were never front of mind. And it wasn't like she'd put them up in the same building her own conglom was located. Secure comms, untraceable funds and chance meetings always lent an aura of plausible deniability to such ventures. Especially when said ventures might involve breaches of either ethics, law or both.

This was definitely both.

On the bright side, his contact managed to get them the entire 52nd floor. It actually used to be the observation deck when the building was new and tall, back some time in the 2000s or 2010s. The proliferation of other conglom skyscrapers around it—taller, glassier, just generally better—made the deck an afterthought. So they basically had office space plus a massive balcony surrounding it.

Chrys VanDerKamp was waiting there for them when they arrived. "Good to see you again, Harry!" she said, extending her hand as Harry, Greene and Huntington got off the elevator. "Glad you could come out here."

"Good to see you, Chrys," Harry smiled, taking her hand. She had a firm grip and a smile that might be called "perky" if not for the steel behind the eyes and the self-aware curl at the very edge of her lips. Chrys had served as Harry's deputy at Billiton MinMetals prior to his Mars assignment, and her star had risen sharply since. Of course, Harry had taken it upon himself to keep her working nose-to-the-grindstone while he was her boss, then received a lot of credit—some of it even deserved—when she began her ascent. The fact that the tables were turned now was a bit awkward for Harry, but it seemed not to faze the younger woman.

She waved everyone in and Harry made the introductions. Greene seemed almost like his old charming self, while Huntington was at least more restrained. When they saw the new quantum computing rig Chrys had acquired for them, they immediately peeled off and began unpacking, leaving Harry and Chrys to walk the old observation deck.

"How's your tennis game, Chrys? You still as good as I remember?" Harry asked.

"Better than yours, unless you suddenly got talent," she replied, then dropped the business smile. "So what the hell happened, Harry? You went from director to VP to EVP in two years and now you're basically an internationally wanted criminal. That's pretty special."

Harry gave her a sidelong glance. "You know what happened, otherwise I wouldn't be here."

This earned him a shrug. "Honestly, all I have are rumors. Aliens? Other dimensions? A pre-industrial Earth ripe for the picking? Just finding out how much is real and how much is bullshit is worth the price of admission. So here we are. Now, how's this going to be more like Mars and a *lot* less like Egypt?"

Harry plopped down on an old plastic bench, and Chrys slid down next to him, sweeping her long brown hair from her face and smoothing out her suit. Harry knew her clothes cost some serious terras; he had a number of suits from that label at one point. "On Mars, we had someone who was in touch with the other side. She was getting info on how to make the portal work. In Egypt, we had an artifact, but no real link. We thought we had enough data to make it work, but without the link, we didn't. And it went south."

Chrys nodded, keeping up an imperturbable cool. "And so now, what? You have a link to the 'other side' again?"

"Sounds crazy, doesn't it?"

"More than a little."

Harry smiled ruefully. "Those two in there are working with the guys that took over *Tienlong* from the Chinese. We believe the Chinese have been in contact with the other side, and we've been getting good working data from them." There were, of course, some things Harry left out of that summary, but there was no use worrying his one and only investor quite yet.

"You know, Harry, they captured *Tienlong*. The crew was found dead. They say the captain snapped after the Enceladus thing and killed everyone, then committed suicide," Chrys said. "So you're saying that's not true."

"Nope, that's just the JSC cover," Harry said. "There's at least one survivor, possibly more. They managed to squeeze off a huge, highly encrypted file right before they were captured. We got that file, which is why we had to get out of Afghanistan, before JSC's jack-boots got there."

Chrys nodded, then stood up, towering over Harry despite her slight frame. "Harry, this needs to work. You need to find a stable portal to the other side. Not some overlap area, not the shit-show that leveled Siwa. A stable portal. I need to march people in and out of there like it's a revolving door. That's the goal. Anything less is failure. And if we fail, I'm out a lot of money. And you…" Her voice trailed off.

"And you recoup your losses by turning me in to whoever pays the most," Harry said.

"You still got it, Harry," Chrys beamed, patting him on the shoulder. "Let me know if you need anything. Use the secure channel, and try to make it after hours. I have an orbital insertion to manage over the next few weeks and it's going to be hectic."

Chrys walked off, leaving Harry on the bench, his back on the cold concrete wall of the observation deck, looking out over Yekaterinburg's skyline. There was a point in his life when Harry could've picked whichever corner office he wanted in any of those buildings. He'd be the one managing....

Harry sat upright and pulled out his phone, pulling it open into a holotablet. It was a matter of five minutes to find out where Chrys was working now—Rossviaz, pretty much the biggest name in satellites. From there, it was even simpler to figure out her next project.

In less than two weeks' time, Rossviaz would be placing 13 satellites into orbit around Venus for the most comprehensive resource mapping expedition ever sent to that little hellhole of a planet. The sats would be constantly circling and twirling around the planet for the next five years, creating an orbital map that could not only pierce Venus' notoriously stubborn cloud-cover, but also could map the surface to within a centimeter—literally. With that kind of map and some serious geological know-how, a smart conglom could figure out the most stable parts of Venus' geography for extraction and exploitation. The margins would be crap, at first, but it opened up the chance for finding the unexpected, landing the big haul.

It was a huge gamble. But with Chrys' company owning the gaming table, she wasn't going to be the one gambling. It was guys like his old employers—Billiton and Total-Suez—who might take a shot at mining Venus.

Harry smiled. He'd like to think he had a hand in Chrys' acumen, but knew that she was at least this good on her own.

And if Harry and his "team"—if you could call them that—could recreate a stable portal, then it wasn't just a pristine, pre-industrial Earth that was up for grabs. Harry had managed to read excerpts from that journal Jain and Diaz found on Mars. That Weatherby guy had described Venus as a lush jungle world, rich with resources.

Perfect.

There was no doubt that Chrys would want—and get—her cut of whatever such a stable portal would bring them on either Earth or Venus. But ultimately, Harry had the tech. She didn't.

Greene poked his head outside onto the observation deck. "Harry, c'mere a second. We have some things we're going to need to get up and running."

Harry nodded and Greene disappeared inside the building again. Correction: Greene had the tech. And Harry didn't quite have Greene in his pocket.

Not yet.

Harry got up and looked out over Yekaterinburg one more time. At least now he knew what the playing field looked like. He could see the permutations, get a feel for the players.

He knew what he had to do to win. And that was the biggest hurdle of all.

Maria Diaz shut down the comm station with a look of disgust that Shaila knew all too well. The only real question was what, among so many different candidates, was the source.

"That was CIA," Diaz said, just loud enough for Shaila and Coogan to hear in Ride Station's busy ops center. "They managed to track Harry down to an industrial park outside Kabul, but turns out they up and left just two days ago. Packed up, drove to the airport and got onto a secure corporate jet. Unmarked. Goddamn corporate shield laws!"

Shaila shared a knowing look with Coogan. This wasn't the first time Diaz spouted off against the international conglom system. It probably wouldn't be the last. And it didn't make her wrong, either. "Anything else? Flight plan filed, maybe?"

Diaz called up a map of central Asia. "All we got is that it's a Cessna Longitude Mark VII. So basically, that's anywhere from London to Beijing to Jo'burg."

Shaila could see beads of light flying along the inside Coogan's HUD glasses. "Yes, General, but I think we might want to focus on nations with particularly welcome corporate laws," he said drily. "Plus, Mr. Yu is wanted by the E.U., U.S. and Islamic League. So that would leave us with Russia and China as our two best candidates, with Zimbabwe and Bangladesh right behind."

Diaz smiled over toward Shaila. "And this is why we're still up and running, thanks to this guy. Find him, Jimmy."

Coogan nodded and parked himself at a nearby holostation; a moment later, he was manipulating data and light like a conductor before the London Philharmonic.

"So what do you think?" Diaz asked Shaila. "What did they send?"

Shaila sat down at the console next to Diaz, idly fiddling with the controls as she spoke. "First time this happened, on Mars, Yuna Hiyashi said she had been in contact with the other side. If I'm remembering right, she said she got some help, too, when she built the accelerator that opened the door. Doesn't seem like Harry had that when he tried to pull it off on Egypt, did he?"

"Nope," Diaz replied. "He had some kind of artifact that was throwing off a metric shit-ton of Cherenkov, but far as we know, there was nobody with a line to the other side that we know of. Probably why it blew up to hell and back."

"But there was a portal, briefly. Your report said you saw Finch?"

Diaz smiled. "Yeah, though he looked a lot older. Maybe an older brother or something? Maybe he was trying to do the same thing Harry was. Didn't seem like it was going too well for him, either."

Shaila shuddered involuntarily. She'd seen the holorecordings of the Siwa experiment: mangled, grasping hands trying to claw their way through the unstable portal Harry's team created. "No, it didn't. But maybe the key to creating a stable portal came from Althotas, that ugly fucker from Mars. Yuna seemed to think she was talking to him. Maybe that data in the Enceladus proteins came from him, too."

"And yet we think Stephane was possessed by one of those proteins—or whatever was hooked up to it on the other side," Diaz said, sounding more frustrated. "Fuck it, I don't know, but I bet Stephane knows. Or Rathemas. Whoever that guy is in our brig. I saw the vid of your encounter with him."

"You're thinking that Stephane could be the key to unlocking all this," Shaila said with a frown. "You think he's still in there? That there's anything left of him?"

Diaz leaned forward with a maternal look that Shaila found both comforting and maddening. "I don't know. But you're the only one here who's managed to get a rise out of him. And he might have some intel on this mess."

Shaila nodded. She knew this would be coming. She'd been gearing up for it. "Even if I have to beat it out of him?"

"Preferably not," Diaz replied. "I think we'd both like to get him back intact, somehow."

Shaila stood up. "All right then. Let's do it."

"Whoa, girlie. You have a plan?"

"Of course not," Shaila replied with a slightly pained grin. "But you have Ayim on the science part, and Coogan doing intel on Harry. I need to be doing something useful."

Diaz nodded soberly. "Take a zapper with you. Set it on high. And don't go in there with him, whatever you do."

Shaila nodded and left the ops center, stopping briefly at the new makeshift armory to grab a zapper from one of Major Parrish's team before heading back to the containment area. She found herself gearing up for the encounter, much like she did back when she was a mere ensign flying training missions. The thought of freeing Stephane from… whatever it was…Rathemas? Martians in general?…was all-consuming.

When she entered the lab, she saw the same eager tech on duty. "Hey. Didn't catch your name earlier."

"Julie Chou, ma'am," the young woman said, smiling. "Are you here to see *him* again?" The tech nodded toward the containment cell, where Stephane sat—on the floor now, as someone took the wreckage of his cot away—with the same glazed look as before. Indeed, the cell had undergone a thorough makeover, with anything remotely hard-edged and hefty removed. All that remained was a mattress and pillow. At least the toilet and sink were securely bolted to the floor.

"Yeah, can you give us a minute?"

Julie looked disappointed. "Umm…yeah. Is it OK if I swap stations and monitor from next door?"

Shaila smiled as best she could. "Sure. Knock yourself out. Make sure you record every bit of it."

"Oh, we're doing that already, Commander," Julie replied brightly. "Every movement, all his vitals, every sensor running 24/7."

"Good. I'll take it from here."

Nodding, Julie gathered her datapad and rushed out of the room, likely not wanting to miss anything. For her part, Shaila simply took a seat and did a few breathing exercises—ironically, ones she learned in yoga classes from Yuna Hiyashi back on Mars, before the woman went batshit. Yuna never seemed possessed—not in the sense that Stephane and the other people on *Tienlong* were—but she ended up pretty much "out there" in the end, up until she realized just what she had let loose. And then the creature named Althotas killed her.

Shaking her head, Shaila closed her eyes and focused on her breathing. Memories wouldn't do right now. Focus was primary.

When she opened her eyes, Stephane was staring at her.

Her heart beating, Shaila returned his gaze as steadily as she could. Normally, she could read Stephane like a book. Granted, that was two years of being in a relationship working in her favor, but he wasn't exactly guarded. He was an honest extrovert, his heart on his sleeve. But the eyes staring at Shaila now were unreadable. Nothing in his slack, pale face hinted at anything at all. His eyes were glassy…dead.

She reached over and toggled the comm system so he'd hear everything she said. "Hi, honey."

He twitched. Almost imperceptibly, but it was there. Out of the corner of her eye, she saw a slight fluctuation in his vitals. *Good.*

Shaila got up and slowly walked over to the containment cell's airlock. "I missed you. Thought I'd come back, see how you were."

Stephane looked away, seemingly at a fixed point just above his toilet.

"Sorry about your bed. Diaz probably didn't want you to hurt yourself," she said, right before seizing on an idea. "Well, not quite that. She probably didn't want Rathemas hurting you. I think he's done enough of that, hasn't he?"

A soft beep from the console behind her prompted her to turn around. Another blip in vitals, and this time in the ambient Cherenkov radiation in the room. *Even better*.

When she turned back, Stephane was there—standing, right up against the transparent wall of the containment unit. Looking at her with focused eyes.

It took every ounce of willpower and discipline she could muster not to jump back.

"So…umm…so. Yeah, we had a thought," she stammered, reaching for something in the back of her mind that was bothering her for a while. "You see, we've been looking at the device Rathemas and his friends created. You know, the one hooked up to the Emerald Tablet the Chinese found on Titan. We have some people working on it. Good ones, smart ones. We're trying to figure out why that machine was hooked up to the vats carrying the proteins."

Stephane blinked and twitched slightly.

There were more blips from the console behind Shaila, but she didn't bother to look. Her heart rate was slowing; she was settling into this. Always the pilot, she was beginning to see the outline of the controls in front of her, in this little interaction. She just had to get a feel for them.

"So what was that about? I mean, Rathemas flew the ship right through a massive debris field full of ice and micrometeors. With the doors open. All that water, and all those proteins got in. That's a huge risk. And now all those proteins are just…dead. That's weird. Why go through all the trouble if you're going to kill them?"

Stephane was visibly shaking now, his eyes darting around the room. The effect reminded Shaila of a kid cornered with his hand in the cookie jar. Perfect.

"You know, I'm thinking that the comm blast *Tienlong* sent was related. Maybe those proteins had extradimensional properties, and maybe it was the data they represented—not the actual molecules—that was important. So the data was sent to Earth, to someone else out there, who could use it to open a portal, bring some more baddies from the other side," Shaila said.

Then she paused, watching Stephane as he crossed his arms over his chest, swaying slightly. As if his body was on the verge of somehow getting away from himself.

And that's when she had an idea.

"Holy crap, Stephane. Maybe this is crazy, but hear me out. So Rathemas used the Tablet to pull not only data, but....oh, I don't know, the *essence*...out of those proteins, right. So hell...maybe there's a way we could use that rig to pull this Rathemas bastard out of you."

Stephane stared wide-eyed now, trembling, mouth agape. Shaila felt her datapad vibrate. A moment later, she saw a text from Diaz on it: WHERE DID YOU GET THIS FROM? AYIM LOVES IT.

Shaila smiled and kept going. "Now, I don't know what happens to Rathemas in all that. Maybe he just gets sucked into the Tablet. Maybe we dump him in with what's left of those proteins so he can swim around. Maybe he just dies. Honestly, I hope he just dies. And between you and me, honey, I really, really hope it hurts. A lot."

Stephane abruptly smashed his fist into the transparent wall, inches from Shaila's face, and this time she did jump. But she smiled more broadly, too. It was working.

"Getting antsy in there, Rathemas? Good. Stephane and I are going to kick your ass right out of there," Shaila said, stepping forward once more. "We're going to rip you out and send you screaming into hell, you bastard."

Stephane's head twitched. It looked for all the world like an abortive nod.

"Yeah? Is that you, Stephane? You ready to kick him out?"

For a long moment, Stephane just stared, bug-eyed and trembling, his fist against the wall. Sweat was beading on his forehead. He staggered back a step. Then another.

And then he screamed something that sounded an awful lot like French before collapsing onto the floor, unconscious.

Fuck. "Julie, get me medical in here now!" Shaila yelled as she knelt on the other side of the barrier, trying to get a better look at Stephane.

Moments later, Julie rushed in. "On their way. His vitals are normalizing," she reported. "This…this is amazing."

Shaila stood slowly. "Yeah. I think it went…well," she said.

"And he said something! That's incredible!"

"You know French?"

Julie nodded. "Hard to make out, but I think it was something like '*moi mont*' or…well, something like that. There was something before it I couldn't make out."

"What's it mean?"

"Me. Me or my. And…rise. Or soar."

A cold shiver ran up Shaila's spine. "'Watch me soar.'"

Julie was calling up reams of data on her console. "*Regarde-moi mont*. Yeah, maybe. We'll have to clean up the audio some."

Now Shaila was the one trembling—so much so, she had a hard time activating her comm. "Jain to Diaz. Tell Ayim we need to figure out how to hook Stephane up to that Tablet thing.

"I think it'll work."

CHAPTER 9

May 9, 1809

"All hands report ready, my Lord. No report from the lookouts," Capt. Searle said crisply, standing tall upon the quarterdeck of HMS *Victory* while Weatherby paced back and forth on the lee side.

"Very good. Thank you, Captain," Weatherby muttered, then pulled out his own glass and looked over to larboard. "Where the hell *are* they?"

They had been at sea for more than twenty hours, having sailed shortly after midday the day prior. Weatherby stationed his ships—only four other ships of the line, with perhaps a half-dozen frigates and brigs—at the very edge of the Firth of Forth, spread as wide as could be managed while still within signaling distance. And there they stayed, hoping beyond hope that the French were indeed heading for Edinburgh, rather than on some other mission to which the purpose might elude them.

Sleep, of course, eluded Weatherby as well. For the younger officers aboard *Victory*, rest was no issue at all, for their worlds were much smaller. Ensure the readiness of your division. Manage your watch crisply and to the first lieutenant's liking. Watch the men for signs of drunkenness or lax discipline.

Weatherby remembered those days well, walking the deck of HMS *Daedalus* and thinking only of the tasks at hand, the day's watch, the respect of his men and his peers. Now, with the defense of Scotland—and the Prince Regent himself—in his hands, Weatherby found himself wistful for those simpler days.

But then he remembered Mars, and the alien warlord that burst through and shattered the boundaries between worlds, and knew that it was never, ever, so simple as that. Like all memories, it was but a reconstruction of an ill-remembered time, filtered through the prism of intention, desire and regret.

Weatherby was distracted from his musings by the arrival of Finch, sauntering up the stairs to the quarterdeck. "Any luck?"

"None," Weatherby said, continuing with his pacing. "There is too much ocean, too many potential targets. We may defend Edinburgh, but they may yet try for Aberdeen instead, or even Inverness. Or south to Berwick. They could simply have made for the poles and the Void to reinforce Venus instead. Damn them, we simply do not know!"

Finch just smiled. "Would you like to?"

"Like to what?"

"Like to know where the French are."

Weatherby stopped pacing and turned to eye his friend closely. Finch had the insouciant look upon his face he often wore when he was about to pull out some alchemical trump. Yet he continued to grow more pallid and wan, so much so that Weatherby had begun to suspect Finch had lapsed into his former drug-addled ways. "You worry me, Finch. You look unwell."

Finch waved it aside. "I'm perfectly fine, Tom. Now, shall we find the French?"

The alchemist turned and waved to someone on the maindeck. A moment later, two men were carrying a table and mirror up the stairs to the quarterdeck, while a third bore an odd sort of helmet made of leather and bits of metal and wire, along with a visor of smoked glass and other, unidentifiable bits.

"This again, Doctor?" Searle asked, his hands upon his hips. "Must we clutter the quarterdeck with such things whilst the very enemy may come into view at any moment?"

Finch regarded the captain with ill-disguised disdain. "My dear Captain Searle, this is *how* the enemy will come into view."

Weatherby shook his head. "Finch, I'm not wearing that…thing."

"I will," Finch sighed, positioning himself above the mirror. "This experiment started as a way for you to communicate directly with your captains during a fleet engagement. Unfortunately, we've not yet had time to test that aspect further. Since then, I've amended this working to create a kind of far-seeing device, one that should allow me to gain a broader view of the horizon and, if all goes well, pinpoint the location of the French. Now, help me orient this to true north, so that I don't send us off onto an ill-fated course."

Finch's helpers—the few alchemists' mates assigned to the ship—looked to Weatherby and Searle first, knowing Finch was trying the patience of the ship's true masters. It was Searle who spoke first. "Are you sure this damnable working of yours won't damage my ship?"

Finch merely smiled. "How can a bit of alchemical clairvoyance damage a ship at all, Captain?"

Searle looked to Weatherby with a frown, but the admiral was merely smiling. "If anyone could damage a first-rate ship-of-the-line with a mirror and a helmet, it's you, Finch," Weatherby said. "Go on, then. Show us. And Captain Searle, you may station fire crews as you see fit."

To Weatherby's amusement, *Victory*'s captain did just that, ordering a line of buckets readied. The admiral had seen enough of Finch's workings to know that it was highly unlikely that a gout of flame would shoot from the mirror—or from Finch's head, now adorned with the queer helmet—but the possibility of an unforeseen incident was certainly a concern. Finch was one of the foremost alchemists of his day, but his methods of experimentation were occasionally reckless. One time, many years ago, the very figurehead of one of Weatherby's ships—along with most of the fo'c'sle—was blown four hundred yards away by one of Finch's errant workings.

This time, however, Finch merely stood over the table, his hands extended over the mirror, and began an incantation in a language Weatherby did not recognize. Usually, alchemists in the employ of His Majesty's Royal Navy used the approved workings written in English, Latin or, on occasion, Greek. But this was nothing like those tongues.

Then a black cloud appeared in the mirror, slowly expanding to cover the entire surface of the glass in pitch blackness. For a moment, Weatherby thought he caught glimpses of stars, as if the mirror was reflecting the very Void. But then it devolved into a whirling, inky darkness.

And then Finch looked up suddenly, smiling. "They're coming from the north and east, roughly…that way," he said, pointing. "Only four large ships, a few others. And…. yes, there's another four large ones coming from the south and east. That way. A few frigates with them as well."

Weatherby followed Finch's finger. "They likely wanted to draw our defenses out toward one group, so the other could come into the harbor," he said. "I imagine their holds are packed with those infernal *Corps Éternel* soldiers."

Searle nodded, though he still looked skeptical. "Orders, Admiral?"

Weatherby turned to Finch. "Which group is closer?"

"The northern group. They seem to have the wind," Finch said.

"As would we should we attack them first, then pivot to the other group," Searle added.

Weatherby considered this a moment, then decided. "Captain, signal the fleet. We sail north to engage the enemy. Have a brig and frigate fall back to Edinburgh and tell them of our course, then stay to help defend the city if needed." He then turned to Finch. "If Edinburgh is indeed attacked, could you have some knowledge of it with your working here?"

Finch reached up and removed his odd headgear, showing his face even more pallid and sweaty than before. "I believe so, my Lord. Though I will need rest in between."

"So I see," Weatherby murmured. "Get below and rest. We'll have need of you to tend the wounded from the coming engagement. And by God, I do hope you're right, for we leave Edinburgh exposed to do this."

Finch smiled wanly. "I'm right, Tom. I swear it."

Weatherby nodded, and Finch went below, leaning upon one of his alchemist's mates for support. Weatherby pulled a small pocket-journal from his coat, along with a pencil, and made a note to himself to discuss this working in great detail with his wife and step-son, for it seemed Finch's bouts of anemic sallowness were at times tied to his workings. He also made a note to have someone search Finch's quarters for signs of his return to the lure of Venusian opiates, just to be cautious.

It was but four hours later when the lookouts first caught sight of the French fleet, well off the coast of Arbroath. As it happened, Finch's mystical reconnaissance turned out to be correct, though he did confuse a fourth-rate for a smaller ship; while brilliant in the research and execution of the mystic sciences, Finch was always a poor naval officer. The odds were roughly even, for while Weatherby had more guns and one more ship, the French had the weather gage and the knowledge that there were a second group of their fellows making for Edinburgh.

But Weatherby nonetheless sought to maximize whatever advantages he had. Well prior to the sighting, he had ordered his ships to form a single line in order to obfuscate the number of ships he could bring to bear. So it was that the ships now sailed straight for a scattered group of French vessels, which were spending critical time and effort forming their own line of battle.

And it was but one line, as Weatherby had hoped. Thus, he could put his plan into action. "Captain Searle, signal the fleet. Form the second line."

In moments, half the ships in Weatherby's line—every other ship, in fact—split off from the line and sailed roughly two hundred yards before forming up again. So whereas Weatherby had but one line prior, he now had two, and they would now maneuver to place the French line between them, catching them in a cross-fire.

But the French commander, it seemed, was a versatile strategist and, much to Weatherby's consternation, split off his own ships into two lines, sending one to Weatherby's larboard side, potentially leading *Victory* and three other ships into a cross-fire of their own.

"Damn him," Weatherby muttered as he peered through his glass. "Starboard line, continue forward. Signal the larboard line that we'll take the van, and they are to follow us."

Searle had the signals run up, and soon *Victory* was peeling off away from the second British line, drawing that portion of the French squadron with them. Weatherby had hoped his trickery would even the odds, but now it seemed a fair fight would be at hand, and the casualties would be high. There would be no flight from it.

Flight.

Weatherby snapped his glass shut with a smile. "Signal our line! Rig for Void!"

Searle was stopped in his tracks. "My Lord? We are fleeing?"

"Not at all. But be quick. Signal the line!"

Searle gave the order, and but three minutes later, HMS *Victory* and three other ships began to slowly rise from the sea to the sky, and thence into the Void. Except....

"Now come about east! Prepare for keelfall! Signal the line!" Weatherby shouted.

Searle, to his great credit, passed along the order before commenting. "My Lord Admiral, we shall burn all of our Mercurium to do this."

Weatherby smiled. "Then it is a fine thing we managed to save Elizabeth Mercuris, is it not? Now run out the guns and prepare to fire at my command."

The turn, combined with the order to descend, caused the four English ships to essentially jump over the second French line—as well as the first line and that of their English fellows as well. *Victory* and the other ships splashed down on the other side of four French ships, immediately catching them in between.

"FIRE!" Weatherby roared.

A moment later, more than fifty guns poured iron and alchemy into the nearest French ship, burning through wood and men with equal, deadly efficiency. Upon the other side, HMS *Mars* likewise fired, capturing the French vessel in a horrid cross-fire. Already, sickly green flame burst through the French gunports; inside, Weatherby knew, would be an abattoir of wood, iron, fire and flesh.

Looking aft, Weatherby saw three other pairs of English ships tearing into the line. One French vessel, a stately old 74 by the look of her, exploded into a greenish-red ball of flame almost immediately, her magazine having been caught. Masts fell while the men on deck screamed and dove overboard, preferring the cold embrace of the sea over fiery death.

The French did not even have time to run out their guns against *Victory* and the other English ships that had taken to the sky. But there were signs of damage on the other English line; *Mars* had taken heavy cannon fire to her gun decks, and her foremast was listing forward at a dangerous angle.

"Report, Captain?" Weatherby asked, more for the formality of it than anything else.

"Our line reports damage amidships from shrapnel and the like, minor injuries," *Victory*'s captain said. "Our other line endured more fire, but all report ready to continue."

But the other French line, as it happened, had little appetite for further engagement with Weatherby's leap-frogging squadron, and continued south and west toward Edinburgh. "They're likely linking up with their fellows," Searle said. "Shall we pursue, sir?"

"For now, full sail in pursuit," Weatherby said. "Engage with chase guns if we come into range. In the meantime, have Dr. Finch meet me in the hold if you please."

"What of the French ships?" Searle asked, turning to regard the blazing hulks. The men aboard were struggling unsuccessfully to contain the fires, and there were many men in the water besides.

Weatherby sighed. "Trail lines aft. Perhaps we may save some yet. But…we must continue." Searle nodded gravely in understanding, and Weatherby made for the bowels of the ship, trying not to be sickened at this violation of the laws of the sea. As much as he wanted to help those men, the preservation of his country—or what was left to him of it—was of a far greater and more immediate concern.

Minutes later, Weatherby watched Finch descend the wooden stairs into *Victory*'s hold, where were housed the lodestones that guaranteed the ship's air, warmth and gravity in the chill of the Void. Yet there were other alchemical workings stored there as well. Finch paused to check on the nearest lodestone, muttering to himself as was his wont of late. Weatherby heard something about "souls," but could not piece together the rest.

"Finch?"

The alchemist stood and smiled once more. "That was quite a trick, Tom," he said by way of greeting; they were alone but for a few able seamen, and formality was often wasted on Finch to begin with. "Good thinking."

Weatherby forced a smile. "I enjoy catching the French unawares. Now, we need to talk about the Mercurium."

Mercurium enabled ships to rise into the Void through alchemical means, rather than through the traditional method of sailing into the aurorae at the poles of Earth, or whichever other world they were upon. The French, without reliable sources of Mercurium, were forced to make for the poles each time, making it relatively easy for the English Royal Navy to patrol the northern regions of Earth—or, more often, the polar regions of the Void—in order to thwart them.

But it was a finite resource that required reapplication to a ship's hull and sails, and they had just wasted a great deal of it, which is why Finch looked perplexed. "Still planning on making for the Void? I doubt we'd be able to. An abortive rising like that burns through a great deal of it—it was as if we had ascended a dozen times."

"I know," Weatherby replied. "Could we do it again?"

At this, Finch shrugged. "That depends. To what degree?"

Weatherby explained his plan, and Finch listened with incredulity and a growing smile. Soon, the alchemist was casting about the hold for his stores.

"It's going to be a tight thing," Finch warned, though he seemed freshly energized by the prospects. "The Mercurium will most likely be spent, and I shall have to rely on other workings to keep us aloft. Even then, we could very well plummet from the sky at any moment."

Weatherby, having given his orders, made for the stairs and the decks above. "Then we shall aim to land atop their ships," he said, only half-joking. "Whatever it takes to stop them."

Philip and Elizabeth watched from the parapets of Edinburgh Castle as the sun set over the mountains to their left. To the right, the waters of the Firth of Forth glistened. There was no sight of the French—or of Weatherby's fleet.

"They found them and engaged," Philip said, adopting the naval terminology with only a small amount of confidence. "They're likely managing the prizes and helping the French survivors now. I'm sure we'll see them tomorrow."

Elizabeth looked at him with a small smile and a hard eye. "You're horrible at this, you know."

"At what?"

"Being at all reassuring."

Philip gave her a lopsided grin and was about to say something he thought quite witty, but suddenly spotted sails upon the water, far in the distance. "I dare say they are returned now, my Lady!" he exclaimed.

Elizabeth turned and smiled…but the joy quickly faded. "I do not see *Victory* among them," she said quietly. "I would know her lines anywhere."

It was in that moment that a miniscule puff of smoke was seen from the lead ship, followed by a small popping sound that carried across the water toward the castle. It was a cannon shot.

"The French," Philip whispered.

Seconds later, bells rang throughout the city and the streets below the castle were flooded with people rushing about—soldiers rushing to the shoreline, all others rushing for the security of the castle walls. The castle had withstood assault from sea and land for centuries, though none imagined but a few short years ago that such shelter would be required once more.

Philip and Elizabeth were soon joined at the lookout by the Prince Regent's retinue, including Lord Castlereagh and Anne, the latter continuing to serve as His Royal Highness' adviser on all things alchemical and mystical. Together, they watched six French ships of the line—double-decked warships, all—and several brigs and frigates fire long range upon the docks at Leith and the defensive batteries set upon the small isle of Inchkeith. The castle's cannons were already firing warning shots into the water despite the range.

Below, Philip and Elizabeth could see line after line of red-coated soldiers massing upon the wharves. In the midst of such a gathering, it would seem a massive throng. From above, they seemed all too few, and tiny compared to the force carried by the French warships.

"How many men do we have, Castlereagh?" the Prince Regent asked.

"Two thousand, sire. Wellesley is rallying them to shore right now," the minster responded. His tone was not one of confidence. "I am not a naval man, but I imagine those ships could easily carry twice as many."

Prince George nodded as he surveyed the defenses. The calculus of his thinking was writ upon his face, and although he was often considered something of a dilettante by some, those around him could see George's resolve—and the weight of his responsibilities—in his faraway gaze. Finally, he turned to Anne. "My Lady," he said quietly. "I hope it is most premature, but I am sorry for your loss. And I must ask you to nonetheless aid in the defense of the city."

Anne stood tall and stone-faced; Philip looked on with sorrow and pride, while Elizabeth allowed a tear to fall silently for her father. "I am at your service, sire. By your leave, I shall take charge of the alchemists within the palace and ensure enough supply to repel a siege."

The prince nodded and looked out once again at the scene unfolding below. The French ships now dominated the harbor. Several smaller ships stood watch at the mouth of the Forth, the first line of defense in what the French likely hoped would be their beachhead—and the ultimate defeat of England.

Anne watched as well, seemingly unable or unwilling to move, and Philip's heart broke at the sight of her. Always strong, always certain, Anne now stood silently as the French ships drew closer. It was as though she awaited one more miracle, a sign that her husband was not lost, but would somehow, in some wholly inscrutable manner, arrive to turn the tide.

Finally, with a sigh and a tear falling down her cheek, she turned to depart, aware that she had duties remaining to her. But she stopped again, looking not at the water, but at the sky toward the west, where the sun was settling below the mountains. And to Philip's great surprise, she smiled.

"Oh, dear God in Heaven," she breathed.

There was a light.

Several lights.

And as they grew larger, shapes surrounded those lights. It was if they had wings.

"What is that?" the prince demanded as all eyes turned toward the heavens.

They weren't wings after all. They were sails.

There, swooping in from the heavens, was the triple-decked, 100-gun wooden monstrosity that was HMS *Victory*, with several more ships behind her—all aloft, all flying with planesails unfurled, bobbing unsteadily in the breeze, looking as ungainly as a seal out of water.

"Sire," Anne said quietly, but with pride, "I must regretfully decline your condolences at this time."

By this point, all upon the walls were transfixed at the sight of the English squadron swooping down upon the French, and the Prince Regent bore upon his face a grand smile indeed. "There's no regret to be had," he replied. "Go, my Lady, and attend to the workings. Hopefully, the tide will have turned."

Anne gratefully rushed off, leaving Philip and Elizabeth with the Prince Regent and Castlereagh, watching as *Victory* and her squadron flew low over the city, their planes nearly horizontal as the ships tried to catch as much of the wind as possible to arrest their fall.

Admiral Weatherby, it seemed, wanted to stay aloft until the last possible moment, for not only were the planesails extended, but also the ruddersail—massive sails hanging at least fifty feet below the keel that would catch the Solar Wind and provide a ship in the Void with direction. And the sails were working just as well aloft as in the Void, it seemed. As Philip looked out into the sky, he imagined that Finch had managed an extension of Mercurium's innate characteristics, allowing short periods of flight by arresting the usual Void-going and keel-falling properties inherent to the mystical practices surrounding the Royal Navy's— Philip's thoughts were wholly interrupted by a huge spray of water from the Firth of Forth, for *Victory* had finally made keelfall, ruining her ruddersail in the process but landing nearly amidships with the largest of the French vessels. A moment later, *Victory*'s guns flashed. White puffs from the English ship were followed by black smoke from the French, just as the sound of the shot washed over the walls of Edinburgh Castle. Other English ships landed, with one unfortunate brig nearly capsizing as it did so, ultimately colliding head-on with a larger French vessel. Almost immediately, fires broke out aboard both ships.

Having made short work of her first target, *Victory* had sailed onward toward another large French ship, with alchemical fire pouring forth from her gun ports. Similarly, HMS *Mars* and the other English vessels had seized the upper hand, seriously damaging much of the French fleet. The ships would not be taken as prizes, not so close to shore, and not with so many undead soldiers aboard. Fire would be the only answer, for it was sure to destroy as many of the abominable *Corps Éternel* as possible. Even so, Philip knew the patrols along the shorelines would increase in coming days, for there would be stragglers, perhaps entire squads, of sodden but still-animated corpses wading out of the river.

Victory had, by this time, landed several shots into her second opponent, and of the dozen French ships that had sailed into the Firth of Forth, seven were already ablaze. The remaining ships—only one of which was a two-deck gunship—had already turned about and were making for the open ocean.

"If the admiral keeps this up these last-minute heroics," the Prince Regent said, turning toward Philip and Elizabeth with a paternal smile, "he shall no doubt cause my heart an arrest." The prince turned to Castlereagh. "Bring me the message papers for *Victory* so I may write the admiral a personal commendation.

"'Tis a far better thing than to write a eulogy."

CHAPTER 10

January 17, 2135

"**W**ith all commendation for your enterprising and wholly meritorious innovation…."

Gerald Ayim looked up from his holocontrols in confusion. "Excuse me, Commander?"

Shaila Jain looked at him blankly for a moment, then realized that the thought that occurred to her out of the blue must've come out her mouth without her realizing. *Really not good*, she thought. *Keep it together.*

"Sorry, Doctor. Thinking out loud about something," she muttered, turning her attention back to Stephane, whose glassy, now-angry glare was fixed solely on her. "Just distracted. Sure you understand."

The physicist nodded, though his understanding was, at best, partial. "Of course, Commander. I hope this innovation does work," he said brightly as he hooked wired pads to Stephane's forehead. Stephane flinched after each application.

And behind his head, out of view, the Emerald Tablet glowed an angry pale green. Shaila could swear it was *pulsing* somehow, and the erratic variation in the energies coming out of it, as measured by the bank of sensors around it, backed that up. They had to take him out of containment to conduct the experiment, but it was the DAEDALUS team's professional opinion that whatever afflicted him was not contagious…probably. Still, Diaz ordered a maximum of three people in with Stephane and the machine at all times, and Diaz wasn't going to put Stephane through the experiment without being present. Neither was Shaila.

To Shaila's surprise, it took very little convincing for Diaz to agree to hook Stephane up to the Emerald Tablet device, even though it came down to a hunch. "I monitored your interview with him," Diaz reminded her. "If it pisses him off, it's got to be good, right?"

The idea that this could also harm Stephane was unspoken, except for a long glance they shared before Diaz gave the go-ahead. It was a risk, and one that would ultimately hang around Diaz' neck should it go south. But Stephane had spoken French for the first time since his possession on Titan, and the fact that what he said was meaningful in a way only Shaila would understand…. She was grateful that, of all the two centuries' worth of science fiction she made him watch, he had latched onto one of the more obscure ones.

"All right, Doctor," Diaz said now, standing over Stephane's prone and strapped-down body. "Run it by us one last time for the record." *The record*, of course, was the bank of holorecorders and sensors and God-knows-what devices around them, the ones that would exonerate or condemn them once the inquiries started.

Ayim cleared his throat. "We currently theorize that this man," he began, nodding at Stephane, "used this so-called 'Emerald Tablet' device to download information stored within protein chains drawn from the waters of Enceladus, both before and after the planet's destruction. We believe these proteins—and/or the data which they carried—existed in quantum superpositioning between two dimensions, allowing for a certain amount of information to be shared between both dimensions. We also currently theorize that one of these proteins has infected this man, and that the data stored therein may be acting as a kind of interdimensional virus, somehow possessing him with a heretofore unknown alien intelligence." He paused. "I still can't believe I'm saying all that."

"Yes, you can," Diaz snapped. It sounded like an order.

"Yes, of course. While very implausible, it is the only explanation that fits all of the facts as we know them," Ayim said quickly. "Now, where was I? Oh, yes. It is our belief that if this device can 'download' and decrypt data stored on other Enceladan proteins, and breaking them down in the process, then it may be possible to do the same here. Whether we recover any data, I cannot say, though we have replaced the comm relay section of the device with an optical holodata storage unit, so we may capture whatever information we can. More importantly for Dr. Durand here, we may be able to break down the protein that is anchoring him to whatever intelligence currently possesses him. We hope that this will free him from that influence, ideally without damaging the proteins that make up his own DNA."

And there's the catch, Shaila thought.

Diaz looked over at Shaila, who nodded. The fact that Stephane was indeed somehow possessed by an alien intelligence was the single biggest military secret in the Solar System; gaining next-of-kin consent for an experiment such as this was impossible. So it fell to Shaila to give the go-ahead. Both she and Diaz figured she was close enough, though she had never broached the idea to Stephane while they were together. Or, rather, while he was himself.

Let them sue, Shaila thought. *I know he's in there. I know he wants out.*

"All right, team. Julie, how are we looking?" Diaz asked.

The tech replied over the comm; she was in the other room, monitoring the sensors. "We're…fine, I guess, General. Commander Jain, would you mind taking a step closer to Dr. Durand for me?"

To Shaila's surprise, she found herself at least a good two strides away from Stephane, almost in the corner of the room. She attributed it to nerves, but also to the glare he continued to fix her whenever she was within range of his eyes. "Sure," she said flatly, and took a step forward. "Why?"

"Wow. Take another step, would you?" Julie asked.

Frowning, Shaila stepped closer still, but behind Stephane's head. "What's going on?" she demanded.

"Interesting," Julie said absently. "It looks like the ambient Cherenkov radiation in the room is increasing whenever you get closer, while the Cherenkov radiation coming off the subject is *decreasing*."

"What does that mean?" Diaz snapped.

Ayim grabbed another sensor pad and moved toward Shaila with it. "It means we need to have a look at you as well, Commander," he replied. "I don't know why, but something is going on between you two."

Diaz suddenly brightened. "Could it be their relationship, Doctor? Maybe Stephane is in there trying to kick the other guy out. Shaila could be a positive influence on that."

The physicist finished taping a sensor to Shaila's head, then turned to Diaz with a look of patient, paternal disbelief on his face. "There is no scientific basis to make that kind of assumption, General. That is why we measure and study."

"You're a real buzzkill, Gerry," Diaz said, giving Shaila a wink. "I vote love."

Ayim shrugged as he fussed with the last of the connections between his equipment, the Tablet and his subjects. "As you wish, General. I believe we are ready. Shall we proceed?"

Diaz nodded. "By the authority granted me by the President of the United States, you are authorized to proceed, Doctor," she said formally, likely for the benefit of the recording devices and as a way to defer blame to a higher authority. "Good luck."

With a nod and the press of a button, Ayim activated the Emerald Tablet device. The slab started to glow even brighter.

And then Stephane screamed—an unearthly scream that seemed to permeate the room with an eerie resonance, even as it caused all three observers to jump out of their skins.

Reflexively, Shaila reached out and took Stephane's hand.

And her eyes suddenly filled with a green-white glow, blinding her.

Shaila stood on the edge of a cliff. Behind her was a verdant field, covered in wildflowers and grasses, with an impossibly blue sky above her and a sun that seemed to shower the land with golden peace. Over the side of the cliff below her—far below, in fact, at least a kilometer—was a dark, blasted plain, covered in dark rocks and gray desert dirt, with clouds the color of coal and a river of black water running through it.

And though it had to be at least three kilometers away, if not more, Shaila could clearly see someone standing there, wearing a very dark outfit, something that looked like it came from…Weatherby's era. *My God.*

"Weatherby?"

The man turned, and Shaila saw it wasn't a uniform, but merely a very dark suit. And the pallid man wearing it wasn't Weatherby. It was Andrew Finch.

"You!" Finch exclaimed, the distance between them suddenly immaterial and unimportant. "What are you doing here?" Then a thought crossed Finch's face, and he grew wide-eyed. "You have the Tablet."

"We do, but Stephane is infected," Shaila replied. It was the only thing she could think of. "Something possessed him. The Martians from your world." She felt like she was shouting through gauze, even though her voice sounded very normal. And she was surprised, at such a distance, that she could see his face so clearly. It was so much older than she remembered. Lined, weathered, worn.

"Venus," Finch said. "They're focusing on Venus."

He suddenly looked wearier, sicklier. It was jarring. Shaila struggled to concentrate. "What? The Martians? Why Venus?" Shaila demanded.

"Souls. There's a soul in him. That's what they need. Souls!" Now Finch looked excited. It was as if he slipped on a new mask every time he talked.

"I don't get it. Souls? What are you talking about?"

Now Finch looked worried, urgent. "Go to Venus. Go to Venus!"

"Venus?!"

Suddenly, the green-white light flashed brighter behind Shaila, and a tide of billowing darkness—as if leaden clouds suddenly mushroomed into being—rolled up behind Finch. Then all was light and dark, somehow at the same time. And then dark.

"Shaila! Talk to me, Shaila!"

Shaila opened her eyes to see Diaz hovering over her, looking worried. Then it occurred to her she was flat on her back.

"General, please step away," came another voice. It was Julie, sounding surprisingly commanding and in charge. Diaz faded from view, replaced by a masked and gloved Julie.

"What happened?" Shaila murmured.

"Easy," Julie said as she waved a diagnostic sensor over Shaila's head. "Yeah, it looks like the Cherenkov radiation isn't staying there. It's fading," she called out.

"Same with Durand," Ayim responded from…somewhere else. "His levels are down sixty percent from before. But…yes, they are still there."

Shaila edged herself up onto her elbows. She was on the floor of the lab, next to Stephane's cot. "I touched him," she said. "I touched him, and…"

"And you started shouting at someone," Diaz finished. "So was Stephane. It was freaky as fuck. Who were you shouting at? We heard you say 'Weatherby.'"

This puzzled Shaila. "I wasn't shouting. I was talking to… well, I was talking to Andrew Finch, actually."

"Come again?" Diaz said, perhaps a little louder than was necessary.

"Finch. From Mars. And he knew we have the Emerald Tablet. He…he told me to go to Venus."

Diaz looked over at Julie and Ayim, who both gave the general a very neutral look. Shaila had seen it many times before on the faces of doctors and soldiers alike: *Fuck if I know, boss. I don't like it any more than you do.* "All right, Jain. Let's get you on your feet."

Shaila reached up for the general's offered hand and easily stood. She wasn't dizzy, or nauseous, or anything, really. It was as if she had simply been moved from one place to another, and back again. Disconcerting but ultimately… anticlimactic. "I'm good, thanks," Shaila said, extricating her hand from Diaz'. "You mentioned some readings off me?"

"Oh, definitely," Julie answered, earning her a cross look from Diaz. "I haven't checked yet, but it looked like when you touched the subject here, you suddenly gave off a huge Cherenkov pulse from your head—likely from your parietal lobe—and dropped to the floor. Then you started shouting about Martians and Venus."

A moan came from where Stephane lay. Ayim gasped. "General!"

Before Diaz could respond, Shaila essentially shoved Julie out of the way. "What is it?" Shaila demanded.

Strong hands grabbed her arms. "Jain, don't touch him," Diaz ordered from behind her. "Gerry, what's up?"

For once, the physicist looked utterly baffled. "I don't understand how this can be," he said quietly. "It didn't work. The Cherenkov levels are lower, but…"

"Shay."

Everyone in the room froze. It was hoarse and quiet, but it was Stephane's voice. And it sounded like…Stephane's voice. Not Rathemas'. Not anything else.

Shaila shrugged off Diaz' now-lax grip and rushed to his bedside, still mindful of Diaz' warnings not to touch him. "Stephane?"

His face still looked sweaty and pallid, his hair was slicked onto his forehead. But his eyes—they were red. They were swollen and half-open.

But they were his.

"Hello," he said weakly.

Shaila's hand flew to her lips, her other hand gripping the railing of his cot. "Hey," she replied quietly, tentatively—unwilling to test the moment too much, lest it slip away.

"You messaged me every day from *Armstrong*, on the way back from Saturn, yes?" he said, his voice getting a touch stronger.

"I did, Stephane. I did."

He smiled. "I thought it was a dream. It wasn't. I'm glad."

Shaila blinked her way through tears. "Is…is he gone?"

A shadow crossed over Stephane's eyes. "No."

The room was silent, except for a single wracking sob from Shaila.

"He is still in here," Stephane said finally. "With me. But…for now…I think I have him. For now. I can't say… how long…he will….be…"

Stephane drifted off to sleep, and Ayim and Julie rushed forward to conduct their research. Diaz took Shaila by the hand and gently led her out of the room, walking her to an unused office next door. There, Shaila finally let out all those months of rage and sorrow and anger as Diaz held her and let her cry. And cry more. Even the Air Force general herself ended up shedding a few tears.

It was worth it.

Harry Yu was working his comms, trying to rebuild any sort of professional network beyond what Chrys VanDer-Kamp could offer, when he noticed the silence and stillness in the room.

Typically, Greene and Huntington would be moving about, talking to each other, dialing up streams of holo-data that prompted all kinds of computer-generated light and noise. Their computer models were constantly being updated, showing the various configurations of particle accelerators they were trying. A few looked odd—it seemed Greene was experimenting with scales both tiny and immense as he worked—but there was always something running in the background, using the quantum computers to cycle through billions of potential scenarios every second.

Harry looked up. The noises had stopped. The holoscreens were frozen.

So were Green and Huntington.

The two former DAEDALUS members sat quietly, staring off into space immediately ahead of them. Both looked pale, and Greene had a few beads of sweat developing on his forehead. They sat…and stared.

"Guys?" Harry said finally. "Hello?"

Nothing. Just staring.

"Guys?"

Harry stood up and tentatively walked toward their workstations. They remained completely, unnaturally still. Even their eyes were locked on a fixed point, and Harry had to lean over and look at Greene's eyes to see that, yes, he still blinked.

"Guys, this is creepy as fuck. Is this how you do it? Is this how you're in touch with the other side?" Harry asked, knowing just how insane it sounded. But the more he had thought about it, the more he came to believe that Greene and Huntington were not only in touch with the other dimension, but likely under the influence of whatever was on the other side.

And there were safeguards in place for that.

Harry pulled his datapad out of his pocket and quickly sent a series of six numbers to a predetermined destination. Maybe this was just some kind of hiccup, or maybe Greene and Huntington were gone, or done, or whatever. Didn't matter.

When he looked up, Huntington was standing right in front of him, smiling her feral, harrowing smile. "Thanks for the help, Harry," she said. To Harry's ears, it wasn't exactly heartfelt.

Then there was a loud click, and Harry felt a sharp, impossibly blinding pain blossom in his chest. And his heart started knocking around in his chest as if it wanted to burst out at all costs.

"Shit," Harry said quietly before he slumped to his knees.

Huntington turned to Greene. "It's time."

Greene was already packing up. As Harry fell onto his side, he could see Greene placing a number of data storage drives in a backpack. "We're good. Everything is uploaded. The hardware on the satellites checks out."

The satellites, Harry thought. Paying attention to his surroundings was surprisingly easy for him in that moment. It kept his mind off the fact that he was probably dying from a gunshot to the chest. He coughed up blood, feeling it trickle from the corner of his mouth down his cheek to the shoddy carpeting beneath him. *The satellites. They knew what Chrys was doing.*

Harry wondered if his former protégé knew about whatever Greene and Huntington were talking about. Maybe this was her screwing him over now, or maybe she was about to get screwed over like he just was. Maybe she'd get shot. Maybe...

The thoughts deteriorated. His heart fluttered. He tried to focus on its rhythm, but in one cold moment, his last conscious one, he realized it wasn't beating anymore.

CHAPTER 11

May 12, 1809

Lady Anne Weatherby strode through the halls of Edinburgh Castle as though a woman possessed, her skirts gathered up in her hands so that she might walk faster. Indeed, only her son could keep pace, for he was a young man still, and while of a scholarly bent, took pains to exercise regularly. Yet even he hurried himself, for Anne was preternaturally healthy due to both mindful habit and alchemical improvement. The fact that such care and effort made her look half her forty-six years was but a bonus.

At the moment, however, the Lady Anne did not seem to care one whit about health or appearance, and those that saw her knew it from her face; the courtiers and servants in the halls of the Royal Palace scattered as she approached, as if she had Moses himself by her side, parting the seas of humanity before her.

So it was that when she entered one of the many small sitting rooms within the palace—one taken over by Lord Castlereagh as his temporary office—Lord Weatherby knew his wife had much upon her mind, and would not be dissuaded from speaking with him in whichever moment she chose, no matter if she interrupted conversation about hunting or the highest affairs of state.

"My Lord," Anne said as she entered, Philip trotting behind her. "I would speak with you if you have a moment for me."

Weatherby looked to Castlereagh, and the minister had a look upon his face of both surprise and amusement. "See to your wife, my Lord Admiral," Castlereagh said gently. "Wellesley shan't win Yorkshire whilst you are gone, I'm sure."

"My thanks, Lord Minister," Weatherby said formally. "If I am to be long, I shall send Captain Searle in my place to discuss the health of our fleet. Now," he added, turning to Anne, "shall we retire elsewhere, my love?"

Anne merely smile grimly, then turned and stalked out of the room as quickly and abruptly as she entered, forcing Weatherby himself to quicken his pace as if he were a chastened midshipman rather than one of the senior-most admirals of His Majesty's Navy. Thankfully, Anne saw fit to simply dodge into an empty salon quite near to Castlereagh's office, whereupon she waited for her husband with her hands upon her hips, and her son looking slightly winded—and worried—beside her.

Weatherby shut the door behind him and opened his mouth to speak, but Anne surpassed him in this. "We need to search Finch's rooms," she stated bluntly.

Immediately, Weatherby shared the concern evident upon the faces of his wife and step-son. "Lord in Heaven, is he afflicted again?" he said.

"No, no," Anne said with a dismissive wave of her hand as she found a seat upon a finely wrought sofa. "Would that it were. I fear it is far more serious than mere drugs, though I'll wager there is a form of addiction at play as well."

Thoroughly confused, Weatherby ventured into the room and sat across from his wife, leaning forward. "I do not take your meaning, Anne. Please…what is wrong with him? He is my oldest, dearest friend, and I worry overmuch about him as it stands."

Anne nodded, and glanced over to Philip, who spoke in her stead. "Have you experienced Uncle Andrew's ability to move between places in an instant?"

"Move between places?" Weatherby asked. "This is how he transported you from Oxford to Edinburgh, was it not?"

"It was, my Lord. But the nature of said transport was like nothing I had ever seen from any practitioner of the Great Work," he replied. "There is nothing of it in my father's journals, and Mother can confirm that if such ability was within the grasp of the Count St. Germain, it was something he never showed."

"And you know how much Francis loved to show off," Anne added with a small smile. She was quite sanguine about the facets of her late husband's character, both good and ill.

"Yes, of course," Weatherby said quickly, clamping down upon a growing unease within his breast. "Yet is not Finch one of the foremost alchemists of our time? Did he not find a way—and quickly, I might add—to give our ships stability and speed so that they may race to Edinburgh to defeat the French invasion without flying off into the Void?"

"Aye, and that's the rub!" Anne said. "The Void-going properties of Mercurium would not allow such movement on its own, and both Philip and I analyzed the stores aboard *Victory* just this morning. There was nothing within its alchemical labs that would allow Finch to create such a feat!"

Weatherby frowned, sitting back and crossing his arms across his chest. "And how is it that my wife and step-son, neither of whom have any authority aboard my flagship or the Royal Navy at large, were able to conduct such an examination aboard *Victory*?"

There was another dismissive wave of Anne's hand, though with a touch of red upon her cheeks to accompany it. "We lied and told the officer on duty we were there upon your errand," Anne replied quickly. "That's not the important part."

"Is it not?" Weatherby said, a bit of thunder entering his voice. "Would not it have been meet for you to approach me with your concerns first, instead of violating the security of His Majesty's Navy?"

"Damn it all, Tom!" Anne said tersely. "We think Finch has *The Book of the Dead*!"

And thus did silence reign in the room for several long moments as Weatherby's consternation grew into wonderment, then fear, then around to anger once more, though the target of his ire shifted considerably. "Explain how you have come to this," he said quietly, but with all the urgency and authority that came with an inviolable order.

Philip cleared his throat. "Are you familiar with the current theories in alchemical circles regarding the nature of souls, and of life after death, my Lord?" Philip waited for Weatherby to respond, but from the look upon his stepfather's face, it was quite evident he had no notion of it. "The current thinking is that there is a kind of shadow-world attached to our own, a dark mirror in which life is death and light is dark and the souls of those who passed on may yet dwell if they do not enter immediately into the Lord's saving graces."

Weatherby shook his head. "How is it that you wonder-workers even have time for such investigations?" he asked, his frustration evident. "And to what end?"

"Tom," Anne said gently, putting her hand upon his knee, "some of these notions stem directly from our encounter upon Mars, those many years ago. You were there, my love. Can you not contemplate the idea of other places between the folds and creases of our own worlds?"

This settled Weatherby to a large degree, and he felt somewhat guilty for being obstinate. "So, then. You have posited the Afterlife and believe it may be a place not unlike that which we encountered on Mars."

Anne shot her son a small grin. "I told you he'd grasp it, Philip."

For his part, Philip turned bright red, but soldiered on regardless. "Yes, well, it is this underworld that I believe your daughter and I glimpsed as we were whisked from Oxford to Edinburgh. We—that is, Mother and I—believe that by traversing the underworld in the manner of the ancient Egyptians as described in their legendry, we would cover vast distances in mere moments. Furthermore, if your ships' lodestones were placed within the underworld—both partially and quite temporarily—they might indeed fly through the air rather than ascending directly into the Void as they should have."

Weatherby thought back to the first of the two battles off Scotland in which *Victory* leapt from one place upon the ocean to another. It was a violent movement that threatened to tear the ship asunder. Yet by the time Finch had conducted his alterations to the lodestones some hours later, the flight from the North Sea to the Firth of Forth for the second battle was smooth in comparison.

He looked at his wife and step-son carefully. Anne had always complained of Finch's propensities for what she called irresponsible experimentation, but in this she had admitted a maternal bent toward him. Plus, Anne and Finch had collaborated on more than a few papers submitted to the Royal Society over the years. As for Philip, Weatherby knew he held his "uncle" in the utmost esteem, bordering upon hero-worship. For the two of them to be in agreement in this matter, and knowing full well Weatherby's own sense of brotherhood with the accused, things must be serious indeed.

"I believe we would need to broach our concerns before the Prince Regent's household before conducting a search," Anne said. "Shall I—"

"No need," Weatherby interrupted. "Finch remains my fleet alchemist, and while that carries a certain rank and privilege, he remains a member of the Royal Navy under my command. I authorize you, as my personal agents in this matter, to take it upon yourselves to conduct this search. I should wish it that it be done with discretion and without Andrew's knowledge, for if you are wrong—and I pray to God you are—then I do not wish to create a rift between Andrew and ourselves where there needn't be one. And if you are right, you are the only ones I would trust to properly secure this artifact. Tell no one other than myself should you find it, for if the Prince Regent discovered Finch had withheld such a critical alchemical weapon from him, it would mean the noose for him and naught but abuse for the *Book*."

Both Anne and Philip nodded soberly. "How should we go about it, my Lord?" Philip asked. "Do you know where Uncle Andrew is at the moment?"

Just then, a knock upon the door interrupted them, causing all within the small salon to jump as if they were scared. "Come," Weatherby ordered.

A midshipman peeked his head through the door. "My humblest apologies, my Lord Admiral, but Dr. Finch has been seeking you out. He has been in consultations with Ambassador Vellusk, and they wish you and Lord Castlereagh to attend them at your earliest convenience."

Weatherby nodded and waved the boy off. "Convenience indeed," he quipped. "Very well. You two have your orders. 'Tis obvious you may carry them out now. Come to me forthwith should you find your suspicions confirmed."

Philip nodded, while Anne gave Weatherby a wry smile. "Does this mean we are now, at long last, part of the Navy, my Lord?"

This elicited a small smile from Weatherby in return. "My ingenious plans have finally come to fruition after three decades," he said gently. "You know I am no master of timing in such matters."

"You never were, my love, but I shall happily follow you now," she replied, then turned and gathered her son with a wave of her hand as she departed the salon.

The midshipman was awaiting Weatherby within the ornate hallway of the palace, and he allowed the boy to lead him to wherever Finch and Vellusk had entrenched themselves. It worried Weatherby no small amount that Finch might withhold *The Book of the Dead* for himself and whatever researches he had hoped to engage upon. The fact that the book could create soldiers from corpses made it, in Weatherby's estimation, an inherently evil artifact. Furthermore, it could represent otherworldly alchemy, as Finch himself had once opined, and thus become a gateway to another incursion from the ancient Martians, the Xan partisans, the future humanity he glimpsed long ago—or perhaps something far worse.

For what if the souls of the dead could come forth into the world of the living? Weatherby imagined Finch would be enamored of such a prospect. And as much as he loved Finch and would swear his long-time friend was a genius of the highest caliber, Finch was not, in the end, possessed of great amounts of wisdom.

On the other hand, Finch had yet to produce an animated corpse-soldier of his own making, so perhaps he was more judicious with his inquiries than Anne and Phillip were giving him credit for? But then, if he had the book, could he not easily devise a manner by which to readily destroy the infernal *Corps Éternel*?

Weatherby's head was quickly swimming in whats and wherefores by the time the mid had led him to a small library near the palace's ballroom. The young man knocked on his admiral's behalf, then held the door for Weatherby to enter. Inside, he found Finch and Vellusk there, with piles of unshelved books between them.

"Ah, there you are, Tom!" Finch said cheerfully, his demeanor far less sickly than it was aboard ship two days prior; it made Weatherby fervently wish his wife and step-son to be wholly mistaken. "We have much to discuss!"

Weatherby gingerly entered the room, which looked as if a hurricane of paper and leather covers had been loosed upon it. "And much to clean when you are done, Doctor. Of course, Ambassador, you are most welcome, and it is a great pleasure to see you once more. May God keep you in health and spirit."

Vellusk bowed deeply toward Weatherby, appreciative as always for the over-mannered speech that too few humans bothered with, even though it was a mere drop in a bucket compared to the Xan's own formalities—some of which could take the better part of an afternoon to wade through. "You are most kind, Lord Admiral," Vellusk replied in pleasant song. "I am heartened to see you in good health after your encounter with the French of late."

There were more such pleasantries—a full five minutes' worth, during which Finch ignored them both and point-edly kept his nose in books—until finally Vellusk invited Weatherby to sit so that he may hear tell of their researches.

"You are familiar, of course, with the idea of memory vaults, as we have seen it together within the Venusian culture first hand," Finch began. "There have been several expeditions and embassies to the Venusian people, both before and after our time there back in '79, during which the concept has been explored further. However, I believe our own Gar'uk might explain things quite simply."

It was then that Weatherby realized that Gar'uk was indeed in the room, quietly reading in the corner and shielded from view by the piles of books and papers strewn about.

"Does no one consult me on any matter regarding my command anymore?" Weatherby huffed. "He is my valet, Finch, not your research assistant."

At this, Gar'uk stood and walked to Weatherby, whereupon he bowed deeply. "I am sorry, Lord Admiral," the Venusian croaked solemnly, and with great dignity. "If I have not been good in my duty, you must tell me now so I can make better."

Weatherby opened his mouth to begin, but found that there had been nothing to indicate that Gar'uk had performed his duty in any way other than exacting. "You have done your duty well, my old friend," he said to Gar'uk in the most gentle of tones. "And I am grateful you chose to assist Dr. Finch and the ambassador."

Gar'uk straightened up and appeared to smile—something he was culturally and physiologically disinclined to do, but tried for the benefit of the humans around him. "They would be lost in long words without one of me to tell them."

At this, Weatherby grinned genuinely. "Of that, I have no doubt. So tell me what you have found, good Gar'uk."

"When we of Va'har'a die," he began, using the native name for Venus, "our souls, what you call memories, all that we are, these go to our priests. The priests carry them to our vaults. There, our memories are at rest, and they can be used by those still living. All of our history is there in our vaults. If one of our people has ever seen something, it can be known to all."

Weatherby nodded. "Simple enough, then. And I suppose there might be some value to the French, though this does not explain Berthollet and Cagliostro, and their enthusiasm for it."

Finch grinned widely. "And that is where two experts on alchemy may come in handy, Tom," he said. "For we may obtain an understanding of these memory vaults that can be applied to modern sensibilities and theories on the Great Work."

Vellusk cleared his throat, which sounded like a wheezing flute. "We cannot say truly what the alchemical implications may be, I am most sorry to say," Vellusk sang cautiously. "However, we may state with certainty that there are many good reasons the French—and the wayward citizens of Great Xanath—may wish access to the racial and cultural memories of the Venusian people."

"Such as?" Weatherby asked, all pretense of politesse forgotten, replaced by strategic inquiry and concern.

"There were Venusians present throughout the wars between our people and those you call Martians," Vellusk sang, notes of martialry and sadness in his voice. "The Martians and the Xan alternatively allied themselves with, or enslaved, the primitive Venusian tribes through the centuries of our struggle. There were Venusians who saw the holocausts on Titan, the destruction of Phaeton, the razing of the Martian surface. There were those who were present—as servants or even military leaders—when Althotas met with his war councils, or when we met with ours.

"And," Vellusk added ominously, "there were Venusians present when Althotas first enchanted the Emerald Tablet and *The Book of the Dead*, and when Althotas himself was first imprisoned in the world between worlds."

And as alarming as this was to Weatherby, one thought stood out. "Gar'uk, all your memories of our time together would enter into this vault when you pass on?"

Gar'uk nodded. "But I will not go to the vaults."

"Why?"

The old Venusian tried to smile again, and it came off fairly well this time. "If the French win the vaults from my people, they could find my memories. Then they know how you think and plan, and they will find a way to kill you. I will not let this happen."

Weatherby placed his hand upon the lizard-man's shoulder. "You are a true and loyal friend, Gar'uk of Venus. I shall not forget this sacrifice."

Finch stood, looking rather pallid once more. "Tom, you don't really know the half of it."

"Do tell," the admiral replied, feeling somewhat annoyed with his friend.

"It's not a matter of their *memories* being placed into the vault. The translation doesn't come across well, because to the Venusians, it appears to them that they are seeing the memories of their ancestors when they visit the vaults," Finch said. "But really, the Venusians have somehow found a way to house not just memories, but a portion—or all, really—of a Venusian's spirit or soul within an alchemical construct, one that allows for access to their very consciousness, really."

Weatherby thought on this. "Gar'uk, whatever memories you have of me, I cannot allow you to endanger your afterlife in this regard. I hereby—"

Then the potential of what he said hit Weatherby like a thunderbolt.

"It's not just what's in the vaults, then, is it," the admiral said. "It's the vaults themselves that the French want. The memories are fine. But the capacity to create a kind of afterlife?"

Finch smiled. "Not bad for an old sailor. That's indeed the biggest problem here."

Vellusk's garments began to ripple in excitement—or concern, perhaps. "They have but a fragment of *The Book of the Dead*, enough to create their abominable soldiers. But with the vaults in hand, they could not only find memories of Venusians dealing with the *Book*, but by examining the vaults themselves, they could come to a greater understanding of death and the afterlife, and their alchemical workings could become far stronger—and darker."

Weatherby eyed Finch most closely as he continued on with his questions, and saw little in the way of guilt or concern in his friend's eyes. "Would the vaults have value to us as well?" Weatherby asked pointedly. "For example, could we find ideas therein to counteract the working that created the *Corps Éternel*?"

Finch shrugged. "It's possible, but that knowledge is counter to the knowledge that I saw in *The Book of the Dead.* Such a working would be within the purview of the Emerald Tablet, and we currently do not have access to that."

Weatherby smirked. "Access? It's in a thousand pieces in a blasted temple on Titan. Not even Vellusk's worthy people could piece it together."

"Then I dare say we may find some use for the vaults, but I would strongly suggest that we ally ourselves with the Venusians against the French, rather than take the vaults for ourselves," Vellusk sang. "England, as I see it, needs all the allies it can get."

Weatherby nodded. "Yes, of course. Having been invaded, I do not wish to in turn invade another sovereign people," he said. "But tell me, gentlemen, what is the worst of this? Say the French obtain the archive of memories—souls, if you will—from the Venusians. If fortune favors them, what do they gain?"

Finch answered, as he knew the thrust of Weatherby's argument. "They not only gain an entire species' worth of history and knowledge, which may include heretofore unknown alchemical insight and power, but they also gain insight into methods they might use to access the world of the afterlife or, perhaps, even access other worlds entirely—such as the one Althotas was imprisoned within, or even the future worlds we saw upon Mars."

Vellusk nodded beneath his voluminous robes. "These vaults, in their own way, allow consciousness to pass onto other dimensions of being, my Lord Weatherby. Thus, this primitive alchemy can be strengthened or altered into a pathway to any number of other realities, including the one in which Althotas may remain in wait."

A rap upon the door interrupted them. Gar'uk dutifully rushed to answer, whereupon he allowed Anne and Philip entrance. Weatherby looked over and found them both to be grim-faced and determined. A quick nod from Anne was all Weatherby needed.

"Dr. Finch, we must speak with you on an urgent matter," Anne said coldly. "And I'm quite glad you're here, Ambassador Vellusk. Perhaps you can help us discern why Dr. Finch might have *this* in his quarters."

Philip came up behind his mother and placed a large, linen-wrapped package upon a table in the room. Weatherby watched Finch turn several shades more pale, his eyes growing wider.

"This is not what it seems," Finch said, altogether too quickly.

Weatherby calmly rose and went to the table, whereupon he unwrapped the linen from the ebon-covered book therein. "Well, Doctor, then perhaps you may elucidate. Is this not *The Book of the Dead*?"

"Well, yes, it is, Tom, but—"

"And it *seems* to me that it is indeed in your possession," Weatherby continued, his voice rising. "Is that the case, Doctor?"

Finch began to grow agitated and slightly possessed of panic. "Yes, yes, Tom, I've been keeping it quite safe, I assure you. I—"

"Quite safe!" Weatherby spat. "It is, by your own account, one of the greatest alchemical treasures the world has ever seen! And you told me to my face—more than once, Finch! To my very face! You told me it was lost, and here it is, found in your rooms, which is certainly not, in any rational opinion, safe!"

"Tom," Finch said weakly. "If I did not keep it…"

"If you did not keep it, would England still stand?" Weatherby roared. "Would we not have found a way to defeat the *Corps Éternel*, despite what you have said? How many have died because you kept this! You hoard your knowledge like an old, corrupt dragon with gold, just as Franklin once warned us would be our downfall!"

Finch looked stricken, and indeed placed a hand upon the chair before him to support himself. "It is too dangerous for others, Tom," Finch said. "It would corrupt us. Look what a mere fragment did to the French! And there is more. It is a way to communicate! I have done so with the others!"

Weatherby was about to speak, but was silenced by a surprising interruption from Vellusk. "What others?" the ambassador sang, loudly and with great anger.

"The others from our future!" Finch replied. "They have the Tablet, or an aspect of it! I....wait...." He suddenly looked as though he could see the very Void before his eyes. "Go to Venus. Go to Venus!"

At this, Finch's legs gave out from under him, and he collapsed to the floor, still looking as though he was seeing leagues away. Or perhaps his mind was leagues away, Weatherby could not say. And despite his rage against the man he called friend, he nonetheless rushed to Finch's side. "Anne, help him!" Weatherby cried.

She, too, rushed over, but they found Finch in a state of near catatonia. "I cannot say what has befallen him," she said after several long minutes, spent in awkward silence. "We need time to study what this damned book has done to him."

Weatherby turned to address Ambassador Vellusk, who was practically vibrating with intensity. "Ambassador Vellusk, my very wise and very good friend. It is only this day we began to suspect Dr. Finch's possession of this artifact, and I must apologize, humbly, on his behalf, and for myself. And for all England."

This helped Vellusk somewhat, though he still appeared quite agitated. "And what shall be done with this fell book?" he sang, notes of both dread and rage within his voices.

"I shall keep it locked away with the utmost security, and I shall hold the only key," Weatherby said. "Only Anne and Philip will be allowed to study it, and only should you be consulted first. You or one of your representatives may be present at all times while it is examined."

Vellusk seemed to pause a moment before responding. "This is acceptable, Admiral Weatherby, but I urge you to keep this matter most private," the Xan sang. "If your Prince Regent discovers this is here, I fear that his lust for vengeance and hatred of the French will cause him to make ill use of it. And if my people were to discover it, it would only add credence to the belief, currently in the minority, that humanity plays with powers they cannot understand and harness."

Weatherby had already thought of this, and the decision—the right one, he felt, but one that was wholly imperfect and in violation of several sacred vows—had already been made. "The existence of this damnable book remains secret to those in this room," he said, gathering the attention of the others with the authority in his voice. "We must come to understand how it has affected Finch, whether he is to remain in our trust, and whether it can be used to reverse the evils of Napoleon's alchemists. And if they are indeed going to Venus, I dare say we must convince the Prince Regent to mount an assault there.

"And we must not tell him the real reason why," Weatherby said sadly.

CHAPTER 12

January 18, 2135

Shaila still couldn't sleep. But at least, she figured, it was good to have different reasons.

A few days ago, she was angry and frustrated and wanting to do *something* worthwhile. Now, she was far less angry, though the frustration and the need to be elsewhere was still paramount.

Being locked in containment will do that to a person.

Shortly after she left Stephane and huddled with Diaz for her crying jag—a hugely embarrassing crying jag, she felt—Ayim and Julie had come in and gently requested she undergo more testing. Of course she agreed, because she was just as concerned about her blackout, and her vision of Andrew Finch, as they were.

However, they turned out to be far *more* concerned. Because they ushered her into a spare containment unit and locked her the hell down while they figured out why touching Stephane had created a massive Cherenkov radiation spike in addition to her rapid unconsciousness.

On the bright side, the monitors in her unit—on the other side of the clear barrier, granted, but still—were focused on Stephane. And that was a far better view than space.

So she watched.

Stephane remained in bed over the past sixteen hours, but he resumed consciousness for at least part of the time. He still looked like he'd been through the wringer, but Shaila knew it was *him*, and not someone else in that room. Spending two years in a relationship with someone—and a full six months on an interplanetary mission as part of that—was more than enough time to recognize the subtle movements and quirks associated with that person. The way he cocked his head when presented with something different, the way he ran his hand through his hair when thinking…it was all there. The DAEDALUS team had placed some of his personal effects from *Armstrong* in with him now, conveniently within reach, and he picked them up and turned them over in his hands. He had a few ancient paperback books, at least a century old, mostly French authors like Dumas and Hugo and Le Clezio. They gave him a datapad—almost certainly not networked. And there was a holopic of he and Shaila from when they visited Paris after finally finishing their debriefing after the *Daedalus* incident on Mars.

Shaila smiled at that. The trip itself was infuriating. Stephane had insisted on organizing everything, which meant they ended up crashing at a friend's apartment and sleeping on an inflatable mattress in a closet of a room. They were up until 3 a.m. drinking wine—good wine, it should be said—and laughing at jokes in French that Shaila couldn't really follow. Stephane had insisted on taking her to the Eiffel Tower, Notre Dame, the Louvre, you name it. There was a river cruise on the Seine done on the cheap, which meant an engine malfunction and an extra two hours on a smelly river in the heat of the day.

If it were anyone else, Shaila would've left after the first night. With him, it was somehow the best vacation of her life—though she'd never admit it to him. She got to see him away from work and crisis, and found him to be generous, gregarious and surprisingly soulful—almost the exact opposite of the playboy dilettante she had first pegged him for on Mars.

She was still afraid to believe he was truly back. Maybe he wasn't. Maybe this was some sort of ruse. The alien intelligence inside him could be playing them, trying to lull them into complacency. Maybe it really was him, but he could be swallowed up by that…*thing*…at any moment, lost to her forever.

She tried not to think about it too hard. And besides, she had her own issues—those odd voices in her mind, stretching back more than two and a half years. Stretching back to a cave on Mars and a journal from an impressionable, young Lt. Weatherby, improbably sitting in a pile of rust-red rubble.

"Jain."

Shaila's reverie was interrupted by Maria Diaz, standing on the other side of the containment barrier. She didn't even hear the general enter the room, which probably wasn't good.

"General," she replied, rushing to her feet.

Diaz looked concerned. "Another one?"

"No, ma'am, just thinking," Shaila said, nodding toward the holomonitor.

That won her a small smile from the general. "Figured you'd want to keep an eye on him. He's doing well, by the way."

"Thank you, ma'am. How do you mean 'well?'"

Diaz pulled over a chair and took a seat in front of her. "Well, his rad levels are stable, for the most part. There's some peaks and valleys, and it tends to correspond with his periods of unconsciousness or inactivity. Nothing anywhere near the levels he hit when he was infected...well, hell, he really was possessed, wasn't he?"

Shaila shrugged. "Let's stick with 'infected,' ma'am."

"So what's *your* explanation, Commander?" Diaz' face took a hard turn at this, leaving Shaila immediately worried.

"I...don't understand, ma'am."

Diaz frowned. "Here's my problem, Jain. When you touched Stephane, there was a kind of...reaction. In that moment, there were *three* huge spikes in Cherenkov radiation in the room. One was from the Tablet, or whatever the fuck that stone is. One was leeching out of Stephane's neural pathways. And one...was from *your* brain. Just like his."

Shaila nodded. "I assumed as much. I've no idea why, though."

"*Why* isn't something we're going to really get out of this, Jain. We still don't know half of what's going on. Ayim's got all kinds of theories, most of which make zero sense to me. Some stuff about 'quantum mind' and 'parallelisms' and God knows what. The plain-English version, though, is that like attracts like. The reaction may have happened because you've had your own…interactions, I guess…with the other side."

Shaila sat down slowly on her cot, a shiver running up her spine. "You think I'm infected, ma'am?"

"You tell me."

"Not that I'm aware."

Diaz smirked. "Good answer. And probably truthful. But not entirely."

Now Shaila was thrown for a loop. "Come again?" she asked, the heat starting to rise around her collar.

"After Ayim talked my ear off for an hour, I had Jimmy run some database searches. He pulled all the sensor data from McAuliffe Base on Mars, including exteriors and pressure suit data, as well as all the data off *Armstrong* and wherever else we could find you over the past two and a half years. We managed to match up where you were, in physical space, with the sensor data around you. Guess what we found."

It wasn't a tough guess. "Cherenkov radiation."

"Bingo. Not a lot—in most cases, it barely registered at all, and never set off any alarms. Just a ping, here and there, weeks or months apart. There were a few on Mars, naturally, and it was tough to work through all the ambient radiation that fuck-all caused. But it was there on *Armstrong*, and right before the tiger stripes blew on Enceladus. Little hits, here and there. And when we pulled the holovid, we saw you were distracted or spaced for a second or two." Diaz stood up and walked right up to the clear barrier of the containment unit. "So if you've got anything you wanna say, Commander, I suggest it comes out here and now, before I have to make a report on it. Because if I do have to make a report, you're pretty much gonna be a guinea pig for the rest of your natural life."

Shaila nodded slowly. "It was nothing, really. Didn't seem like it at the time, anyway."

"Go on."

"Just little moments, I guess. Visions? I don't know. Just moments where something just came to me out of the blue. I thought I saw Weatherby's journal during that first quake on Mars, but it wasn't there—not until that second time, anyway. I had this…dream, or imagining, or something…about the tiger stripes going before they happened. Lately, it's been words, like the stuff we saw in Weatherby's journal, but not his writing. Same wording, that old-time stuff."

Diaz nodded slowly. "Times and places, then."

"Yeah…and you sound like you knew the answer before you asked."

The general stood and walked over to the comm panel. "Gerry, you catch all that?"

Ayim's voice came in over the loudspeakers. "I did, General. All readings normal."

"Readings?" Shaila asked. She was starting to feel exposed, and a little violated. "Permission to ask what the hell's going on, General."

Diaz ignored her. "How about now, Gerry?"

"Zero Cherenkov, General. Though she's starting to get agitated."

"Roger that," Diaz said. She turned and smiled at Shaila. "For once, that fuse of yours is actually helping you."

And then Shaila realized what was happening. "You're worried that if I get pissed off enough…"

"Yep. And your vitals are already past where Stephane's were when you goaded him that first time," Diaz replied. "So I think we're good." The general turned back to the comm. "Gerry, why don't you come in here and tell Jain what we're thinking."

It took several awkward seconds—in which Diaz smiled somewhat apologetically and Shaila simply stood with her arms crossed, feeling irritated—before Ayim entered. "Well done, Commander! I think with our observations of the past day, along with your little test just now and all of the data the general recovered, I do believe—tentatively, mind you—that you are not infected."

Shaila stood stock still for a moment until the laughter she was trying to contain burst forth. "Jesus Christ, we really are in the dark here, aren't we."

At this, Ayim looked slightly perturbed. "We are gathering evidence and data and building working theories, Commander. And you were a part of that. I apologize if you feel somehow slighted in all this, but as the general pointed out, you did withhold pertinent information regarding your…condition. Your experiences, if you will."

Diaz shot Shaila a told-you-so look which prompted her to stifle her laughs and back down. "All right. Fine. What's going on, then?"

Ayim pulled up another chair to the barrier of the containment cell. "Oh, it's quite interesting, I assure you. You see, in basic quantum physics, a physical system—say, an electron or proton—exists partly in all of its physical states simultaneously. That's quantum superposition. Only when that physical system is directly observed does it give us a view to only one of its potential states. Are you with me so far?"

Shaila nodded tentatively. "Mostly."

"So let us say, then, that two entire dimensions existed for a finite amount of time in superposition. Now, there is no fundamental way we can reasonably observe the state of every single particle in that crossover, now can we? That would be impossible! Not even the most advanced sensor system, attached to the most powerful computer, could observe every subatomic particle that came into superposition with particles from the other dimension back on Mars—and that was only a limited area! So it was quite possible for the two dimensions to come together. More importantly, it is also quite possible that there could remain a kind of quantum entanglement in those areas of time and space where the crossover occurred."

"Which is why we still have particle acceleration experiments going on at McAuliffe," Diaz added, "and we're studying what happened in Egypt last year, too."

"Right. Time and place," Shaila said. "And now you think it's somehow personal to me?"

Ayim grinned widely. "You are one of only three people living who were present when the first recorded crossover occurred on Mars. And you and Dr. Durand were both present on Titan as well, which was most certainly another interdimensional crossover, if the chamber you discovered there is any indication.

"Now, given your presence at these various crossover events, it is my theory—and I believe the evidence we've gathered is beginning to back this up—that your neural pathways are entangled somehow with the other dimension at the quantum level. And that's *very* exciting, isn't it?"

Shaila frowned. "You're lucky there's a barrier here, Doctor."

"Oh, I am sorry! I didn't mean to imply that this was not a burden on you, Commander. I'm sure it is. But it could very well be extremely beneficial to us as well in figuring out what has happened to the data retrieved from the Enceladus organisms, and who on Earth received them," Ayim said.

Shaila looked from Diaz to Ayim and back again. "You think…you're thinking I can tap into this somehow. That I can see what might go down next?"

"Either you or Dr. Durand, yes," Ayim said. "I would suggest Dr. Conti or our Chinese guest, but they remain in comas and completely unresponsive. We have detected no radiation surges from either of them, and I am left to wonder whether the transmission from *Tienlong* stripped them of their active infection, or somehow the injuries they sustained from our boarding parties did the trick.

"But anyway, you and Dr. Durand are our best candidates, because you both seem to have a degree of Cherenkov radiation inherent in your condition, which we believe is the calling card for dimensional displacement. Now, the artifact from Titan may be the appropriate conduit, either by focusing on what is occurring in *this* dimension, or by using it as a kind of comm system to perhaps glean information from the *other* dimension, to which we are, at this point and for all intents and purposes going forward, entangled on a quantum level."

Shaila let this sink in for a moment, then looked to Diaz suspiciously. "You were with us on Mars. You saw Weatherby and Finch and Anne Baker there. Why isn't this happening to you?"

Diaz shrugged. "I ran the same location-sensor sweep on myself and Durand, too. You were the only one who had the Cherenkov matches. You had that very first reaction, during the first quake on Mars, so our best guess is that you were basically at ground zero for the entanglement."

"Wrong place, wrong time," Shaila summarized. "Figures. So what's the deal now? Am I still stuck in solitary here?"

"There are a few more tests I wish to run," Ayim said. "We're going to do a full map of your neural pathways—should take no more than a few hours. And when you are released, I will ask you to wear a very sensitive radiation sensor on the back of your neck. The general and Dr. Durand will be wearing one as well."

"And Stephane's will also have a built-in zapper, in case he…relapses," Diaz said. "Figure if he gets taken over again, we'll need to take him down. Gently."

Shaila nodded, but inside, she was pretty furious at Diaz for even thinking it. But then…she was probably right. Damn her. "All right. And after that? Do I end up hooked up to the Tablet to try to chat with someone?"

"All in good time," Ayim said. "We will need several days, if not weeks, of further study before we are willing to do that."

Any further conversation was interrupted by the comm. "Coogan to Diaz. Respond, please."

Diaz reached over to the comm panel. "I'm here, Jimmy."

"Ma'am. We have a hit on the potential whereabouts of Mr. Yu."

Shaila and Diaz traded a wide-eyed look. "I'll be damned. Where?"

"Ekaterinburg, Russia," Coogan replied. "A hospital there accessed his global medical records database seven hours ago."

"And why did it take us seven fucking hours to get that info, Jimmy?" Diaz groused.

"The Russians, ma'am. They do participate in the global medical database network, but they do so on a time delay, probably to frustrate outside intel."

"Dammit. He's probably already gone."

"No, ma'am, I suspect he's still there," Coogan said, a hint of satisfaction couched in his perfect English accent. "He was brought in 14 hours ago in suspended animation. Gunshot to the chest. The surgical procedure they listed in his file is both risky and time-consuming, and recovery is at least two days."

Diaz grinned. "Finally, some luck. Well, for us. Seems like he's having a really shitty day. Jimmy, have the team prep *Hadfield*. We're leaving in 20 minutes. I want Parrish and his team aboard. You'll stay here and run the show. Diaz out." She then turned to Jain. "You're probably going to make my life a fucking misery unless I let you come along."

That earned the general a genuine smile. "Absolutely, ma'am."

The general looked thoughtful for a moment. "We still need tests. And honestly, I'm still worried about you. I don't know if you're a risk. *But*…if you get fitted for a sensor with a zapper in it, you can come along."

Shaila figured this was coming. "Understood. Just don't get carried away with the trigger, ma'am."

Diaz reached over and tapped in the keycode to open the containment barrier. "Gerry, get her sensor fitted. She's back on duty."

January 20, 2135

Harry Yu's first conscious thought was surprise at actually having a conscious thought, something akin to: *Holy fuck, am I alive?!*

Then the worry set in. He could hear sounds, but they were unfocused, fuzzy. There were some electronic noises, but he couldn't tell if they came from comms or computers or cars. Finally, he surmised sensors, given that by this point he figured out he was horizontal, likely on a bed.

Then he remembered what happened to him and his heart began to beat faster. That actually hurt, however; he could feel the muscles around his ribcage were sore, and his heart and lungs felt...messed with. Violated. It was as if someone had reached in and reorganized things. Not entirely surprising, he supposed. He'd been shot, after all.

And that started his heart beating hard again, which made him more rueful. *How do you go from senior conglom exec to internationally wanted criminal and gunshot victim in six months, anyway?*

Once he calmed himself down—bitching about things in his head wouldn't do him any good, after all—he decided to figure out where he was. It took what seemed like an age just to find his eyelids, let alone force them open.

White walls, trimmed with beige. Random holopicture of flowers on the wall. Electronic equipment.

Hospital. That made sense.

A voice shook him out of his slow, methodical observations. "Jesus, Harry, you sure know how to pick 'em."

With great effort and focus—or what felt like it, at any rate—Harry slowly turned his head in the direction of the voice. There, sitting in a chair next to his bed was Chrys, his backer, with datapad in hand and a look of both consternation and sympathy on her face.

"Yeah," he croaked quietly. "Nuts."

Chrys nodded grimly. "You want the download now, or should I wait until you're up for it?"

It took several seconds for him to register what she said, and several more to interpret it. Given that she was there, in his hospital room, rather than running her ops and making money, chances are something went south on her end as well. "Now," Harry replied.

Chrys nodded. "Well, first you got shot, of course. Bullet nearly went straight through your heart, and they had to freeze you in place before moving you. You're lucky I got a building with gunshot detectors all over. Ambulance was there in four minutes. Saved your life."

Harry managed a small smile. "Owe you one."

"You owe me a shit-ton more than that," she grumbled. "Your *team* there, Greene and that other woman, they screwed me over. They fucked with my satellites. I'm out trillions of terras."

This took even longer to digest, and when Harry finally got there, he felt his heart racing again. "You...went backdoor."

At this, Chrys gave him a small, lopsided grin. "Yeah, I did. Total end-around on you. I contacted them just about the same time as I contacted you. I knew what you were trying to do for Total-Suez—open the door to whatever place is on the other side, exploit the hell out of it. Your intel from the Mars fiasco made the rounds with a few people. I read about what Venus was supposed to be like, and figured it'd be absolutely perfect. So I had Greene do up some extra hardware for the sats so maybe we could experiment on a larger scale, without the repercussions of opening some kind of fucked-up portal right here on Earth. But as it turns out, Greene rewrote the entire software command structure to lock us out of the project entirely. So now I got a dozen sats heading for Venus with God-knows-what on board, and I have no control over them."

Harry took all this in, his mind fighting against anesthesia and medication in order to focus. For the first time, he noticed that Chrys looked horrible—dark circles under her eyes, disheveled hair, no makeup, wrinkled suit. *Good.* "You...screwed me. You screwed us both."

"Hey, if you didn't have homicidal whack-jobs on your team, this wouldn't be an issue, Harry," she replied, only slightly defensively. "Give me straight-up capitalists any day. I pay, they produce. But this, this is some left-field shit. And now I'm on the hook with my conglom because of your people."

"And I got shot."

"And you got shot," she replied with a sigh. "So you don't have your accelerator project, and I don't have my sats. We're both screwed."

Harry thought about this again, all the while all-too-conscious of his uncomfortable heartbeat inside his ravaged chest. "Anything on our computers?"

She shook her head. "Nothing. They erased everything. We can't even reconstruct what was there. They were thorough. Only positive I can see here is that Greene needs a big-ass comm dish to get commands over to the sats. He might have control, but he can't talk to them unless he has a corporate-quality interplanetary comm rig, or he somehow gets a lot closer to them."

Harry was about to reply when there was a perfunctory knock on the door. By the time he turned his head to reply, it was already opened.

Maria Diaz and Shaila Jain walked in.

"Fuck," Harry whispered.

To her credit, Diaz looked suitably concerned with his wellbeing. Shaila, as he had come to expect, seemed almost disappointed she couldn't shoot him again.

"Christ, Harry. You really screwed the pooch this time," Diaz said by way of greeting. She looked annoyingly maternal about it.

Harry started to laugh, but his chest muscles protested fiercely, leaving him gasping. "Everyone…says that."

Diaz turned to Chrys. "Miss VanDerKamp, we couldn't help but overhear your problems."

Chrys gave Diaz a once-over, stopping at the two general's stars on her uniform. "Couldn't help it?"

Shaila held up a datapad with a satisfied smirk. "Fine, we spied. Welcome to Russia."

Chrys turned to shoot Harry a deadly look before replying. "That won't hold up in corporate court, you know."

Diaz nodded. "Good thing this isn't going to court. We got more important things to do, like fixing the fuck-all you just got us into." She turned to Harry. "You realize now what's going on, don't you?"

Harry managed a nod. "They're...opening it up...on Venus."

"And who's 'they,' Harry?" Shaila prodded.

"Greene. Huntington."

Diaz stared, wide-eyed, and took several seconds to respond. "They're alive? I thought we lost them in Egypt!"

"Alive, but...they're...not..." Harry paused. He didn't have words for it.

To her credit, the general recovered quickly. "Right. They're not themselves. That actually makes more sense to me than you might think. OK, then. You two are about to spill everything you got. Miss VanDerKamp, you're going to cooperate, as will your conglom, or I'll make damn sure the only project you'll get to manage again is lunch rush at McDonald's. How many days until those sats reach Venus?"

Chrys stared hard at Diaz, who stared right back. Finally, the exec relented. "Nine."

"Thank you," Diaz said. "Means we got nine days to get there and stop all this. Otherwise, it's going to be Mars all over again...and probably a whole lot worse."

CHAPTER 13

May 14, 1809

"Lord Weatherby, I assure you whilst I feel your information is of the highest validity, I cannot simply allow you to take half my fleet to Venus whilst we prepare to retake England—our very homeland!—and drive the foul French from our shores!"

George, Prince of Wales and Prince Regent-in-Exile on behalf of the captive King George III, paced his council chamber with an energy typically reserved for infantry drills—or, in the prince's case, a particularly high-stakes game of cards. His agitation was understandable, certainly, for there in the room were his two most trusted military advisers—Lord Admiral Thomas Weatherby and General Sir Arthur Wellesley—advocating two entirely different things, neither of which assured success by any reliable measure.

But the potential to retake England, no matter the cost, was the most deciding factor. And even Weatherby had to admit he would choose similarly if in the prince's position—though the prince did not, and would not, have all the information available to Weatherby.

"Sire, I wish it were otherwise, but it is my belief that if we can defeat the French upon Venus, our chances of success south of Hadrian's Wall shall be vastly improved," Weatherby said. "Without the bulk of their fleet, they cannot be resupplied. Our people continue to resist the occupation, and without supplies, the French are weakened."

Wellesley cleared his throat. "With utmost respect to Lord Weatherby, sire, the bulk of the French forces require neither food nor water, and even should they run out of munitions, they remain impervious to most types of injury. There will be no greater opportunity to fight them than the summer months, when our troops will require little in the way of additional supply themselves. Plus, the ships of His Majesty's Navy can provide a great deal of firepower as we land, especially should we take the mouth of the Thames. They may sail as far as Windsor, allowing us a foothold in the south and the liberation of London itself!"

Weatherby did his best not to scowl at Wellesley. "The general is, of course, an exceptional tactician, and I do believe we can provide his foothold in the south with but a few of our ships. Meanwhile, the bulk of the fleet can make for Venus and easily eradicate the rest of the French fleet. From there, we can even return to provide support as needed, whereas they will have none. And it is quite well proven that our facility upon sea or Void is far superior to theirs. Best to crush them on Venus, or in the Void, rather than in the Channel or the North Sea, where they then might simply escape to the Continent and resupply. Sire, I urge—"

"Enough!" George cried, placing his hands to his ears. "I have had enough of both of you!" This silenced both commanders long enough for the Prince Regent to produce a letter from his coat pocket. "Do either of you know what this is?"

Wellesley stared with furrowed brow, but Weatherby recognized the large, looping script upon the page. "It is from the Xan, I take it."

"Yes, from the damnable Saturn-dwellers! And they have the temerity to tell me how and when they shall assist us, and upon what conditions. Your friend Vellusk," the prince raged, focusing on Weatherby, "says there may be a way to counteract the alchemy that has raised the *Corps Éternel*, but he says his people may require particular plants and other obscure alchemical items from Venus. Lord Weatherby, I swear to you, if you are somehow complicit in this, or your wife for that matter, I shall execute you for treason. I swear I shall behead you myself."

Weatherby was taken aback by the Prince Regent's anger, and more so by the obscured truth of his words. And so he set his course upon the most dangerous course of his life. "I swear to you, sire, upon my life and those of my family, that while Vellusk and I may both seek the Green Planet, he has not shared the contents of this letter with me."

This was, of course, a true statement in the narrowest of definitions, as Weatherby was in another room whilst Vellusk wrote his letter. But in the spirit of his prince's question, Weatherby felt he well and truly lied and sinned, and could but hope that it was for the greater good.

Prince George's eyes narrowed. "And so I shall take you at your word, as you have served with naught but honor and success. But on your head be it, Thomas. I must now acquiesce to the Xan's requests in order to garner their aid, and I will not stand for any betrayal or deviancies on their part. This Venusian gambit of yours had best bear fruit, and quickly." Wellesley made to speak, but George silenced him with but a look, one of fire and fury barely contained. "Now, Lord Weatherby, you have thirty-two ships of the line currently blockading England and defending Scotland and Ireland, correct?"

"Yes, sire," Weatherby responded quietly. "At least twice as many more frigates, brigs and sloops as well."

George put his hands upon the council table and studied the maps carefully thereupon. "Very well. We will need every ship that can carry men southward. I can spare you *Victory* and four other ships of the line, along with a half-dozen smaller ships for your fleet. There can be no more. If you cannot move the French from Venus with this, or the odds are stacked too greatly against you, I expect you to return to Earth and England forthwith to aid in the recapture of our home. Do I make myself clear, my Lord Admiral?"

Too few! All too few! Weatherby thought. But there truly was nothing for it. "I will either claim victory or return to assist Sir Arthur in his campaign, sire. I promise you."

"Then you will immediately prepare for your departure. Send me another admiral so we may continue our preparations for the assault on England, and be sure the defense of Edinburgh and Glasgow are well in hand before you go," the Prince Regent ordered.

"By your leave then, Your Highness, I shall send you Admiral Saumarez forthwith," Weatherby said as his picked up his hat. "God save you and King George."

To Weatherby's great surprise, the prince offered his hand. "I know not what strange workings are afoot with the Xan and Venus, but I do trust you, Thomas. Destroy the French fleet, gather what the Xan require and hurry back to us safely."

Weatherby took his prince's hand with gratitude. "I shall." He turned to Wellesley, but found the general pointedly studying the maps upon the table, and so took his leave without further word.

Outside the chamber, he found Philip waiting for him. "Well?"

"We are to make for Venus with but a handful of ships," Weatherby said without breaking stride, forcing Philip to rush to keep up. "And so we shall likely face a French fleet at least three times our size in the Void, making keel-fall nearly impossible. Then there's the trek through the jungle to the memory vault, held by a race of beings that may or may not be amenable to our presence there. And of course, Berthollet and Cagliostro will likely have surmised our intentions and have a veritable army waiting for us."

Philip took all this in for a few moments. "So this is somewhat worse than usual then, Father?"

Weatherby grinned. "Only slightly. How fares Dr. Finch?"

At this, Philip's humor quickly waned. "We have placed *The Book of the Dead* in a container we believe will isolate its mystical properties from its surroundings. And indeed, we have seen Uncle Andrew regain some of his color and vitality. Naturally, that makes us loath to study it further. And Ambassador Vellusk insists Mother and I should not conduct any researches until the book is away from Earth, lest it somehow release energies that either harm living beings or strengthen the French forces."

Weatherby nodded. "That seems prudent. And as for 'Uncle' Andrew, damn him, he shall not set eyes upon it again."

Philip stopped and took Weatherby's arm in hand. "Father, please, a word about Andrew."

With consternation, Weatherby looked around to ensure no others were about in the palace corridor. "There is little more to be said, Philip. I have decided."

"But Uncle Andrew managed to contain the book's energies, and learned from them, for more than a decade," Philip protested quietly and reasonably. "There are none others alive, except for Berthollet, who know such lore as well as he. He has made some remarkable advances in the Great Work through his research."

"And he lied to me," Weatherby snapped. "To my *face*, Philip. How can I countenance this?"

"Father," Philip said gently. "He believed the course before him required secrecy and, yes, deception. And for a decade, no one else has so much as seen the book. He has protected its secrets from our enemies and sought to use them on behalf of England. Has he not been by your side since Egypt?"

"He lied," Weatherby said simply, though the conviction of his words was on the wane.

"And this is different from the course you just set for yourself now, with the Prince Regent?" Philip asked, gently enough so that Weatherby heard his beloved wife's voice in his.

And so the protest died before it was brought to the old admiral's lips. "By God, you are your mother's son."

Philip smirked, another echo of Anne in his face. "And I am as much yours as well, for your example is a fine one indeed."

Weatherby clasped his shoulder. "Thank you, Philip. Now go make preparations to depart. Since Dr. Finch, either by taint of illness or suspicion, cannot remain my fleet alchemist, I am appointing you to the position in his stead. Report to *Victory* and ensure all is in order. When

I've ascertained the composition of the rest of our squadron, I will send you the names so you may prepare those ships as well."

Philip blinked with surprise. "But I've no training at this, my Lord. I'm not even in the Navy!"

"You are now," Weatherby quipped. "You may appoint an assistant, and I've no doubt you will have your mother on hand as well. Go. You have work to do."

Philip straightened up and made a salute that, admittedly, would've had a midshipman whipped, then departed quickly. Shaking his head, Weatherby watched him go wistfully. There was a time when he was that young, and the responsibilities of command were a joy, not a burden.

Those times were long past, it seemed.

Weatherby made his way to the wing of the old castle in which he and his family and retinue were housed, stopping at a door that was locked from the outside—Finch's quarters. There were two Marines stationed there as well, and they smartly snapped to attention as he approached. Weatherby nodded, and one of them produced a key and unlocked the door, opening it so that he might enter.

Inside, Weatherby found Finch lolling on the bed, one leg dangling off, his clothing disheveled. For a moment, Weatherby's mind flashed back to their very first meeting, having discovered Finch in a decrepit boarding house upon Elizabeth Mercuris, drugged on Venusian extracts and wholly unsuited to his assignment as alchemist aboard HMS *Daedalus*.

But Finch was reading now, rather than inhaling from a hookah. And his color had improved substantially since then, and even somewhat from a few days prior.

"Thomas!" Finch cried with delight, slamming the book closed and scrambling to his feet. "Thank God you're here. Sit with me and let me explain."

Weatherby held up his hand. "No, Doctor. Not this time."

"But, Tom! I am the same Andrew you've always known. Surely this is naught but a mistake. I apologize for keeping you in the dark, of course."

"In the dark?" Weatherby shouted. "You lied to me, damn you! You earned my trust, time and again, and then for a decade—a full decade or more!—you have concealed the truth. Lied to my very face. Sat upon a treasure we may have used to liberate England years ago!"

Finch's face took a hard turn. "And who would have used it? The Prince Regent? He would've created his own fell abominations to fight the French, as you well know! Wellesley? He'd gladly lead an army of revenants if it brought him glory! You, Tom? What would you have done? Would you have used the book in such a way? And if the French made further strides, would you have met them? Would you have condemned the world to darkness and allowed the very Underworld to seep into the land of the living?"

Weatherby grabbed Finch by his shirt. "I don't know, damn you! I don't know! But you never gave me the choice, did you? No! You never sought my counsel! You never allowed me yours! Do you not see it? What might we have done together, years ago, had you but trusted me in the way I trusted you? We will never know! And now, because of you, I've broken all my oaths to King and Country so that we may make one final, impossible effort at stopping a war we may have already long ended!"

Weatherby released Finch with a shove, and the latter man had no words with which to reply. Instead he stood, hurt and angry and dismayed, and the two stared at each other for what seemed an eternity.

Finally, the admiral spoke once more. "Due to illness, you are no longer my fleet alchemist. Philip, the Count St. Germain, has taken your position. You will be brought aboard *Victory* so that Philip may aid you in regaining your health. Do you understand me?"

"I do," Finch said, defeated.

"Once aboard and once we are assured of your health once more, you will aid the Count and his duly appointed representatives, likely including the Lady Weatherby and Ambassador Vellusk, by telling them all you know of the book, and of the researches you have conducted with it.

All of it, without omission. If I find you have withheld anything more at this juncture, I will court-martial you and, if you are found guilty, I will sentence you to hang upon the yardarm. I will do this by my own hand if need be. Do you really, *truly* understand me now?"

An errant tear escaped Finch's eye as he nodded. "I see you clearly, Tom. And I am truly sorry."

Weatherby shook his head. "I have chosen a life of service to England, Andrew. My life *is* pain, save for when I am ashore with my wife and daughter and step-son. Do not apologize to me. Think instead of those thousands who have perished defending England while you hid the book in your sea chest all this time. Think of what a wiser course of action may have done, and then make your apologies to the ghosts of the fallen."

Before Finch could respond, Weatherby turned on his heel and stalked out the door, nearly colliding with his daughter.

"Father!" she said with a smile. "You must mind your step, lest you trample all before you. I—" Her kindly jibe immediately faded upon seeing his face. "My God, what is it?"

Weatherby opened his mouth to speak, but a wave of sadness washed over him, and he could not find his voice. Seeing this, Elizabeth took his hand and guided him to the family's sitting room, where she gently placed him upon a couch and sat next to him in silence, his hand remaining in hers.

And there they sat for a long while, with silent tears streaming down Weatherby's face, with only his daughter's presence keeping him from a totality of gloom and anguish.

CHAPTER 14

January 26, 2135

A s it happened, Shaila hated being on a ship she wasn't flying.

Having been the pilot and second-in-command of *Armstrong* for a year, she found it oddly annoying not to have a ship's holocontrols at her fingertips. She wasn't even technically in the chain of command, since she and the rest of DAEDALUS were officially passengers aboard *Hadfield* as it zoomed toward Venus at maximum speed. Some kid named Baines was at the controls; Shaila had no idea who he was, and he looked way, *way* too young to be flying anything with wings, let alone a state-of-the-art mid-system ship like *Hadfield*.

But Diaz had her seconded to DAEDALUS for "the extent of the current mission," which meant that she was basically off the books as far as Joint Space Command was concerned. Shaila was kind of surprised at how quickly and efficiently Diaz had not just become the head of a completely black-ops program, but how she seemed to embody the role as if she were born for it. And maybe that was it, that Diaz was really the woman you wanted in charge when the shit hit the fan. Shaila thought so.

But it was hard to have confidence in anything—in the pilot, in her boss—when there was just way too much unknown out there. Nobody was sure whether the Emerald Tablet would be of any use, or whether Stephane was truly out from under the influence of the Enceladan viruses. Nobody knew what the signal was from *Tienlong* to Greene and Huntington, though there were theories, and nobody could seem to find the two former DAEDALUS members. Diaz and Coogan seemed to have every national intelligence agency and private security contractor on Earth and the Moon looking for them, but they disappeared with an efficiency that was both startling and damned frustrating.

They would be Earth's problem anyway. *Hadfield* was going to Venus.

Coogan and Chrys VanDerKamp spent most of their time trying to hack their way into the command-and-control functions of Chrys' satellites, but Greene and Huntington had been extraordinarily thorough in their rewrites. Nearly all of *Hadfield*'s quantum computing power—and some heavy processing power borrowed from Earth as well—was thrown at the encryption used on the satellites, but not only were there multiple firewalls, but the team was beginning to get a sense that the sats' underlying operating system had been extensively rewritten, and that the interface/symbology used to do it was completely different from anything ever written before.

It was as if aliens had recoded the software in their language—which at this point was a distinct possibility.

All this was incredibly worrisome, but Diaz had thankfully given Shaila a pretty big to-do item to keep her focused: Preparing both ship and team for the possibility of a second interdimensional incursion, this time on Venus instead of Mars.

The hope was that the team could simply shut down the satellite array, even if they had to manually power down each bird—or just shoot it out of orbit. The latter wasn't the ideal solution, since there were a couple of small research stations in orbit around the planet that probably wouldn't like being pummeled with debris. But if it was a choice between evacuating the research stations or opening up a portal to another dimension—and possibly freeing more unfriendly alien life forms—the stations would be evacuated.

Of course, there was the chance that Greene and Huntington would try to do something on the surface of Venus itself. Not impossible, but it would be extremely tricky. And it was up to Shaila to ensure the team could go planet-side if need be.

Unlike Mars, with its light gravity, very low atmospheric pressure and cold temperatures, Venus was a fucking hellhole. The atmospheric pressure was 92 times that of Earth's surface, and it had temperatures that could reach nearly 500 degrees Celsius at the equator. And even if you managed not to be crushed or fried the moment you entered the atmosphere, Venus' gravity, 90 percent that of Earth, didn't make it particularly easy to get around while carrying a bunch of life support.

Oh, and you had to get through an upper atmosphere laden with sulfuric acid. Again, hellhole.

Thankfully, the first few missions to Venus had come up with a solution: the Venus-Surface Exploration Vehicle, or V-SEV. And Shaila had to admit, they were pretty damn cool.

The V-SEV looked like a four-meter tall robot. The torso was large enough for two people to sit, one in front of the other. The forward personnel would pilot the arms and legs of the vehicle during transit, allowing it to "walk" across the Venusian surface, while the rear personnel would be in charge of sensors and experiments, including the operation of the arms while at a standstill. The V-SEV boasted laser drills on both arms, as well as pincer-like hands that could take samples and either store them in a carrier or crush them for on-site analysis.

The V-SEV's ceramic-titanium composite shell allowed it to withstand both heat and pressure, and it was powered by a small fusion reactor attached to its back like a giant backpack. It had enough air and food storage aboard to last two days on the surface.

Of course, getting onto—and off of—Venus was the trick, as most spacecraft couldn't manage the planet's harsh environment. That went for *Hadfield* as well. So the V-SEVs were dropped to the surface in one-use ceramic-composite capsules lined with a micron-thin layer of stainless steel to repel the sulfuric acid in the atmosphere. Once the capsule made it through the upper and middle atmospheres, they were designed to crack and flake away at a particular temperature, leaving the V-SEVs exposed to the elements but ultimately in one piece. At the last moment, giant airbags deployed around them to cushion the final landing. These bags could only withstand the heat of Venus for about five minutes, after which they basically disintegrated, allowing the V-SEVs to begin roaming.

Pickup was a little trickier. The mothership would drop booster rocket rigs into the upper atmosphere, attached once again to parachutes. Meanwhile, a carbon-ceramic cable would drop from the booster rigs to the Venusian surface, allowing the V-SEVs to grab them and attach them to the chassis. Once attached, the boosters would fire, launching out of the atmosphere and into orbit. Venus' temperature and air pressure decreased substantially after a certain point, which made it no harder on the V-SEVs to rocket out of the atmosphere than to simply walk around on the surface. There would be some minor chassis damage to the V-SEVs due to the acid, but critical life-support systems would remain intact.

There were six V-SEVs aboard *Hadfield*, and there was a squad of Marines busy training up on them en route to Venus. Shaila had always wanted to pilot one. Just not under these particular circumstances.

"Why is it that every time I go to a new planet, fucking shit blows up?" she groused one day to Stephane.

Of course, she immediately felt guilty for it. While Shaila still wore her radiation detector-slash-zapper on her neck, she was still part of DAEDALUS and given free rein aboard ship. Stephane was out of containment, but he was confined to quarters aboard *Hadfield*, even though he too wore the same device at the base of his skull. There had been some concern about bringing him along in the first place, but Diaz and Ayim felt that if he could provide any intel—either through the use of the Emerald Tablet or simply through the constant wrestling match he seemed to endure while keeping Rathemas at bay—it would be worth it.

And yet he seemed to be holding up well. "Really, *chéri*, I was the one to blow up Enceladus. Not you," Stephane said with a small, sad smile. "I didn't want to, but...I guess I did."

"It wasn't you," Shaila insisted, taking his hand and kissing it. "It was that thing inside you. And I know Ayim's working hard to get it out of you for good."

"I don't think it'll be out of me for good until this is all over," Stephane said. "Do you know how Mars started changing slowly, starting with that earthquake three days before Weatherby showed up? I feel like that's happening here. Something is...happening. I cannot say why I know this, but it is. Has there been any change on the surface of Venus?"

Shaila shook her head. "No. We're on it. If things cool down there, we'll know about it. What do you think is happening?"

Stephane shrugged. "Hell, I don't know. Something. Some big thing. If I probe any more, I'm scared Rathemas will get a...what do you say...a foothold. His foot in the door. I need to keep him locked away. Do you understand? I don't know if I'm making any sense."

Shaila squeezed his hand. "You are. I get it. I mean, I can't really get what you've been through, but I know you went through a lot. Whatever you have to do, you do it."

"I will," he said, then stole a glance at the clock in his room. "I wish you could stay longer."

Shaila stood. "I know. '30-minute visits for now.' Want to be sure you have a handle on things."

"I do. You believe me, don't you?"

"I believe you, honey. But I'm not in command. Diaz is. And that's probably a good thing, you know?"

"I suppose." He gave her a smile and kissed her hand before releasing it. "When this is all done, you and I, we're taking a very long vacation together. Someplace warm with no need for a lot of clothes, yes?"

That's my Stephane, she thought. "Deal. Rest up."

Shaila floated out of his quarters and into the corridor, propelling herself toward the lab section. *Hadfield* was designed for pretty much any short-term mission between Mars and Mercury, be it corporate, scientific or military. It could even run cargo in a pinch, but JSC would be pretty irked at such a petty use; that's what contractors were for. *Hadfield* was as state-of-the-art as governments could afford, with engines that rivaled *Armstrong*'s for speed. Whatever mission JSC had left to it, at least beyond ferrying corporate exploitation teams around the inner Solar System, *Hadfield* was the ship for the job.

It was but a few meters before Shaila arrived at the lab compartment, which despite the cramped quarters—it was roughly the size of an apartment kitchen—contained some of the best scientific gear around, and thanks to the gravity, on every available surface. Inside, Ayim was continuing to put the Emerald Tablet through its paces.

"Ah, Commander! Don't move!" Ayim said, holding a hand out to stop her at the door. He floated up toward the ceiling and a panel of holodisplays.

"What? What's wrong?" Shaila asked.

"Nothing! Nothing at all. Now, if you would, please proceed one meter into the laboratory," the scientist replied. "And then stay there."

With a smirk on her face, Shaila pushed herself through the door, then grabbed a handhold to arrest her momentum. "All right, I'll bite. What are we doing to the Tablet today?"

"Radiation testing, Commander. I'm trying a broad spectrum of radiation, some dangerous, some not, to see if there is any reaction. Your presence, as you know, can be an important variable in such an experiment. Very well, proceed another meter closer to the tablet."

Shaila did so, which quickly had Ayim frowning. "What is it?" she demanded.

"There is nothing at all," Ayim said, shaking his head. "It has become imperturbable. Ever since the experiment with Dr. Durand, it has been dormant. You aren't experiencing any more auditory or visual stimuli, are you?"

"Nice way of putting it. And no."

"Neither has Dr. Durand. In fact, his brainwave activity has stabilized to a very large degree, even in sleep."

Shaila's ears pricked up. "So he's clear, then? That thing is out of him?"

"Oh, no! No, that isn't the case at all," Ayim said with a chuckle. Then he saw Shaila's face, and immediately straightened up as best he could in zero-g. "Right. Terribly sorry. No, his brainwave patterns aren't *normal*. He has a great degree of increased activity in his parietal lobe and there is still trace amounts of Cherenkov radiation coming from somewhere within his neural pathways. He is most assuredly still under some kind of external influence, since we cannot pinpoint a source for this activity. Yet I would say that he is better. He reports no issues sleeping, nor any instances of any interference with his conscious thinking."

"So Rathemas is as dormant as the Tablet," Shaila said simply. "I don't like it."

"Now, Commander, I still find it difficult to ascribe names and consciousness to whatever has affected Dr. Durand, but—"

Shaila held up her hand to silence him; they'd had this conversation already while aboard. "It has a name because it's real. Because I've seen one like it."

"Yes, of course. Apologies, Commander," Ayim said primly. "Was there something you required?"

"I need to assess whether it's safe for Stephane to land on Venus if we need him down there. V-SEV co-pilot only, no controls."

Ayim's eyes bugged out. "I would recommend strongly against that, Commander! There is no way of telling how an extradimensional incursion would affect him. Perhaps he might remain dormant, but perhaps the energies there and his proximity to them…well, I simply cannot say. Even in your experience, there is no precedence for this!"

Shaila nodded. "Kind of what I thought, then. Send that formal recommendation to Diaz and CC myself on it. Best be on the record about such things." Before Ayim could respond further, Shaila turned and left the lab.

Having Stephane planet-side was, of course, a really bad idea, but she wondered if it might also be the last piece of the puzzle. She had her own pet theories, of course, regarding quantum entanglement and place—completely untested and uninformed, of course—that made her wonder whether having her and Stephane together on Venus might trigger something positive. Perhaps she or Stephane, or both of them, might garner insights into the aliens' goals or motives, or perhaps he might communicate the way Shaila seemed to chat with Andrew Finch from the other side.

Or maybe Rathemas would take over once more and everything would go to hell. Hard to say. The worst was that she knew she was potentially using the man she loved as a guinea pig. No matter what the stakes, that wasn't easy. She figured Stephane would agree, because that's the kind of man he was. But shit...it wasn't easy. As for Diaz, well, Shaila hadn't really told her yet. The general would probably shoot it down anyway, but one battle at a time.

"Commander Jain, report to CIC at once. Repeat, Commander Jain to CIC at once."

Shaila tabbed the comm on her datapad even as she propelled herself back down the corridor. "Acknowledged." It was a bit superfluous, as she was in the CIC within fifteen seconds, but military habits die hard.

She saw Diaz and Coogan looking at the large holodisplay in the middle of the room. "Looks like we got some company, Jain," the general said. "Got a ship behind us, just spotted on short-range sensors. Our course was supposed to take us well away from all the pre-registered flight plans. It'll overtake us in about ten minutes, which is pretty impressive. Trying to ID now. Jimmy, what we got?"

Coogan flicked a file from his datapad to the holodisplay, where a list of missions and vehicles appeared. "Three potentials here, General, depending on flight path and orbitals: A Virgin Galactic tour with 37 passengers, a Russian cargo ship en route to the Stanford University orbital outpost, or a Chinese something-or-other they don't care to tell us about, as usual. I've sent out comms to all three to confirm where their ships are, but it'll take a few minutes to get back to us. I've also pinged the bogey; no response."

Shaila studied the data and did some fast math in her head. "Each one of those would have to have altered their flight plans to be where they are right now," she said. "Could be as simple as a longer fuel burn or a different departure. Is the cargo ship automated?"

Coogan checked his data. "Outbound, yes. It's bringing a few students back on return."

"So they all have atmo," Diaz said. "All slightly off-sked, but not by much. I dated a Virgin pilot once. She told me they're always running late because of the fat cats they bring on. Always burning fuel to catch up. Figure the others would do the same."

"Or it could be corporate. Off the books," Chrys said from a nearby ops station. "I have a query into the corp-net. But it'll take a few to get a reply."

"Thank you," Diaz said simply. "Hopefully not. Meantime, Jimmy, get Lt. Baines up here in the cockpit, in case we have to move."

"I can do that," Shaila said.

Diaz smiled. "Not your job, Commander."

A moment later, the cherub-faced Baines slid into the pilot's seat. "Baines reporting in, ready on the controls. We may be experiencing a little turbulence, so please return to your seats, buckle your seatbelts and return your tray tables to their upright positions."

Shaila had to admit, the cocky little bastard had a pair of brass ones to banter like that on an open comm, especially with a two-star commanding the mission. And knowing Diaz, she probably liked him for it. It was probably why Diaz liked Shaila so much, after all.

The minutes ticked by. *Hadfield* received comms from the Chinese, Russians and Virgin, with all three reporting their ships on course. None reported spotting *Hadfield* on sensors, either. The latest flight plans for each ship were included, and all three remained suspects since their last reported position could coincide with that of the unknown ship had they made course corrections in flight.

"I'd like to believe it's probably nothing," Coogan said as he wrapped up his comm report, "but I'd like to think I know better by now. Orders, ma'am?"

Diaz floated over the holodisplay, studying the trajectories of the two ships. "How close are we talking here? Fifty klicks?"

"Fifty-seven, ma'am," Coogan replied.

"And no response on comms, even on emergency channels?"

"No, ma'am. Fifty seconds to intercept."

After a few more seconds, Diaz nodded at Jain, who floated over toward the cockpit, her fingers dancing across her datapad. "Baines, let's give these guys some space. Come to course...2-5-1 mark 3 and give me a 20-second burn on top of that."

"Yes, Commander," the lieutenant said. "New course and burn in 10 seconds. Nine—wait! Bogey is changing course! Repeat, bogey is changing course!"

"Shit," Shaila said. "Time to intercept?"

"Eight seconds!" Baines shouted.

"Full right thrusters, up full on the yoke! Now!"

"What the hell are you doing?" the pilot shouted from the jump-seat of the Virgin Galactic ship's cockpit. "You're going to get us all killed!"

Maggie Huntington just smiled. "You know, I really didn't get far in my pilot certification," she mused. "But I got one hell of an overqualified navigator."

From the co-pilot's station, Evan Greene was crunching numbers on a datapad, his blood-shot eyes darting quickly through the digits. "All right. Come about to 2-1-8 mark 7 and let's do a two-minute burn. That should get us there at least six hours before they arrive, even if they burn all their fuel too."

The pilot in the jump-seat—strapped down quite firmly and involuntarily—looked aghast. "You're burning all our fuel? You're going to strand us around Venus?! Why the *hell* do you want to lock us in orbit around Venus without goddamn fuel?"

Greene looked over at Huntington, who returned his gaze with a shrug. She then pulled out her pistol and shot the pilot in the head.

"These creatures complain a lot," she said.

"That they do," Greene replied. "But I don't think we need the rest any more. What did you do with the passengers?"

Huntington called up a map on the cockpit's HUD. "Herded them into the dining room. It's been about three hours. Figure they'll try to do something stupid before long."

Greene nodded. "A false fire alarm should do the trick. It'll cut off life support and vent the room to space."

"Shitty way to go," Huntington observed.

"In a few days, they'll probably see it as a blessing," Greene said with a smile.

A moment later, they were the only two left alive on the Virgin Galactic ship.

"Stay on top of things here," Greene said. "I have to finish the work on the comm system. I want to be able to transmit to the satellites the moment we're in range."

CHAPTER 15

May 28, 1809

The sight of Weatherby's entire family in the great cabin aboard HMS *Victory* was both comforting and highly disconcerting. The former, of course, because what he had said to Finch was absolutely correct, for it was naught but his family—his dearest wife, their truly remarkable and wholly commendable children—that gave him comfort aside from duty.

The latter, of course, because their next rendezvous would be with the French fleet. And that meeting would be dire indeed.

"Father, I continue to wonder as to the motivations of Berthollet and Cagliostro," Elizabeth said in between mouthfuls of lamb and potatoes. It was, of course, the admiral's prerogative to bring aboard victuals befitting his station, and while Weatherby typically eschewed such fine fare on his own, having Anne and the children with him was another story altogether.

"How so, my love?" he asked.

Elizabeth straightened in her seat. "In the brief amount of time we spoke with Cagliostro while at Oxford, it seemed that he was quite regretful of his past actions. Would you not agree, Philip?"

The new fleet alchemist nearly choked on his wine at being called out. "I…that is certainly one possible interpretation," he allowed.

"And you've yet to supply others," Elizabeth shot back in the manner of an irritated sibling. "Anyway, I should think that Cagliostro, having been so rudely tossed aside by Althotas on Mars, and then stripped of his power, would be loath to resume any sort of association with him."

Weatherby shrugged, but favored his daughter with a smile. "I cannot discern the motivations of men such as he.

I should never want to rule the universe. I just wish to live quietly within it."

Elizabeth remained undaunted. "But what of Napoleon, then? Why should the Emperor wish to summon an unreliable ally while he has the partisan Xan with him? Napoleon certainly is not one who would share power easily, and this Althotas seems rather the same."

Weatherby considered this, as well as the one who said it. Having Anne with him on this mission was practically commonplace at this point in his life, for it seemed the former Miss Baker had made a lifelong decision to run toward danger, rather than away from it, and he could not countenance denying her at this point. Philip, of course, was a man and a fine alchemist besides, and while he would worry over him, the son of Count St. Germain was quite capable of taking care of himself.

But Elizabeth...there had been a very long, overwrought argument there, in their chambers at Edinburgh Castle, about her joining them. Yet with Finch deemed quite untrustworthy, Elizabeth's studies into the Venusians and Xan were such that she was expert in many areas, including the language of the Venusians. Even Gar'uk, when uncomfortably pressed into service to bolster Weatherby's argument against her coming, was forced to admit that the girl's knowledge of dialects, and her diction given even the most difficult vocabulary, was extraordinary. And Vellusk noted that she had a fine singing voice indeed.

Anne had remained silent on the issue—Elizabeth was not properly her daughter, after all—but it took but a glance for Weatherby to realize that he was well outgunned within his own family on the matter. And now, looking at her across the table in his own cabin, all he could do was to pray that no harm would befall her in the duty she had chosen for herself.

"Father?"

Weatherby smiled as he came out of his reverie. "My dear, it is very possible that the French aims have very little to do with Althotas. However, we are left with naught but conjecture until we make keel-fall tomorrow. In the meantime, how fare you in determining our ultimate destination?"

Elizabeth nodded primly and pulled a sheaf of papers off a nearby chair. "Gar'uk and I have been studying the geography of the Va'hak'ri territory. Gar'uk, of course, was young when he last visited, and only knows the trail starts from the beach where you and Uncle Andrew—I mean, Dr. Finch—appeared back in '79."

"My dear, we still love Andrew, even with all we have learned of late," Anne said gently. Weatherby merely frowned; Finch was confined to quarters on his orders, and was not welcome to dinner. Elizabeth, for her part, decided simply to continue on.

"Yes, well, all we know is that there is a mountain upon which the vault stands. Originally, we had thought Mount Ar'ak'a would be a likely destination, but even though the volcano is now dormant, I thought it highly unlikely that the ancient Venusians would build such a structure there. So I believe the most likely candidate would be here," Elizabeth said, pointing at a map. "It is two days' journey from the shore, in the very heart of the jungle."

Weatherby motioned for the map, which Elizabeth offered him as he put on his spectacles—yet another nod to advancing age. "This is probably the worst place on Venus it could possibly be located," he said after studying it for several long moments. "There is but one realistic trail there, and it goes through a massive…what is this? A meadow of some kind?"

Gar'uk came over from his post by the wall and looked at the map. "Yes. Clear area. Few trees. A long walk from one end to the other. If we no like who we see there, we kill them."

"Of course you do," Weatherby said, amused fatigue in his voice, for nothing, it seemed would be easy at this point. "And where might we gain safe passage for this journey, Gar'uk?"

"At the village."

Weatherby looked to Elizabeth for clarification, to which she replied: "The village Cagliostro destroyed in '79. We can assume, I believe, it has been rebuilt. The Va'hak'ri remain a key part of Venusian culture, so a village such as this would certainly be appropriate as a kind of customs agency for passage."

The admiral, meanwhile, continued to study the map. "The French holdings here to the south…is there a trail to the mountain from there?"

Gar'uk studied the map once more. "No, but they can make trail. Long walk, but land is flat. Use swords and axes to cut trees….yes, they can if they wish."

"And so…if the French have made progress in their research, then they may very well have located the vault already," Weatherby said glumly. "They may be there in force."

Anne placed her hand on his. "Then we'll meet them in the field and take it from them," she said gently but firmly, for she was accustomed to her husband's occasional melancholies.

Before Weatherby could respond, the ships bell began to ring insistently, followed a moment later by the sound of the marine drummer beating to quarters. Weatherby rose and grabbed his hat, already proffered by Gar'uk. "Philip, with me. Anne, take Elizabeth with you to the cockpit so she may assist as she's able."

Anne immediately rose from the table and took Elizabeth's hand in hers. The young woman seemed slightly shocked at the sudden burst of movement; no doubt Anne would explain all in due course. For now, Weatherby caught his wife's gaze and issued a silent plea: *Keep her safe.* Anne smiled and nodded, then hurried out and down toward the bowels of the ship, which was the safest place to be at the moment. Of course, safety was relative. The bells and drums would not be necessary unless a potential enemy was spotted.

Weatherby buttoned his coat and strode forth onto the main deck, where he was saluted by all in view, then turned and made his way up to the quarterdeck, where stood Searle and his officers. Philip saluted Searle and the others—there were a few private lessons with the admiral to better acclimate him to the expectations of the service—and Weatherby received salutes in turn. "Captain?" the admiral asked.

"Three ships sighted, my Lord Admiral," Searle reported, pointing off into the Void, two points to starboard, then again three points larboard. Between those two points, Venus loomed before them, already filling a quarter of the Void in their eyes. "I would assume French pickets, but they appear to be advancing upon us rather than retreating to inform their fellows."

Weatherby took out his glass and looked off into the distance. They were mere points of light, but that would change within the next thirty minutes, maybe less. "They seem to be within signaling distance, but just barely. Where are we?" asked the admiral.

"We have *Mars* and *Kent* to starboard, my Lord, with *Thunderer* and *Agamemnon* to larboard," Searle said. "Spread wide so as to extend our pickets as well. But I do not know if we can close up in time, given they have yet to see some of our signals."

The admiral frowned, for this was his own stratagem come back to haunt him. In the Void, he had taken to spreading out his ships in order to gather more intelligence, for the French typically traveled in tight formations. Once sighted, the British captains knew to swarm to the static French formations, allowing for a scattered but effective approach against a single group of targets. Now, however, their enemy would come upon all sides as well, and Weatherby's ships were so far apart, they might not be able to coordinate their activities.

"Why must the French decide to innovate today, of all days?" Weatherby groused. "Signal the fleet to form up. Hopefully they shall see it in time. I—"

Then the worst sort of thought occurred to him. One he was sure he might regret at some point, sooner or later. He could only pray it would be later.

"Lieutenant St. Germain," Weatherby said, turning to Philip. "Bring Dr. Finch to the quarterdeck at once. And tell him to bring the equipment we used off Edinburgh. Now. Go."

As Philip dashed off, fairly plowing into a couple of midshipmen in the process. Searle turned his back toward the other officers and faced Weatherby, lowering his voice to a bare whisper. "I cannot think this a good idea, my Lord, and my apologies for saying so."

"And what other options might we have, Captain?" the admiral replied, quietly but with steel. "I see none other than retreat and regroup, and I assure you that time is not with us to make that a possibility."

Searle frowned. "I…I shall be here in case you need me, my Lord."

Weatherby put his hand on the man's shoulder and favored him with a grim half-smile. "Should this not work, you shall take command of the fleet and, with whatever you have left, make for Venus with all due haste. Vellusk and the Lady Weatherby will advise you on your course afterward."

"I pray it will not come to that, my Lord."

Weatherby spied Finch making his way out of the fo'c'sle, looking to the quarterdeck with an eager look upon his face and several alchemists' mates in his wake. "So do I, Captain."

Mere minutes later, Weatherby watched as dispassionately as possible as Finch set up his table and mirror on *Victory*'s quarterdeck, with both Philip and Anne supervising him. Searle had far less dispassion upon his face, looking between Finch and his creation with both immense concern and barely concealed anger, for the captain had been told of Finch's betrayal and had suggested to his admiral that the yardarm was fair recompense for the alchemist's crimes.

Instead, however, Weatherby would seek to take advantage of Finch's forbidden researches in order to defeat the French. The old admiral wondered just how complicit he would become in his friend's crimes.

"Tell me how this truly works, Doctor," Weatherby said, no small measure of malice in his voice. "And tell it true, with Philip and Anne here listening. Leave no detail out."

Finch kept his eyes upon his work, lining up his table and mirror just so, in alignment with the stars of the Void above and in consultation with a thick leather-bound book. "Yes, well, as you may have now surmised, this working does indeed make use of the world of *Maat*, the Egyptian Underworld—though I do believe it needs a better name, wouldn't you say?—to provide a kind of clairvoyance to the wearer of this device."

With that, Finch offered Weatherby the leather-and-glass rig, which the latter accepted gingerly. "So I shall be entering the Underworld, shall I?"

"Oh, no! Of course not!" Finch said quickly, snatching the device from Weatherby's hands in order to adjust it. Finch's hands were all aflutter, and his mien was one of nervous energy and deference. "Through the working upon these lenses and the mirror, you are merely peering into *Maat*, rather than bodily entering it. Because the energies of the Underworld touch upon every part of our world, and both space and time are constricted and, I believe, quite meaningless there, you can use those energies as a conduit to peer upon whatever you wish—such as the Void around your captains' ships."

Anne was nodding slowly. "And he needn't be in contact with them to do this, for he can simply view the area around them, using them as an anchor in our reality, yes?"

"Exactly!" Finch said. "Of course, you'll need to contact them mentally. That's simply done by saying their name and focusing on their face, then speaking the message. Then say their name again to break contact, lest they all hear each other and it becomes a perfect jumble."

Finch slipped the device over Weatherby's head, ignoring the deathly, angry look his superior officer and friend showed him. "If the French have a similar device, Finch, can they not see and hear my plans as I communicate them?"

"No, it doesn't work like that, Tom....my Lord Admiral," Finch said quickly. "Though if they had thought of this innovation, I would likely commend them highly as it took me several months of research with the *Book* to figure..." Finch allowed his voice to drift away upon seeing the faces of those he loved and cared for favoring him with naught but disdain. "I shall be right here if you have need of me, my Lord," he added quietly.

"Very well," Weatherby said tersely. "So I shall begin by focusing on HMS *Mars*, which ought to be –"

Weatherby gasped as the mirror below filled with stars and, a moment later, that fine vessel appeared as if it were off his larboard side, with full sail and guns out. "Dear God," he breathed. "Now for *Thunderer*." Another stream of stars went by, and Patrick O'Brian's ship came into view. Soon, Weatherby had found every ship in his fleet. He called out a relative position upon each and had one of Searle's lieutenants mark them accordingly on a rough map.

"Now, where are the French?" Weatherby muttered. "Finch, how do I find the bloody French?"

"You must see them from the eyes of your men, or the minds of your captains," Finch said gently. "I think you shall have to ask."

Weatherby frowned. He was not at all enamored of the idea of being a voice in his captains' head. Having been a captain himself, he knew full well that his voice—imagined, of course—was already there, berating or encouraging them, depending on their wont. But...there was nothing for it.

"You and I will have a long, long talk about responsibility once again, Doctor," Weatherby groused before closing his eyes and clearing his mind. "Patrick O'Brian. Paddy, it's Tom. This is a genuine message. It's Finch's doing. Can you hear me?"

Weatherby spoke the words aloud, but the reply came as a tentative whisper in his mind. "*Lord Weatherby? Is that you? I can hear you. Do I need to speak aloud or can you hear my very thoughts?*" Immediately after hearing this, a jolt of pain lanced through Weatherby's head; it seemed the working exacted quite a toll indeed.

"I've no idea, Paddy, but I can hear you," Weatherby said, gritting his teeth through the pain and yet, oddly, somewhat amused that his officers on the quarterdeck were forced to listen to but one side of a conversation. "However you are communicating, continue it. Where are the French?"

As it happened, *Thunderer* had spotted two French ships, a third-rate and a frigate. From there, Weatherby touched the minds of his other captains—engaging in long and often-times frustrating conversations in the process, accompanied by continued aches in his head—until he had a complete picture of the field of battle before him.

"I believe we have but seven French ships, including three ships of the line. Our best stratagem will be for as many of us to set upon single ships as possible," Weatherby said, both to his captain aboard *Victory* and, he hoped, to his other captains. By now, he felt completely fatigued—and the battle had yet to even start. He could only hope to remain standing throughout the engagement. "O'Brian, take *Thunderer* and make for the 74 nearest you. *Kent*, set your course three points to starboard and two down upon your planes, and adjust when you see both the French and *Thunderer*. I shall send *Agamemnon* and *Enterprise* to join you. Meanwhile, Captain Searle will take *Victory* and engage four points to larboard. We should find a first-rate of ninety guns there, and I shall bring *Mars* and *Surprise* to join us."

And with that, Weatherby allowed himself a few moments of quiet to mollify his aching head and to gather his wits about him for another spate of communication, should it come to that.

Searle posted lookouts to both sides of the ship specifically to look for *Mars* and the 28-gun frigate *Surprise*, and was not disappointed. HMS *Mars* appeared within a point of where Weatherby had predicted, while the frigate *Surprise* was even more precise. Meanwhile, a single point of light ahead grew in size and soon revealed itself to be a substantial three-decked vessel flying the French tricolor.

"Traditional signals should work now, I believe," Weatherby said, using his kerchief to wipe the sweat from his brow. "Signal our compatriots. *Mars* shall take the larboard side, we shall fire upon the starboard. And have *Surprise* come up upon her keel and fire upward."

It was, in the end, no contest at all.

The French ship attempted to maneuver but was taken by surprise, and Weatherby's captains were able to adjust well enough. *Victory* and *Mars* raked the French ships with massive broadsides, while the French—split between two enemies—could only manage a small barrage on either side. *Victory* shuddered with the impact of several shots, but Weatherby could see that Searle's gunners aimed true, for there were several holes rent in the side of the French as it flew past. Weatherby could only imagine the damage *Surprise* had done to the French's underbelly.

All upon the quarterdeck wheeled around and pulled their glasses to see the effects of the strategy. Smoke poured from several gaping holes in the French vessel, both upon the sides and from her keel. One mast was listing to starboard, and both her planesails were in tatters. Open flames could be seen from inside the windows of her stern, and there were several men dangling over the sides on lifelines.

The admiral snapped his glass shut. "Very well, then," he said grimly, turning back to his map and mirror and, with substantially more confidence, donning the lenses once more. "I shall contact *Thunderer* and, if they have fared as well as we, select new targets. Captain, give me a damage report on *Victory* when you have it."

Yet before Weatherby could focus his mind upon his captain and friend O'Brian, there were shouts from the topmast and forward—more ships spotted.

Weatherby tore off Finch's goggles and used his own glass to look, and felt his stomach sink. "Dear God, have we fallen into a trap?" he muttered.

During the battle, the Royal Navy ships had continued to travel toward Venus at a very high speed, and the green, cloud-shrouded planet began to obscure more and more of their view. But now, from either side of the world before them, more French ships were spotted—at least three clusters of them, coming from larboard, starboard and above.

"Captain, I need numbers for these contacts," Weatherby said as he snapped his glass shut, and wrestled with putting his headgear on once more. "I shall warn the others and see what their lookouts may find as well."

The news was far from good. Each of the three clusters of French coming toward them had two ships of the line and at least four other vessels, which meant they were more than a match for Weatherby's own groupings. The admiral's mind raced, even as pain seemed to emanate from his very skull. The French had at least half again as many ships, with at least a third more guns. They could be more flexible, darting around the Void to pick off their English targets as if they were hunting grouse.

So we must be larger game, then, he thought suddenly.

"I'm telling *Thunderer* and *Agamemnon* to signal the others and form up on *Victory*," Weatherby said to his officers. "Captain Searle, identify the very nearest group of French ships and make for them, full sail, royals and stud'sels. Signal *Mars* and *Surprise* to follow suit."

Weatherby returned to the mirror upon the table before him and added instructions to his captains as to how they should form up, for the old admiral had a very specific plan in mind for maximizing his guns. He was in the midst of explaining it to the captain of *Kent* when the mirror before him burst with a strange blue light, causing his eyes to water as he turned away suddenly.

"Finch!" he cried. "What was that?"

The alchemist scurried over to the table and, using a strange eye-piece of his own, peered into it. "My God," Finch said quietly and reverently, which was wholly opposite his normal demeanor. "Look at it, Tom."

Weatherby turned back and saw that the starfield before him had several new additions; in his mind, he could hear the confusion in his captains' minds as well. A lookout upon *Agamemnon* had seen one of the unknown marks up close, and found it to be a metal object some twenty feet long, shaped like a coffin, with insect-like, yet rectangular, wings protruding from it and two large concave plates attached at either end.

"What just happened, Finch?" Weatherby demanded. "There are several new…things…out there."

Before Finch could answer, they were interrupted by a cry from Searle. "Full down on the planes! NOW!"

Reflexively, Weatherby grabbed for the railing of the quarterdeck with one hand and at Finch's wrist with the other. The gravity upon *Victory* shifted greatly as the maneuver prompted the massive *Victory* to begin a steep dive. And just overhead, Weatherby saw a massive object nearly scrape the top of the mainmast. It was similar in metallic design to what the lookouts had seen—but several times larger.

It was so close, in fact, that Weatherby could see the markings upon it—including a flag painted upon the side, in an all-too-familiar pattern of stripes and stars.

"They're here again," Weatherby said, amazed. "Dear God. Are we too late?"

CHAPTER 16

January 29, 2135

I t didn't take long for *Hadfield* to discover the malfeasance aboard the Virgin Galactic liner. Baines managed to avoid collision with ease, but then required an additional thirty-second burn to get the ship back on course—and they lost several hours on the other ship.

Of course, nobody thought this was coincidence, but confirmation came just a few short hours later—when the first frozen corpse appeared on sensors.

Shaila called up a visual on the first one. She was Asian, probably Korean, somewhere in her 30s, and dressed in an elegant gown that flowed behind her yet was as motionless as her body. She only had one of her stilettos on—the other was probably close by, but too small for sensors to find. The woman's skin was grey and bruised, the result of blood vessels bursting in the vacuum of space, and her eyes were open and milky. Somehow, Shaila expected her to look stricken or horrified, but the woman merely looked as though she was mildly surprised.

After that, Shaila didn't look at any more.

As the first two or three showed up on sensors, Diaz seemed to be inclined to stop and pick them up...but then more and more bodies showed up on the screen, and the entire CIC quickly grew quiet. Finally, the general ordered the position and course of each body calculated and transmitted to Houston. Someone, hopefully, would recover the dead. The perpetrators were heading for Venus, and justice would be better served by capturing them instead of cleaning up their mess.

The problem was finding them. Two days later, their sensors had picked up no trace of the pirated ship.

"Stable orbit, 500 kilometers above the surface," Baines reported from the cockpit. "Sensors running at max."

Diaz nodded and gave a wave toward the cockpit. "All right. Full sensor sweeps with every orbital pass. I want Venus mapped all over again and I want everything in orbit out to a hundred thousand klicks. If there's so much as a micrometeor out of place, I want to know about it."

Shaila nodded and ensured Diaz' orders were carried out, then turned back to Chrys VanDerKamp, who had been trying for the past twelve hours to uplink with her satellites using a new tack. Long-range hacks hadn't worked, but the satellites also had short-range comms aboard to coordinate their efforts. The hope was that Chrys, with Coogan's help if needed, could use those short-range receivers to beam commands into the satellites' operating system, circumventing the normal I/O interface that had been seemingly given a new operating system. Perhaps by approaching the problem at the hardware level, they could at least cripple the satellites, robbing Greene and Hutchinson of their use.

"I can't even *find* my sats," Chrys said as her fingers flickered over the holocontrols. Screens of data and maps flowed across the air before her, and none were able to wipe the frown off her face. "Hard to send a signal if I can't aim it well enough."

"Can't you just broadcast it wide?" Shaila asked.

Chrys turned to her with a look of disdain. "They're narrow-band laser comms, sat-to-sat only. They're designed to be secure. Otherwise, anybody with a goddamn ham radio could mess with them."

"Try harder," Shaila said icily before leaving the exec to her work. Naturally, Chrys' conglom opted not to allow JSC full access to the satellite array without a representative aboard—as was their right—but Shaila didn't have to like it one bit. She tried to have sympathy for the exec, but the fact was that, to Shaila, she was just as small-minded, and as complicit, as Harry Yu.

"Jimmy, why aren't we finding these sats?" Shaila asked. "We're going at a pretty good clip. Shouldn't we have been in range by now?"

Coogan sat at his ops station and manipulated the holoimage of Venus in front of him. "Our last track on the satellites was here," he said, pointing to several dots in geosynchronous orbit around the planet. "When we entered the atmosphere to brake, we lost them, and we're still not picking them up."

"Debris?" Shaila asked.

"None detected. In fact, if it weren't for several diagnostics on the sensors, I'd question whether they were working properly. I'm not getting anything. I can't even find the Stanford outpost."

Now that got Shaila's attention. Stanford University's orbital labs held twenty souls aboard, the vast majority of them academic researchers. It was an older facility, but it worked well, and it gave the tourists somewhere to visit when they got tired of looking at clouds all day. "Did Stanford report a burn?"

"No, Commander. We should be well within comm range, and we should've gotten a hail by now, but there's nothing." Even Coogan looked concerned, which seemed extraordinarily out of place on his usually placid face.

"What about Cherenkov radiation? Maybe there's been a rift and they got caught in it or something," Shaila said.

"Nothing there either, ma'am."

"Keep trying," she replied, then hit the comm. "Major Parrish, how are we doing on V-SEV readiness?"

A moment later, the marine responded: "All systems ready. We can launch in five if needed."

"Thanks. Jain out." Shaila then turned to Diaz. "General, suggest we hail the Stanford facility. If they're in trouble, we can maybe get a bead on them, even use the V-SEVs to evacuate as needed."

Diaz was reading her own holodisplays and frowning. "Yeah...something's just not right. Where the hell is everything? Did the Virgin ship just come in and blow everything up?"

"We'd see something, ma'am," Shaila replied. "Debris, latent energy readings, something."

"I know," Diaz snapped, then calmed visibly. "Sorry. Send a broad comm out for Stanford."

"Yes, General." Shaila toggled a few keys, then spoke into a mic on the console. "Stanford University Venus Outpost, this is the Joint Space Command Ship *Hadfield*. Come in, Stanford outpost."

To Shaila's surprise, a reply came back within seconds. "*Hadfield*, this is Stanford. Where the heck did you guys come from?"

Diaz and Shaila traded a look. "Stanford, we've been coming in hot for a while now, just made orbit. You should've picked us up hours ago. Over."

"We should've, yeah. We're not getting anything right now. All our sensors went down about six hours ago. All our projects on the surface, stuff up here, nothing."

Shit. "Do you require assistance, Stanford?" Shaila asked.

"Maybe if you got a tech handy or a spare sensor suite. We were showing an incoming before our sensors went down, but we haven't made comm or visual on them since. You might want to check on them first."

"Roger that. We'll survey what we can and get back to you soon. *Hadfield* out." Shaila dropped the link and turned to Diaz. "Ma'am, looks like we need to do a search for…."

Oh, shit. Shit shit shit!

Diaz saw the emotions play out on Shaila's face. "What? What is it?"

Shaila turned to Coogan. "We're being jammed! The whole goddamn system is being jammed! Countermeasures!"

Coogan's fingers flew across his controls. "I believe you may be right, Commander. There's a very low-frequency signal surrounding the system. Trying to place the source now to counter it."

Diaz caught up fast. "Focus on the last known location of those satellites and extrapolate, Jimmy. Only possible source."

Chrys rushed over to Coogan's station, and the two began trading data quickly and furiously. "Confirmed.

Low-frequency signals emanating from projected positions of corporate satellites. Hang on. Engaging countermeasures."

Suddenly, every alarm aboard *Hadfield* went off at once, followed quickly by a half-dozen voices.

"Cherenkov radiation spikes!" Ayim reported. "In orbit and on the surface!"

"Debris, straight ahead, twenty klicks!" Baines reported. "Taking evasive action!"

"Proximity alert! We have another ship within fifty kilometers and closing fast!" Coogan shouted. "They're heading right for us!"

Diaz rushed forward toward the cockpit. "Baines! Evasive burn! Take us to 350 klicks above the surface and prepare for a slingshot into geosynch. We need to get above this crap!"

"Calculating! It'll take a few seconds!" the young pilot replied.

The general then turned to Ayim. "Gerry, report! What's going on with Venus?"

The physicist looked both elated and alarmed. "There is a huge area on the surface, General, covered with vegetation! At least two hundred square kilometers. The area appears to extend upward into orbit, ending at the satellites! I don't know how... It's extraordinary!"

"Roger. Record everything. What about that debris?" Diaz called out toward Coogan.

"Scanning now, General. Appears to be...oak wood. Iron. Hemp fibers. Human remains."

Shaila put it together quickly. "Ship! It's a goddamn shipwreck!" She met eyes with Diaz. "We've just flown into the middle of an overlap!"

Suddenly, *Hadfield* shuddered violently, and more alarms went off. The room's lighting turned red and the data on every screen was replaced with a single message.

COLLISION.
HULL BREACH.

Coogan's hands waved wildly in front of him as he flew through the holographic data before him. "Engines hit," he reported, his usual cool inflected with just a hint of panic. "Offline. Breach in engine room, damage to landing gear, deployment bay and cargo hatch. And…"

His voice trailed off, leaving Shaila and Diaz to look over expectantly at him. "Jimmy?" Diaz asked.

"Life support on critical," he said simply.

Diaz immediately turned toward the cockpit. "Baines! Get us aimed at Stanford! Use chemical thrusters and give me an ETA stat." She turned to Shaila. "Get Ayim in gear. We need him and the Emerald Tablet secured in a V-SEV in case things get worse."

Shaila nodded. A ship like *Hadfield* didn't have lifeboats. The V-SEVs could serve in a pinch, but they had extremely limited maneuvering ability aside from simply landing on the surface of Venus. None of this would go well. "Come on, Doctor. Move your ass," she snapped, grabbing the old scientist by the scruff of his jacket and pulling him toward the doorway of the CIC, with zero-g making it quite easy for her to bodily drag him along.

Shaila and Ayim sped toward the lab, where Ayim carefully undocked the Emerald Tablet from its mechanical cradle—a bit too carefully for Shaila's taste. "Move it, Gerald!" she shouted, but the physicist was intent on making sure the tablet was placed just so, and Shaila floated impatiently for what seemed to be hours, but was only thirty seconds or so.

When they finally opened the door to the lab, Stephane was floating out in the corridor in front of them, a pained and worried look on his face.

It startled the hell out of her.

"Why aren't you in your quarters?" she demanded.

"The locks stopped working when the alarms went off," Stephane said. "Something's happening. I am…*mon dieu*, it's happening again, isn't it?"

Shaila nodded. "You still in the driver's seat?"

Stephane gave her a weak smile. "For now. This is strengthening him. I have this sense that he is happy. Eager? Yes, eager."

Fuck. "All right. Get moving, Durand," she said as Ayim floated up from behind her with the briefcase containing the Tablet. "Deployment bay, now!"

Before they could launch themselves down the corridor, another impact rocked the ship, sending them into the walls and ceiling. More alarms went off, followed by a panicked voice from the CIC which Shaila couldn't place: "Emergency suits! All personnel into emergency suits now!"

Shaila immediately grabbed a handhold on the side of the corridor and gave it a twist, opening a storage locker. Orange emergency pressure suits began spilling out. "Grab 'em and put 'em on!" she shouted.

Stephane immediately took a helmet and put it on, then started shoving his legs into the suit itself. Shaila did likewise—until she saw Ayim just…floating there. Wide-eyed. Panicked beyond all action.

Swearing loudly, Shaila grabbed a third suit and shoved it into Ayim's chest, sending him floating back into the wall. "Gerald. Put this on. NOW."

He looked down at his hand, where he carried the case with the Emerald Tablet. "This…" His voice trailed off. "Can you hold this?"

Shaila snatched the case from him. "Put it ON, Gerald."

The scientist slowly began unfurling the folded up suit. Shaila's every urge was to help him with it, but her training said otherwise—you can't help someone else if you're not secure first. A basic rule since the earliest days of space travel, but it was hard to enforce sometimes. She turned to see Stephane just about sealed up. "Stephane, help him," she ordered as she wrestled with the seals on her own suit.

Then a massive *whoosh* rang through her ears as the ship shuddered a third time, and she felt herself pulled toward the deployment bay.

The ship was falling apart, and the air was going with it.

She grabbed a handhold and, with the other hand still holding the Tablet, she tried to finish her seals. A scream caught her attention—she saw Ayim hurtling past her down the corridor at high speed, limbs flailing through his half-donned emergency suit. His head caught the ceiling hard and the scream stopped instantly, and she watched in horror as his body was carried downward to the bay below.

Then she felt Stephane's hands finishing up her suit seal. "There," he said. "I'm sorry. I couldn't save him."

Shaila nodded and gave his helmet a rap. "You tried," she said, then keyed her comm. "Diaz, this is Jain. We've lost Ayim."

Several long moments passed—in which the two made their way down toward the deployment bay—before Diaz responded. "Roger. Deployment bay is breached into space. Parrish and his team aren't responding. Jimmy and I are heading down there. Let's get the V-SEVs fired up."

A dozen people. "Understood," Shaila said as she floated down to the bay below. On entering, she could see a meter wide hole in the side of the ship. There was blood all around the ragged outer edges of it. There were no people. "Go for V-SEV startup sequence. Where's Baines and the rest of the CIC crew?"

Another long pause, during which Shaila keyed in the command codes for the V-SEVs and watched as they came to life. "Baines sealed himself in the cockpit to try to steer us clear of anything else. The rest…we got VanDerKamp with us. That's it."

Shaila turned and guided Stephane toward one of the V-SEVs. "Shit. Roger that. Let's go one person per V-SEV." Not the optimal operating crew, of course, but Shaila knew that launching four of them would increase the chances of someone surviving the day. She turned to Stephane. "Did you read the manual I sent you on these?"

He shrugged and gave her one of the infuriating grins she had grown to both love and hate. "Some of it. It can't get any worse, yes?"

She grabbed him by the arm and hurled him toward one of the mechs. "You better figure it out fast."

Shaila pushed herself toward another V-SEV and, as she buckled in, saw Diaz, Chrys and Coogan float into the bay. Coogan looked ashen but focused, while Diaz had tear streaks on her face and grimaced in anger and pent-up rage. For her part, Chrys just looked utterly dazed. They immediately made for the other vehicles, with Coogan taking the exec and strapping her into the jump seat of his V-SEV before taking the pilot's chair.

"Baines, you're a brave kid," Diaz said over the comm as she strapped into her own mech.

"I'm an idiot, General," he replied. "But we're in the clear, for now. There's….there's a lot going on out there."

The hatch on Shaila's V-SEV lowered and her ops controls came on. "A lot of what?"

Yet another alarm sounded in her ear, and the HUD on her forward hatch window lit up red: LAUNCH SYSTEMS INOPERATIVE.

"General, we can't launch," Shaila said.

Suddenly, Diaz' V-SEV lurched forward and began to float toward the rent in the side of the ship. "May not need to. Jain, give us a workaround so we can use the launch breaking thrusters in short bursts."

"What the…oh." Shaila grasped it. If the thrusters on the backs and legs of the V-SEVs—normally used for slowing down the atmosphere—could be placed under manual control, then they could maneuver in space. They could at least reach the Stanford outpost, or maybe even one of the satellites.

Maybe they'd even live, at least for a bit longer.

Shaila's fingers danced over the controls for several long seconds. "Hacking it now. Looks like…if I route through the forward gear subroutine….there. Transmitting new code to V-SEVs operating systems. Use your walking controls as thrusters. Left leg forward and back fires left side, same for right. Together to go directionally."

"Good job," Diaz responded. The general had maneuvered her V-SEV toward one of the small rents in the hull. She raised the mech's arm and, a moment later, a panel slid back to reveal the barrel of a laser drill, designed to cut through whatever minerals Venus had handy. She began to cut into the hull of *Hadfield* in a wide arc and, a moment later, a three-meter piece of bent metal floated off into space. "Here's our exit. Let's go."

Shaila watched as the three other V-SEVs floated out the freshly made exit, using the ship itself to push off into space. She started floating across the deployment bay to join them. "Do we make for Stanford, ma'am?"

Then she saw the space around Venus for the first time, and her HUD lit up like a Christmas tree.

There were twenty-six sailing ships in space around her, hanging over Venus like...nothing she could've ever imagined.

And they were trading cannon fire.

CHAPTER 17

May 28, 1809

"What in God's name are *those*?" asked a junior lieutenant as he scanned the larboard side of HMS *Victory* and saw giant metal men floating off in the distance.

Weatherby looked up from his mirror. "I do not know, but we can at least assume they are not allies of the French," he replied. "Now mind your station."

Suitably chagrined, the lieutenant continued his watch, scanning for French ships on the larboard side aft. Weatherby caught Searle eying him closely, and cocked his head—a signal for the captain to approach and speak whatever was evidently in his thoughts.

"Due respect, my Lord Admiral, but how can we assume they are not in league with the French, whatever in God's name they are?" Searle asked quietly.

Weatherby allowed himself a small smile. "If these are the people I encountered on Mars, those many years ago, then they have rules against firing upon anyone without appropriate foreknowledge."

Searle nodded, but seemed unconvinced. "And if they are not those same worthies from before?"

"Then we shall deal with them should they engage, and not before," Weatherby said, turning back to Finch's mirror. He could see that the metal creatures, for want of a better word, had exited the remnants of some form of vessel—a craft that, luckily, had collided with the remnants of a French frigate and seemed to be crippled. A passing French 74 had taken the liberty of firing upon the vessel as the two passed each other, but the metal creatures had not retaliated, so Weatherby's assumption was seemingly safe.

A familiar melody came from the forward part of the quarterdeck. "It has happened once more, my friend Lord Weatherby."

The admiral looked up to see Vellusk there, robed as always, his body quivering under the folds of his raiment. "That would seem to be the most likely explanation," he said, sounding more terse than he might have liked. "At the moment, Ambassador, might I suggest the cockpit as a safer place for you?"

The Xan, however, had already turned to gaze out upon the metal creatures, now floating in the Void. Short bursts of light were emanating from their bodies, seemingly propelling them toward the battle. "They are not of these worlds," he sang.

Weatherby opted to drop the matter, and simply hoped that if Vellusk were to die, it would not cause yet another interplanetary crisis, for there were only so many which could be managed this day. "We have three French ships coming up directly aft, two more to larboard," he told Searle. "Come right full rudder and signal *Agamemnon* and *Enterprise* to form up with us to protect our keel."

Searle barked out the orders as Weatherby turned back toward the mirror, and watched as a drop of his own sweat fell upon the glass. He felt as though his very vitality was being leached from him by the power of this netherworld into which he peered. Perhaps this was why Finch would often look wan and pale, for Weatherby doubted not that his friend's researches would exact an even greater toll.

And Finch seemed to see it as well. "Tom, you must rest," he said. "Our ships are already formed up. Can we not rely on traditional signals now?"

Weatherby gazed into the mirror once more. He had arranged his ships into an intricate pattern which allowed for maximum broadsides while protecting as many keels and upper decks as possible. Some ships were upside-down upon the planetary plane, while others were on their sides. The grouping he had split off would hopefully draw fire away from the others, but he would soon lead those French back into the midst of his fleet, hoping to catch them in the crossfire.

"Perhaps you are right, Doctor. I…wait."

A fourth grouping of French ships now approached from his starboard side, and seemed to be positioning themselves to come alongside. By Weatherby's count, this was very much the bulk of the French fleet—a trap laid for him at the very highest levels of the French Navy. He scanned the starfield before him, looking for an exit strategy.

But there was none. The French were descending upon *Victory* on all sides. And they would of course want to capture her at all costs.

"Captain, load every gun and wait to fire upon my command. Signal the others to do likewise," Weatherby ordered, stripping the goggles from his head once and for all. "Then prepare to repel boarders."

Searle visibly blanched. "Has it come to that, then?" he said quietly.

Weatherby favored him with a small smile and placed his hand on his shoulder. "We are well outgunned, Captain. The French wish to take us as a prize. I have ordered all the other ships in our fleet to our defense, but they will not last long." Weatherby's smile dropped and his eyes grew distant. "I have placed us upon this course, and we must now see it through. Have the men prepare."

With that Weatherby shrugged back into his coat—he had removed it as the strain of Finch's working weighed upon him—and took both his hat and a glass of fortifying port from Gar'uk before starting to make his way below decks.

"Tom," Finch said softly, touching his admiral's arm. "I set us upon this course, not you. I should have told you of the *Book*."

Weatherby glared. "You should have indeed, Doctor. And while I will always consider you a brother, I've no wish for a reconciliation at the moment. I want to see my family."

The admiral turned and marched down the steps toward the maindeck, not looking back to see what he assumed would be Finch's stricken look. Idly, he wondered if their reconciliation would have to wait until the next life. And if that next life would be in *Maat* or, hopefully, somewhere a bit more welcoming.

Weatherby waved off the salutes of his officers and the men of *Victory* as he made his way below. There were gashes and rents in the ship—she had already undergone withering French fire—and the men were bloodied and, in some unfortunate cases, well past saving. Past the three gundecks he went until reaching the very bowels of the ship, where he finally encountered the lantern-lit cockpit, in front of which several dozen casualties were waiting for admittance.

Inside, he could see Anne and Philip now working feverishly to care for the wounded, and Elizabeth bravely helping where she could by bringing fresh bandages and water to the wounded. His daughter looked up as he approached. "Is it over?" she asked, desperation in her voice.

"No, my dear," he said quietly, smoothing her hair. "It is likely we shall be boarded. I am so sorry."

Elizabeth nodded and cleared her throat. "Will they allow us to finish caring for the men, I hope?"

"It is customary," he replied. "I…I am so very, very proud of the fine woman you've become, and I am most sorry that I have led us here."

Elizabeth rose and embraced him. "You are the finest man I know, Father. All you have done has been for the greater good." And with that, she crouched down and returned to care for a man whose left leg and right eye were simply mangled masses of red flesh.

He entered the cockpit itself, where he found both Philip and Anne with blood to their elbows, and several alchemists' mates preparing any number of workings and elixirs. He watched as a man's hand began to slowly grow back under Philip's care, while another yet to be tended to suddenly coughed and breathed his last.

Anne looked up and caught the look in her husband's eye almost immediately. "Is it that bad?"

Weatherby nodded. "I am afraid we may be boarded soon. I will ask the enemy commander to allow you, Philip and Elizabeth your freedom after we strike our colors."

She nodded gravely, while Philip made a redoubled effort to merely focus on his work. "Shall I see you again?" Anne asked.

"I don't know."

Quickly, she moved before him and kissed him deeply, ensuring that her gore-splattered hands did not touch his uniform. "Then that will have to suffice," she said, tears welling in her eyes. "Now go, my Lord Admiral. You're in the way."

He gave her a sad smile, for he was indeed in the way and she was still focused on the lives she could save. Blinking to stave off his own tears, Weatherby nodded at Philip, who returned it in kind, and left the cockpit—only to have a midshipman nearly run into him.

"Captain Searle requests his Lordship upon the quarter-deck," the young boy said breathlessly. "I dare say you won't believe it!"

What now? Weatherby wondered as he dashed off after the mid, climbing four decks as fast as he could until finally reaching the maindeck.

And then he saw.

A French triple-decker—most likely the 118-gun *Ocean*—had come right up alongside *Victory* and was merely hanging there in the Void, not fifty yards off. And yet neither ship had fired.

"Captain Searle!" Weatherby shouted. "Why have we not fired?!"

Searle rushed down from the quarterdeck with Vellusk right behind him. "I do not believe we need to, my Lord Admiral."

Weatherby spun 'round on the man. "What in God's name are you saying?"

Then a great crash came from the other ship, followed by several more. And then there were shouts…and screams.

Finally, *Ocean*'s main deck erupted in an explosion of wood, causing those few left upon the deck to scatter. A cannon shot upward through the resulting hole—so hard and fast that it escaped the French first rate's gravity and sailed off into the Void above.

Then a giant metal claw came out of the hole. And another. Until finally, one of the giant metal creatures pulled itself out onto the deck. It paused, then grasped *Ocean*'s mainmast and tore away half the wood, causing the mast to buckle and fall away—thankfully, away from where *Victory* was.

"The French fired upon those vessels repeatedly," Vellusk sang quietly. "They did not take to it well."

They were suddenly interrupted by a shout from the quarterdeck. "Another French ship coming up starboard side!"

Weatherby wheeled around, feeling suddenly energized. "Ready on the guns! Prepare to repel boarders!"

This other ship was another three-decked gunship, looking to be at about 90 guns. It should have caught *Victory* in a deadly crossfire between two ships, but it had likely been unaware of *Ocean*'s strange fate.

"Admiral, I suggest we wait until she is nearly ready to board," Searle said as the two men took their stations back on the quarterdeck. "We appear adrift, and perhaps we should play along."

Weatherby nodded. "A fine plan, Captain. At your discretion." He then saw Finch slowly packing up his mirror and table, looking utterly morose. "Dr. Finch, please produce some fog in order to shroud our decks. Then report to Lieutenant St. Germain in the cockpit and assist as you're able," he ordered. "I hereby restore you to the rank of alchemist's mate for the present. Captain Searle, make a note in the log when this is over."

Finch blinked several times, looking utterly confused, then caught the glimmer of humor in his old friend's eye, for Weatherby's melancholy had taken a sharp turn after seeing the mechanized beast veritably gut the innards of *Ocean* by itself. "As you wish, my Lord Admiral," Finch replied, tossing off one of his incredibly sloppy salutes. "It's a damn sight better than the brig."

"All hands! Lie low! Hide!" Searle shouted. And to a man, all the seaman abovedecks aboard *Victory* fell to the decks, hiding behind sailcloth and cannon, slipping behind the masts and diving down into hatchways. Below, the midshipmen and junior lieutenants were already distributing pistols, pikes and cutlasses in order to help repel boarders, and some of the smallest and youngest aboard were now quietly and quickly darting about to arm those remaining on the main deck.

Meanwhile, Finch had produced several egg-shaped packets, placing them strategically on the main deck and tossing a few above the fo'c'sle as well. The quarterdeck was left clear, as there were few standing upon it to begin with—and, of course, the officers still needed to see what might be in store.

Finch then said a quick Latin incantation, and the packets began to produce prodigious amounts of black smoke— very nearly the same hue and thickness Weatherby had seen spewing forth from fire-damaged ships. To the French, it might appear that *Victory* was suffering fire damage, which might further lower their guard, even as their vision was obscured.

"Most alchemical smoke is white in nature," Searle noted quietly.

"Finch really is quite talented," Weatherby replied. "At least, when he has his head about him."

Moments later, the French ship edged closer to *Victory*. There were sharpshooters on her main deck, barely visible through the smoke. They wanted the prize, of course, which is what Searle had counted on. But they weren't being quite brash enough for Weatherby's tastes, while his captain's brashness was all too evident.

"FIRE!" Searle shouted.

Immediately, fifty cannon on *Victory*'s larboard side poured iron and alchemical power into the hull of the French ship, while the men in the tops and upon the main deck opened fire with muskets and pistols. Weatherby watched the fog part somewhat, and saw many casualties upon the French decks, along with several large gashes in the enemy hull.

But it was not enough. Grappling hooks and ropes sailed through the fog and caught in the wood of *Victory*, even as the sound of a return broadside deafened all aboard and sent *Victory* shuddering from fo'c'sle to stern. More screams sounded, and this time they were below decks.

Anne. Elizabeth. Philip.

Finch.

Weatherby suddenly cursed himself for his cavalier attitude, for he realized in that moment he had swung from melancholy to over-confidence, ably assisted by Searle's lust for battle and glory.

"Boarders to starboard!" Searle yelled, drawing his sword. "Onward!"

The captain dashed down to the maindeck to join his men, who had opened fire once more at the direction of their squadron leaders. Despite the withering fire, several dozen French began to board *Victory*—for the first time in her illustrious history, if Weatherby's memory served. He slouched slightly, then drew his sword. The silvered blade seemed to cut through the fog with a glow of power all its own, and he knew that many young men would fall before it.

Perhaps he might fall this day as well.

The admiral prepared to move down to the maindeck when he heard the sound of…well, something not normally heard aboard a ship. He could not for the life of him place it, but it was coming from starboard, from *Ocean*.

And there, through the fog, he saw a pair of bright lights making their way toward *Victory*.

The metal beast was coming.

"*Victory*!" Weatherby shouted. "All hands fore and aft at once! All hands, move fore and aft! NOW!"

The two lights arrived amidships. A metal claw—hand?—grasped the railing along the side, crushing it even as the beast pulled itself up onto the deck of England's very flagship. It was, Weatherby could see, a full twelve feet tall, each arm easily the length of a grown man. It had no head, but there appeared to be a port or window in its chest.

And although the fog was still thick, Weatherby saw something—someone—through that window he never thought he'd see again.

"The French are amidships!" Weatherby yelled at the beast. "Their ship is grappling ours!"

The creature turned and strode across *Victory*'s deck in but two steps, then started swinging its arms wildly, sending several Frenchmen flying over the side or across the deck. Searle had ordered his men, now clustered near the fo'c'sle and quarterdeck, to open fire as well.

And in the space of a few moments, the situation became a rout.

Soon, the French were clambering back over the side for the safety of their own ship, even as their fellows were thrown past them by the metal mechanism or were cut down by musket fire.

Then the beast leapt. Short spurts of white fire spewed from its back and legs, and it bridged the Void between the two ships in but a moment.

Weatherby could not see what came next, but could easily imagine it from the sounds of screams and crunching wood.

Searle came back to the quarterdeck, bloodied sword in hand. "Never in all my years at sea and Void have I see anything like that," he breathed. He took a moment to compose himself. "Orders, my Lord Admiral?"

Weatherby nodded. "Have one of the alchemists clear this fog, then signal the rest of the fleet to join us once more. I believe there were three other mechanisms out there, and I will wager they have means to communicate with each other. I expect we have received similar aid elsewhere.

"And Captain, prepare to pipe visitors aboard."

Searle's brow furrowed. "Admiral?"

Before Weatherby could respond, the sound of metal crunching down on wood resounded across *Victory* once more. And there, upon the maindeck, the metal creature stood.

"Belay that last," Weatherby said. "Pass the word for the Lady Weatherby and Dr. Finch at once."

Weatherby waited patiently until his wife and friend joined them from below, with Philip and Elizabeth in tow. Philip approached and saluted smartly. "Do you wish a casualty report, Father…I mean, my Lord Admiral?"

In his haste and zeal to report to his superior officer, the fleet alchemist hadn't bothered to turn forward, as his mother, stepsister and "uncle" had already done. Weatherby simply nodded toward the metal beast, and enjoyed the look on Philip's face immensely as he struggled to come to grips with the sight.

Weatherby then took Anne's hand in his and walked slowly down to the maindeck, where the men of *Victory* slowly surrounded the mechanism. As Weatherby approached, the front of the beast seemed to detach somewhat, and began to rise slowly, as if it were a gunport.

Inside, there was a woman. She had black hair and brown skin, and was dressed in a simple-looking uniform of some kind—one with a Union Jack upon the sleeve.

"Mr. Weatherby, I presume? We had reason to believe you and Dr. Finch were aboard," the woman said with what could only be described as an insouciant grin. This was followed by a slightly perplexed look and a surveying gaze. "How long has it been for you?"

"Thirty years, Lieutenant," Weatherby replied with a smile. "And might I say, you're looking well." Indeed, she looked little changed since they day they had first met, so long ago.

"It's 'Lieutenant Commander' now, actually," the woman said, her smile growing broader. "Less than three years for me." She then spotted Anne by his side and waved. "Hey! You look great for thirty years on! Did you two get together?"

Weatherby smiled as Anne laughed. "Remarkable," Weatherby said. "And yes, I suppose we did. You are aboard HMS *Victory*, Commander. And I am now both an admiral and a baron, in point of fact."

The woman in the mechanism blanched slightly, her grin fading, then gave an unusual but formal salute. "Lord Admiral Weatherby," she said. "Permission to…remain aboard, I suppose."

Weatherby turned to Searle to gain his captain's tacit approval, but the man looked quite dumbfounded, as did so many others aboard. For his part, Weatherby couldn't be happier.

"Permission granted, Lieutenant Commander Jain."

CHAPTER 18

January 29, 2135
May 28, 1809

Shaila looked up at her V-SEV on the deck of the venerable HMS *Victory*—though not as venerable as it was in the 22nd century—and marveled yet again at the direction her life had taken. This time, at least, it was a positive thing.

In the sudden chaos of the overlap, she thought herself lucky to spot the triple-decked gunship in the fray. She figured there were other first rates out there, both English and otherwise, but the black-and-yellow pattern on her sides was just as she remembered it from her first-year cadet visit to Portsmouth, where *Victory* now resided in dry dock.

Well, it resided there back on Earth, in her time and world. In Weatherby's world, he was in *command* of this ship, and so many others. Her head swam, just as it had back on Mars.

"Are you quite all right, Commander?"

Shaila turned to see Miss Baker—wait, no, Lady Weatherby now—looking at her quizzically and with a bemused smile. The woman had been barely eighteen when they last met, and while Weatherby looked every bit of his nearly 50 years, Anne looked no older than Shaila. *Whatever she uses, I got to get me some of that.*

"I'm fine, thanks. It's all just surreal. And this time, I really don't know what we're supposed to be doing here," Shaila said. She turned to look up at the quarterdeck, where Diaz and Weatherby were chatting off to one side. Stephane and Coogan, meanwhile, were still making their way to *Victory* from several hundred kilometers out. Other ships had been dispatched to get them, since for whatever reason—*Alchemy, most likely,* she remembered—the sailing ships traveled much faster in space than the V-SEVs.

"There is an overlap for a reason," Anne replied. "You've brought us your world's version of the Emerald Tablet, while we have our version of *The Book of the Dead*. The mystical and alchemical properties of these two items together would be…honestly, I cannot think of a superlative for it. But to what end do we use this power? That's the question."

Shaila nodded. "There's someone behind all this. Stephane was infected by the Martian intelligence. You remember Greene? He's still infected. He's the one behind the gear that created this overlap, probably."

"My son also suffered from what you call infection, and my first husband died while fighting it," Anne confirmed. "We have been, I think, more successful in staving off another Martian incursion, but I think the French have been playing into their hands all the while."

Shaila stopped and pointed off into space. "Looks like we found our last two mechs," she said. "That would be Stephane and Coogan."

"I remember your Stephane," Anne said. "Did you and he 'get together,' as you put it?"

Shaila turned a bit red. "Yes, ma'am. Though with everything, it certainly hasn't been easy, has it? And Stephane is how we knew you were aboard."

Anne crooked her head slightly, confused. "How is that?"

"Just after we abandoned ship, he said he knew Dr. Finch was aboard, along with *The Book of the Dead*. Can't say how he knows, but…" Shaila's voice trailed off as a pained look came over her face.

"There is a very interesting link between them, then," Anne said. "Come, I'm sure Andrew and the others will want to welcome Stephane, and this new compatriot of yours, Mr. Coogan."

The new compatriot arrived first, and his V-SEV was lashed to the starboard side of *Victory*, amidships. The ship's captain, some guy named Searle, was pretty concerned about the heavy mechs on his wooden decks, and Shaila could certainly understand the concern.

James Coogan was welcomed aboard by an early 19th century admiral and found himself on an open deck overlooking Venus—which he handled like a fucking pro, unsurprisingly. Shaila assumed he'd already had access to all the holos and data involving the *Daedalus* incident, and he had been there for the Siwa thing too. Kid probably looked up 19th century Royal Navy salutes and protocols, just in case, because he seemed completely unflappable.

The same could not be said for Chrys VanDerKamp, who looked flabbergasted the moment she slid out from behind Coogan's seat.

"Jain," Chrys said, sidling up to her after all the introductions were made. "Have I gone completely batshit crazy?"

"Don't know," she replied with a smile. "It's all real. You're looking at Venus with nothing between you and space except a wooden ship. Crazy's not a bad way to go if you need to."

Chrys nodded. "So what do we do now?"

"Don't know that either. If it'll help, maybe we take out your sats, one by one. Last time this happened, though, back on Mars, the devices adapted. Still…you got sensors?"

The exec shrugged. "I got a datapad and whatever the V-SEV has. Maybe I can gin up something."

Shaila nodded and sent Chrys on her way. First rule of command—keep the troops focused, especially when there's uncertainty. If any of them paused too long to ponder it all, the impossibilities would hit them like a freight train and they'd be left completely overwhelmed.

A few minutes later, the final V-SEV was secured to the other side of the ship, and Stephane clambered on board. To Shaila's relief, he looked a bit less strained and more himself. "That was fun," he said as he kissed her. She was a few seconds into the kiss before she remembered they had been under orders not to engage in, as Diaz had put it, "too much fraternization." But the world didn't seem to be ending…yet. So she rolled with it.

"Had fun in the new toy?" Shaila asked.

"It's easier than the manuals said. Though I did feel bad about wrecking my countrymen's ships," he replied. "Don't tell the general, but I only destroyed their masts and sails."

Shaila smiled, and made a note to tell Weatherby instead, as the admiral would probably really want to know the state of his enemy's fleet. "I knew you were a good guy, eh?"

"I'm trying. Moving and acting seems to help," Stephane said. "And…oh…*mon dieu*…there he is."

Stephane had spied Finch walking across the maindeck with a younger man and made for him, and Finch immediately recognized him. "Dr. Durand! So glad you could join us. Might I introduce…."

Then Finch's eyes widened as Stephane approached. And Stephane began to walk more slowly.

"You've been inside *Maat*," Stephane said, his eyes narrowing. "That's what I sensed…. What did you do?"

Finch peered at Stephane with equal amounts of consternation and concern. "I should ask, Durand, what in God's name have you been up to? I…dear God." Finch immediately reached into his pocket and pulled out a strange set of eyeglasses, with a number of hinged and colored lenses on them. He switched between lenses for several long moments, all the while staring directly at Stephane.

"What is he doing?" Stephane asked.

"Beats me, but if they have the *Book of the Dead* like Anne says they do, maybe you're giving off some kind of vibe he can see," Shaila said.

"Vibe?" Stephane asked, confused. "Like that thing you have?"

Shaila smacked him in the arm as she felt her face flush. "Christ, Stephane. Not here!"

Finch finally lifted the lenses from his face. "I suggest, Philip, that this man be placed under immediate armed watch while aboard," he said with a surprising amount of seriousness. "Whilst he remains in control in large part, there is another entity within him, likely of Mars."

"Yes, there is," Stephane said, a hint of combativeness in his voice. "His name is Rathemas, and I am keeping him down right now."

The young man next to him grew wide-eyed at this and nodded, then turned to one of the red-coated marines stationed on deck. "Marine, keep watch over this man until ordered otherwise. I will inform the admiral."

The marine immediately took up a post behind Stephane's left shoulder, about three feet back—plenty of distance for him to shoot if needed. .

"He's got it under control, Dr. Finch," Shaila said, with maybe a little more emphasis than she intended. That's when she noticed his pale, sweaty look. "How about you? What's that book been doing to you?"

And Finch's arched eyebrow showed he got every bit of subtext there was to have. "I assure you, Miss Jain, that *The Book of the Dead*, whilst a powerful artifact, has not led to possession by an outside intelligence. The connection with *Maat* is draining, but it is not consuming my Will," Finch said, a touch defensively. "And Dr. Durand here is, shall we say, not entirely himself. Or, rather, he's quite more than one self."

Shaila restrained herself from wanting to punch Finch in the face, and was about to say something particularly cutting before being interrupted by a young boy dressed up like an officer. *Right. The mids were pretty young back then*, she reminded herself.

"Commander Jain, is it?" he asked, directing the question toward Stephane.

"I'm Commander Jain," Shaila said pointedly. "This is Dr. Durand."

This seemed to catch the midshipman at quite a loss for several seconds until he remembered why he was there. "Right, then. Uh, Commander…you and Dr. Durand have been asked to report to the great cabin. And Dr. Finch and Lieutenant St. Germain as well."

Stephane looked up at the man next to Finch. "St. Germain? Son of the Count?"

The young man stood a touch taller. "Yes, he was my father, God rest him. I am the second Count St. Germain, and fleet alchemist to Admiral Weatherby, my stepfather."

Stephane and Shaila looked at each other in bewilderment. "I think we're going to need a flowchart here," she said quietly as they followed the two alchemists to *Victory*'s great cabin.

They were met at the door by a meter-tall walking lizard. "This way," it croaked.

Even more stunned, the two wordlessly followed the creature into the cabin, where a long table awaited them. Behind this dining room was another room that looked to be the admiral's office and berth. Everything was mahogany and brass and intricately made. It was just as Shaila remembered it from her cadet visit.

Weatherby and Diaz were at the head of the table, with a massive robed figure to Weatherby's right. "Xan?" Stephane whispered.

"Wow, yeah. Probably. Holy shit," Shaila replied.

The room filled up quickly. Weatherby and the Xan were joined by Finch, Anne, the new Count St. Germain and a young woman who turned out to be Weatherby's daughter, Elizabeth. Coogan and VanDerKamp were ushered in as well, and the little lizard-guy—a native Venusian, it turned out—poured wine.

It was incredibly civilized and utterly surreal. *Let's have wine with the aliens. All right then.*

"I am saddened to report that we have lost ninety-three souls aboard *Victory*, and it looks as though *Kent* and *Enterprise* were completely lost to us," Weatherby began, looking tired and drained. "Reports are still coming in from the rest of our fleet, but the damage has been grave. Thankfully, the French have retreated back to the surface in the face of our new allies from… what was your ship again, General Diaz?"

"*Hadfield*," she replied. "Good little ship. Named for an early explorer and educator."

"Yes, *Hadfield*, then. How many aboard?"

The general grimaced. "Twenty-seven. We lost contact with the last man alive on board an hour ago."

Weatherby reached out and placed a hand on Diaz' shoulder. "'Tis a hard thing to lose good men," he said. "My condolences. When the time comes, we shall include the crew of the *Hadfield* in our memorials." The admiral then took a deep breath. "But until such time as such arrangements can be safely made, these events must be put aside as we determine our true course. Perhaps, General, you and Commander Jain might give us a summary of your course since our last meeting, and how you may have come to be with us again?"

The "summary" took well over an hour, with Diaz and Jain providing a précis of the Enceladus crisis and the Siwa fiasco, which apparently dovetailed to a degree with Weatherby's visit to Saturn about a decade ago, as well as Finch's discovery of *The Book of the Dead* in the very same part of Egypt—just three centuries earlier, give or take.

Shaila also caught a very strong sense that Finch had held out on the *Book* from Weatherby, because he was getting a pretty cold shoulder from the admiral and his family, and his seat was at the very end of the table, leaving him with little to say or do unless called upon. Instead, he seemed content to stare out the window past VanDerKamp, who busied herself on her datapad. *I bet she does that in all her meetings*, Shaila thought. *Rude.*

Meantime, Weatherby was rolling with it far better than he had just three years—or three decades—ago. It was odd and extraordinary to see his evolution from a green lieutenant to an experienced admiral in such a truncated fashion, at least for Shaila. She knew intellectually that his three decades in service to King and Country had taken him through the French Revolution and the Napoleonic Wars, but she had *just* interacted with his younger self three years ago in her timeline.

It was tougher for Shaila—and both Stephane and Diaz, it should be said—to grasp just what had happened to Weatherby's world over the past decade. As any good

Englishwoman, Shaila knew her history well. Napoleon bought time through the Peace of Amiens to build his armies and attack, but he could not cross the English Channel because of the power of the English Royal Navy.

In Weatherby's timeline, however, through the power of ancient Egyptian alchemy, Napoleon didn't need to contest the Royal Navy on the Channel—he could just march his goddamn zombie troops under it. So while the Britannia still ruled the sea, at least on Earth, and Nelson got his big victory and martyrdom at Trafalgar, the French were able to use Venus' timber to build more ships, and they needed to put fewer into play to transport their troops.

No wonder Weatherby looked tired.

"So if I am to understand you, it seems that your Dr. Greene, whom you once trusted, turned on you...twice?" Weatherby asked.

Diaz grimaced slightly. "He went to work for the corporates, yeah, and then got possessed by a Martian. And... well, that sounds pretty crazy, but that's what happened."

Vellusk leaned forward slightly. "We were all deceived by the Martians, General Diaz," he sang. "From what I have heard tell at this table, it seems Althotas has played us all for fools, starting with my ancestors more than five millennia ago."

It was the first time the Xan had spoken during the entire conference, and his melodic voices—he had two, and Shaila found the music enrapturing—were undercut with sorrow and foreboding.

"How so, good Vellusk?" Weatherby asked. "Have we not sent Althotas back into his prison once more? In the place between worlds?"

The Xan's robes rustled as he spoke, and Shaila caught a glimpse of both tentacle and snout from under his hood's shadows. "I fear the Xan had the first role to play here. The presence of an Emerald Tablet from another universe confirms it in my mind."

From the end of the table, Finch gasped. "Oh...I see it. Dear God...."

Weatherby grimaced. "Be so good as to explain, one of you," he said impatiently.

Vellusk's robes rustled again. "Of course, my good friend and brave admiral. Millennia ago, we imprisoned Althotas in a pocket real, a space between universes. But now that I see the Emerald Tablet—something we ourselves destroyed a decade ago on Titan—in the hands of these people, and I cannot help but wonder if our great working those thousands of years past had a hand in our current situation. It is but theory, but I believe that our working actually sundered our universe in two—the worlds of our own experience, Admiral, and the universe known to General Diaz and Commander Jain and their fellows."

Finch picked up the thread excitedly. "But there were objects of alchemical power—the Emerald Tablet and *The Book of the Dead*—that could not so easily be sundered. So they were duplicated instead, in each of the universes," he said. "And perhaps…when Althotas was defeated on Mars, his experience in the combined worlds led to him to better understand the nature of his prison?" Vellusk nodded at Finch, who pressed on. "I believe Althotas likely seeks to combine your Tablet and our *Book*, along with the souls of his kin once imprisoned on Enceladus."

There was a long silence at the table as everyone digested the alien's words. Stephane finally spoke up. "This feels right. I think us coming here is part of the plan. I think he wants the Tablet and the *Book* to do something."

Weatherby stared hard at the Frenchman; Philip and Finch had briefed him before the meeting began. "So then do we not simply destroy both items and be done with it?"

The admiral looked at each face at the table, and most seemed to be on board with the idea to some degree or another—Shaila, for her part, wanted to see them vaporized yesterday, and even Finch was slowly nodding. But Coogan raised his hand after a moment to get their attention. "If I may, Admiral? General?"

Both Diaz and Weatherby nodded, and Coogan rose to place his datapad in the center of the table. Shaila smiled;

the 19th century was about to get its first look at holotechnology. A moment later, an image of Venus a meter wide was hovering in the air over the pad, and there were more than a few gasps around the room.

"I had been backing up Dr. Ayim's work periodically, under General Diaz' orders, and managed to do a final grab of his sensor programming before we left *Hadfield*," Coogan said. "The thing is, there is no real connection between the *Book* and the Tablet and the satellites that likely caused the dimensional overlap we're experiencing right now. So if we destroy these two items, it's quite possible they would have no effect on whatever's going on."

"Then we go after the sats," Chrys said dully. "Blow them up with cannonballs or something."

Coogan shrugged. "We could, but the thing is, the Cherenkov energy signatures aren't 100 percent right when it comes to that, either. Yeah, the satellites are focusing the power, but just like General Diaz and Commander Jain saw on Mars, there's more energy here than can be accounted for. Destroying the satellites doesn't take out all the power, and may have unexpected consequences. Maybe the overlap spreads uncontrollably, or collapses around us."

"But we're in the overlap now. So there's already two dimensions. Shouldn't we be able to trace the energy coming from the second dimension and close it up?" Shaila asked.

"Ideally, but we can't," Coogan said. "Ambassador Vellusk noted that Althotas is trapped 'between universes,' or in some sort of pocket dimension. That means there's a third possible locale, and that may be the source of the energy."

Weatherby looked at Anne and Finch in turn, and both nodded back at him. "I dare say he may be right," Anne said. "We did, after all, give him a source of power on Mars by throwing the alchemical essences of the Known Worlds into the vortex with him as he was defeated."

Shaila and Weatherby both bristled at this. "It seemed the best option at the time," the admiral said curtly.

"I'd do it again," Shaila confirmed.

"And it worked!" Finch hastened to add. "But it also allowed him different pathways in which he might work his will. So he used the alchemical energies he gained to affect Enceladus and the temple in Egypt. He may have directed us—all of us—to these treasures. So yes, he has a plan for the tablet and book. Perhaps he needs to destroy them to fulfill his ends. Perhaps we can use them against him. But again, I cannot say."

"Greene knows," Diaz said simply. "And so does Cagliostro and this Berthollet guy. We find them, we find out what they're doing, and we find a workaround to stop them." She turned to Coogan and Chrys. "Where are we on sensors?"

The exec straightened up in her chair and seemed a little gratified to be asked something. "We can only boost the V-SEV sensor array so much before we start burning it out. We're only good to about ten kilometers. That's it."

"I can't believe you've adopted that damned French measurement," Weatherby groused quietly. "What is that…six miles?"

"Yes, sir," Chrys said.

"So your electronic eyes, then, are only a little better than our lookouts this time," the admiral said. "Elizabeth here has identified a potential site for the Venusian memory vault we discussed. At the least, your 'sensors' may very well detect occult energies from it before we even reach it, which would at least help us know we were in the right place. I would not be surprised in the slightest if your Greene and his cohort had somehow found the French as well."

Weatherby looked to Diaz, who nodded. "I agree, Admiral Weatherby. Looks like we need to go planetside and search up close. Jain, get the V-SEVs up and running, and check with *Victory*'s first lieutenant to see where he wants them when we…well, how does this ship get down to the surface, anyway?"

Finch smiled. "Oh, you're going to love it."

CHAPTER 19

January 29, 2135
May 28, 1809

Shaila and Stephane—accompanied by their ever-present Royal Marine guard—stood upon the quarterdeck of HMS *Victory* as she began her descent into the green-orange clouds of Venus. On either side of the ship, the rest of Weatherby's fleet began to ready for "keel-fall" by tucking in the sails on their rudders and unfurling their plane sales parallel to the deck. The sails on all the ships were also drawn upward at an angle to further provide drag.

A moment later, *Victory* disappeared into the clouds, and all they could see was a lime green mist around them.

"Venus' clouds are supposed to be made of sulfuric acid," Stephane said quietly. "The winds here should be roaring at 360 kilometers an hour. And the atmosphere pressure…" He took a sniff of the air. "It simply smells humid and green, like a swamp."

The ship suddenly lurched under them, buffeted by a series of sharp gusts. "Well, the winds are still impressive," Shaila said. "Happy the acid's not here."

She was also happy for the lines that secured her to the ship's mizzenmast, helpfully provided by the little lizard guy—Weatherby's valet, a Venusian named Gar'uk. Officers in the Royal Navy enjoyed some serious comforts three hundred years ago, unlike the modern Navy. Shaila wondered, as she saw the admiral calmly sipping tea with Diaz and Vellusk nearby, what this older Weatherby thought of his station and his crew. She remembered the young lieutenant of a few years ago caring for the handful of men he commanded. How do you extend that to a fleet of ships with three thousand men aboard?

Suddenly, Elizabeth Weatherby lurched toward them, caught off-guard by the pitching, rolling deck. "So sorry," she said after nearly colliding with Shaila. "I cannot say how Father abides this every time he visits a new world!"

Shaila helped the young woman to the railing. She looked pale and wild-eyed and kept glancing over to her father, who stood tall on the quarterdeck, resplendent in his spotless uniform. "Your first time?" Shaila asked.

Elizabeth nodded. "Is this the first world you've visited as well, Miss Jain?"

"No, I've hit up a few," Shaila smiled. "Jupiter, Mars, Saturn. Now Venus. Though we don't exactly use wooden ships to do it."

"And you are an officer in His Majesty's Navy?"

"*Her* Majesty's Navy," Shaila corrected. "We got a new queen a few months ago. And yeah, I'm a lieutenant commander. Roughly equivalent to being a first lieutenant on a good-sized frigate."

Elizabeth gazed at her in wonderment. "I should very much like to be of your time, Lieutenant Commander. It took all of Father's contacts and Lady Anne's persuasiveness for me to be accepted at Oxford—which lasted only until the French took the town."

"I think your father would miss you if we took you back with us," Stephane said with a gentle smile. "That is, of course, if we make it back ourselves...."

Shaila glared at him. "Jesus, Stephane. It'll be fine. It worked out before."

He simply stared off to starboard, into the swirling green clouds.

Then suddenly, the clouds disappeared, and all of Venus was spread below them. And even though she had seen snow on Enceladus and the great hydrocarbon lakes on Titan, it still took Shaila's breath away.

Below, a lush green land stretched before them. It was almost completely forested, even the very tops of the mountains off to their west. There were rivers and lakes, and a vast ocean off to the east, the waters of which were an unusual brighter shade of green. Above, the disc of the sun—easily a third larger than could be seen from Earth—was swathed in rich orange-lime clouds, the light diffused across the horizon.

"Captain Searle!" Weatherby shouted over the winds that still swept across and under the ship. "Signal the fleet! We shall cross over land and make keel-fall in the bay below! Any lookouts there will think we would come by sea, so we must endeavor to disappoint them!"

Shaila watched as Searle relayed the orders—hugely formal, so inefficient!—and the junior officers rushed to implement them. A young lieutenant and a midshipman were huddled over a signal-flag book, piecing together the appropriate order to the other ships, while Searle's first lieutenant got *Victory* heading in the right direction. Soon, the massive warship had arced in the sky and now had nothing but green jungle under its keel as it continued its somewhat-controlled descent from space.

"You know, seeing ground below the keel is more fucked up than seeing Venus from space," Shaila said nervously, causing Elizabeth's eyes to widen. "Sorry for the language," she added.

"Not at all," the young woman said with a bright smile. "I should say, I do not give a…a *damn* how you speak. A woman's speech should be as…*hell* free as a man's!"

Shaila burst out laughing. "I couldn't agree more, but you need practice, Miss Weatherby. And I really suggest you stay out of earshot of your parents, just in case. Don't want them thinking I'm a bad influence."

Stephane actually brightened somewhat at this. "She is, though. In a great way."

Any further conversation was interrupted by a flurry of shouts and running crewmen. There were indeed ships in the bay where they hoped to land.

"How many? Do we have a flag?" Searle shouted.

"Aye, sir! French!" came the word from the lookouts. "A third-rate, a frigates and two brigs!"

Searle turned to Weatherby, who nodded. "Prepare to engage. Focus on the brigs and frigate," the admiral ordered. "We do not want the French to learn of our location quite yet."

"Aye, my Lord Admiral," Searle said, then turned to his first lieutenant. "Beat to quarters! Run out the guns!"

Shaila felt the deck below her vibrate as *Victory*'s crew opened a hundred gunports, and ran out a hundred cannon. All were loaded and ready to fire. It was funny to think that she could unleash nearly as much raw firepower from a 22nd century fighter/bomber with the flick of a switch, but she was nonetheless impressed at the efficiency of eight hundred men, acting in concert.

"Let us try to make keel-fall in front of that brig," Weatherby said, pointing to the ship furthest out. "We can contain her or destroy her as needed and bottle up the rest of the bay."

"Anything you want us to do, Admiral Weatherby?" Diaz asked, handing off her delicate teacup to Gar'uk.

Weatherby and Searle traded looks. "Can your vehicles be dropped upon land?"

Diaz waved Shaila over to join the conversation. "How high up can we survive a drop?" she asked.

Shaila took out her datapad and linked it to the operating systems of the four V-SEVs. "We have enough thrusters to go from 100 meters, ma'am. Any more we'd have to deploy the airbags."

Searle bent over the map table on the quarterdeck and quickly penciled out some equations; Shaila noticed he was faster than she would've been. "They'll make the beach, but barely."

Diaz nodded. "Good enough. Jain, get everyone suited up. We'll secure the beach. All right with you, Admiral?"

"It is indeed, General Diaz," Weatherby said. "Godspeed to you."

Shaila and Stephane followed Diaz to the maindeck, where Chrys and Coogan were already working on their V-SEV. Everyone clambered aboard their mechs, which had been brought onto the deck and laid out horizontally during the descent to better distribute the weight. It made for awkward going, and added a new wrinkle to their plans—especially as they continued to barrel forward toward the bay.

"Um…Shay, how do I get this thing standing up?" Stephane asked over the comm.

Shaila thought about it for a moment as she powered her systems up. "Just wait there. I'll give you a hand. Once you're up, get right up close to the side and get ready to hit thrusters. We gotta roll in….90 seconds."

There was silence after that as the group from *Hadfield* prepared their V-SEVs. All systems were functioning normally, and Shaila was sure to seal herself in as if she were going onto the surface of *her* Venus. If they missed the beach and landed in the bay, she was sure the seawater would play havoc with the mech's systems if it got in. She then panicked a moment about the mechs being waterproof, but quickly dismissed it out of hand, remembering that they were designed to be completely airtight and to resist atmospheric pressures comparable to the lowest depths of Earth's oceans.

Shaila tucked her mech's legs under it, then used its arms to push it into a kind of squatting position. She felt the machinery tremble a bit as she got it into a standing position—it wasn't used to being deployed in such a way. Once upright, she turned to Stephane's mech and reached for its outstretched claw, pulling it up far more easily. To her left, she saw Coogan giving Diaz a similar helping hand. A moment later, all four mechs were at *Victory*'s maindeck railings, two to a side.

"Coming up on target. Ready to jump off on my mark, then hit your thrusters to get clear of the ship," Shaila said. "Three, two, one….MARK."

A second later, she was falling straight down, and numerous alarms and warning messages popped up on the heads-up display before her. "Yes, I know this is sub-optimal deployment," she groused quietly as she got her mech upright and fired thrusters.

A burst of noise from the comms startled her. "I have negative thrusters! Repeat, negative thrusters!" Coogan shouted.

"Deploy airbags!" Diaz ordered.

From her hatch window, Shaila could see Coogan's mech tumbling toward Venus out of control—and much further out than the rest of them.

"Unresponsive! We hit the side of—"

Shaila saw a splash about 50 meters out to sea, and a moment later, HMS *Victory* splashed down further out, creating a massive spray and wake that obscured everything else. Then her HUD interrupted her view with the tracking information she needed to touch down safely. Shaking her head, she quickly reversed her thrusters in order to make a safe landing on the sandy Venusian beach.

"Jain to Coogan. Come in, Coogan," she said.

There was no response.

"Scanning now," Stephane said; Shaila could see on her display that both he and Diaz landed safely, about 10 meters from one another on the beach. "The V-SEV is about twenty meters under the water. No movement, no life signs."

"Can the sensors penetrate inside the V-SEVs, Jain?" Diaz asked.

"No idea, ma'am. I—wait. We have three bogeys on the beach, running toward the tree line to the south." Shaila turned and zoomed in on them. "Blue uniforms, officer with a red collar. Presumed French."

"Get after them, Jain," Diaz ordered. "I'll go after Coogan and VanDerKamp. Stephane, guard this goddamn beach."

Shaila grasped the controls inside her cockpit and urged the V-SEV forward, its broad metal feet gaining surprisingly good traction in the sand as it headed down the beach toward the trees. In fact, the vehicle was handling better than Shaila remembered from her simulator training. The damn thing weighed tons; it should not feel spring-loaded.

Then she remembered: She wasn't on *her* Venus. The simulator had simulated the dense atmospheric pressure of the Venus she knew, which had made her feel like she was piloting through gravy. Yet on *this* Venus, there was a mere fraction of the pressure.

And it made piloting the V-SEV seem like driving a performance sports car. Within moments, she managed to get the mech up to a decent jog, crashing through the verdant undergrowth near the treeline with abandon.

Thankfully, a jogging V-SEV with a 2.5-meter gait matched up well against running humans. She started wondering how to subdue the French without much injury, given that they had abandoned *Hadfield* without taking any nonlethal microwave weapons with them. And the V-SEVs weren't subtle, no matter the atmospheric pressure.

Then one of the dots on her tracking grid vanished. And others appeared, with the word UNKNOWN FAUNA next to them.

She looked up to see one of the Frenchmen on the ground about ten meters in front of her with a spear sticking out of his chest. His hands clutched the shaft, even as Shaila watched his vitals slow, then cease.

The dots representing her other two targets winked out a few moments later, while the UNKNOWN FAUNA bogeys faded out of sensor range just as quickly as they entered it.

Having met Gar'uk a few hours ago, Shaila had a pretty good idea of what just happened.

"Jain to Diaz. French targets neutralized by third party. Over."

There was a fairly long lag before Diaz responded. "Roger that. Come on back. You see 'em?"

"Negative, ma'am," Shaila said as she piloted her V-SEV around and headed back to the beach. "I can report that one target was eliminated with a primitive spear."

"Understood," Diaz said. "You think they're on our side?"

"Doubt it, ma'am. We have no comms with them. The French may have simply entered a well-defended territory," Shaila said. "How are Coogan and VanDerKamp?"

"Alive. Get back here."

Shaila put her V-SEV back into a jog, and arrived at the beach to find the British RAF officer and the corporate exec on the beach, unconscious and soaked. Diaz was just opening her hatch and scrambling out, while Stephane still remained aboard his mech, his window aimed at the forest.

"General?" Shaila asked as she opened her hatch.

"Their mech shorted out," Diaz said. "I think they hit a few cannon on their way off *Victory*, sprung a leak somewhere. They were filling up with water when I got there. Had to rip open the hatch, grab them fast and hit thrusters to get them up and out."

Shaila hurried over, her V-SEV's first aid kit in hand. "Electrical too?"

"Yeah, they got zapped *and* drowned," Diaz muttered, grabbing the kit to supplement her own. "Alive, but barely. I'm hoping our resident alchemists can whip up a magic potion or something. Help me get them stabilized and chilled."

The two officers worked fast to put their colleagues in a short-term stasis. They injected them with medications designed to slow bodily functions considerably, and then began wrapping them in a thin, chemical-laced foil. Once completely wrapped—except for a small breathing tube—a small electric charge would interact with the chemicals in the foil, cooling them down to just a few degrees above zero and stemming the worst of whatever injuries they had.

As they worked, the booms of the battle in the bay echoed across the beach. Shaila could see that one of the brigs nearest *Victory* already flew a white flag, while the second was in flames. Another English ship—she thought it might be HMS *Thunderer*—was engaged with the French 74 and seemed to have an edge, aided by *Surprise* and another English ship.

By the time Shaila and Diaz had the two fully stabilized, the battle at sea was over. A brig and the 74 had struck their colors; the rest of the French ships were ablaze. There were also flames aboard two of Weatherby's ships, and even *Victory* was looking a little worse for wear. Meanwhile, a few hardy survivors started coming ashore, drenched and exhausted, and Diaz directed them to different parts of the beach—French toward the center, farthest away from the tree line, and English survivors to a point a good 50 meters away.

"Durand, get down here and speak French to these guys," Diaz ordered. "Shaila, saddle up and use the sensors to keep watch."

Shaila and Stephane passed each other on the beach, and she noted he looked drawn again. "You all right?"

He shrugged. "I get the sense that Rathemas is…happy? Somehow…yes, he's happy. He's fighting me less and he's happy to be here. That seems bad to me."

Shaila put a hand on his shoulder. "Me too. We need to tell Weatherby and the alchemists when they get here. Meantime, go help Diaz translate."

Stephane nodded and, a few seconds later, was yelling orders at the French survivors, who looked more and more confused. Shaila couldn't blame them, of course—two women ordering them around on a beach, backed up by metal giants, then some guy gets out and barks at you in your own language. All that after you had your ship shot up from under you? Even in this dimension, that was a weird day.

Shaila climbed up into her V-SEV and brought it online again. She felt very discomfited by Stephane's revelation, much more so than she let on. The whole situation seemed a bit too pat, that they would come together, each bringing with them one of the two sacred alchemical objects needed to do…well, whatever they'd do. Probably not great. She wondered if Greene and Huntington would be in contact with the French—Cagliostro again, or this Berthollet guy—and whether the French were once again in contact with Althotas. She wondered what the data was that Greene and Huntington brought with them, and just what they planned to do with it. After all, they were already in overlapping dimensions. What more could they…?

A beep from Shaila's sensor grabbed her attention, and she called up the terrain grid on her display. One of the

UNKNOWN FAUNA contacts was back, at the very edge of her sensor range, deep within the jungle.

"Jain to Diaz, I have sensor contact with an unknown bogey, possibly one of the Venusians. Over."

"How far out?" Diaz asked.

"About two klicks and closing. Sensors aren't picking them up further out. Wonder why."

Stephane chimed in. "If they are Venus people, they would be cold-blooded, yes? Lizards. They would mix well with the background. And they are small."

"Good thinking. Roger that," Shaila said. "At least we have…crap. We have a half-dozen now. Coming at us in a couple groups, to the north and south."

"Keep me posted. Do not engage unless you see them on the beach," Diaz ordered.

The number of contacts grew regularly and substantially in the time it took for HMS *Victory* to launch a number of boats toward the crescent-shaped beach. In the meantime, there were about fifty exhausted Frenchmen on the beach now, along with twenty English survivors, many of whom Diaz pressed into service as guards, even though they weren't in any better shape than the French.

"I think the Admiral and his family are in the landing party," Stephane said. "I can tell Finch is with them as well. We should've given them a comm."

"Yeah, well, we've never been on Venus before," Shaila groused. She had powered up the V-SEV's laser drill which, while a huge drain on the vehicle's power reserves, would probably cut through dozens of hostiles at a time. Hopefully, they wouldn't be hostile.

"Stephane, grab any spare headsets from our V-SEVs," Diaz ordered. "Let's not make the same mistake twice."

"We may not get a chance," Shaila replied. "I now count three hundred bogeys, about five meters from the tree line.

"We're surrounded."

CHAPTER 20

January 29, 2135
May 28, 1809

Weatherby had come ashore quite willing and ready to vent his fury upon his guests from the future, for it was that one of their metal vehicles—metal ogres, more in fact—had upon exiting off the sides of the ship severely damaged eight gun placements upon *Victory*'s larboard side and, more importantly, injured some thirty-two men, two of whom were upon death's door.

Then he saw two of General Diaz' people, mummified in queer metal wraps, and came to quickly understand that the targets of his wrath were themselves among the most unfortunate.

And there were, perhaps, more misfortunes.

"We are surrounded, you say?" Weatherby asked Diaz. "Could you not have signaled before....ah. Of course. You've not any flags."

Diaz handed over one of the strange headpieces Weatherby had worn those many years ago on Mars. "Sorry. No flags. And we didn't think to give you one of these before we jumped ship. I have two others. Who gets them?"

Weatherby looked over his landing party, which consisted of Anne and their two children, along with Finch, Gar'uk and several Royal Marines. Philip might have been a better option, but he was quite busy treating Diaz' fallen comrades and the English injured on the beach. "Sadly, I fear we must give one to our Dr. Finch, simply based on prior experience. And given that we are likely well outnumbered by Venusians...."

Elizabeth stepped forward to interrupt her father. "I will take the other device," she said. "It is for communication, is it not?"

Weatherby turned toward her with a smile but also exasperation. "My dear girl, it is not as though you may use these to communicate with the Venusians." He then paused and turned toward Diaz. "That is correct, yes?"

"Right, but if your girl here is the expert she says she is, having her keyed in to Shaila on the sensors might not be a bad idea," Diaz said, handing the headset to Elizabeth. "We'll be able to tell you what we're seeing and whether what we do from here on out has any impact, one way or the other."

Weatherby looked over to Anne, who nodded with a small smile, while Elizabeth simply took the headset and placed it upon her head, doing her best to emulate her father's actions in doing so. "So now what do I do?" she asked.

"I hear you, Elizabeth," Shaila said. "I'm in one of our vehicles, the one facing the jungle. Our sensors are showing at least 300 creatures out there right now—mostly small, but a few really big ones as well."

Elizabeth nodded. "Yes, those would be the *sek'hatk* mounts. Large saurians used as steeds by some of the Venusian chieftains. How many 'big ones' do you see?"

"Screening now…we have six large targets."

Elizabeth relayed this information to her parents. "My guess is that we have representatives from at least three different social groupings, possibly as many as six, perhaps even more, depending on whether the French have left them alone or actively mistreated them," she said. "Even the honored Va'hak'ri are reported to have but three *sek'hatk* among their warriors."

Anne nodded. "In our years here on Venus, we never saw more than two of these in one place. They are only for the greatest of the tribes. And given that these Venusians before us are working in concert, and not at each other's throats…"

Weatherby finished her thought. "Yes, they likely have had a run-in with the French already, for that would certainly unite them. And they would wish to determine whether we represent another threat. Do they recognize the differences in uniforms by now, do you think?"

"If the Va'hak'ri are among them, then yes, they will have a lore-master who would likely have enough experience to tell English from French," Elizabeth replied. "It's been reported that the red coats of His Majesty's soldiers are known to a number of tribes, so we may wish to bring more Marines ashore at our earliest opportunity."

"It seems we were right to bring you along," Weatherby said to his daughter. "Might you suggest a course of action, Miss Weatherby?"

At this Elizabeth smiled, then traded whispers with her stepmother for several moments. Weatherby knew Anne had lived on Venus for a number of years, and interacted with the Venusians—yet her focus, and that of her first husband, was on alchemy, not the culture of the lizard-creatures. Still, Anne was the most knowledgeable alchemist among them, save for Finch, and had Elizabeth's trust besides.

"I think we have a plan," Elizabeth said finally. "There is an introductory ritual that, while somewhat difficult, is one of utmost respect and friendship. It is called the *dul'kat*, and…"

Gar'uk suddenly let out a shrill bark unlike anything Weatherby had ever heard. "You cannot do *dul'kat*!" he said. "You will be hurt!"

Weatherby turned quickly back to his daughter. "I will not allow you to be harmed by them, Elizabeth."

"No, Father, they will not hurt me," she said, a slight quaver in her voice. "You see, the *dul'kat* is a greeting of immense supplication, and it is the height of rudeness to interrupt once it has begun. What I think Gar'uk takes issue with is that the supplicant must bleed onto the ground while making the introduction."

Weatherby looked stunned. "And so you will….cut yourself?"

Anne placed her hand on Weatherby's arm. "I will be right there with her. As soon as we are welcomed, I will stanch the bleeding and give her an elixir to build up her blood quickly."

"Just how much blood loss are we talking here?" Diaz asked.

Elizabeth straightened up and put on a brave face indeed. "I must open an artery and let it flow until either I am welcomed or I pass out."

"It is a test, as with many Venusian traditions. She must be seen as worthy of sacrificing herself for her purpose," Anne added. "I promise she will not endure lasting harm. And I would add that a human, even a woman of her young years, contains a substantially higher amount of blood than even the largest, most powerful Venusian warrior."

"I will do it," Gar'uk said. "I will give the *dul'kat*. Elizabeth will not need to."

At this, Elizabeth and Gar'uk entered into what appeared to be a most spirited discussion in Venusian, with Anne chiming in now and again. After several minutes, Weatherby waved Finch over to him. "Pray tell what my wife and daughter are saying to my valet," he said quietly and with no small amount of frustration.

"Well, my Venusian is not as good as Elizabeth's, that much is certain, but my understanding is that the primary supplicant must be of a chieftain's bloodline—and you would qualify as that chieftain, of course," Finch said. "Gar'uk, as it happens, is also of a chieftain's bloodline, but as he's not actually acting on behalf of *his* chieftain, there is some question as to whether Gar'uk would be an acceptable substitute."

"What do you think of it all?" Weatherby asked.

"Are you trusting me now?"

Weatherby glared at him. "This is my daughter, talking of spilling her own blood on this forsaken beach for our cause. So answer the dammed question, Doctor."

Finch's face reddened as he cast his eyes downward. "I am sorry, Tom. I'm no expert, but it seems Elizabeth has the better chance."

Weatherby nodded. "And I cannot go in her stead? I'm the chieftain, after all."

"The Venusians are very precise when it comes to language. If you erred but once, you would be shot through the heart with an arrow before you realized your mistake."

"Can you give her something for the pain of it?" Weatherby asked, a father's plea in his voice.

"Of course, Tom," Finch said gently. "I can accompany her and Anne if you like."

Weatherby's hard stare softened. "I appreciate that, perhaps more than you know. But I am her father, and as brilliant a woman as she is now, she is my little girl, Andrew. I will be at her side, along with Anne."

Finch nodded, and Weatherby intervened in the growing argument. "Enough! Elizabeth….report to Dr. Finch so that he and Lady Anne may prepare you for this ordeal. Gar'uk, you will work with Elizabeth in the next few minutes to ensure her pronunciation of this ritual is *exactly* what is required. Lieutenant Commander Jain, if you can hear me, do you have an update on the numbers of Venusians before us?"

Shaila's voice crackled into Weatherby's ear. "Pushing four hundred now. At least seven large contacts as well. Lizard-horses, I guess."

"Very well. Please stay in contact once our introduction begins. If there is any hostile movement, I would like to hear of it quickly."

"Understood, Admiral," Shaila said. "I won't let them get near her. In fact, if General Diaz approves, I can walk up right behind you in this rig. Should be nice and intimidating."

Weatherby conferred with Diaz—and Elizabeth, as it was her life at stake—and it was agreed that there could be no harm in allowing Shaila to accompany them in her bipedal vehicle. So several minutes later, a most unusual group walked up the beach toward the tree line. In the middle was Elizabeth, a small dirk in her left hand. Weatherby held her right hand—a bit too tightly, she had to warn him at one point—and Anne was at her left, a bandage and curatives at the ready. Gar'uk insisted on accompanying them and, if necessary, performing the ritual himself if needed.

And Shaila tromped along slowly, about ten feet back, in her vehicle. "I see a group of two dozen targets breaking off from the main group and heading for the tree line," she reported. "Six of the larger targets are with them."

"Are they advancing as if to attack?" Weatherby asked, still quite unused to speaking to a disembodied voice in his ear.

"No, sir. Moving slowly. Just like we are."

"Very good. Please continue to update me, if you please, Miss Jain."

"Understood, Admiral. And you're a brave young lady, Miss Weatherby."

"I thank you, Commander Jain. And I am most pleased you are here," Elizabeth said, her voice somewhat unsteady. "I believe this patch of sand here, nearest the trees, will be an appropriate place. That stone there, Gar'uk—is it what I think it is?"

The little Venusian croaked in agreement. "It is a marker. This is where Va'hak'ri land begins. Good place for *dul'kat*."

Elizabeth nodded and placed a hand on the marker for a moment. She then knelt upon the sand of the beach and began to speak loudly in Venusian, a language well known for its clicks and guttural sounds, ones that do not come easily to mankind's physical makeup. And yet she continued on for several minutes, with Gar'uk nodding at several points.

"The welcome committee is about five meters off. Standing still and listening," Shaila reported. "So far, so good."

"Thank you, Commander," Weatherby whispered before turning to his wife. "When does she…?"

Anne took his hand in hers. "Soon, my love. She is so very brave—truly her father's daughter," she said with a sad smile.

Before Weatherby could comment further, Elizabeth cried out in a series of groans and barks, then held the blade to her wrist. She hesitated a moment—and who would not?—then drew it down and across her wrist. Weatherby gasped and made to rush forward, but was held firmly, and with surprising strength, by his wife. "Let her be," Anne whispered.

And so Elizabeth watched a moment, her face wide-eyed and pale, as her blood, her very life, began to ooze forth from the wound upon her wrist. Then she began her chanting anew, her voice still strong amongst the rustling trees and lapping waves of the beach.

"How long?" Weatherby asked. He caught his hand trembling and clenched it into a fist.

"Until they are satisfied," Anne replied gently.

"Please help her as soon as we are able," he pleaded.

"Of course, my love. But we must wait now. This is truly the test for her—dedication to her cause, respect for the tribes."

Weatherby watched as the small crimson stain on the beach next to Elizabeth's left hand grew wider, and could not help but wonder just how much sacrifice would satisfy the Venusians. He had great respect for their peoples and cultures, as all civilized men would, but the father in him wished nothing more than to rescue his daughter, savage bloodletting rituals be damned to Hell as they properly should.

More minutes went by, and Elizabeth's voice started to weaken somewhat, her body swaying slightly. It took all of Weatherby's three decades of naval discipline not to rush forward to put a stop to the madness of it all, to take his daughter in his arms and forget all that hung in the balance. He simply gripped Anne's hand tighter...and waited.

Elizabeth finally swayed forward, placing her uninjured hand upon the sand to balance herself. At this, even Anne tensed, and Weatherby finally took two steps forward. But he was stopped by Shaila's voice in his ear. "I got three targets advancing to the tree line now, all riders."

Anne and Weatherby rushed forward just as the Venusians emerged from the jungle onto the beach. They were large for their kind, nearly approaching four feet in height.

They had the beaks and neck-frills common to the lizard-kind, as well as bulbous green eyes with vertical black slits in them. Each wore elaborate necklaces of shell and feathers, with similar headgear, and all wore wood-and-hide armor. They carried shields of similar make, adorned with painted markings of an unintelligible nature, and bore wicked-looking spears.

Their steeds were short-legged lizards roughly the size of ponies. The *sek'hatk* had heads that seemed almost snake-like except for the rows of ridges atop their brows stretching down their elongated necks. They had similarly long tails and very stout bodies. They too were adorned with shell-and-feather decoration, and were controlled with bridles upon their broad snouts.

The leader of the group barked several words in Venusian, at which Elizabeth stopped her chanting and looked back to her father with a nod. Weatherby and Anne rushed forward, the latter immediately giving Elizabeth an elixir and binding her wound with deft efficiency.

Then the Venusian spoke. "We know of you, English chief. You are Weatherby."

Surprised, Weatherby nonetheless bowed. "I am he, and I am at your service…my fellow chief."

"The blood of your kin honors us. We know of you in the Va'hak'ri tribe from the time many suns past. Your name carries good words with it."

"And all who know of the Va'hak'ri know you to be worthy of great honor," Weatherby replied, secretly stealing a glance over at his daughter and wife. Anne nodded with a small smile—Elizabeth would recover.

"What is it you wish of us?" the Venusian demanded.

"I seek an audience with your leaders. We believe the French have come to uncover your memory vaults, and do so for dread purpose," the admiral said.

At this, the Venusian leader took to chattering with the two others who flanked him, and soon a flurry of croaks and gestures began to volley among them—some of which,

Weatherby felt, did not include the sort of warmth and fellowship he had hoped for.

"Our medicine tells us there are two among you who have touched upon evil," the chieftain finally replied. "It is only your ritual that has kept us from attacking."

Durand and Finch. "They are as much victims of plot and plan as your people," Weatherby replied. "We are part of some larger scheme. We must, your people and mine, divine the truth of it."

There were several more croaks and grunts between the Venusians, then the leader let out a shrill cry. He then stared forward at Weatherby with what could only be described as a glare of anger.

And Shaila's voice entered Weatherby's ear once more. "Admiral, all targets now advancing to the tree line. Repeat, I have at least four hundred targets making for you—fast."

Weatherby returned the chieftain's gaze. "I swear upon my life, we have come in peace!"

The chieftain nodded. "And that is what the French say to us. You will now come with us. If you attack us, we will kill you."

Suddenly, hundreds of lizard-men emerged from the underbrush, spears at the ready. There were cries from the beach behind Weatherby as both the French and English survivors began moving as far away from the advancing warriors as possible.

"Admiral, whatever you're doing isn't working," Diaz said over the communications link. "Jain, status."

"Lasers at 100 percent, targets acquired," Shaila replied. "Give the word."

"No!" Weatherby cried out, reflexively placing a hand over his earpiece. "Do not attack!"

The Venusian straightened up on his mount. "You will come with us?"

Weatherby nodded, unbuckling his sword from his side and placing it upon the sand of the beach. "We will. You may take us to your people."

As the Venusian warriors swept across the beach, Weatherby spoke into his headset once more. "General, please inform my men to stand down. And I suggest you do the same. I fear we must become captives here in order to have any chance of winning the Venusians as allies."

There was silence for a long moment before Diaz responded. "All right. Helluva gambit, though. Due respect, Admiral, but I don't like this."

"Quite all right, General. Neither do I."

CHAPTER 21

S haila guided her V-SEV carefully through the jungles of Venus, hoping that she wouldn't step on one of the little alien lizard people underfoot and grateful she had been able to stay in her mech in the first place. Having not really seen her inside it, they may have simply assumed that she and her mech were one and the same—just a large, clunky metal creature.

Diaz and Stephane hadn't been so lucky. Shortly after Weatherby surrendered to them, the Venusians surged onto the beach, taking everyone captive at spear-point. Stephane and the general had tried to climb back aboard their V-SEVs, but the little lizards weren't having it. At least the battle survivors were allowed to remain, along with an alchemist's mate and a junior officer. Shaila hoped Coogan and Chrys would be OK, and that the first-aid deep freeze was something the surgeon-alchemists on board *Victory* knew how to manage. If nothing else, Vellusk had remained aboard ship, and the Xan were far more advanced than the English. He could probably figure it out.

"Strange-ass flora here," Diaz commented over the comm. "Something tried to wrap around my leg just now. Gross."

Elizabeth, now feeling better under her stepmother's care, chimed in. "There are some who say the plant life on Venus are actually multiple manifestations of a single being, that the planet itself is largely alive. The activity you've seen may support that theory."

Shaila's sensors were lit up with all the plant life around her. There were thousands of different potential classifications, and a few that stumped the onboard computers.

Dutifully, Shaila logged all the unknowns in memory, and further backed-up all her holo and sensor logs too.

To her surprise, that data wasn't just backed up. It was *uploaded* somewhere.

"Jain to Diaz, routine memory backup just uploaded itself to unknown client. Over."

"Come again?"

"Ma'am, I went to back up my V-SEV's logs and vids, and not only did it save local, but it uploaded somewhere else. You think it's *Hadfield*?"

"Doubt it," Diaz responded. "I saw her get pretty beaten up in the battle. There's been no word from Baines. But… aw, shit, Jain. We still got Stanford up there!"

Shaila could've face-palmed herself if her hands weren't busy at the controls. In the complete chaos of the overlap, the loss of the *Hadfield* and the battles with the French, they had forgotten about the academic outpost in orbit around Venus. She did a quick check of her comms. "That's a negative on Stanford, ma'am. Long-range, we're keyed to *Hadfield*. Looks like the data flow is going to a short-range target."

And then it hit her: "Ma'am, we may be transmitting to Greene."

Diaz took several seconds to respond. "Get our shit encrypted ASAP, Jain, and then see if you can triangulate the location of the upload destination. Then while we're walking here, figure out how to get long-range comms keyed up to Stanford. Maybe they can help us."

"Could use a co-pilot, ma'am," Shaila said as she tried to begin the encryption process while still keeping her V-SEV moving. "Lots to do."

"Yeah, well, I got a half-dozen Gila monsters around me with spears, and they have twice that with Stephane. Do your best."

The encryption was the easy part, in fact. Within a few minutes, the data transfer stopped. Shaila then tried to tri-angulate on the source, based on the V-SEV's movements, but only managed to center in on an area 25 kilometers north, and some 50 kilometers wide. In that jungle, it was worse than a needle in a haystack.

Putting that aside for the moment, Shaila then started to reprogram her mech's long-range transmitter, opening it up beyond the official-use frequencies employed by governments and congloms. It nearly burned out the module, but Shaila soon picked up a signal she was able to lock onto.

"….Hadfield…this is Stanford Uni….post. To any…of the wreck….come in…."

"Stanford Outpost, this is Lieutenant Commander Shaila Jain on the surface of Venus. Transmitting on multiple frequencies. Please come in, over."

The computers aboard both the outpost and her mech adjusted far more quickly than their human operators could; a moment later, they had a common frequency. "Commander Jain, this is Dr. Brian Rios aboard Stanford's Venus outpost. Can you hear me?"

Shaila smiled and opened her channel to Diaz as well. "Stanford, I hear you five by five. I got Major General Maria Diaz online as well. What's your status? Over."

"You wouldn't believe me if I told you," Rios replied.

Diaz chimed in. "Dr. Rios, I'm walking out in the open on Venus, in the middle of the jungle, taken prisoner by three-foot-tall lizard people and walking next to an early 19th century English admiral. So I say again, what's *your* status? Over!"

Jesus, boss, Shaila thought. *So much for operational security.*

To the Stanford guy's credit, he came back within fifteen seconds. "Well, ah, that actually confirms what we're seeing up here. We have, ah, several wooden vessels up here with us. They've left us alone, mostly. It seems the people on the ships are repairing them. In space. With no suits on. And they have gravity."

"Right, we were there for that part," Shaila said. "What are you seeing on the planet?"

"Oh, of course. There's a roughly circular area about 500 kilometers in diameter in which atmospheric composition, atmospheric pressure, temperature and geological composition are near Earth-normal, and there's an absolute ton of life readings in that area. There's a lot of ambient radiation being thrown off at the edges, and that radiation seems to be directed, back and forth, from a series of satellites that came into orbit a few days ago."

"Doctor, can you account for 100 percent of the energy between the ground and the satellites?" Diaz asked.

"Account for it? Well, I…hang on…now that you mention it…no. There's a discrepancy between what's coming off the satellites and what's emanating from the location below. There's extra energy there which can't be sourced. What the hell is *that* about?"

"Classified for now," Diaz snapped. "Just keep us posted if you see any change there."

"Well, it is growing," Rios responded. "About a kilometer a minute. In roughly 16 Earth-days, the whole planet will be covered. Oh, and there's another ship down there. I mean, a real ship. A spaceship."

That got Shaila's attention. "Did it identify?"

"No, but transponder said it was a Virgin Galactic shuttle. It arrived before everything hit the fan, settled into a high orbit, then decided to break orbit a few hours ago. Flew right into the affected geological area. We think it may have landed. Sending you coordinates now. Looks to be maybe 30 to 40 kilometers from your location."

"There you go. Thought that was it. Stanford, sending you encryption key now. Let's keep all future communications just between us, all right?" Shaila said.

"And avoid contact with the Virgin craft at all costs. Attempt no search and rescue. We need you guys to stay put up there and be our eyes," Diaz added.

"Understood, General. No comms except you, no EVA. Any estimate on when we might get things put back together?" Rios asked, a plaintive sound in his voice.

"Anywhere between now and never, inclusive," Diaz deadpanned. "Hang in there. Diaz and Jain out."

Shaila killed the long-range comms. "Do we try to split off and investigate the Virgin ship?" she asked.

"Negative. We're playing the negotiation card here with the little guys. Let's not mess with that. And open up comms so we can update Admiral Weatherby here, who's starting to look at me cross-eyed."

The two officers updated Weatherby, who agreed that an attempt to check out the Virgin ship would only anger the Venusians. They had to play the situation out before making their next move, and that meant going to wherever the Venusians were taking them.

As it happened, their destination was a small village, set into a picturesque clearing, surrounded by verdant trees and colorful undergrowth. The buildings were made of mud-brick and thatch, with doors barely a meter and a half high and open windows a half-meter wide, but large enough to hold a generously sized Venusian family, given their small statures. The village seemed, by Venusian standards, to be a relatively new affair, for the undergrowth between the neatly made buildings was trampled down but not worn away. A large fire-pit dominated the center of the village.

When Weatherby asked Elizabeth, she confirmed his thoughts. "When several tribes gather, they often create a village in a neutral territory where their elders can meet. This is done to debate matters of great import to the tribes—and the arrival of the French might certainly qualify, Father," she said. "Oh, and yes, there are Va'hak'ri here! I recognize that fellow's beadwork as such. That may help us, given your history with them."

"One can only hope," Weatherby replied. "I wonder if we might even see a few of the creatures we encountered back in '79."

Unfortunately, it was too much to ask. Turned out that the current chief of the Va'hak'ri tribe was the grandson of the creature Weatherby and Finch encountered thirty years prior—Shaila remembered it from Weatherby's transdimensional journal, found on Mars during the *Daedalus* incident. But like the warrior on the beach, the chief—who had a headdress half his own height and enough necklaces to make a Mardi Gras attendee blush—seemed to know Weatherby and Finch. Unfortunately, he didn't know English, leaving Elizabeth to translate.

"We are welcomed, but the elder says these are dark times, and only Weatherby and his companions would be given such honor. And yes, I've already told him the honor is truly ours, and a number of other ritual greetings I'm sure you'd wish to make properly, Father."

Weatherby nodded. "Thank you, my dear. Once the pleasantries are completed, do ask whether they have encountered the French, and inquire as to the safety of their memory vault and other ritualized areas, if you please."

After a flurry of Venusian grunts and grumbles—truly, Weatherby could not understand how Elizabeth managed such expertise with the language—it was discovered that the French had indeed been in contact, in the person of Berthollet and a small escort of troops, all hale and healthy humans. There was no sign of Cagliostro, nor of any *Corps Éternel* soldiers—and Elizabeth reported that the Venusians appeared greatly agitated at the mention of either.

"So they have not been fully apprised of the French numbers here," Anne mused. "Not surprising, really. I should think they would have a great cultural aversion to the walking dead, given their near worship of Nature itself."

"I think most folks have a good solid aversion to zombies," Diaz quipped. "Question is, where are Berthollet and the French now?"

After more discussion and translation, it was determined that the French had set up shop about 20 kilometers to the south and east, near a wide river that then led out into the ocean. It wasn't near any Spanish or Dutch outposts, and it was close enough to water for the French to make a run for it as needed.

They had also been seen in a clearing about 20 kilometers directly east—in between the Va'hak'ri village and one of their memory vault sites. "Their scouts say the vault itself is watched but remains untouched," Elizabeth said. "The clearing, I believe, is the one Gar'uk discussed before, in that it is a highly defensible place, a vale between two large mountains, with a wide meadow therein."

Weatherby's eyes narrowed as he studied a Royal Geographic Society map of the area. "There really is nothing stopping the French from taking the vault," he muttered. "What are they waiting on?"

"Looks to me like they're defending it," Shaila said from inside her mech. "I managed to patch into the Stanford sensors, got a good picture of the area, even some life-signs there. Not detecting anything beyond that clearing."

Weatherby turned to Anne and Finch. "Do you think they have already obtained what they have come for?" he asked.

Finch shrugged. "It may take them several days, perhaps even weeks, to conduct the experiments necessary to take full advantage of the Venusian alchemy inside those vaults. They may simply wish to deny them to us, or perhaps they are still engaged inside, and need the soldiers to watch their backs. And before you ask, yes, I fully believe Berthollet and Cagliostro could enter the memory vaults without anyone the wiser, with all due respect to the Venusians and their abilities."

Weatherby straightened up. "We must proceed forward and, with the Venusians' help, take the clearing and the vaults from the French. Only then can we bring the Tablet and *Book* there, and figure out what fell plot the French have concocted with Althotas this time. Elizabeth, please convey this to them."

She did, but to Weatherby's great surprise, he received nothing but a terse decline, followed by several questions on the part of the Venusians.

"They have no wish to become embroiled in our quarrels," Elizabeth explained. "More importantly, though with respect to you, Father, they wish to know why you have brought two...oh, I am struggling with the interpretation here. I suppose the closest I can get is 'alien warrior outsiders.'"

Weatherby cast around, looking at the people with him, as did Diaz. "You think he means me and Durand, Miss Weatherby?" Diaz asked.

"Dr. Durand, yes. But not you. They mean Dr. Durand… and Uncle Andrew."

Weatherby turned to Finch. "You and your thrice-damned research," he said, angry and tired. "What have you done now?"

Finch raised his hands and backed up slightly. "I promise you, I've no idea," he said. "Obviously, there is something they can detect as it relates to *The Book of the Dead*. Perhaps if we showed them?"

"Um, negative on that," Diaz snapped. "If we have two of the biggest sacred whatsits in the universe with us, we don't go bragging. Obviously, something in that book has rubbed off on you, Dr. Finch. And I'm starting to wonder if it's on par with what we're seeing out of Dr. Durand here."

Listening to the conversation over her comm, Shaila was beginning to wish she could jump out of the V-SEV and drag Stephane back inside with her. Instead, she switched over to a private channel with him. "How are you doing, honey?"

"I am…struggling a little, yes?" he replied quietly, whispering over the channel. "Rathemas doesn't like this. He's impatient to get past this. Afraid of something. I don't know what."

"Can you keep him down?" Shaila asked.

"So long as these lizard-people don't do something strange, I think so. But I'd like to hurry this up," he replied.

Meantime, Diaz and Weatherby were busy arguing with Finch, until finally Weatherby raised his hand. "Enough of this! General Diaz, would you submit Dr. Durand for examination by the Venusians? Perhaps they may find something to help him."

"You going to guarantee they won't spear him in the face, Admiral?" she replied, hands on her hips.

Weatherby's brow wrinkled. "You know I cannot. But I shall order Dr. Finch to undergo the same examination. They may be satisfied by this, and more importantly, they may be inclined to assist afterward."

Finch opened his mouth to object—and Anne seemed pretty willing to question her husband on it, too—but one look from Weatherby silenced them both. The admiral then turned to Stephane, and grabbed Finch's arm to drag him over as well. "I cannot, I realize, actually order either of you to submit yourselves to the Venusians so we may answer their questions—or even have some of our questions answered regarding whatever has ailed you both. But I will ask it of you freely, and pray you agree."

Stephane didn't hesitate. "I want this thing out of me. Maybe they can do it, yes? I will let them see me."

Finch was less convinced. "Tom, I swear to you on thirty years of friendship, I am not afflicted by my research in any way. But…for the greater good, yes, they can look me over, for all the good it will do them."

Once decided, and translated for the Venusians, the chieftain and one of their shamans took Stephane and Finch away. To Shaila's consternation, Stephane was forced to leave his headset behind, so she was just as much in the dark as the rest of them. Surrounded by a half-dozen warriors, the two men were taken into a long, low hut at the center of the village.

"They say they will strive to understand why the alien darkness is with our friends, and whether they can be saved," Elizabeth translated. "If they cannot somehow improve them, well…I am quite afraid as to their fates, Father."

"So am I," Shaila chimed in. "Permission to get down there, General Diaz."

"Sorry, Jain. Need you to stay put. If the Venusians decide not to let you back in, we're out a major advantage. Don't worry, I'll keep a sharp eye out for him," she replied.

And so they waited. And waited more. The Sun slipped below the horizon, leaving a greenish glow in its wake, until finally the clouds formed a dense, dark gloom above the jungle. A surprising number of plants had phosphorescent qualities to them, and the Venusians seemed to gather these up and use them for lighting inside their huts. Outside, bonfires and torches lent an eerie quality to the proceedings, and made the little lizard warriors seem scarier and more formidable than they might've been otherwise.

Finally, as the dinner hour neared, Stephane and Finch emerged from the hut. Actually, they were shoved out the door, and marched angrily toward Weatherby and the others at spearpoint.

"What is the meaning of this treatment?" Weatherby demanded, casting around for Elizabeth to translate. "Why do you handle my friends in such a manner?"

"Jain, heat up your drills in case this gets ugly," Diaz said quietly over the comm.

"Bringing laser drills online," Shaila replied. "With pleasure."

The Venusian warriors shoved Stephane and Finch into the central part of the village once more, and with a final push, sent them to the ground at Weatherby's feet. Meanwhile, the elder and his shaman rushed up, gesticulating and shouting in stream of croaks and squawks.

"They claim we have brought evil to their land, and want nothing more to do with us," Elizabeth reported. "Out of respect for Father's past deeds, we will not be slain, but we must leave this place, and never set foot upon Venus again while Doctors Finch and Durand are among us. I assume they mean while they are so afflicted."

Stephane, meanwhile, shook his head and seemed to be coming out of a daze or trance, while Finch simply looked put out. "They have no conception," he muttered. "They wish to stick their heads in the sand and be done with us."

"They were there!" added Stephane, who was wild-eyed, pasty and drawn as he staggered toward Diaz. "They were there and they saw what happened, yet they do nothing!"

Diaz caught Stephane and helped prop him up. "Both of you, shut up and report. Thirty seconds. Go."

Finch opened his mouth but hesitated, whereas Stephane knew the drill. "They know that Rathemas is inside me. While their shaman did his...something, ritual, whatever... we saw what happened back on Mars long ago, when the Xan attacked. Althotas ripped the souls from his *own followers* and hid them elsewhere. The Venusians know I have one of the souls, and they believe Finch is the...doorway? Corridor? Conduit! Yes, conduit."

Finch shook his head dismissively. "I am not possessed by any power, so how can I be the conduit? It is folly."

Beside Weatherby, Anne gasped suddenly. "Oh, Lord. I see it now. Oh, Finch, I see what you've done!"

Hands on his hips, Finch turned on Anne. "What, then? What have I done, except to further Mankind's knowledge of the Great Work beyond even that of your late husband, then? Tell me, for everyone thinks I'm naught but a criminal in this!"

"Not a criminal, but a fool, and a damned fool besides," she replied, spitting the words. "You entered *Maat* every time you employed a working that used knowledge gleaned from *The Book of the Dead*. That underworld was, in part, where the souls Althotas ripped from his followers were stored! So you, over the years, have been chipping away at that opening, just as surely as Berthollet has in animating his legions. In fact, you yourself have traveled through *Maat* in order to speed yourself and our ships through time and space!"

"And you have placed me within reach of it as well," Weatherby added, realization dawning on him. "Dear God, Finch, I am complicit in this as well!"

Finch started to argue the point, then stopped. "Oh...I see it. Dear God in Heaven, I see the connection now," he whispered. A moment later, his knees gave way and he tumbled onto the ground.

"Yes!" Stephane cried out. "You're the doorway, and Rathemas wants to use both of us to walk through! Only here, on Venus, where it's overlapped, can he do this now!"

Anne looked up at Weatherby. "I fear we have walked straight into whatever Althotas' plans are. And the Venusians are too scared to help us put things right."

Weatherby surveyed the lizard-men before him with growing agitation. "Then we must do it without them, damn them to Hell."

Elizabeth stepped over to him. "Father, please. Allow me to stay and argue for us. If we act without their support, all chance of alliance, now and in the future, will be lost!"

"And what do I care?" Weatherby thundered. "They prefer to cower in the trees while the fate of the Known World hangs in the balance! Meanwhile, Cagliostro and Berthollet *have* their precious memory vaults. There are renegades from the future running about transforming Venus, and the warlord Althotas is nigh! We must assault the French and put an end to this—now!"

Tears welled in his daughter's eyes. "Please, Father. I wish to stay. I can try to make them see reason. I have performed the *dul'kat* and they cannot harm me now because of it."

Weatherby cast around, frustrated, then laid eyes on Philip. "Lieutenant St. Germain. You will remain here with your stepsister. If they so much as lift a finger toward either of you, I command you to secure her safely and make for the beach with all haste. Do you understand?"

Stunned at Weatherby's anger, Philip could only nod as his stepfather turned on his heel and stalked off away from the village, a collection of 19th and 22nd century compatriots looking after him in confusion and concern.

CHAPTER 22

January 30, 2135
May 29, 1809

Weatherby stalked the beach impatiently, waiting for men and matériel to be brought by boat to shore. He had not slept and had eaten very little since the morning, and could see that all around him were shying away from him and his anger.

Except for Shaila Jain.

"She's going to be fine," Shaila said. "She's a super-smart kid."

Weatherby waved his hand. "I've no doubt as to Elizabeth's safety at this point. The Venusians are a primitive sort, but the honor of the Va'hak'ri is not in question. And I've great faith in Philip as well. Should the Venusians seek vengeance after we engage the French, I dare say he is quite capable of removing her from harm."

At this Shaila looked troubled. "Hadn't thought of that. She checked in over the comm about an hour ago. All's well, but she's still getting stonewalled. You want one of us to go get her?"

"No, Lieutenant Commander. I've no doubt the French will meet us on the field with superior numbers. It is likely they have spies within the Venusian camps. All of the European powers have links to the various tribes the Venusians have assembled. When we take the field, I believe your mechanisms will be critical to winning the day. I suggest you ensure the Emerald Tablet is secure aboard one of your machines. And please ask General Diaz to ready them. I hope to leave in an hour's time."

Shaila looked rather unconvinced, but nodded. "Aye, sir."

As she walked off, Weatherby looked on after her. It would not be seemly in His Majesty's Navy for a lieutenant—or lieutenant commander, which was a wholly unusual rank—to speak so frankly to an admiral. Yet he found himself thrown back in time to when he was a mere lieutenant, and she was the elder of the two. Furthermore, she was not technically under his command, and although he could press the matter, for she was indeed of the Royal Navy of some place and time, he felt it a losing cause.

There were more than enough losing causes to be had, it seemed.

A fresh-faced lieutenant approached and saluted smartly. "We've emptied the ships of marines and have supplemented their ranks with able seamen, my Lord Admiral," the man said—what *was* his name? Weatherby could not recall.

"Cannon?" Weatherby asked.

"If you wish to depart forthwith, my Lord, there will be but eight, along with their crews. Any more would require dispatching the boats another time, and loading them has proven to be more difficult than anticipated."

"It will have to do," Weatherby said. "Prepare the men and cannon to break camp and march as soon as possible."

The young man saluted and ran off, leaving Weatherby feeling old and unsuited to the task ahead. His exhaustion weighed heavily upon him, for it was well past midnight now, and they would not reach the clearing and the French lines until after dawn. Gar'uk had brought coffee from *Victory* to fortify him, but even his favorite beverage seemed only to add to his nerves rather than his wakefulness.

"You are frustrated, my friend," sang Vellusk, who somehow had managed to come up behind Weatherby unnoticed, despite his prodigious height.

Weatherby turned and did his best to be diplomatic, knowing what a premium the Xan placed on manners. "I am, my wise friend. I apologize. In most of the battles I have fought on behalf of my King and Country, my goals were very clear. And even on Mars, we knew full well that we had to interrupt Althotas' ritual, and had the means to do so. But here…here, our course takes us off the map."

Vellusk nodded as he began to walk alongside Weatherby. "I should like to say something wise and helpful here, but I am most aggrieved that I am unable to do so," he sang. "I have consulted with the Lady Weatherby and Doctors Finch and Durand regarding the Emerald Tablet and *The Book of the Dead*. There are, of course, a variety of ways in which they might be used in conjunction with the memory vault, but I feel as though we are missing something. We are unable to say for certain what the French plan may be."

"And what if we destroy them?" Weatherby asked. "Be done with it. Would that not stymie the French?"

"I would advise against it," Vellusk sang, notes of concern and sorrow in his melodies. "We discussed this as well, but what if their loss is the edge the French seek? Or General Diaz' former colleagues, for that matter? Without knowing, such a course would be rash indeed, and very possibly fatal."

"They could be the key to Althotas' masterstroke," Weatherby countered.

"Or the key to his undoing," Vellusk sang.

Weatherby slumped a bit. "You are, of course, quite right. And I've no doubt the impulse to destroy these items stems simply from my desire to be done with all this."

The admiral kicked an errant stone across the beach in frustration.

"You are a wise man, Thomas," Vellusk sang. "Much wiser than some of my compatriots, I am afraid. We have worked hard to ensure that the partisans among us—those for whom the ways of war are welcome—are being dealt with. And we have given your Wellesley some small aid that should nonetheless turn the tide against the foul revenants. But when it comes to this battle, I must leave it in your hands. We Xan have our own conflicts to resolve amongst ourselves. And with that, I shall take the Lady Anne's advice and depart." The Xan then laughed, which sounded like wind chimes upon a spring breeze. "Besides, if you are indeed marching into battle, even if I wished to march with you, I shall be quite useless."

Weatherby's first instinct was to insist otherwise, but he quickly realized that it was merely the truth; Vellusk was the product of a pacifist society, and he really *would* be in the way. So he simply thanked the ambassador for his counsel yet again, and managed to extract himself from the Xan's ritualized farewells in just short of five minutes, which likely was a record of some sort.

Just as Vellusk departed, Weatherby's attention was drawn to the northern edge of the beach, where one of the bipedal mechanical beasts came crashing through the jungle. So wrapped up in his own thoughts, and in the preparation of his forces, he hadn't noticed that one of the three metal giants was missing. He tapped the button on the headset he still wore. "Who just arrived, and from whence?" he demanded.

"It's Diaz, Admiral. While you were setting up your guys, I did a little recon to where the Virgin Galactic ship was reported. It's there and it's empty. Greene and Huntington are on the move, but no idea where."

Weatherby sighed. On top of everything else, two more individuals possessed by the very ghosts of Mars were loose somewhere in the blasted jungle—a mishap simply waiting to happen, no doubt. "Very well. I request you prepare your vehicles for battle as best you can. We shall be leaving shortly."

"Roger that, Admiral. Diaz out."

With a sigh, he tapped the button again, having become rather used to the instantaneous communication the headset afforded him. He thought of calling Elizabeth on the device, but his facility with these "comms" was not up to the task. Shaila had assured him that she would make contact regularly. It was another thing, small but so very, very important, out of his control.

Weatherby walked over to the small camp table where Anne was working with Finch and Stephane. "Please tell me, my Lady, that there is some small progress to report."

"No, love, we have little to add to what we already know," Anne replied, her eyes on the table with the Tablet and

Book before her. "It seems Dr. Durand is much discomfited by proximity to these objects, and tells us that he is loath to touch them directly, for the creature inside him, this Rathemas, apparently wishes him to do so."

Weatherby looked at Stephane, who stood quietly, his arms cradled, face drawn. Finch, meanwhile, seemed agitated, his hands fluttering around a pencil and notebook but with precious few notes. "What say you, Dr. Finch?"

"Damn it to Hell, I've not the slightest," Finch said, tossing the pencil and notebook to the table. "Something tells me that these will play such a critical role in the hours to come, but for good or ill I cannot say, and the notion of it is vague intuition, nothing more."

"That's not good enough, Doctor," Weatherby said sharply.

Finch seemed as though he was about to retort, but thought better of it. "We shall keep working," he said simply.

Weatherby shook his head. "There is no time. We have eight cannon. We shall need them to produce as much destructive power as you're able by the time we arrive at the clearing. Suspend your work here, and join Lady Anne in preparing for battle. Dr. Durand, are you able to operate your...vehicle?"

"Yes, sir," he replied steadily. "If you feel this battle will help get Rathemas out of me, I'll do whatever you say."

That prompted a small smile from Weatherby. "Your commander is General Diaz, not myself, but I thank you nonetheless. I suggest you report to her and ready yourself."

As Finch and Stephane took their leave, Anne paused to address her husband. "Tom, are you sure this is the right course? I do not know what meeting the French will accomplish."

"No, I am not sure!" he barked. "I am sure of nothing! I know not what will happen. But even if the answers aren't in the damned Venusian vaults, at least we will know that much, and can find answers elsewhere. It is the only course I can see, so I shall embark up on it, madam!"

Anne's eyes flashed in anger, for it was a very rare thing for Weatherby to be so curt with her. "Sir, do not mistake my question for doubt about you!" she said quietly, but with no small amount of venom. "We simply do not know what will come of this, and some of these men here will die because of this course."

"Men die all the time because of my orders!" Weatherby hissed. "And I thank God Almighty that he has seen fit to haunt me with their faces as I sleep, for otherwise what sort of monster would I be if I did not care? Do not come to me with men's lives, madam, for I have each soul weighed upon me, and yet I still stand, and still do as I must. Would you cripple me with indecisiveness now, at the hour when decisions are hardest?"

Taken aback, Anne nonetheless stood her ground. "If you must know, Tom, I fear that you have embarked upon this course to assuage your own guilt, not to add to it with men's lives. More and more, the French draw closer to the Crown in Edinburgh. More and more, we are at our wit's end. And yet, I ask you, what will this onslaught accomplish that a reconnaissance would not?"

"It will result in fewer French!" Weatherby raged. "And yes, that is a horrible thing to say, but if I can remove even a hundred of these damnable revenants from the Known Worlds through this action, then I shall do it! We will fight through them to get to the vault because it is the right thing to do! And then we shall figure out whether or not we can save all of Mankind or whether it shall be in vain!"

With that, the two of them stood staring at each other, both trembling and engulfed in anger and sorrow and remorse. Finally, Weatherby spoke once more, managing his words carefully. "I apologize, my Lady," he replied. "We must do our duty to England, and to Mankind, and it falls upon me to decide. And so I have. Please, if you will, assist Finch with his preparations. We will have need of your talents if we are to succeed."

Quite unable to face his wife any further, Weatherby nodded and turned, walking briskly back down the beach where the marine commanders awaited him. He did not care to look back, for he was certain the look upon Anne's face would wreck him as surely as any Void storm.

"How's the admiral holding up?" Diaz asked as the remaining crew of the *Hadfield* huddled on the beach.

Shaila turned to follow Diaz' gaze and saw Weatherby and Anne in what seemed to be an argument. "Honestly? Stressed out of his mind. He's keeping it together, but it's not been easy."

"His daughter and step-son are with hundreds of Venusians with spears, his wife is about to go into battle with him—I wouldn't expect him to be happy," Stephane said. "And really, we don't even know if we'll find anything we need at these memory vaults."

Diaz paused and looked down at the sandy beach. "I gotta say, I'm not exactly thrilled about this. Yeah, we helped out the English because we got good facial-recognition on Weatherby. That was my call, and I think it was the right one at the time. We had an ally under duress, and rules of engagement are clear on that one. But this battle? I have some doubts. This is a straight-up battle of the Napoleonic Wars, and even though the French supposedly have zombies or whatever, it's still human against human for the most part. I like Weatherby, and in most cases I'd definitely consider him an allied commander. But for this, not sure we should be in the mix."

"What's the alternative, then?" Shaila asked. "We could try to find Greene and Huntington on our own, but tracking them in this jungle is pretty close to impossible. And really, the whole idea is to get to the Venusian memory vault. If that's what's going to stop Althotas, and the French are resisting it, then they're aiding and abetting an alien power. Seems pretty straightforward to me."

"These are my countrymen, and I have no wish to hurt them, but I find myself agreeing with Shay here," Stephane said. "We have the Emerald Tablet as well, and if we aren't there when they reach the Vault, then they may not be able to stop Althotas—and get Rathemas out of my head."

"And if Althotas needs the tablet to win, we could end up giving it to him on a silver platter," Diaz sighed. "We don't even know if the French are defending a key objective or just some goddamn ammo depot."

Stephane shook his head. "I can't say how I know this, but I feel like Rathemas *wants* us to get to the memory vault. There's something there he needs."

"So we shouldn't go?" Shaila asked.

"No, I don't mean that," Stephane said. "He wants to go there, but he also seems nervous about us going. So maybe getting there is both a good idea and bad? I think it depends on what we do there, whether we win or not. Either way, if this is how he gets out of me, then I'm really very OK with it."

Diaz gave him a little smile. "Fair point. And if he gets out of you, maybe we get a chance to put a laser through his skull."

"I'd like that quite a lot," Stephane agreed.

With a sigh, Diaz straightened up. "OK, decision time. Jain, keep the Tablet in your V-SEV. Security of the object is top priority. If your V-SEV is compromised or damaged, sit tight and wait for Durand or I to come get you. Now, I know we went to bat for Weatherby out in space, but knowing just how much we're in the dark here, I'm not real excited about engaging enemy combatants directly. We're not here to re-fight the Napoleonic Wars. So we'll head for the vault, but we will not, repeat *not*, engage French personnel."

"Roger that," Shaila said. "But do zombies count?"

The general raised an eyebrow at this and thought it out for a few moments before replying. "Maybe not. Anne told me they're really dead, animated by…well, magic, I guess. So if the French have zombies with them, they're fair game. But until we have proof that the main body of French troops are complicit in whatever Althotas is up to, hands off the living French guys."

"*Très bon*, General," Stephane said with a smile. "Thank you for that."

Diaz clapped him on the shoulder. "No worries. One final thing about our friends here. I'm hoping Admiral Weatherby isn't going to get all Captain Ahab on this quest, but he's looking pretty stressed. If he goes off, we may need to withdraw and find our own answers. I know he's a good guy, but he's an *allied* commander, not actually on our team. If I feel we need to pull out, we will.

"And as for Finch, if this book starts to make him squirrelly, we may have to put him down. We clear on that?"

Shaila nodded. It seemed Finch was keeping it together, but with all the mystical bullshit flying around, it seemed prudent to have a fallback in place.

Stephane, though, looked troubled. "And if I start acting 'squirrelly,' General? Do you put me down too?"

Diaz held up her datapad. "You still got your collar on, Durand. If Rathemas acts up, you'll be out cold in seconds. Now, get your V-SEVs warmed up. Jain, I'll need you to work on a hack to get the most out of our lasers once we engage. Dismissed."

Shaila and Stephane headed to their V-SEVs. "You're doing good," she told him. "We won't have to zap you."

He gave her a sad smile. "So far, so good. But please, knock me out if he comes through. I don't want to experience that again."

She stopped him and gave him a short but passionate kiss. "You got this. I won't need to. Now...saddle up. We may have some zombies to fry."

CHAPTER 23

January 30, 2135
May 29, 1809

And so it comes to this, Weatherby thought as he looked across the shaded glen toward the French lines.

They were in a vale, one with a fine clearing therein, though a portion of that was swamp and muck. A brook provided the water for the bog, which drained off behind Weatherby and away from the trail that brought his men there. There were trees and vines surrounding the clearing, radiant in their riot of colors—blues, reds, yellows and at least a score of different greens.

And like a sickly cancer, an infection upon the very face of life, the blue coats and grey flesh of the *Corps Éternel* stood out among the greenery of the Venusian fauna. There were living men among them, of course, notable for their nervous movement and shouts filled with bravado, whereas their expired fellows remained both silent and stock-still.

Soldiers without fear, Weatherby thought. *To think we shall face such an unthinking, horrific enemy as that*. And according to his advance scouts, there were at least two thousand such abominations within the French ranks, with a hundred more living officers among them and some twenty cannon.

He took a moment to mark this place in his memory, for there was the fear that Anne was indeed right about his motivations—he found women in general, and Anne in particular, knew more of men's minds than men themselves. And if he was indeed wrong, and lived to make his regrets, he wished to remember well his folly amongst such natural beauty.

Weatherby then turned to survey his own men, a mere three hundred strong, and did his level best to mark their faces in his mind as well. His marines stood out with their red coats and finery, while the able seamen with them remained less conspicuous in their shipboard clothing. The eight cannon they managed to bring were well placed, and he knew *Victory*'s men could fire and reload at least triple the rate of the French artillerists. They would have to, would there be any chance of evening the odds.

The ground shook beside him as Shaila approached in her "mech," whatever such a word meant—mechanical, certainly, though he could see no gears nor levers upon the giant skeleton encasing her. The hatch atop the metal giant opened, and he could see his counterpart therein, wearing the headset that allowed her to talk with her fellows.

"Reporting for duty, my Lord Admiral," she said with a hint of a smile. "General Diaz and Dr. Durand have taken flanking positions on either side of your front line."

Weatherby nodded. "Thank you, Commander. If your.... mechanism...can withstand the assault, I should like you in the vanguard."

Shaila nodded. "Aye, sir," she replied. "I don't think anything they have will be a problem."

Weatherby examined the hatch as best he could, though it was a good six feet above his head. "The glass? Would that not be a problem?"

"No, sir. If it can withstand the pressure on Venus—my Venus—it can manage pretty much anything these guys throw at us. Only a direct hit would worry me."

"Then I shall not worry, either," Weatherby said. "Though that is probably something of an untruth."

A young midshipman ran up. "My Lord Admiral, I—" The boy stopped to stare at Shaila's V-SEV. "I—"

Weatherby allowed the boy several moments to take in the 12-foot-tall monstrosity before tapping him on the shoulder. "You were saying?"

"Sorry, my Lord. All report ready. The Lady Weatherby instructed me specifically to remind you to give her and Dr. Finch time to fire before your flanks advance."

"Very well. Anything else?"

The boy looked down upon his shoes at this, his face reddening. "The lady asked me to extend other messages as well, though I dare say t'was none of my business to hear them, my Lord."

Weatherby managed a smile, though he knew their last words upon the beach were less than ideal. As much as he wanted to know what she said, now was not the time. "I take your meaning well enough. You are discharged from that task. Stay with me in case I've need of a runner."

He was interrupted by Shaila. "Admiral, looks like the French are moving. Diaz and Durand reporting it too. They're advancing."

Weatherby sighed. "Very well. I suggest you seal your hatches, Commander, and prepare to advance as well. Our van will be behind you."

Shaila tossed off a casual salute. "Tell them not to get underfoot. I won't be able to see them. Otherwise, I'll pave the road for you." And with that, the queer glass-and-metal hatch once again lowered over her body, leaving her sitting inside the belly of the metal giant she piloted so deftly.

"Truly amazing," Weatherby muttered, before turning to his men and drawing his sword high. "Englishmen! These French before us hold fell secrets that will aid those left at home! Victory here saves all England! Our lands, our families, our people now rely on us! Today, we start France on its road to defeat!"

The men cheered loudly, and Weatherby saw even the most fearful faces gain new heart, even as his own heart sank. Some of those cheering would be dead soon, and at his command. He offered a silent prayer that their deaths would have meaning beyond the words he would next yell. "Now! For God and King! For England! CHARGE!"

Weatherby drew his sword and tapped the flat of the blade on Shaila's V-SEV, and the giant metal suit immediately started striding forward, even as the first rounds of musket fire could be heard whizzing past. The admiral pointed his sword forward, and began jogging, lines of marines and sailors behind him.

For England, he thought. *For home.*

"All right, I'm on the move," Shaila said over the comm, "and I got a bunch of guys with muskets behind me. Over." Shaila's HUD immediately pointed out the location of Stephane and Diaz, to her far left and right, respectively, and she could see them moving as well, identified as blue dots, with dozens of white dots behind them in neat lines. Ahead, the computer helpfully pointed out movement, though it was having a hard time properly identifying the *Corps Éternel*. It settled on another "UNKNOWN FAUNA" designation.

"Roger that," Diaz replied. "Getting some musket fire. No damage. Powering up the laser drills now. Remember, aim only for the zombies. Kicking and stomping works, too."

Shaila flipped a switch to fire up her own drills. "Durand, report."

"I'm here," he replied, sounded determined. "Ready to fight."

I bet you are, Shaila thought. "Roger. Don't get carried away, honey."

"I am perfectly calm," Stephane protested, a hint of humor in his voice. "But I'd be lying if I said I wasn't looking forward to this a little bit, yes?"

Shaila's reply was cut short by her HUD readout, which saw a few of the white dots behind her winking out. "They're taking heavy fire," she said. "We're starting to lose 'em."

"Double time," Diaz ordered. "Get to the French lines and start cutting."

Shaila pushed her yoke forward and felt the V-SEV respond quickly, charging across the glen and leaving the English lines behind her. It was but the work of thirty seconds to get to the first lines of kneeling French soldiers. She saw a few scatter—the living ones—while the rest still went through the rote motions of firing, reloading and firing again.

Shaila turned to her left, toward Stephane, and fired up her right drill. Looking out her starboard window, she saw the red line cut through the first two undead soldiers like butter, severing heads and arms from torsos with ease. "Lasers are effective. Repeat, lasers are effective. Let's go."

She once again started up, using her laser to cut through the first two rows of soldiers. Ten, twenty, thirty—they went down wordlessly, passively, continuing to fire their muskets even as their legs were cut out from under them. They didn't move, didn't flee.

It was creepy as hell.

"Laser power down to 30 percent," Diaz said. "I'm shutting down to recharge. Suggest you do the same and start clobbering instead."

"Roger that," Shaila replied, shutting down her drills. She then turned right and waded into the French lines, swinging the V-SEV's arms wildly so as to strike as many French soldiers as possible. A few more started running—again, the living ones, it seemed—while the *Corps Éternel* were starting to form lines for what seemed to be bayonet charges. *For all the good it will do them.*

"Um, Shay? I am seeing some living French soldiers with ropes and chains," Stephane reported over the comm. "I think…wait…they're going for the legs! Shay, they're going to try to take us down!"

Ahead, Shaila could see several undead soldiers carrying long lengths of rope and chain, spreading out as much as possible. "I see it. I hate it when they get clever."

"Cut the chatter, Jain," Diaz ordered. "If they take you down, sit tight. Do *not*, repeat, do *not* get out of your V-SEV. Acknowledge and confirm."

Both Shaila and Stephane acknowledged, but continued to fight on. Shaila could see Stephane's V-SEV in the distance, and noticed he was swinging and stomping hard, wading in almost heedlessly—probably too fast for him to be making best use of his HUD. She was about to chide him for it when a huge gout of flame erupted from behind her, sending her sensor alarms screeching. "What the hell was that?"

"Alchemy, I think," Diaz replied. "They managed to take out a couple hundred with those blasts. Not bad."

And indeed, Shaila could see several undead soldiers now on fire, toppling over or simply crouched down, ablaze in the undergrowth—which was also starting to catch. "Guys, if you can, try to stomp out some of these fires as you go so our guys don't get torched," she said.

On her tactical map, she could see rows and rows of UNKNOWN FAUNA falling ahead of her—but the white dots behind were easily at two-thirds of what they were just a few minutes ago. And there were a lot more unknowns than friendlies. She redoubled her efforts, following Stephane's example by charging hard into the nearest mass of French soldiers, stomping and swinging wildly. A few of them started climbing the chassis, and one managed to even reach her hatch, peering through the window with hollow eyes, sunken cheeks and dried, peeled-back lips.

She used a pincer to pluck the fucker off and throw him twenty meters away. *Gross.*

Suddenly, her HUD erupted in light, and several alarms went off. On either side of the glen, hundreds upon hundreds of new dots appeared. It took the computer several seconds to identify them, and when it did, all it came up with was UNKNOWN FAUNA-2. It also helpfully relabeled the *Corps Éternel* as UNKNOWN FAUNA-1.

"What the hell is *that*?" Shaila said. "Jain here. We got new bogies at three and nine. Anyone have eyes on them? Over."

Before anyone responded, she felt her V-SEV start to tip. More alarms went off, and the cameras helpfully showed what the computer had labeled MULTIPLE OBSTRUC-TIONS—several French soldiers, both living and dead, were pulling on her V-SEV's legs with ropes.

She swung the vehicle's arms wildly, but it was no use. She pitched forward, the ground rushing up to meet her windows.

Weatherby was covered with black ichor and red blood from the battle, nicked and scratched but mostly hale, and was able to pause long enough to witness Shaila's vehicle fall before he could identify the source. Then the chains and ropes became visible, and soon discovered the French were truly learning to become adaptable yet again, with unfortunate timing on their part.

"To the metal giant!" he shouted, rushing forward. Several marines and sailors accompanied him, and it was the work of but a bloody, swirling minute before the intrepid French were scattered or slain, though it cost him two of his small squad.

"You two! Untangle the ropes and chains. Let us see if we can get her upright again!" Weatherby ordered the two closest men, even as he cast his eye around for more targets. "The rest of you, reload and ready!"

As his men carried out his orders, Weatherby clambered up onto one of the giant's metal legs. He could see the battle going poorly indeed, with hundreds of French before him in neat rows, marching forward with eerie symmetry. Behind him, his men fought bravely, but he had lost at least a hundred thus far, even though he estimated more than five hundred casualties among the French, largely due to Finch and Anne's alchemy, along with the beams of light from Jain, Diaz and Durand. To Weatherby's left and right, the other two metal giants fought on, and he could even see some of his men working on a flanking maneuver to take down more of the French as they advanced.

It would not be enough. The calculus was against him. Too many French, not nearly enough men and cannon. Were the odds even, he might cut through them like a scythe through wheat, but whereas his living soldiers might cut down a dozen undying creatures, they were far more susceptible to wounds. The French had only to be lucky once.

He wished to sound a retreat, and to go back and ensure Anne was safe. But he could not, for if but one of Jain's people in their sturdy vehicles could push forward past the French, they had a chance to reach the ruins in time, to try to figure out the French plot, if there was one, and perhaps to send Althotas to his death once and for all.

And if that happened, perhaps England could be liberated. Perhaps.

"It's been freed, my Lord," one of his men said.

Weatherby looked down to see the vehicles limbs were untangled, and jumped off it just as it started to move. "Commander Jain!" he shouted, "Are you quite all right?"

Slowly, the metal giant rose onto all fours, to the point where he could see through the hatch windows once more. Inside, Shaila Jain hung there in her harness, but raised her hand and thumb to him. He could only assume from her demeanor, and lack of further signaling, that this was a positive thing.

"Admiral!"

Weatherby turned once more, and saw a long line of French troops, several rows deep, advancing on their position. He looked about and saw but thirty or forty Englishmen behind him. *So be it.* "Form a line and prepare to fire!"

To a man, his soldiers and sailors quickly settled into ranks and aimed, using the still-prone vehicle as cover. Weatherby drew his last pistol and himself took aim.

"Ready! Aim!—"

The first rows of French soldiers fell before he could give the order to fire.

"*What?*"

More were felled.

By spears and arrows.

"My Lord! 'Tis the Venusians!" a marine shouted.

And so it was, for Weatherby soon heard the alien croaking and creaking that was the Venusian battle cry. To his left, several dozen warriors swung down from the trees on vines, spears at the ready, and fell upon the French with vigor, tearing at the revenants' undead flesh with claw and beak and primitive weapons. To the right, a larger group of warriors erupted from the underbrush and descended into the clearing en masse, aiming for the back ranks of the French forces. There, they too fell upon the French, aiming squarely for the revenants and swarming over them, using their sheer numbers to make up for their diminutive size.

And that left the first few ranks facing Weatherby vulnerable once more.

The admiral turned back to his men, a smile upon his face. *Thank you, Elizabeth.* "FIRE!"

Thirty muskets spoke as one, and a moment later, a score of French *Corps Éternel* dropped. Those still moving were soon set upon by the Venusians, who tore into the French with spear and claw—and with surprising, savage efficacy.

For the first time in what seemed an age, Weatherby allowed himself to feel just a small glimmer of hope.

"CHARGE!"

"The Venusians!" Stephane shouted over the comm. "They're joining the fight after all!"

Shaila managed to get her V-SEV into a kneeling position and surveyed the scene in front of her. "Roger that. And they got balls, I'll give 'em that," she replied as she watched three small anthropomorphic lizards jump onto a zombified soldier and bring him down with stone axes and spears. In three years of strange sights, it was most definitely one of the stranger ones.

"Confirmed. I'm calling them as friendlies," Diaz replied. "They're only going after the dead guys. Repeat. The little lizard-men are friendlies. Get to the center of the French lines so we don't cut or step on any allies here."

Shaila managed to get her V-SEV on its feet once more and did a quick diagnostic—it would limp a bit, but it was mobile enough. "Roger. Proceeding forward. Meet you at grid number 34-27."

She didn't quite know how they knew to avoid the V-SEVs, but it seemed the Venusians either sensed that the mechs were friendly, or just hated the French zombies a whole lot. Either way, the little lizard-people scattered quickly before her, leaving the undead soldiers to be kicked and swept aside as she moved. In fact, it seemed a group of UNIDENTIFIED FAUNA-2 were trailing her mech and attacking whatever UNIDENTIFIED FAUNA-1 were still kicking as she passed.

And that worked just fine by her.

After a few minutes, Shaila managed to rendezvous with Diaz and Stephane toward the eastern side of the glen, though by this time, several lines of French troops were advancing on them with more ropes and chains. Shaila checked her drill power—it was back up to 67 percent. "General, suggest we go back-to-back and fire up the lasers again."

"Roger that," Diaz said. "Stephane, stay where you are and fire up your drills. We'll come up on your position and protect your back."

Shaila and Diaz maneuvered so that the three V-SEVs were standing in a triangle, arms and drills extended. "Ready when you are, General," Stephane said.

"Light 'em up," Diaz ordered.

The laser drills flashed...and the *Corps Éternel* proved to be less-than-eternal. The beams easily cut through several ranks of soldiers at a pass, leaving twitching masses of still-animated body parts on the ground, which was quickly turning black with whatever passed for their blood.

"God, these things are awful," Shaila said.

"Their blood has been infused with the energies of the Egyptian Underworld," Stephane said, sounding slightly distant. "They have the Void inside them, animating them and....my God, I don't want to know these things anymore."

"You OK, Durand?" Diaz asked.

"I am, but I want to get to the memory vault," Stephane said. "Can—"

Suddenly, with a earth-shattering boom, Stephane's mech began to topple over onto Shaila's. "I'm hit! A cannon ball, I think! Not stabilizing!"

Shaila, in turn, stepped forward and managed not to fall with him, though it looked like a piece of Stephane's vehicle caught the arm of her V-SEV, ripping through the connectors and rendering it useless for the time being. "Stephane, you goddamn stay put and stay in your V-SEV, you read me?"

"Ow. I'm not going anywhere," Stephane said. "Power is offline, systems are rebooting."

Shaila turned and saw Diaz' V-SEV heading off east. "I saw the shot. I'm gonna go try to take out some artillery. Jain, keep Durand clear of pests."

"Acknowledged," she replied. She continued to use her lasers in a wide swath—but quickly shut them down when she saw a squad of English and Venusians heading toward her position.

"Looks like our pals are catching up. That must be a good sign," she said. She pushed forward a few paces to knock several dozen *Corps Éternel* aside; they had turned to fire on the English, which made them easy pickings.

The group's leader jogged up behind her and gave her a jaunty salute—and she swore angrily when she realized who it was. She flipped on her outside speakers. "Dammit, Lieutenant, what the hell are you doing? Where's Elizabeth?"

Philip St. Germain's smile grew slightly wider, even though his left arm was hanging limply by his side. "I believe we are fighting, my Lady Commander. And thanks to her persuasiveness, our new allies have escorted her to the safekeeping of my mother."

Kids. "All right. Form up behind me, then. Use the other V-SEV as cover so you can fire without getting trampled or shot."

"The other what?"

Shaila groaned. "V-SEV. The thing I'm in. There's one on the ground that's damaged. Use it as armor and hide behind it as you shoot the bad guys. Got it?"

Philip nodded. "Very good. Come on, men! Follow me!"

To be fair, it seemed the group of bedraggled soldiers and sailors following Philip went along without so much as a peep of discontent. Shaila wondered if Philip had suddenly developed a sense of leadership. Then Philip pulled a flask from his coat and, wisely using the V-SEV as cover, tossed it toward a group of French soldiers. In an instant, the ground started...writhing. Vines and tendrils grew, leaves sprouted, trees grew larger—and soon the French were entangled up to their necks in the brightly-colored Venusian undergrowth, which had grown to twenty times its normal size. *Alchemy works too, I guess*, Shaila thought. *That's pretty impressive.*

Then the Venusians descended and, a moment later, the French troops were relieved of their heads. The vines retreated, and their corpses fell. Shaila wasn't sure whether to feel elated or grossed out.

Diaz, meanwhile, was busy kicking over cannon after cannon behind the French lines—she had managed to avoid the shots going in, then quickly skirted around to attack from the side. In fact, the general had picked up a cannon in each of her V-SEV's pincers, and was busy swinging them around like clubs.

"General Diaz, ma'am, you're having way too much fun," Shaila said.

"Lasers are busy recharging. Don't you ever improvise?" Diaz responded. "Now shut up and find some targets, Commander."

But there were few targets to be had now. Line after line of Venusian warriors were now surging past her, chasing the retreating French. The little critters were fast, and quickly jumped on and took down the remaining French zombies. Behind the Venusians, the English staggered forward, picking off the last pockets of resistance, living or undead.

And in the distance, Shaila could see Weatherby walking toward her, three Venusians beside him. The lizard people were decked out in headdresses, beads and other primitive gear. As they walked toward her, she could see Weatherby gesturing toward her V-SEV. The Venusians' faces were unreadable to Shaila, but she hoped they'd be suitably impressed.

"Stephane, how we doing?"

"Reboot keeps failing and looping. I don't know what's wrong."

"Roger that. Coming back to your position. Let's see if we can get you going again."

But it wasn't happening, even after Shaila climbed out, manually opened Stephane's entry hatch and spent twenty minutes going through the guts of his V-SEV. It would take at least an hour to debug the computers, let alone fix whatever damage the cannon shot and the fall caused.

"So," Weatherby said, approaching the V-SEVs after conferring with the Venusians and Diaz. "I take it cannon shot is indeed something you might've been worried about, Commander?"

Shaila grimaced at him. "Probably, but I think we did all right, with due respect, Admiral."

"Quite well, and I thank you for it. You are unharmed?"

Stephane nodded, as did Shaila. "We're fine. How bad were you hit?"

Weatherby grimaced. "We've but sixty men left, and only one cannon, which we shall leave behind. Your General Diaz tells me that time is of the essence. She has been in contact with your compatriots in the Void. The devices—satellites, I believe she said—have substantially accelerated their efforts to widen the portal between our worlds. We now have but hours before the world is completely consumed."

Shaila looked around at the injured, thirsty, exhausted men under Weatherby's command. "We're still a ways off. Some of them won't make it."

Weatherby regarded them with sadness and resolve upon his face. "I'm afraid you're right. I....wait. Can your devices pull a wagon?"

Shaila frowned. "A wagon? Really?" But then she spotted what caught Weatherby's attention—a small cluster of wagons off at the edge of the forest, probably the supply train for the defeated French forces. "Yeah, I bet they could."

Weatherby turned to one of his men. "Find Lady Anne. She has some experience with these matters. Tell her we need to harness those wagons to the metal giants. Go!"

It was a tall order, but with Anne and Philip overseeing the hasty renovation of the wagons—and with Elizabeth translating so that the Venusians might lend a hand—a total of four wagons were reinforced with additional wood for cover and loaded with men. There were small-arms gunports spaced out regularly, and one of the wagons was loaded with the last surviving cannon and all remaining shot—a lucky happenstance indeed. Each V-SEV could tow two of the wagons, hitched to each other, without a major loss of speed.

And Anne had made it all happen in an hour. Shaila wondered if there was some sort of alchemy that allowed the former Miss Baker to whip the troops into shape like that, but decided that she was pretty formidable on her own. Shaila figured that if Anne had been from the 22nd century, she might outrank Diaz.

The unusual caravan started off into the jungle once more, and Shaila thought the sight of V-SEVs towing wagons as probably the most absurd thing in the Solar System—except for the fact that the Venusian warriors had taken to climbing all over the V-SEVs, and refused to budge. So when they powered up and started moving, each V-SEV was covered in at least a dozen lizard-men.

"This can't get any weirder," Shaila told Stephane as they set off. With Stephane's V-SEV down, he joined her in the jumpseat, making for cramped quarters.

"It can," he said tiredly. "And it will. Just wait until we get to the vault."

CHAPTER 24

January 30, 2135
May 29, 1809

It is exceedingly impolite to refuse a gift, and not simply amongst fellow men. Within the Venusian culture, refusing a gift is tantamount to a declaration of hostilities. The Va'hak'ri tell of great wars in ancient days, fought because gifts were refused—even inadvertently called into question as to their quality or provenance.

And so with that in mind, Weatherby rode toward the Venusian memory vault upon one of the Venusians' queer *sek'hatk* mounts. Given its relatively small size, Weatherby had thought to decline, but it was fortunate that Elizabeth was by his side to translate, as well as to warn him of the repercussions of refusal. To the admiral's great surprise and mild consternation, the saurian mount was surprisingly strong, much in the way of the Icelandic ponies he had read about years ago. Except, of course, that these steeds had scales and frills rather than horsehair and manes.

"Did you name him yet, Admiral?" Shaila asked in his ear, where the headset remained.

Despite his exhaustion and doubt, Weatherby smiled at the quip—and the insouciance behind it. There were times when Weatherby wondered whether Shaila Jain was actually part of a real military organization. "I'm quite hopeful, Commander, that this is a mere passing acquaintance that will absolve me of actually keeping, let alone naming, this poor creature. That said, given the odor this fine steed seems to produce, a number of monikers do come to mind—few of them complimentary."

There was a short pause on the other end before she replied. "You're using big words just to mess with me now, aren't you."

"Only because I've found your 22nd century grasp of vocabulary alarming, Miss Jain. Shall we not seek to better one another in the time we have together?" Weatherby's smile grew broader as he said this. Throughout his long and storied career, Weatherby had noticed his propensity for good humor after an engagement. He felt it was, at times, unseemly that the natural reaction to winning a battle was joviality, especially given the heavy losses on both sides. However, it was, he found, human nature to feel awash in relief and good humor at the prospect of having survived, and contented himself in knowing that, in his experience, he was not the only one to react in such a way. Besides, with work still to be done, now was not the time to grieve for the fallen or feel his customary guilt—and the men needed to see him in good spirits.

"I don't see how—wait." Shaila said, interrupting herself. "Admiral, I have twenty-seven contacts ahead, roughly two kilometers—sorry 1.2 miles—ahead. There's a clearing there as well, and some sort of large stone structure." The woman's voice had changed from relaxed to respectful in mere moments—a sign, surely, that something was afoot. "There's a handful of unidentified targets, but it looks like seventeen of them are human."

"Very well, Commander. Please pass on my request to General Diaz that you ready your vehicles for battle," Weatherby said. "It seems like we may have arrived at the French camp. So…um…Weatherby out, I believe?"

He heard a chuckle on the other end. "Roger that, Admiral. Jain out."

Weatherby turned to his surviving marine commander—a lieutenant by the name of Cook now, as his two superiors had perished in the battle—and ordered him to ready the men. He then had the wagons unhitched from the giant metal vehicles. One wagon had their lone remaining cannon aboard, with its muzzle pointed out the end, so Weatherby requested Diaz and Shaila to bring that wagon forward so it might provide fire support.

As this was happening, the marine commander had thoughtfully sent a scout ahead—the same midshipman Weatherby had used as a runner, as it happened. The admiral had forgotten about the lad, to his chagrin, but was quite pleased to see the mid alive after the battle.

"There's a ruin up ahead, my Lord," the boy said breathlessly. "It looks like a pyramid, but made of steps instead of slanted walls. There's a clearing there too, but no huts or anything. Looks like there may have been buildings at one point, but not anymore. The French have tents set up there. They have about ten of those revenant guards, the dead ones. Some living soldiers, too, and then a handful of gentlemen all dressed up fancy. A couple of them were going in and out of the pyramid. There's an opening at the base of it."

Weatherby turned to Finch, who had come up to hear the report. "Doctor, does that not sound familiar?"

The alchemist nodded. "It does indeed. Rather like what we saw in '79, last we were here. It makes sense. I believe we saw one of their alchemists or shamans or whatever take the memories out of dead warriors then. They're probably stored in the pyramid. That's likely the vault."

"Actually, uncle, I should say the vault would be *under* the pyramid," Elizabeth corrected. "The Venusians still to this day do not have the ability to work stone on such a scale as to create pyramids. The structure is likely Martian or Saturnian in origin, and abandoned thousands of years ago. The Venusians would likely find a way to burrow under the floor inside the structure."

"Why burrow?" Diaz asked over the comm. "Why not just use the building as is?"

Elizabeth reflexively put her hand to hear headset as she replied. "Because while the tribes can appreciate the defensibility of stone structures, they also see relics of the other Known Worlds as not trustworthy. So they would create their own spaces inside the structure—underneath most likely. The 1794 expedition to the *Ve'lak'tha* ruins near Puerto Verde found—"

"Yes, thank you, my dear," Weatherby interrupted, prompting a blush from Elizabeth. "General Diaz, shall we plan our attack?"

"Roger that, Admiral. Seems like the main force here are zombies, with some non-combatants as well. I'd rather capture than kill. We want answers, after all."

"Agreed, General," Weatherby said. "What do you have in mind?"

Shaila guided her V-SEV down the rutted wagon-trail, a series of ropes in her mech's "hand" that allowed her to tow the wagon behind. Diaz took up the rear in her own V-SEV.

"You know, Shay, there will be more *Corps Éternel* here at some point," Stephane said from behind her. "I would imagine that they would guard other approaches to the memory vault just as well as the approach we went through."

She smiled at this, because it was the same conversation Shaila, Diaz and Weatherby had *before* they faced off in the clearing and the Venusians saved their collective asses. "I know, honey. That's why we gotta get in, figure this out, and get out fast before the cavalry arrives. Literally, I suppose."

"Cut the chatter, you two," Diaz said over the comm. "I'm detecting a lot more movement in the clearing now. They spotted us."

It would be hard to miss us, Shaila thought as she gave the four-meter-tall V-SEV more speed. Ahead, she could see a line of soldiers forming about thirty meters away, in the center of the clearing. Behind them, French officers and civilians were rushing around—many of them into the huge pyramid behind them.

"Pyramids," Stephane said, humor in his voice. "Why is it always pyramids?"

"Well, they're easy for primitive cultures to build," Shaila noted as she tugged the cannon into position at the trail head, giving Diaz enough room to join her in front of it.

"Of course, there's always the ancient astronaut theory, and—dammit. They've opened fire."

Shaila saw puffs of white smoke erupt from the muskets in front of her. A split second later, a handful of pings on the outer hull of her V-SEV indicated the French had good aim. Of course, a vehicle designed to drop from space and handle Venus' harsh environment was a good bet against 19th century muskets. She looked at her readouts and confirmed that the soldiers in front of her were zombies. Only the officer with them was among the living.

"General, permission to engage," Shaila said. "I can target the zombies and spare the officer from this angle."

"Granted," Diaz said.

A moment later, Shaila charged forward toward the French line, and an angry red beam shot out from the forearm of the V-SEV, slicing the *Corps Éternel* in half as they reloaded and stopped within a few centimeters of the French officer, who looked on in shocked horror.

"Targets eliminated," Shaila reported. "Admiral Weatherby, you're up."

"Thank you, Commander," he replied over the comm.

Suddenly, a swarm of red-coated marines and Venusian warriors burst out of the jungle from all sides of the clearing. Weatherby and Finch positioned themselves directly in front of the pyramid entrance, thus intercepting the most obvious line of retreat—and bagging several Frenchmen in the process.

The remaining French dropped their weapons—except for the one commanding the *Corps Éternel* that Shaila had just cut down. He was still staring at the V-SEVs. *We may need to get that poor guy some help*, Shaila thought.

To Weatherby's great pleasure, the remaining French at the encampment were by no means patriots, at least when faced with capture, and a few discussed freely their aims and compatriots. Of course, the metal vehicles brought by Shaila and Diaz were perhaps far more persuasive in interrogation than his stern questioning.

Sadly, the news was nowhere near as accommodating as its sources. And as much as Weatherby wished to immediately enter the pyramid, he instead posted sentries at the portal so he might confer with his subordinates and allies as to the defense of their position.

"We are told that, shortly after our earlier engagement, runners warned the encampment here of the losses, and word has already been sent to reinforce this area," Weatherby said grimly to his makeshift war council, which included his alchemists, the 22nd century officers and several Venusian chieftains, with Elizabeth translating. "There are at least another thousand revenants at their disposal, and may be here at any time, for they can move as fast as horses without tiring."

This prompted croaking and chirping among the Venusians. "The chiefs wish to convey that their alliance remains with you, Father," Elizabeth said with a wry smile. "Seeing the French use revenants, and then finding them here at their sacred site, has aggrieved them greatly."

"Please convey my utmost gratitude as you see fit," Weatherby said. "And we shall make the best use of them as we may. Of course, I dare say even with their courage, this small band will not be enough."

Diaz nodded. "We got one cannon, about sixty humans and maybe three hundred Venusians at this point, plus we're down a V-SEV. We can't take on another thousand zombies like we did last time and expect to come out on top. We're going to need to take up defensive positions, and we're going to need a plan."

"What did you have in mind, General?" Weatherby asked.

Diaz nodded at Shaila, who held her datapad in the palm of her hand and activated the holoprojector. A miniaturized layout of the clearing sprang forth. "We took the opportunity to do a little recon while you were rounding up the French. This pyramid is old and crumbling, but sensors say it's structurally sound inside. Outside, it provides plenty of cover for snipers, and there are few cracks on the upper tiers where you could take cover if you needed to.

"So here's the plan. We want to put one of the V-SEVs on the first tier up, above the door, and the second one actually blocking the door once we're all inside. That creates a bottleneck that protects us and maximizes what real firepower we have. General Diaz can link the two mechs so that one fires while the other recharges lasers, so that we always have a laser going.

"We have one cannon left, and apparently we have alchemists who can make it sing," Shaila said with a nod toward Anne and Philip. "I want to place that on the same tier as the V-SEV, preferably right between its legs so that the gun crew can use it for cover. Same idea…blast as many of them as possible. Ideally, the cannon can aim for whatever artillery the French roll in here, because if they bring any, this whole plan goes pear-shaped fast."

Shaila then pointed to the upper tiers of the pyramid. "Your marines are used to firing from the tops, if I remember my naval history lectures. So we place your best shooters up higher, using the rubble up there as cover. They take out command-and-control, the officers, just like they would aboard ship. Again, if the French bring artillery, snipers need to focus on gun crews and help neutralize them fast. If the cannon are in place and start firing on the pyramid itself, our defense goes out the window and we all get buried."

Another stream of chatter erupted from the Venusians. "The chiefs would like you to know that they are warriors, and do not hide behind stone. They will face their enemy in the open," Elizabeth said. "So sorry, Commander."

"Not at all," Shaila smiled. "We want them to do their thing. We just need them to wait. Let the French march into the clearing and begin to assault the pyramid. Then, when the bulk of the French are inside, I need the chiefs to send their troops in from beyond the tree line and encircle the French as best they can. Pick them off at the edges and herd them toward the center so that there are more troops bumping up against each other than there are fighting any of us."

Shaila tapped a few keys on her datapad to reenact her plan with the aid of holographics as Elizabeth translated. Suddenly, the Venusians started chattering amongst themselves and, a moment later, they were jumping up and down and making what could only be considered battle cries. "Much better," Elizabeth confirmed.

"Good. We're going to need you to get into some detail with them about avoiding line-of-fire," Shaila said. She then noted the look on Elizabeth's face. "Right. We need to explain to them how the laser and cannon will work so they don't get in the way. Anyway, we think with this set-up, General Diaz can hold the clearing long enough for the rest of us to get in there and figure out what the French are doing, and stop them if possible."

Weatherby turned to Diaz. "It seems a sound plan. Are you comfortable with sharing command with Lieutenant Cook, Madam General?"

Diaz raised an eyebrow at Weatherby and turned toward the obviously green lieutenant who had inherited command from his deceased superiors. "What's your name again, Lieutenant?"

The young man, who looked barely out of his teens, straightened up and looked Diaz in the eye. "Lieutenant Samuel Cook, my Lady."

"You understand, Lieutenant Cook, that this plan maximizes our assets and relies on coordination, and that your admiral here endorses it?" she asked in her best no-nonsense tone.

"Yes, my Lady," Cook replied, slightly nervous now.

"All right then. I hope you take my suggestions under immediate advisement and decide quickly as to the merits. And you can just call me 'General,' since I've been fighting wars and commanding men for a good three-plus decades. We clear?"

"Quite so, General," the young man said, saluting for good measure and seeming to be extraordinarily uncomfortable now.

Diaz turned to Weatherby. "I think we're good."

Weatherby could not help but smile. "So you shall have all our soldiers and cannon. Lieutenant St. Germain will remain at the gun so he may provide as much support as possible. If it is quite all right with you, I would ask that Elizabeth be placed inside your second vehicle, which I believe would be the safest place for her during the engagement."

"Agreed. We can rig a speaker, too, so she can call out commands to the Venusians when the time's right for them to pounce," Diaz added. "She can keep her headset so she and I can chat beforehand."

"Very well. I entrust her to your safekeeping. I…" Weatherby paused. "Well, I am sure I need not say more."

This prompted a rare smile from Diaz. "I'll take care of her as if she were my own, Admiral."

Weatherby cleared his throat and regained his composure. "I thank you, General. And so that leaves the Lady Weatherby and Dr. Finch to accompany me into the pyramid, along with Gar'uk. I assume Commander Jain and Dr. Durand will be joining us?"

Shaila nodded. "We have the Emerald Tablet in a secure container. I assume we'll want to bring *The Book of the Dead* as well."

Finch looked alarmed at this. "Do we think it wise? Can we not secure them elsewhere? We've no idea what we may find below."

Weatherby turned to Anne, who simply shrugged. "On the other hand, if these artifacts are the key to stopping whatever Cagliostro and Althotas have planned, we may miss a singular opportunity. It is an incredible risk either way," she said.

Stephane stepped forward, his eyes somewhat glassy. "She's right. Rathemas wants both these items. And he wants to be down there, but…I feel as though he's afraid. That we've come further than he expected, maybe. That we'll figure it out, whatever 'it' is. I think we should bring the book and tablet."

Weatherby hung his head for several moments before finally looking up at his companions. "Very well. We shall bring them. Anne, my love, you must carry the book, for I do not think it wise for either Finch or myself to carry it. I'm sorry."

She gave him a small, sad smile. "We all have our burdens in this, Tom. I am glad to take it now."

He stared at her for what seemed an eternity before chaining his emotions once more and simply nodding at her. "Yes, very well then. Commander, I suggest you carry the Tablet. We will need you to keep a weather eye upon Dr. Durand as well. I will find two men we might bring with us for support. But that will have to do."

Weatherby stood straight. "Thank you, all of you. We have much to attend to. General, if you please, begin your preparations. Everyone else, with me.

"And God save us all."

CHAPTER 25

January 30, 2135
May 29, 1809

Shaila entered the pyramid through a decrepit, crumbling portal lined with inscrutable carvings. She expected to traverse a long corridor before getting into the center chamber, like the old pyramids of Egypt she visited as a schoolchild. Or the one on Mars, for that matter.

So when, after only five meters, she entered into a vaulted space—the hollow interior of the pyramid, buttressed and soaring—she gasped. It was as if the entire pyramid was hollowed out or inverted, with each outside step visible on the inside. An intricate network of buttresses kept the space free and clear, and there were some breathtakingly beautiful carvings—each several meters high—on many of the inverted steps.

"Who the hell built this?" she breathed. "It's incredible!"

"Likely the Xan," Finch replied, holding a lit torch aloft. "This is beyond the construction the Royal Geographic Society has documented on Mars. A shame the French were the first Earthmen to gain access here."

Gar'uk clambered ahead with another torch, providing more light. The very top seemed to be open to the sky and covered by some form of cupola, bathing the grey stone in an overall greenish light. "Yes, from long ago," he croaked. "When the others were here, when they brought war to our lands."

Stephane stumbled as he entered the room, then cast his eyes higher. "Yes, the Venusians…they were part of the war long ago."

Shaila turned back to him. "Stephane?"

He gave her a little smile. "Sorry. I saw a little of that when the lizard-people were examining me. It was…weird.

But I could see the Martians and the Xan. They used the Venusians. Warriors, or slaves. Probably both."

Weatherby and Anne entered last, with his two marines before him. "All quite interesting, no doubt, but I think it best that we try to find entrance to whichever part of this structure the Venusians have claimed for their memory vault. Conduct a search for anything in the walls and floor that may lead downward."

The group spread out in the cavernous room. There were few structures inside, though the rather large altarpiece in the front—easily two meters high, now cracked and crumbling in the middle—definitely stood out. It was on a dais, and seemed to be the obvious place. Shaila and Stephane made their way over to it, with Finch in tow.

"This looks somewhat similar to what I saw in Egypt," Finch said. "There was a trapdoor under the altar. Perhaps?"

The alchemist climbed the stairs to the altar and began searching around the base of it. Shaila could see more runes and sigils on it; unlike the carvings on Mars, there were no real images or pictures she could make out, though the stone was pretty weathered. She looked up to find that the altar was right above the opening atop the pyramid, and figured millennia of rain had a lot to do with the altar's erosion.

"Yes! Here!" Finch called. "A small opening—even the Venusians would have to crouch down to enter!"

Shaila and Stephane came up behind him and saw a small hole in the ground, no more than a half-meter in diameter. It was surrounded by crumbled stones of various sizes. "Tight fit," she said, pulling out her datapad and activating sensors. "Looks like it widens out a bit down there, but we don't have a lot of leeway."

Stephane pointed to the floor of the dais. "These are footprints, no? This must be the place. The French have been here."

"All right then. Looks like we do the squeeze," Shaila said.

Weatherby had Gar'uk go first, armed with a pistol to hold off any potential trouble while the rest of the group made their way inside. It took a few tries for Shaila to get through there with the Emerald Tablet in tow, but she managed to drag it behind her as she squeezed through a space about three meters long, sharply sloping downward behind the altar and dais.

And she ended up in a corridor no more than a meter and a half high. "I'm going to get claustrophobic quick," she muttered, using her datapad as a flashlight to help with her footing. Stephane nearly collided with her on his way down, but soon everyone was huddled in the small, rough-hewn hallway.

"Onward," Weatherby ordered quietly. "Weapons at the ready."

Shaila drew a pistol, loaned by one of the marines above, and followed Gar'uk down the corridor. The stonework was very rough and looked to be hand-carved. There were no runes or features of any kind. She figured it was done by the Venusians after the Xan left—for whatever reasons they left in the first place.

After about forty meters of winding, gently sloping corridor, Gar'uk hissed and raised a claw. They all stopped, and the little Venusian pointed ahead. "I hear."

A low hum seemed to permeate the walls at this point, though the source couldn't be placed. Likewise, there seemed to be a faint light coming from ahead, though to Shaila it was barely discernible—it felt like a trick of the eyes. But she figured Gar'uk probably had better vision. At least, it seemed reasonable to presume that.

Shaila turned back toward Weatherby. "Plan?" she whispered.

"Gar'uk shall move ahead and provide us with reconnaissance," Weatherby said. "The rest of us shall prepare for the worst. Finch, you and Lady Anne shall provide us with alchemical means of either distraction or subdual, while the rest of us ready ourselves for battle if need be."

It took the little Venusian little more than a few minutes to scurry forward and report back. There were but three men in the chamber—two older gentleman and a French officer. Unfortunately, there were also a dozen *Corps Éter-nel* soldiers therein.

"Very well, then. I assume a typical working to simply stun adversaries will not be effective against the revenants?" Weatherby asked Anne.

It was Finch who responded, however. "Typically, yes, but I believe I can create an admixture that would have the same effect on the revenants without harming the living. If I can have but a moment, I—"

The admiral cut him off with a sharp gesture. "No, Doctor. Your workings with regard to revenants and your other researches are part and parcel of this. We shall not meddle in these matters any longer. Lady Anne?"

Looking perplexed, she looked at both Weatherby and Finch. "I do not know whether this proposed working will actually touch upon the forces of *Maat* as others have," she said slowly. "Perhaps there is merit to this. If Dr. Finch may take a moment to explain—"

"No!" Weatherby hissed. "I will not chance it. Prepare an alchemical fog, then, that will mask only the doorway. Then we attack. Make ready."

Finch turned to Shaila with a helpless look, but all she could do was shrug. It was obvious at this point that Finch had used up whatever trust Weatherby had in him, but she was far from being an expert on 19th century alchemy. Instead, she drew her pistol and motioned for Stephane to stay put. There were at least eleven combatants in the room ahead, and only Weatherby, Shaila and the two marines were armed.

That is, until she saw Anne produce a sword as well. Shaila was about to speak up when she remembered Anne's skill from their battles on Mars. *Hell, she's probably better with it than I am.*

With Weatherby in the lead, the group proceeded quietly down the corridor. They started to hear some voices ahead, echoing off the stone walls. Finally, Weatherby put his hand up to stop the group. The room was right around the bend. The admiral extended his hand, and Finch placed a small cloth satchel in it. With a quick scan of his troops, Weatherby then hurled it around the corner. With a soft plop and a hiss, smoke started edging upward into the corridor.

"Now!" he hissed.

Shaila allowed the marines and Anne to move past her—she only had one real shot, and was mindful of Weatherby's warning about the Tablet. She had no doubt the guys inside would love to nab it if they could. So she edged forward as the sound of cries and steel rang out from behind the curtain of white fog.

"Arrêté! Corps, arrêté!"

What the...?

She turned back toward Stephane, who looked equally confused as the sounds of combat ceased. The French had ordered their *Corps Éternel* to stop fighting.

Motioning for Stephane to stay put, Shaila hugged the wall of the low corridor and poked her head into the fog. It took a moment for her to find the very edge of the alchemical effect, but when she did, she saw Weatherby, Anne and the marines pointing muskets and swords at two men, while the zombie soldiers were literally frozen in mid-strike. And they were all in the middle of one of the strangest chambers Shaila had ever seen.

The room was a kind of rough tunnel extending at least forty meters out. The top of the arc was easily six meters high and wide, and the walls seemed to be of the same rough-hewn make as the hallway. But lining those walls were shelves made of sticks and logs, lashed together by what looked like vines.

And on the shelves were glowing silver orbs.

Each sphere was no larger than a baseball, but seemed to have a variable light inside it, as if a twinkling star could be seen up close. They were kept several rows deep on each shelf—and each wall was stacked with at least 30 shelves. They extended down both walls...all the way to the end of the room.

There were tens of thousands of them—perhaps more. Perhaps millions.

About six meters from the doorway was a circle on the floor made of piled stone, rising about a half-meter from the floor. Shaila could see a dull, silvery liquid inside. And on either side of it stood two men. One was tall and heavy set, with a florid, long face and swept-back grey hair. He wore the clothes of an early 19th century gentlemen, well embroidered and shiny where appropriate. The other was much older, clad all in black, with a wreath of white, unkempt hair around the crown of his head. His face was wide and full and heavily wrinkled, and his eyes were slightly bulbous.

Even though he had aged thirty years, Shaila would never fail to recognize Cagliostro, the man who nearly started an alien invasion of the Solar System.

Naturally, she felt pretty good about pointing her pistol at him.

"Given that the Lady Anne Weatherby is with you, I can only assume you are Admiral Lord Weatherby," the first man said in accented English. "I pray you, lower your weapons! We have much to discuss and precious little time to do so."

Weatherby was not in the mood to acquiesce. "And I can only assume you are Jean-Claude Berthollet, so you'll forgive me if my weapons remain as they are, for it was your men who attacked my fleet in the Void yesterday and again, mere hours ago, in the jungles here!"

Another man stepped forward from where the *Corps Éternel* had halted. The man was tall and mostly bald, and wore the most ornate military uniform Shaila had ever seen. "Those were on my orders, my Lord Admiral, as there is a state of war between England and France," the man said. "I am, however, open to a truce between our local forces while Dr. Berthollet explains our…situation."

"And you are?" Weatherby demanded.

"Louis-Nicolas Davout, Duke of Auerstädt, Marshal of the Empire and servant to His Imperial Majesty, Napoleon."

Shaila saw a look of surprise on Weatherby's face—the Frenchman had to be a major player in the Napoleonic Wars. "The last we had heard, you were in London," Weatherby ventured. "It is no doubt highly significant that you are here, your Grace." He finally lowered his sword. "For the moment, we are in a state of truce, but only within this room. We will discuss the present situation, and then, if there can be no accord, you may revive your accursed soldiers and we shall see who prevails."

Davout smirked. "A fine plan, my Lord." The marshal then barked out several rapid orders in French, at which the zombies animated and returned to at-ease positions on either side of the doorway, a kind of macabre honor guard.

Then Shaila noticed Cagliostro staring at her, and realized she was still pointing a gun at him. Reluctantly, she lowered it—but he kept staring.

"What?" she demanded.

"You...you're from the other realm, are you not?" Cagliostro asked in his Italian-accented English. "I saw you on Mars!"

She narrowed her eyes at him. "Yeah, I was there. Commander Shaila Jain. We stopped your ass from unleashing Althotas on the world. We should've hauled you back to our 'realm' and put you on trial for war crimes and attempted genocide."

Cagliostro he turned to Berthollet. "Dear God, it is happening again, Berthollet! They are here! I warned you this was possible! They have meddled in these matters a second time and created another convergence! It is just as Althotas would have wished!"

Berthollet frowned at Shaila, then turned to Weatherby. "Before we can begin negotiations in earnest, Lord Weatherby, I should wish to know why you would take such a hazardous and irresponsible step by creating another convergence!"

At this, Anne practically lunged toward Berthollet. "You know full well that we did not do this!" she countered. "It is you who unleashed *The Book of the Dead* into the world and created these fell soldiers. And with each one you create, the space between worlds gets smaller!"

Weatherby shook his head. "Please! Wait, my love, I beg you." He placed a hand on her shoulder, which she shrugged off violently, but nonetheless stopped for the moment as he continued. "You're saying that you have not created a convergence, and I swear upon my honor that we have not done so ourselves."

"So you say, but is it true that Andrew Finch possesses *The Book of the Dead*?" Berthollet asked. "For I have seen his workings of late, and they would be nigh impossible without it."

Finch stepped forward. "Yes, I have the book. And yes, I have used a modicum of its power, as you have," he said, standing tall but contrite. "It is possible—though still not proven—that our use of these powers, yours and mine, may have weakened the border between worlds. We come seeking the truth of the matter."

"Yes, yes, we're well aware of this possibility," Berthollet said with a dismissive wave. "But that in and of itself cannot create a convergence. It would take either the alchemical essences of the Known Worlds—which were destroyed with Althotas on Mars—or a combination of *The Book of the Dead* and the Emerald Tablet. That is why we are here, you fools. The Venusians were *there* when Althotas created those fell artifacts, and they were there when he was banished to the world between worlds."

"Their memories of these events are here, in the memory vaults," Cagliostro added. "We hope that these memories will give us the information we need."

"To bring him back?" Weatherby demanded.

"God, no, Weatherby!" Davout thundered. "To shut him away forever!"

"But with you here, and the convergence in place, all he would need are the two artifacts, the book and the Tablet," Berthollet said. "And we fear his agents could be anywhere. Indeed, they could be you!"

Shaila's stomach dropped as Weatherby turned to her in horror. It was their worst fear confirmed. *All he needs are the book and the Tablet. And we brought them here.*

Suddenly, Shaila's headset crackled. "Diaz to Jain. Diaz to Jain. Enemy is here. Repeat, enemy is here. We got about a thousand goddamn zombies out here and we are engaging. Over."

CHAPTER 26

January 30, 2135
May 29, 1809

Diaz watched stoically as line after line of *Corps Éternel* soldiers marched into the clearing. They spread out like the precision drill teams she had seen in her academy days at Colorado Springs, with muskets over their shoulders and feet moving in unnervingly precise lockstep. And they moved *fast*—it was like she was watching a parade in fast-forward.

"Hold fire," Diaz ordered. She had given Elizabeth's headset to Philip so they could coordinate better, then rigged the comms in the other V-SEV so that she wouldn't need one. "I want to see how these guys line up."

And line up they did. They emerged from the jungle five abreast, then quickly formed larger lines in the clearing that spread out and pivoted toward the pyramid. There were easily fifty troops in each row, at perfect arm's length. And they kept coming.

"Holding fire. Cannon is ready," Philip replied. "Lookouts report several cannon coming down the trail now. Six…no, eight pieces."

"Aw, hell. Why not, right? Jesus," Diaz responded. "I'm going to try to disable the guns while they're in transit. If I can't, hold fire until the guns have stopped moving before you hit 'em."

"We shall concentrate fire upon the *Corps Éternel* until you tell us otherwise, Madam General," Philip responded, "and allow our Venusian compatriots to attack at the flanks and rear."

Diaz powered up the lasers on both V-SEVs. "Call me 'madam' again, Lieutenant, and I'll beat you something fierce," she said with a grin.

It took a moment for the young man to reply. "I certainly meant no disrespect," he said, a touch of petulance in his voice.

"I know. Don't worry about it. Let's get to work. Fire when ready."

Above Diaz' V-SEV, a huge blast shook the foundations of the pyramid as a gout of bluish flame shot out in a wide arc across the clearing, and at least two dozen zombies went down in flames, literally. Meanwhile, Diaz targeted the first cannon she saw, rolling up toward the clearing from the trail. She took aim and fired—and found the laser was going to take a while to cut through the thick iron of the cannon.

Thankfully, it cut through the wooden wheels just fine. A second later, the artillery piece dropped through the wooden wreckage onto the ground—effectively blocking the other artillery from entering the clearing and approaching the pyramid.

"Hot damn!" Diaz whooped. "Lieutenant, I suggest you have your snipers commence firing. Elizabeth, as soon as you see the last soldiers come off the trail, signal the Venusians to attack.

"We might get out of this looking good after all," she added.

Diaz began slicing through the enemy lines with her laser—failing to notice two small targets edging around the back of the pyramid.

Weatherby stood across from Berthollet and Davout with his arms folded. "You'll forgive me, gentlemen, if I cannot quite believe your assertion that the presence of the Emerald Tablet and *The Book of the Dead* in this place is in error, for our own alchemists believe that these two artifacts may be used *against* Althotas with great efficacy."

"Just as a child may use a loaded gun when placed before him," Berthollet sneered. "Not well. And if there is a soldier there with him, who should make better use of it?"

Shaila stepped forward. "Fine, but where is he, then? If he's not here to use the damn things, and if you guys are all excited about keeping Althotas out of our worlds, then let's take them and get to work. Seal it up. Banish him. Whatever."

"That is not the entirety of our mission, young lady," Davout said. "It is, of course, imperative to ensure Althotas does not enter our realms again. But the Emperor himself has commanded that we find a method to permanently banish the Martian that does not reduce the effectiveness of the *Corps Éternel*."

Weatherby narrowed his eyes at the French marshal. "And so you and your Emperor would risk the Known Worlds in order to keep your foul soldiers," he said. "That cannot stand. We have the book and the Tablet, and by God, we will use them to defeat Althotas, and your creations can go to Hell where they belong!"

The two sides stared for a few long moments before Anne stepped forward and ventured an idea. "Gentlemen, perhaps we may yet come to an accord. Of course, we retain the book and the Tablet, and have no intention of surrendering them to you," she said, walking around the room slowly, apparently deep in thought. "Of course, with this convergence occurring, I would suggest time is of the essence. Therefore, I would like to conduct my researches here in this chamber, with Dr. Finch assisting me. As might I suggest that you may continue your inquiries here as well, so long as you do not hinder ours. Should either of us find a solution, we may implement it as we see fit—again, without interference. And of course, we shall all agree that this chamber is of utmost importance to the Venusian people, and should be treated with all due care and respect."

Davout and Berthollet looked at each other, surprise and confusion writ upon their faces, while Cagliostro seemed almost giddy at the prospect. Meanwhile, Weatherby positioned himself just in front of three of the revenants, and gave Shaila what he hoped to be a most meaningful look. To her credit, the young woman gave a slow nod of her head and slowly walked toward two others, bringing one of the marines closer with a subtle gesture.

After conferring briefly, Davout looked up and smiled. "While that is indeed a most fair-minded solution, Lady Weatherby, I am afraid we must decline. Above, our reinforcements are well on their way, and even with your fantastical vehicles, our sheer numbers may yet turn the tide. And as for this room, well…" Davout made a show of unsheathing his blade. "You are outnumbered. *Corps, attaque!*"

Utterly predictable, Weatherby thought. With one swift motion, he drew his alchemically enhanced sword and swung in a wide arc, neatly slicing three of the revenants in half before they could move. Shaila was less fortunate, however, for her pistol shot hit her target in the jaw, rather than the forehead, and the creature began to grapple her in its clawed, shriveled hands, even as its jawbone dangled from its shattered face.

A scream to Weatherby's right sent a shiver down his spine; he turned to see one of his marines impaled on a bayonet, while another revenant twisted the poor man's neck in a wholly unnatural way. With a sharp crack, the deed was done, and the man slumped to the ground, his head at an ugly angle from the rest of him.

Weatherby bent down to grab one of the severed revenant's muskets. "Jain!" he cried, throwing the weapon toward her. Despite her predicament, she managed to catch it with one free hand, then sent the butt of the weapon into her revenant's head, or what remained of it, stunning it long enough to free her. She then drove the bayonet through its throat and twisted, severing the head and sending the body collapsing to the floor.

A gunshot rang out, and Weatherby turned to see Stephane at the door, holding another musket. His heart stopped a moment—at whom did he aim?—but was relieved to find that the Frenchman had successfully shot a revenant making for Anne, and she was able to finish off the creature with her sword.

Weatherby was about to move forward to engage the rest of the revenants when several more shots rang out in dizzying succession. He wheeled about to find Stephane being pushed to the floor, and two other people walking into the room with what could only be firearms from some unimagined future—jet black and small and, it seemed, capable of firing rounds at an incredible pace.

"Greene!" Shaila cried out. She raised her musket toward him, but the silver-haired man immediately pointed his weapon at her—and she immediately thought better of it.

"Enough!" Greene shouted. "Throw down your weapons!" He then said something in a language Weatherby could not fathom, and the revenants immediately stopped fighting, once again frozen in place.

Undeterred, the remaining marine set his bayonet and charged Greene and his companion, an African woman of surpassing physical strength. The woman fired her weapon at the marine, and the man's chest exploded with what seemed to be at least seven different bullet wounds. He fell wordlessly to the floor.

"Anybody else gonna be an idiot today?" the woman hissed. Her brow was dappled in sweat, her eyes were wide, and the near rictus-grin she bore chilled Weatherby to his bones.

Evan Greene walked over to Weatherby. Like the woman, he too seemed…strained. His eyes were bloodshot, with dark circles under them, and he seemed coated in a thin veil of perspiration. And his smile was only slightly less disconcerting. "You look old, Mr. Weatherby. I guess it's been a while. Your sword, if you please. I know how dangerous that thing is."

Weatherby looked around and saw the woman with her weapon now aimed at Anne, whose face bore a look of anger and horror both. With a grimace, Weatherby flipped his sword around in his hand and presented it to Greene. "At least I, Doctor, can blame my appearance on the passage of time. You do not have such an excuse at your disposal."

Greene took the blade with a grin. "It's these bodies. They're soft. Sure, they can contain a human spirit just fine. But a Martian soul? It's a tight fit." He then turned to Shaila.

"Really good of you to bring the Emerald Tablet with you, Shay."

Shaila's look would've made most grown men cower. "You can go to Hell."

"Working on it," Greene quipped. "Maggie, do you sense it? I think the book's here too."

The African woman—her name was Huntington, Weatherby remembered—gazed around the room a moment before settling back on Anne. "It's in her pack." She then grabbed Anne's arm and roughly spun her around, tearing Anne's pack from her shoulders and shoving her to the floor. "Yeah, it's in here. He's going to be pleased."

Greene laughed. "I can't believe you guys. This was too easy." He walked over, wrenched the case containing the Tablet from Shaila and proceeded to the pool in the middle of the room. "You really played your parts well. All of you!"

"Then perhaps you might illuminate us as to our folly," Finch said icily.

Greene and Huntington began to unpack the artifacts, one on each side of the pool. "I really wish we could just shoot these fuckers now," Huntington said as she stood back up and covered the room with her weapon.

"That's not the plan," Greene said softly as he began unspooling wires from his own pack. "Althotas wants them to see this."

Huntington looked over to Davout. "What about him? He's not part of the brief."

Greene looked up briefly at the French marshal. "No, I guess he's not."

With an awful grin, Huntington aimed her weapon at Davout and pulled the trigger, releasing another volley of rounds into the stunned officer. He was struck several times and immediately fell backward. The man coughed once, turned his head briefly toward Weatherby…and died.

"What is it, then, that the ascended master wishes us to see?" Cagliostro asked with surprising deference, a change in demeanor that immediately repelled Weatherby.

It seemed neither Greene nor Huntington was falling for it. "You failed once already, Cagliostro," Greene said as he began attaching wires to both the Tablet and the book. "I suppose you did your best. Maybe Althotas will keep you around. Like a pet or something."

"What are you doing?" Weatherby demanded. He saw Greene now attaching wires to one of the "datapads" Shaila and her compatriots used. "What do you hope to accomplish here?"

Greene looked up and smiled again. "This."

He pressed a few keys on his datapad, and both the Emerald Tablet and *The Book of the Dead* began to glow—the Tablet in a bright greenish-yellow, and the book in a black-purple emanation that seemed to draw light in rather than cast it.

Weatherby heard a soft tone from Shaila's direction. Heedless of the revenants around her, she pulled out her datapad and examined it. "Oh, my God. They're transmitting something. From the satellites."

A moment later, the remaining revenants in the room began to tremble.

Then they screamed—an unholy, utterly unintelligible cry that seemed to come from the darkest places of all Creation.

What was that old phrase? Shooting fish in a barrel? Diaz smiled as another line of zombie soldiers were sliced in half by her V-SEV's laser. Her plan to alternate between vehicles was working out fairly well, though she figured she had maybe three or four more shifts between the two before both lasers would need a serious recharge. By then, with any luck, the French would run out of bodies to throw at them.

And at least the French had the decency to line them up nice and neat for her to mow down. *Gotta love 19th century infantry tactics.*

Another boom echoed above her, and this time a single cannon ball was launched into the middle of the French lines. The resulting explosion produced a ring of fire that took out another twenty targets. At the edges of the French lines, the Venusians were giving it their all. It took three or four warriors to take down a single revenant. The little lizard guys were getting pretty efficient at it, though their losses were starting to pile up a bit more than anyone would've liked.

It was going to be close, no matter what. Still, if she had to mobilize her V-SEV and go storming in, she wanted as many of the goddamn zombies down as possible.

Then suddenly, the French *Corps Éternel* stopped fighting.

"Lieutenant, what the hell am I seeing here?" Diaz asked over the comm as she watched five hundred zombies begin to quake…and scream something completely inhuman.

"I…I cannot say, General," Philip replied. "This is…this is wrong. Something is happening."

"No shit," she replied, pausing to allow her lasers a chance to recharge a bit. "But what is it? They running out of juice? Giving up? Dying?"

"No, General, I…oh, dear God in Heaven."

Diaz quickly pulled up a holocam shot on her HUD and zoomed in on a small group of zombies. They had stopped shaking and screaming, and were now…looking around. They were looking at the muskets in their hands, the clothing they wore, the faces of their comrades.

"Oh, fuck me. They're waking up," she breathed.

A few of them started talking…shouting, really. Diaz couldn't hear, but from what she could see, the zombies were definitely communicating with one another. She panned her camera over to two living French officers—and they looked horrified.

A moment later, they were swarmed by their formerly docile troops…and literally torn limb from limb.

"Oh, fuck. Lieutenant, I need you double-time on that gun. Fire at the biggest groupings you can find. Now!"

But the *Corps Éternel* were no longer as compliant in their own destruction as they were a few moments prior. At least half of them began running—and running *fast*—toward the pyramid. And they were running in zigzags and jagged lines, toward and away from each other all at once.

They were dodging.

The other half started in on the Venusians, hacking at them with bayonets or simply tearing the poor things apart with their bare hands. They were strong before, but now...

Diaz powered up the lasers on both V-SEVs and started firing in wide arcs. "Kid, get off a last shot and then take cover," Diaz ordered. "Get Elizabeth out of her V-SEV and bring her and as many men as you can inside the pyramid. Hopefully we can hold them off at the door."

With a grimace, Diaz pushed her V-SEV forward a few meters to clear the way for what she hoped wouldn't be a futile retreat.

May 29, 1809

Sir Arthur Wellesley looked over his maps and, for the first time in years, dared to hope.

"Your warriors are most efficient, as are your weapons, my lady," he said to the robed, hooded Xan towering over him to his right. "I had thought the small handful that accompanied you were too few, but...I was wrong, and I apologize."

The Xan bowed. "Your apology is appreciated, but the gesture is most unnecessary," the creature sang. Her name was Arkhest, and her title was that of "battle-art master" of the Xan. "Our weapons simply rob the revenants of their alchemical properties long enough to give those poor souls their proper rest."

"Indeed," Wellesley said, noncommittal. Arkhest had a penchant for understatement, for the queer firearms employed by the two dozen Xan she brought with her could immobilize a dozen revenants at a shot, allowing the English to come behind them with bayonets and fire to finish the job.

Wellesley had launched his attack at Colwyn Bay, sailing from Edinburgh and traveling north through the Orkneys to avoid detection. Once he landed his force, resistance was light until they reached the outskirts of Shrewsbury. However, the Battle of Shrewsbury went well enough to send the French retreating east and south, and Wellesley had pressed forward to the town of Dudley, where they now faced resistance.

The real prize would be Birmingham, on the other side of this particular battle. If they were able to secure themselves there, they would have numerous options—Bristol, Oxford, Northampton. Once cut off from the south, the French forces in the North would be faced with a second front, commanded by the Prince Regent himself, heading down from Hadrian's Wall through Yorkshire.

It would work. It had to.

A young runner dashed up to the command post. "General Wellesley!" he panted. "The revenants! They are…they are attacking!"

Wellesley looked at the boy with a mix of astonishment and annoyance. "Of course they are, boy! That's why we're here!"

"No, sir! No…they're different! They've attacked the French officers! They've broken ranks and…"

Screams echoed from the field in front of them, and Wellesley saw a wave of *Corps Éternel* surging forward haphazardly. They ran in groups of three or four and dispatched those before them with not only their amazing strength, but also an agility that he had never seen from the revenants before. They were no longer mindless undead.

They were feral beasts. Hunters. And they were coming up fast.

"To arms!" Wellesley cried. "Fire all cannon at the oncoming French!"

Arkhest crouched down beside him. "Your men," she sang quietly, mournfully.

Wellesley sighed. "They will die faster than at the hands of those creatures," he said.

He then turned to his artillery commander. "FIRE AT WILL!"

Wellesley turned back to Arkhest, but she was already gone, a blur of robes heading out to meet the horde head on.

He drew his sword. "CHARGE!"

CHAPTER 27

January 30, 2135
May 29, 1809

"This is not good at all," Shaila breathed as she helped Stephane to his feet. Thankfully, Greene and Huntington simply hit him in the head rather than shooting him, and that was about all the good news Shaila expected at this point.

Above her, two zombies stood watching. And yes, they were *watching*. Dead eyes, milky and cold, set inside withered faces with grinning, lipless teeth looked down at them. Their fists clenched over and over and they shifted from foot to foot—they were itching for a fight. Whatever they might have been, they were sure as hell alive now...or as close as they'd been to living for quite a while.

Two other revenants shoved Berthollet toward Weatherby, Finch and Anne, while the rest held them at gunpoint and seemed to regard them as little more than gnats. In an odd way, it was the same look Huntington had on her face as she covered the room with her AK-740—a Russian-made semi-auto that could fire five rounds each second. And the ammo belts she wore were evidence that she wasn't afraid to waste bullets.

"Will one of you learned alchemists do me the honor of explaining what has happened?" Weatherby said softly as Greene continued his work on the Emerald Tablet and *The Book of the Dead* in the middle of the room.

"Somehow, the convergence of the two realms, along with the realm of *Maat*, has allowed these revenants to acquire... souls, I suppose," Finch ventured. "I can only assume they are Martian souls, or the souls of some allied force. His device—the datapad, I believe you call it—was likely linked to an exterior source, and needed but the power of these two artifacts to complete the working."

Greene stood up from his work. "Very good, Dr. Finch. Shame you stuck with these guys. You'd be a great asset to us."

"Thank you, but I shall continue to 'stick with these guys,'" he replied, venom in his voice.

"Your call. You already helped the cause a lot, anyway. By now, every revenant in Napoleon's army has become one of us—the great race of Mars, reborn on Earth. And armed to the teeth," Greene said. "Finch's research and workings opened the door, and this French guy here provided the empty vessels." Greene pointed at Berthollet, who, to his credit, looked aghast.

"And the souls? Where did they come from?" Anne asked.

"You can thank Jain and Durand here for that," Greene replied with a magnanimous wave of his hand. "They went to Enceladus and allowed one of our great leaders, Rathemas, to enter this world through a little microscopic virus. Rathemas took over Stephane, then blew up Enceladus to free the rest."

"Right," Stephane said angrily. "But how did you get those viruses into these zombies? I didn't do that."

"But you did! And you did *so* well. We're really proud of you, champ," Huntington replied. "The viruses were just codes—strands of genetic material that represented ancient alchemical principles. While Rathemas was inside you, he took those codes and used the Emerald Tablet to translate them into data—data that could actually exist in both worlds thanks to the Tablet—then transmitted them to us on Earth. And we brought them here, where we set up the convergence in the one place where we could find willing bodies for them. And the one place where Althotas can arise once more."

Weatherby stood dejected. "We played right into your hands."

"You bet," Greene said cheerily. "You all did. We knew Diaz and Jain would follow us to Venus to figure out what we wanted with the satellites—which we needed to create the convergence just like Yuna Hiyashi did back on Mars.

And Althotas seeded ideas in the mind of our friend Cagliostro here—dreams and whatnot, the stuff that he used to do—but in a way that made this idiot think he was *stopping* us, rather than helping. Because we knew he felt burned the last time. Which makes it so cute that you're playing nice now, Cagliostro."

The old alchemist merely hung his head and trembled slightly.

"Once there was an overlap, we knew you guys would meet up," Huntington added. "Just like the old days. Get the band back together and play the greatest hits. Use the items *we needed* to try to stop us. God, you're so fucking predictable."

"So the book and the Tablet—they *can* stop you," Shaila ventured.

Greene held up a finger. "Don't even try, Jain. Althotas may want you alive to see his return, but if you get in the way, I'm happy to apologize to him for killing you beforehand." The possessed physicist suddenly stopped and smiled. "I guess part of me is still a holovision host. Always explaining. But Althotas really wanted you to know just how badly you fucked up.

"And now, all we need is Doctors Finch and Durand, and we'll be all set," Greene added. He then hissed a stream of commands to the zombies, who immediately grabbed Finch and Stephane and dragged them toward the pool.

"What do you need them for?" Shaila shouted. A zombie reached out and punched her in the face for her trouble. She staggered, but remained standing. "And fuck you, mate," she added.

The zombie smiled. It was one of the worst things she'd ever seen.

"Tired of explaining now, Jain," Greene said as he took more wiring out of his bag. "If it were really up to us, you'd all be dead by now. Althotas is a little old-school, I guess. It's not just about him winning. It's about you *losing*."

The two zombies forced Finch and Stephane toward the pool. Finch was shoved toward *The Book of the Dead*, while

Stephane was dragged toward the Tablet. Shaila looked on in horror as Stephane began to sweat profusely, his eyes widened to an almost unnatural degree, his skin growing sallow.

Rathemas clearly wanted out.

Finch seemed to be undergoing something as well. His skin grew exceptionally pale, the circles under his eyes growing unusually dark in the span of a few seconds. He was sweating, but the look on his face was one of utter confusion. Shaila wondered if some part of Finch found the whole thing fascinating.

"What do they intend?" Weatherby asked his wife.

Anne watched as both men were forced to the ground, and Greene began placing wires on their palms, foreheads and chests. "Durand carries the soul of Rathemas, and Finch has apparently become something of a conduit for dark energies from the land of *Maat* beyond death. If Dr. Greene is to revive Rathemas—or Althotas, for that matter—both Finch and Durand must release the energies they've held from their respective objects."

"Will they survive?" Shaila asked, fearing the answer.

"I cannot say," Anne said quietly.

Weatherby turned to Berthollet and spoke sternly. "*Monsieur*, your marshal is dead and your troops turned against you. If you've any notion of reversing this disaster, I would hear it now."

The French alchemist watched as Cagliostro staggered toward the pool and, to his evident shock, began helping Greene. "That spineless fool," he muttered. "So committed to stopping Althotas he was—I even used the Great Work to ascertain the truth of his words! And now he meekly becomes a lap dog for the dictator to come."

Shaila turned on Berthollet as well, grabbing him by the lapel of his greatcoat. "Hey! The admiral asked you a question. Answer it," she hissed.

Stunned, Berthollet stared at Shaila for a long moment before replying. "I…well, I…nobody can know for certain! The answer lies in the memories of the Venusians here, I have no doubt, waiting for us to view and interpret them. But if I were to hazard a guess, I would say one or both of those men would have to die before this Greene person finishes his rituals—ideally, they should die just before the rituals are fully resolved."

"Not good enough," Shaila growled, grabbing Berthollet's coat with both hands now. "Try again."

This time, Berthollet's stare grew hard. "Mishandling me will not alter the laws of the Great Work, woman!"

Suddenly, Shaila was wrenched away from Berthollet by a strong hand at her shoulder—one that managed to throw her halfway across the room and flat on her back. When she looked up, she saw Huntington standing over her with that creepy, wolf-smile on her face and the barrel of her gun right at her forehead. "We've never met. Diaz talked highly of you. Kind of makes me want to shoot you right here and now."

Shaila edged up onto her elbows. "Diaz spoke highly of you, too. Shame if she could see you now. Probably make the tough old bitch cry. She's a softie when it comes down to it."

Any further conversation was cut short by a scream.

Turning toward the pool, Shaila saw Stephane writhing on the ground next to the Emerald Tablet, which now glowed even brighter. Strands of light snaked through the wires connecting him to the object, and when Stephane opened his eyes, the light was in there as well.

"Oh, God, no. Please, God, no," Shaila said.

Finch also convulsed suddenly, his look of confusion giving way to pain. His eyes grew completely black, and when his mouth opened, his scream was a bare hiss. A black mist escaped his mouth and rose into the air for a moment... before snaking into the pool between the two men.

Greene viewed all of this dispassionately, looking at one man, then the other, then the datapad in his hands. Shaila saw him tapping on the screen, and when he did, one or the other man jerked and convulsed even harder—and Greene's face started to grow concerned. "Mags, get over here," he ordered.

"What?" Huntington demanded as she crossed the room in an almost unnatural blur.

Greene glared at Finch. "This one's too strong. Either that, or he didn't go far enough in his work with the book. Either way, he's fighting the connection between the book, the tablet and the pool. He's getting in the way."

"Fuck. Why didn't we try to infect him?" Huntington spat.

"We didn't have the means. The Siwa experiment... wait! We can still infect him!" Greene scrambled over to Stephane and began tapping furiously on his datapad. "If we draw Rathemas out of Durand and transfer him over to Finch...it might work!"

"That might kill him," Huntington warned. "Don't we need him alive?"

"Only if Rathemas were still inside him," Greene said as he adjusted wires, his hands flying at high speed now. "But with Rathemas inside Finch, Finch can be the conduit for both light and dark. And if Durand dies, well...too bad."

Suddenly, Stephane let out another scream, an unearthly echo of pure pain and pure rage. His mouth opened so wide, Shaila thought his jaw would dislodge. His eyes shone with alien light and his hands started fluttering around his chest. Shaila started to get up and run toward him, but she was intercepted by Weatherby, who practically had to tackle her in order to stop her. "They'll kill you," he said as gently as possible.

"Don't care. Let me go," she said dully, trying to squirm her way out as the tears began to well in her eyes.

"They will kill you and you will not be able to avenge him," Weatherby said. He was soon joined by Anne, and between the two of them they managed to at least keep Shaila in one place.

"I believe I have seen this before, long ago with Philip," Anne said in a rush. "He may yet survive. Philip did, and he was but a boy at the time. Stay your hand. He may soon be out of danger."

"Or dead," Shaila growled. "Let me go! I—oh, God. Oh, God, what is that?"

Weatherby and Anne turned to look at Stephane. He was on his side on the floor, writhing, and his mouth continued to open wide.

Then a hand reached out of his mouth—a green, taloned hand covered in glowing slime.

Another hand soon joined the first, both clawing at the air before the fingers wrapped themselves around each side of Stephane's mouth. Then the crown of a head appeared, pushing through with its dull dark eyes, its tiny nasal slits, its maw of teeth biting and gnashing as it exited its host.

It was a Martian.

It was Rathemas.

Soon, spindly arms emerged as well and the whole of the alien began to grow to enormous size as it left its host. Its torso was bony and ribbed in odd ways, and its legs were long and sinewy. Finally, the creature withdrew one taloned foot, then another, and Stephane slumped to the floor of the vault like a worn coverall, and the Martian grew to its full three-meter height.

"I NEED A HOST," the creature demanded, turning toward Green. "WHERE IS MY HOST?"

For the first time since he arrived, Greene looked properly scared. "That one, my Lord Rathemas!" he cried, pointing toward Finch. "He is the gateway to the underworld where Althotas lies in exile, but he is fighting it! He is too strong!"

Rathemas smiled a truly terrible smile, full of teeth and hatred and sadistic joy. "HE IS NOT STRONG ENOUGH. PREPARE HIM."

Huntington grabbed Finch's face in both hands and forced open his mouth.

"Finch…" Weatherby breathed. "I am so sorry."

It took only a few seconds for Rathemas to enter Finch. The creature practically dove into Finch's mouth in a flash of green-yellow light, and the alchemist immediately began convulsing violently, green light coming from his eyes and black mist once more flowing from his mouth.

Shaila turned to look at Stephane, unmoving on the floor. *Please breathe please breathe please please breathe come on breathe.*

His chest moved up and down once. Then again. Slowly. But regularly.

And in that moment, something clicked inside Shaila. She realized that with Stephane the focus of Greene's attention, she'd been paralyzed with fear and anger. She accepted the situation instead of acting, all because of Stephane. But Stephane was safe. Rathemas was out of him, finally. She felt like an idiot, but she felt free, too.

Next.

She immediately scanned the room. There were five zombie-guards left—two behind her and Weatherby and Anne, one over by Berthollet, and the fifth near the pool. And all of them, every single one, was watching Rathemas take over Finch.

Shaila put her finger to her headset. "Jain to Diaz. Come in. What's your status? Requesting assistance. Over."

It took several seconds for Diaz' voice to come through. "Jain, I've got an utter shit show out here. We got a fuck-ton of zombies now acting like goddamn ninja warriors. Heavy losses. I'm barricading our survivors in the pyramid. Going to blast the entrance so the rock fall will keep 'em safe inside. And then I'll be out of laser power and my main power just kicked into emergency reserves. So what's *your* goddamn status?"

"Greene and Huntington just released Martian souls into the zombies, they've pulled Rathemas out of Stephane and into Finch, and it looks like they're going to bring Althotas back any minute now," she replied quietly and quickly. "Roger your status. We'll manage in here. Over."

Diaz actually laughed at that, the kind of hopeless laughter reserved for the worst situations. "Well, fuck. Hurry it up then, will ya? Diaz out."

Shaila turned to Weatherby. "Diaz is losing badly out there. We have to do something."

Weatherby looked around, a pained look on his face. "Dying now is not going to help," the admiral said, glancing at Anne. "They have us by the heel."

"So let's not die," Shaila replied. "Three of us against five zombies and Huntington. Greene's too busy to help. Not impossible. They're distracted. Options?"

Anne raised an eyebrow at this, then a look dawned on her face. "Oh! I may have something." She rustled around her skirts for a moment before pulling out a vial and a small stone. "Curative here, blessed lapis lazuli here. With the right incantation, I could strike nearly everyone in here blind for...well, at least several moments."

"Do it," Weatherby said, seeming to gain strength from her. "Quickly, my love."

Finch had stopped twitching and was now lying on his back on the stone floor. The green light now seemed to emanate from his very skin, while the dark mist now seemed to be a torrent of inky blackness flowing into the pool.

And the zombies—and Huntington—were all watching raptly.

"Ready," Anne said after whispering a prayer over her concoction. "Be sure to avert your eyes. I cannot say how long you'll have."

Weatherby turned to Shaila. "Grab the weapons and fight, then?"

"You and Anne, yeah. I'm going to take on Huntington. We have to get that gun out of commission or this fight ends way too fast."

Weatherby turned and nodded. "Now."

Anne threw her elixir into the center of the room and, a moment later, the revenants staggered slightly and began casting about blindly. Without looking back, Shaila dashed across the room and tackled Huntington, sending both of them sprawling to the floor near Stephane. Shaila immediately scrambled for the gun, which had clattered across the floor next to them. But strong hands grabbed at her clothes, pulling her back across the floor as if she were a doll.

"You stupid little bitch," Huntington growled. "I'm gonna enjoy beating the shit out of you now."

Shaila flipped onto her back to see Huntington over her, her fist already cocked. Without thinking, she rolled away as quick as she could—and toward the gun again. Inches from her head, Huntington's fist hit the stone floor, hard enough so that Shaila heard something crack. Her opponent's unearthly howl of pain and rage confirmed it was bone, though Shaila figured she was strong enough to crack stone. Thank God for Anne's concoction, because if Huntington had been able to see, Shaila would be dead.

This is so dumb, Shaila thought as she scrambled across the floor on all fours toward the weapon. She felt a hand on her clothes again and swore—Huntington was still strong enough to stop her with only one good hand and managed to claw blindly at her.

Shaila turned and brought her boot up, catching Huntington across the jaw. Her grip loosened a moment, long enough for Shaila to grab her hand and twist for all her might. She heard a pop and smiled.

Then Huntington's other fist—the one that just pummeled stone—slammed into her cheekbone. Shaila's vision was instantly darkened and blurred, the entire side of her face was lanced with pain.

But there was no second hit coming. Shaila shook her head to clear it and saw Huntington with a pained, angry look on her face. Her hand was covered in blood, with fingers sticking out at ugly, stomach-churning angles. The former DAEDALUS member tried to cradle her fist with her other hand, but could only use it below her sprained wrist.

Shaila turned back on all fours and started scrambling for the gun again, even as the floor of the room seemed to pitch under her in a wave of disorientation and nausea. *Concussion*, Shaila's rational brain told her. *Not good. Get the gun.*

She crawled past Stephane's body—*still breathing? Still breathing*—and clambered up to the AK-740.

Then a buckled shoe stepped on it.

She looked up and saw Greene standing over her, smiling his infuriating holovision smile.

"Valiant effort," he said. "The blindness thing was cool. Didn't last very long, though."

He reached down, grabbed her by the scruff of her coverall…and threw her.

Five meters later, she hit the floor, knocking Weatherby over.

"Oh, hell," Shaila muttered, then winced. Easily a couple cracked ribs, plus she landed on her left elbow, which was ablaze with pain and likely useless. "Weatherby?"

The admiral looked up to see a zombie pointing his musket at them. Anne had been fighting another, but saw what had happened and dropped her bayonet in supplication.

"A good try, but not enough," Weatherby said softly, and with pain. Shaila could see blood coming from his right shoulder. "I suppose he wasn't quite busy."

Greene, meanwhile, picked up the gun, then went back to his work. He hissed something in that strange language and the zombies motioned for Weatherby and Shaila to get up against the wall. A moment later, Anne and Berthollet— who had avoided fighting at all—joined them.

Huntington staggered over to Greene and stood in front of the pool. "She got me good. Not sure I'm going to be much more help here."

Greene looked up. "You did well. When Althotas arrives and the floodgates open, you'll get a better body. You ready?"

Huntington nodded.

Without so much as a facial tic, Greene shot her in the chest. She keeled over into the pool.

And the dark, shining water began to roil.

At that moment, Finch slowly sat up. His skin was white as snow, but covered in a thin, oily film that matted his hair to his head. His eyes, blinking as though he had just awakened, shone with light.

"It is done," he said to Greene, a thick black mist trickling out as he spoke. "Althotas awaits."

CHAPTER 28

January 30, 2135
May 29, 1809

Maria Diaz piloted her V-SEV like a woman possessed, stomping through the masses of living zombies and swinging her mech's arms and feet wildly. Each step threatened to topple the vehicle, but that was because there was a half-alive body underneath. She had shut off the power alarms several minutes ago—she knew she'd run out of juice long before she ran out of targets.

The snipers atop the pyramid were now engaged in hand-to-hand combat, as the hordes of possessed zombies quickly scaled the sides of the ziggurat, helping each other up the two-meter high stones. Others were busy moving rubble away from the entrance, and it was these Diaz tried to focus on, if only to give Philip, Elizabeth and the few others she could save just a little more time to live.

She tried hailing Shaila a few times, but it seemed a handful of enterprising zombies managed to climb the chassis of her V-SEV and were now busy ripping apart anything they could get their withered hands on—including the antenna. Diaz knew it would take more strength than even these bastards had to rip into the cockpit, but they were trying their damnedest anyway. *Let 'em try*, she figured. *I can stay in here all day.*

Even after the laser gave out, she continued to fight, and accounted for at least fifty additional casualties. She could see the Venusians on her HUD map, their little white lights blinking out far too rapidly as the *Corps Éternel* blew through them. The little lizards did their best, but for every zombie that went down, at least two Venusians went with them.

She reached down with the V-SEV's claw and grabbed a zombie by the head, crushing its skull with ease, while stomping another into the Venusian dirt. Yet they kept coming—at least three hundred remained, and they were highly mobile, elusive and fighting like demons.

Suddenly, all her readouts went red, and a single message popped up on her HUD. RESERVES SPENT. REFUGE-IN-PLACE ACTIVATED.

One by one, she heard and felt the V-SEV's systems shutting down. The controls stopped responding and the vehicle went completely still. Her HUD winked out, followed by all other interior lights. Only one small screen—an ancient LED used for backup—remained active. And all it displayed was the time left before life support would fail: 59 minutes and counting.

She tried her comm one more time, diverting remaining power to do so. "This is Diaz. To whoever's listening, my V-SEV went into refuge mode. I'm out of the game. Repeat, my power is gone and I'm no longer able to act. Over."

To her surprise, she caught a few snippets of a reply. "Diaz...inside...barricaded in but...coming through the roof...will continue on...."

It was Philip. Diaz looked up and saw a number of zombies hurtling themselves through the open space on the roof of the pyramid. Others on the ground had found some rope and were beginning to bring it up the side of the pyramid.

She looked at the LED again. Forty-three minutes now. Apparently the comms drained power fast.

"Goddammit," she breathed. "Guess I'm not getting any younger. Or older."

She began to manually override the refuge mode in order to pop the hatch. She'd probably die out there, but there were plenty of muskets strewn across the ground, along with spears and a couple of swords.

The least she could do was take a few more sons of bitches with her.

Weatherby watched as Anne tried to staunch the bleeding in his shoulder, which had been run through by one of the French revenants—well, former French, as they likely held little allegiance to any country at this point. The awakened undead had paid for the blow with his head, shorn clean off by Weatherby even though he used only a common blade, as his alchemically enhanced sword remained too close to the pool to be retrieved.

Anne paused a moment to look behind her, and Weatherby followed her gaze to find Greene embracing Finch as though they were long-lost brothers. Perhaps they were.

"Are you OK?" Greene asked.

Finch cocked his head in an unsettlingly Finch-like way. "I cannot say. This creature's dabblings with *The Book of the Dead* made him a perfect vehicle for the transfer, but he is also strong-willed. He…" Finch paused a moment and cast around blankly. "Do we have Venusian extracts around? He was once addicted to them. It might quiet him."

Greene shook his head and looked toward the now-roiling pool. "No time. Can you finish this, Lord Rathemas?"

Finch nodded and walked over to the pool, taking off his coat and kneeling before it. "I can. I've waited six thousand years. I shan't wait any longer."

And then Finch opened his mouth and vomited forth a stream of blackness that was something between a liquid and a gas, which fell directly into the pool.

"What the hell is that?" Shaila asked, her voice slightly slurred. It struck Weatherby as though she may have taken a sharp blow to the head. "What's he doing?"

Weatherby looked to Anne, who simply looked distressed. "I haven't the faintest notion, my love," she replied to his unasked question. "He is…possessed, yes. And Rathemas is channeling whatever residual darkness Finch's researches accrued within him. But to what end?"

Berthollet harrumphed, and Weatherby was astonished that the man could retain his hauteur even in moments such as these. "Isn't it obvious? The Venusian memory vault preserves the memories of the dead. As such, that pool—linked to all these orbs—is not only a repository of remembrances, but a physical and occult link to the underworld. This fellow," he added, pointing to Greene, "has found a way to use the book and Tablet to create an additional link to the realm in which Althotas has been exiled."

Shaila slumped a bit. "Jailbreak."

"Crass, but not inaccurate," Berthollet confirmed. "This is what we had come here to prevent, so that we might continue to utilize the *Corps Éternel* without hazard."

Weatherby watched as Cagliostro approached Finch, kneeling next to him and placing a grandfatherly hand on his back. "We were all deceived. Whether Cagliostro played you for a fool or is only a turncoat at the end, we are well on course for defeat. Commander Jain, how fare you?"

Shaila gave him a weak smile. "Ready to go at your order, Admiral."

She looked glassy-eyed and was leaning against a wall for support. "Ready" would have to remain subjective if they were to somehow turn the tide.

"There are but two revenants now," Anne whispered. "The African woman is gone. We may yet prevail if we can but—"

A rumble permeated the room, cutting off Anne's thought. Finch staggered back away from the pool, which now looked to be at a high boil, the dark, shining liquid now overflowing and spattering on the stone floor. Greene quickly scurried to the Emerald Tablet, disconnecting some of the wires, then ran over to *The Book of the Dead* to do the same. "A little too much," he shouted over at Finch. "The satellites are feeding more energy than I thought. We might be able to salvage some of the artifacts' power!"

Finch held his hands to his head, his eyes screwed shut, grimacing in pain. "Yes... salvage. Well done. Althotas... will...be pleased."

Weatherby looked long at his oldest, dearest friend, then over to Anne and Berthollet. "What is it? What ails him?"

"How should I know?" Berthollet protested. "It's his own damnable fault."

Without thinking, Anne reached over and slapped Berthollet across the face. "Shut up. You, sir, are not helping." She then studied Finch carefully. "I dare say...he's in there,

Tom. Andrew. He's in there and I'll wager he's fighting this somehow."

The rumbling stopped, and a moan could be heard from across the room. Shaila pushed past the revenants and rushed haphazardly toward Stephane, who had begun to awaken. One of the revenants slowly walked toward them, gun raised, while the other remained guarding Weatherby, Anne and Berthollet.

"Jain!" Weatherby cried. "Don't!"

But she wasn't trying for an attack. She slid to the floor next to Stephane and cradled his head. His hands fluttered about and his eyes remained half-open. But alive he was, and Shaila began to whisper to him gently, stroking his hair. Somehow, the revenants decided not to shoot her, probably because Althotas still wanted them to see whatever was coming next.

Finch, for his part, simply stood swaying slightly as Greene's fingers danced over his datapad. "Almost there," the former physicist said, excitement in his voice. "Power levels are high. Should be any moment now."

Then a clawed hand shot upward out of the pool. It was massive, the splayed fingers easily six inches long each, tipped with jagged, wicked barbs. It was covered in the same dark, silvery liquid as the pool, but as the liquid ran downward, Weatherby could see green scales beneath.

"Althotas," Weatherby breathed. "We are finished."

A second hand thrust upward from the pool, and both began grasping, finally finding purchase at the stony walls. Then the crest of a bulbous head appeared, followed by eyes as black as night itself.

"My Lord Althotas!" Cagliostro said in a quavering voice, immediately falling to his knees and prostrating himself before the pool. Greene also knelt, but kept one eye upon his datapad, tapping occasionally as needed, while Finch simply swayed more, hugging himself, a look of grim consternation upon his face.

"I AM FREED," came a voice from the pool, sounding like a swarm of bees with suddenly found articulation. "I AM FREED!"

And slowly, with great purpose and dread, Althotas arose from the pool of memories, reborn unto the Known Worlds. His wide eyes sat above a wicked maw, his green, sinewy, scaly limbs pulling himself upward. First one leg, then the other, lifted out of the pool and onto the floor of the chamber with a sickening squelch. And finally he drew himself up to his full height—nine feet tall if an inch, powerfully muscled and inhumanly proportioned. His limbs were long, his torso slight, but there was no doubt as to his physical power.

Althotas scanned the room, looking down upon the Emerald Tablet and *The Book of the Dead* with a smile. "THE SEEDS OF MY AWAKENING," he said. "WHO HAS BROUGHT THEM FORTH?"

Greene finally put his datapad down and stepped forward, taking Finch's arm and bringing him along. "We have, Lord Althotas. I am your humble servant, while here is Rathemas, your most trusted lieutenant!" Greene said. "We hope you find pleasure in our working."

Althotas surveyed Finch closely, even crouching down to look him in the eye. "YOU ARE UNWELL, FAVORED ONE."

Finch nodded. "This vessel…powerful…I…my Lord…" Finch's trembling and swaying worsened. "Help me."

Althotas simply grinned. "THIS IS BUT A MINOR TEST. YOU CAN DEFEAT A MERE HUMAN." He then turned toward the captives in the room. "AS FOR YOU, YOU HAVE ALL FAILED."

Weatherby stood tall, but found he had no response, for the mere presence of the Martian warlord was the proof of his words. To his left, Weatherby heard Shaila sob. *Show strength*, he thought, but when he turned toward her, he saw her eyes boring into him, even though her face was tear-streaked. She then glanced ever so briefly to her side, where the powerful firearm lay but six or seven feet away from her and Stephane.

Strong indeed.

"While I have breath, I will fight you, creature!" Weatherby said, emboldened. All eyes in the room now turned to him. "Your days are long past. Now is the time of Mankind, and we shall not give it up so easily!"

Greene rushed forward with a look of rage and struck Weatherby across the face. "Show some respect!" he thundered. "You've lost! Know when you've been beaten!"

Anne crouched over Weatherby, who had fallen backward under the onslaught, and he immediately saw the question in her eyes through the pain in his jaw. He nodded slightly, and she wheeled around to face Greene. "You, sir, are a monster and a coward both!" And she lashed out, catching him in the nose. A crunch was heard, and her hand came away bloody. "We shall bow before no one, Man or Martian!"

Greene raised his hand a second time, but was stopped by a metallic click at the other side of the room. He turned—and saw Shaila holding the firearm. But it was not pointed at him.

It was pointed at Althotas.

"Go back to Hell, you son of a bitch."

She fired.

Dozens of bullets lanced into the Martian warlord, prompting an otherworldly scream of pain, like nothing short of the wail of a thousand damned souls. Where the bullets landed, splotches of yellow blood appeared on the creature.

But despite being struck by at least a score of bullets, Althotas was able to keep his feet—and turned toward Shaila with an inarticulate scream of rage.

Not enough, Weatherby thought. And then he saw the revenant nearest him, his alchemical blade in a scabbard at his belt. Immediately, Weatherby lashed out with all his might, shoving the creature to the ground and grasping the hilt, pulling for all he was worth. The revenant clawed and punched at him in a flurry, but Weatherby managed to fall backward—with the blade in his hand.

A moment later, the revenant's head fell to the floor.

Shaila, meanwhile, continued to pour bullets into Althotas, and while the Martian staggered, he continued to push forward toward her. Weatherby saw Greene charge, unseen by her. The admiral moved to intercept him, but was tackled by the other revenant, shoved to the floor and nearly stabbed by the creature's bayonet—which Weatherby sliced in half before it found his heart. He shoved the revenant off him and neatly cleaved its head from its shoulders.

Weatherby turned and saw that Greene had staggered and fallen—Stephane had grasped his ankle and twisted. Finally catching a glimpse of him, Shaila briefly turned her gun in Greene's direction. He stopped moving almost instantly.

But that allowed Althotas to get close enough to swing at Shaila, who had to fall backward to avoid the Martian's claws—claws that were poisoned, Weatherby remembered. The admiral clambered to his feet and rushed forward.

Then Finch stepped in front of him. In his hands was *The Book of the Dead*.

"Tom," he croaked. His pallor was sickly and his hands trembling but his eyes—his eyes were his own. And they pled with his old friend. "Tom...destroy this."

Weatherby needed no further encouragement. He brought his blade down upon the book in Finch's hands, slicing it in twain with a single stroke.

Althotas screamed again and turned toward Weatherby. "WHAT HAVE YOU DONE?"

Finch answered for him. "What I...should've...done... long ago!"

He then tossed the two pieces of *The Book of the Dead* into the pool of memories—which immediately turned pitch black.

Althotas turned and tried to swipe at Finch, but was met with Weatherby's blade. The creature's forearm was severed midway between wrist and elbow.

"We have not failed!" Weatherby bellowed.

Then there was a loud crack from the other side of the pool, and Althotas screamed again—and even with his alien features, there was true panic writ upon his face.

Weatherby saw Anne and Stephane together, with the pieces of the Emerald Tablet at their feet. They had shattered it upon the stony floor—just as Weatherby had done so many years ago. Quickly, the two bent over and began scooping up the green, glowing shards, casting them into the pool as well. And the waters soon began glowing with the same emerald light.

The sound of gunfire rang out again, and more yellow blotches appeared on Althotas' chest and skull. Shaila had regained her footing, and was grimly firing upon the Martian once more—until her bullets were spent, and she cast the weapon to the ground in disgust. "Now what?"

Weatherby ran forward, his blade held high. "Now we finish him!"

But Finch practically tackled him, leaving the two struggling against each other. "No, Tom!" he shouted, his voice straining. "We must…close it. The convergence."

Weatherby struggled to disengage himself from Finch. "How?" he demanded.

Finch simply smiled and clasped Weatherby in a ferocious hug. "I will…make this right," he said. "You are…my brother."

Then Finch disengaged himself from his friend and dashed up to Althotas, shoving him backward with all his might—a considerable might, Weatherby saw, as he was still possessed, at least in part, by the otherworldly Rathemas.

But Finch, it seemed, had taken the upper hand.

Althotas staggered backward, tripping upon the edge of the pool. Finch pushed again, leaping upon the teetering titan and hammering him with his fists, over and over.

Althotas fell backward into the pool, taking Finch with him.

The waters surged and roiled, and all in the room could see Finch and the Martian struggling. Althotas' clawed hands grasped vainly for the stone walls of the pool, while Finch kicked against the very same stone in order to push the warlord back into the water. Finally, Althotas clasped Finch to him as they both sank under the surface with a resounding splash. After this, the struggles grew less intense, and as the waters smoothed, they slowly returned to their dark silvery color.

Weatherby turned toward the others. "Is that...is that it, then?"

Anne smiled, but Shaila and Stephane looked upon each other with fear in their eyes, holding hands, whispering things that, Weatherby felt, he had best not hear.

But still. "What is it?" he asked.

Shaila turned and smiled, and her tear-streaked face was the most heartbreaking look Weatherby had ever seen. "If this is anything like Mars, the overlap will end pretty fast," she said. "And the surface of Venus will kill us instantly." She sniffled and suddenly gave him a proper salute. "An honor serving with you, my Lord Admiral."

She then turned back to Stephane. "I love you."

He smiled. "I love you, too."

Then a blinding white light erupted from the pool, and all those still alive were suddenly blinded.

CHAPTER 29

May 29, 1809

General Wellesley turned his back for a moment to rally what remained of his men, but an unearthly growl prompted him to turn back—and swing wildly. Thankfully, the blade connected with the French revenant about to assault him, and the creature was dispatched quickly, though further soiling the general's fine red coat with more blackish ichor. To his right, the brave Arkhest moved fluidly through the French lines, her robes twirling about her as she used the swords she carried to cut her way through the masses of the damned like a scythe in the fields.

But it was not enough. Wellesley's forces were decimated by two-thirds, their retreat cut off. They were surrounded. Furthermore, Arkhest was the only Xan the general could see—all the others had quickly fallen to savage, massed assaults by the former *Corps Éternel* after they…changed. The Xan were torn limb from limb by the hordes of newly angered revenants. Wellesley was sure he would take the images—and the sounds of the Xan's disharmonic screams—to his grave.

He also assumed he would be in his grave in short order.

"Follow me!" he cried, rallying a small group of red-clad soldiers behind him. "We must punch through their lines! For England!"

The general ran forward, his blade held high, and cried out incoherently with a growing, bubbling rage. If he were to die, it would be forward, on true English soil, with the blood of his enemies on his hands.

Suddenly, the revenants…collapsed.

As if they were puppets without their strings, the entirety of the *Corps Éternel* simply collapsed into heaps of dead flesh and soiled uniforms. Wellesley's run became a jog, and then a walk, until he reached the first rank of the now-fallen French. He poked one with a sword, and found there was no reaction. He then sliced the head clean off. Its fellows did not seek vengeance.

Arkhest came up to his side. "It would appear the power animating them has been...removed," the Xan battle master sang.

"Will it return?" Wellesley demanded.

"I cannot say, but if it does, it shan't be a thing done quickly, I would think," Arkhest replied, notes of amazement and growing joy in her voice.

Wellesley turned back to his men. "Burn them. Every last one. Send messengers to Edinburgh to report what has happened, then prepare runners to move south to report further. Should the rest of the revenants be found like this, they must be burned. Go!"

The men scurried off to procure torches and oil, and Wellesley visibly slumped as he regarded his fallen foes. "Thank God," he whispered.

He then found himself thinking of Lord Weatherby, who insisted he would find a way to stop the revenants. Perhaps he had.

Wellesley still didn't like the man. But he was grateful.

January 30, 2135
May 29, 1809

Maria Diaz parried a bayonet with her forearm, grasping the weapon and using the zombie's momentum to send him crashing into the one next to him. She used the sword she had found to hack an arm off, then a head.

And she kept moving. For how long, though, she couldn't say.

Exhausted and covered in black blood, Diaz kept moving forward toward the pyramid, step by bloody step. Every meter, it seemed, she was set upon by more goddamn zombies. They were maddened and savage as hell and wailing something completely awful, but remained untrained, at least by 22nd century standards. She was able to cut through them decently, though had taken a bayonet slice to the side and a few other minor wounds.

You're not gonna make it, she said to herself.

Shut up! she replied.

Another three zombies came charging forward, and she adjusted her stance so that she wouldn't be fighting on the severely sprained ankle she got a few zombies ago. She pulled out her last pistol and readied her sword.

Then a white light blasted through the top of the pyramid, blinding her.

She couldn't tell if it was good or bad, so she waited.

Shaila opened her eyes.

Stephane still had his closed.

She looked around and saw Weatherby and Anne looking at her, their faces stricken. The bodies of zombies and people and former friends were everywhere. Finch was gone.

She turned back to Stephane. His eyes were open now.

"Alive?" he asked.

"Think so," she replied, grinning widely. "Umm…yeah. Alive!"

Despite her injuries, Shaila pulled Stephane closer and hugged him fiercely, ignoring the pain lancing through nearly every part of her body. "You OK? Tell me you're OK."

He laughed. "I am sore and feel sick and I have a headache and I am completely wonderful," he said quietly. "He's gone."

They hugged tighter.

"OK, OK," Shaila finally said. "Not out of the woods yet." She tapped her headset. "Jain to Diaz. Report."

The general came on almost immediately. "Since when do I report to *you*?" She sounded elated. "But if you must know, all the goddamn zombies just keeled over. Every single one. Your status? Over."

Shaila smiled. "Althotas is gone. The artifacts are both destroyed. Honestly, I thought the overlap would snap back, but it isn't."

Diaz suddenly became all business. "We need to get back in the V-SEVs. We don't know how long we have."

"Actually, we have two days," Stephane said, smiling. He held up Greene's datapad. "It's still linked to the satellites and to the Virgin ship. The overlap is receding in an orderly fashion. I have no idea why, but it is."

Weatherby looked over to Anne. "How is this possible?"

She looked around, seeming to search the room itself for an answer. "I...I do not know."

"Not sure it matters," Shaila said. "I think we need to get moving, regardless. Admiral, can we get a lift?"

Weatherby smiled. "By all means."

January 31, 2135
May 30, 1809

Weatherby stood upon the quarterdeck of HMS *Victory* and conducted the service that defined much of his career at sea and Void. He had lost count of the number of times, and despite his best efforts, the number and names of those memorialized. He worked hard to ensure that, within himself, the words in the book before him never became rote, that the task he discharged would never become drudgery.

This time, there was no worry of any of that. He felt every moment acutely.

"James Whitlock, post-captain, HMS *Enterprise*. John Roberts, first lieutenant, HMS *Victory*. Margaret Huntington, marine captain, Project DAEDALUS. Dr. Evan Greene, science specialist, Project DAEDALUS," he intoned, at the end of a list that took a full twenty minutes to read. "And..."

He paused, tears welling in his eyes. He stood stock still, trying to rein in emotion, but a single sob betrayed him. Composing himself, he finished: "Andrew Finch, fleet alchemist, HMS *Victory*."

Weatherby felt Anne's hand upon his shoulder, and Elizabeth's hand in his, and drew strength from them both.

"We commit their bodies to the depths, to the ground, to the Void and to the great beyond, indefinable except unto God Himself," Weatherby continued. "The Lord bless them and keep them. The Lord make His face to shine upon them and be gracious unto them. The Lord lift up His countenance upon them, and give them peace. Amen."

"Amen," said the hundreds assembled upon the main deck.

"Dismissed," Capt. Searle ordered, and the crew dispersed.

Weatherby turned and handed the book to Gar'uk, who had survived the invasion of the pyramid along with Elizabeth and Philip. He then extended a hand to Diaz, who had joined him on the quarterdeck, along with Shaila and Stephane. "Thank you for attending, General."

She took his hand warmly. "Thank you, Admiral, for including my people in your prayers. Means a lot to us." The general and her people were wearing their pressure suits, with large backpacks attached, though their helmets were at their side. While the overlap continued to reduce itself at a steady rate, the general did not wish to take chances. "And I am truly sorry about Dr. Finch," she added. "I know he meant a lot to you."

Weatherby nodded and grasped Elizabeth's hand for support. "He was as a brother to me, and I have much I regret with my recent treatment of him," the admiral said. "In the end, he was strong enough to overcome possession, strong enough to sacrifice his life for ours. He was, I believe, the very best of men, and…." Weatherby stopped, feeling as though he was being somewhat maudlin. "…well, I shall miss him greatly."

Diaz nodded and placed a hand on Weatherby's shoulder. "I have no doubt. Thank you, sir. It's been a privilege." They saluted one another, and Diaz picked her way down the stairs to the main deck to await her colleagues.

It was Shaila's turn. "Shame about Berthollet," she said. "That guy was a prick."

Weatherby laughed, despite himself. "I suppose he was, but we remained too evenly matched for us to try to capture him. At least Cagliostro is in our brig. This time, I doubt we shall allow anyone else to have him."

"Good idea," she said. She then embraced him in a hug. "Thank you. You and Finch, you saved us."

Slightly startled, he returned the hug. "Not without your help. My very best to you and Dr. Durand." He gently disengaged her. "I do hope you make an honest man of him at some point," he chided.

She and Stephane both laughed, and Weatherby shook hands with the Frenchman as well. "I think we need a vacation first," Stephane said. "Thank you, Admiral Weatherby."

After exchanging hugs with Anne and Elizabeth, and a few manly handshakes from young Philip, Shaila and Stephane joined Diaz on the main deck. About 200 meters off *Victory*'s larboard side, the Stanford research station floated in space…or the Void. Whichever. When *Victory* first brought them up, the remnants of Project DAEDALUS had used small alchemical lodestones for life support—and rigged a rope bridge, of all things—to get them to the Stanford airlock. After that, the suits felt like a much better choice.

A Royal Navy lieutenant and an honor guard stood at attention as they prepared to disembark. "I could get used to this," Diaz said. "Weatherby's got a valet."

Shaila turned and waved at Weatherby, who returned the gesture. "I think I just want to go home," she said. "All this…I've had enough."

With that, the three JSC astronauts pushed off the side of HMS *Victory* and into space, then jetted toward the Stanford station—and their own time.

CHAPTER 30

March 29, 2136

Maria Diaz shut down the holophone on her desk and leaned back in her chair, exhausted. She had spent this day—and many of the days since her return from Venus—engaged in issuing reports, answering to higher-ups, holding confidential briefings and "doing politics," as she often put it. This latest conference call was with President Weathers' chief of staff, who wanted some political cover when the conglom execs came calling. Chrys VanDerKamp and Harry Yu were going to be charged with a rainbow assortment of crimes, and while the Corporate Court could never be briefed on the exact happenings surrounding the *Tienlong* and Venus, the Weathers administration seemed willing to butt heads with the congloms in order to see justice done.

It was a nice change of pace in Washington. While preparing her reports, Diaz discovered Harry Yu was a top party donor, and she was certain that would buy him at least a partial reprieve. It seemed that the right things were happening.

Earlier in the day, she had to schlep up to Capitol Hill, where she was forced to brief a select group of four senators and six congressmen about Project DAEDALUS and all the recent activity. Thankfully, she had worked with JSC to come up with a pretty airtight cover story, and was able to convince the committee that corporate malfeasance was to blame for everything. Martians? What Martians?

There was a knock on her door. "Come," she said.

Shaila Jain entered in her shipboard khakis. "You asked to see me, ma'am?"

Diaz waved her to a seat. "Yep. How's Steve doing?"

"Frustrated," Shaila said with a brief smile and she took a chair on the other side of Diaz' desk. "How long can one man be debriefed?"

"Getting infected by an alien intelligence, stealing a spaceship and then helping to defeat a Martian? You're lucky *you* only got away with two months."

Shaila frowned. "We just want a break, ma'am."

"And you deserve it," Diaz replied. "So I pulled some strings and got five minutes with the President himself a little while ago. Basically, it comes down to this: Stephane Durand will need to be monitored pretty much for the rest of his life. Nothing we can do about that.

"*However*," Diaz added, speaking over Shaila's budding objection. "So long as he agrees to wear a monitor 24/7, tied into a Project DAEDALUS computer, he can be released to his supervising officer."

"And who's that?" Shaila groused.

"You, of course," Diaz grinned. "You're welcome."

Shaila sat stunned for several moments. "So, that's it then?" Shaila said finally. "He's done? We're done?"

"Well, I hope you two will consider staying on with me," Diaz said. "DAEDALUS is still up and running. Coogan's had enough, and I can't say I blame him, so I need a number two. You're already up for full commander, probably make captain in three or four more. And I figure Steve's learned a lot over the past few years—he'd be one hell of an asset."

Shaila looked pained, so Diaz put her hand up. "You don't need to decide now. My partner's brother has a cabin up in Hyde Park, Vermont. She bullied him into staying clear of it until after Memorial Day. So you and Steve go play house for a couple months, then figure out what you want the rest of your lives to look like."

That got Diaz the smile she hoped for. "Thank you, ma'am," Shaila said. "That really means a lot."

"Get out of here. Send me selfies from the woods or something," Diaz said, rising from her chair to give her friend and subordinate a hug. "Give him my best."

Shaila departed, and Diaz sat back down, looking over yet another report regarding the Venus incident. They still couldn't figure out why the overlap—or convergence, whatever—hadn't snapped back like a rubber band like it did on Mars. Hell, she wasn't going to question it at the time, because Venus' heat and pressure would've turned her into charcoal in a split second. But the latest theory was that *someone* had to have regulated the energy flows between the satellites and the waning energies from the other dimension so that there could be a slower and more orderly collapse of the overlap. The problem was that when the investigators combed through the programming on board the satellites, the Virgin ship, all the datapads—there were no subroutines or coding of any kind to cover that particular situation.

So someone *else* had to be taking that action. There was an intelligence behind the controlled overlap—and Diaz didn't know whose it was.

And that's why Project DAEDALUS would keep going, until someone found the answers.

July 15, 1815

The small boat bobbed in the bay off Rochefort, and the young man commanding it, a Lt. Mott, seemed almost shell-shocked by the man he'd been ordered to ferry. The passenger would've been amused at the young man's reaction had it been nearly any other occasion.

But this was, he was sure, the very end. Napoleon Bonaparte, Emperor of France, was being rowed toward his final captivity.

Napoleon turned and waved at the men of the ship *L'Epervier* and received a cheer in return, though it seemed more a wail, with many men aboard in tears. The gambit had failed. One of many, it seemed, destined to fall to pieces around him.

As the English crew rowed toward HMS *Bellerophon*, Napoleon could not help but reflect. He had been, at one point, the ruler of all Europe. He'd been on his way to crushing the last redoubt of England, had taken most of the continent east of Russia, and had been massing a fresh *Corps Éternel* to march on Moscow itself.

But then…something happened. The *Corps Éternel* fell. Jean-Claude Berthollet had abandoned Napoleon in the wake of the catastrophe and was still unaccounted for, and without their revenant troops, the French were quickly and decisively expelled from England.

Napoleon had held on longer than even he had thought possible, and even mounted the planned invasion of Russia. But the winter was cold, and his soldiers were no longer impervious to conditions. Slowly, inexorably, the various Coalitions and forces arrayed against him chipped away at his shining empire. Finally, a year ago, he found himself the exiled emperor of a spit of land in the middle of the Mediterranean, with little hope of a return to glory.

But there was always hope, and the fleet patrolling Elba was simply not up to the task. Smuggled from exile, Napoleon had tried one last gambit. He quickly deposed the Bourbon king, raised an army, and met the forces commanded by Wellesley—now the Duke of Wellington—in the field near Waterloo.

It was a catastrophe.

As he was rowed toward his fate, Napoleon considered whether he should have asked to be taken to one of the offworld colonies—Ganymede, perhaps, or Venus. He could've taken time, rebuilt his forces. But no...France was in his heart, and he was in France's heart as well. How else to explain his welcome during those brief, glorious hundred days? He was emperor of France, first and foremost.

He turned to regard the coast once more. He would never see his nation again.

The little boat came up alongside *Bellerophon*, and a rope ladder was lowered. Napoleon clambered aboard, where he was met with a rather small and sorry looking honor guard. Even in this, it seemed, England wished to rob him of dignity.

He was greeted by an officer, who extended a hand. "I am Captain Frederick Maitland," the man said in passable French. "I am sorry for the lack of honors at such an early hour."

Napoleon looked about and then took the man's hand. "It is of no concern," he said.

"Please, this way, Your Majesty."

Maitland led Napoleon to the captain's cabin. "This is a handsome chamber," Napoleon said, though he found the cramped quarters anything but. The Emperor had always hated sea travel, and found berths aboard any ship woefully lacking.

Nonetheless, Maitland bowed. "Such as it is, sir, it is at your service while you remain on board the ship I command."

Nodding, Napoleon caught sight of a portrait of a woman upon the wall. "Who is that young lady?"

"My wife," the captain responded.

"Ah! She is both young and pretty," Napoleon said with a small smile, still in command of the charm that had won him a continent. "From whence does she come? Have you any children, Captain?"

Maitland held up his hand. "My apologies, but I am not the man of whom you should ask anything, Your Majesty. There are others here who wish to meet you, and I shall have tea brought shortly."

The captain departed, and Napoleon waited patiently as a couple of seaman—scruffy and filthy and altogether unsuited for proper tea service—deposited a silver tray and cups upon the captain's table.

A moment later, two other people entered the room. One was tall, gray-haired, and dressed in the manner of an English gentleman of standing, and he wore the star of the Order of the Garter upon his coat—a man of singular importance, then. The other was a woman, seeming much younger than the man, pretty and with a look that spoke of great intelligence.

"My apologies, Your Majesty," the man said as he extended his hand. "I simply had to see you for myself."

At this, Napoleon's heart beat a little faster in his chest. A friend? A dire enemy? "And to whom do I have the honor of addressing?"

The man smiled and waved Napoleon toward his chair, then poured the tea for all therein. "We have never met, Your Majesty. But you met a very close, very dear friend of mine a long time ago, and it is in his memory that we come here now."

"He must have been a fine man," Napoleon commented, "for you to come all this way to see me at this hour."

The man sat across from the Emperor. "He was the finest, bravest and truest of men," he said. "His name was Dr. Andrew Finch, and he saved all England—all the Known Worlds—from your *Corps Éternel* and the threat of Althotas."

Napoleon gently placed his cup upon the table, his hand trembling and his heart pounding. "Ah," he said slowly, deliberately. "And I believe I know you now, sir."

"Indeed. I am Thomas Weatherby, and this is my wife Anne," he said. "And as I said, we simply had to see you, to know that this was done."

Napoleon nodded. "And so it is. What is to become of me?"

Weatherby looked grave. "You will be taken to England first, where we shall make a show of consulting our allies as to your disposition. But your final destination has already been decided."

"Where, then?"

Anne pulled out a small map of the Known Worlds from her reticule. "Here, Your Majesty, on the small world known as Flora, within the Rocky Main," she said. "It is barely a world indeed, but one with arable land and a water source. There is a house and farm there, and you and your servants will be made comfortable. We have found debtors willing to work there in exchange for pardon. You will be comfortable."

"And very, very far away," Weatherby added. "Lady Anne here, of course, is King George's court alchemist now. Did you know this?"

"I did," Napoleon said, his hands growing more tremulous.

"Good. She and I will both make sure that when you are exiled to Flora, you will remain there for the rest of your natural days," Weatherby said.

"And now, if you'll excuse us," Anne added, rising, "we must be off."

Napoleon stood. "So quickly? There is much I would wish to know."

Weatherby regarded the French Emperor with a withering stare. "Ask someone else, then."

And with that, the couple left. Napoleon slumped back down in his chair and, a moment later, in a fit of pique, swept the tea service off the table in a single, violent gesture.

ACKNOWLEDGEMENTS

Thomas Weatherby has been with me now for more than 12 years, though it was only in the last four that his story was finally put to the page. With *The Venusian Gambit*, the adventure that started in *The Daedalus Incident* and continued in *The Enceladus Crisis* is now complete. I think it turned out pretty darn well—better than I could've hoped when I first dared to write that first novel—and I'm very gratified with how this trilogy has been received. And for that, I have you, the reader, to thank first and foremost.

Thank you for letting me tell this story to its conclusion. I hope you enjoyed it as much as I did.

Finishing this book, and this trilogy, was immensely satisfying—and bittersweet. Saying goodbye is never easy, but I'd like to think that these characters had a good run. I'll miss them, but it's time to let them go, and to see what other challenges there are for me as a writer.

There's another reason why I'm a little melancholy about wrapping up this series. Those of you who pay attention to such things may have noticed that *The Enceladus Crisis* was dedicated to my mother, and that this book has been dedicated to her memory. Mary Ann Martinez passed away on July 26, 2014, after a long battle with cancer. She fought to the last, and even in the midst of her fight, her encouragement and her pride in this work was a source of inspiration. I thanked her before she passed, but I'm doing so again here. It's only fitting.

As you might imagine, finishing this book over the summer and fall of 2014 was a difficult task, but one made easier with the help and support of so many family and friends. My heartfelt thanks goes out to all of them, and especially to my aunt and uncle, Edee and John Butnor; my cousins John, Courtney and Ashby; my aunt Joan Butnor;

my mother's amazing friends Sheila Mann and Ruth Bolton; and, of course, to my dear friends Karl Isselhardt, John LeMaire and Drew Montgomery.

I also want to thank everyone at my day job, managers and colleagues alike, for such immense support and compassion over the past year—and for all their encouragement in this literary effort since the beginning. You're all fantastic.

The folks at Skyhorse/Night Shade Books are among the finest people I've worked with in over two decades as a writer, and their support and understanding during the summer and fall is doubly appreciated. Cory Allyn's effort may be unseen in this book, but his fingerprints are all over it, and it's a better work because of him. Thanks also go to Jason Katzman and Lauren Burnstein for all their hard work and general awesomeness.

I've thanked Sara Megibow before, but I'm going to do it again. She's a great agent and someone I'm proud to call friend. Never has there been a better advocate for an author.

My thanks also go to the SF/F community at large: authors, reviewers and fans alike. Authors such as Jason M. Hough, Michael R. Underwood, Django Wexler, Beth Cato, Chuck Wendig, Mary Robinette Kowal and so many others have been a source of encouragement and welcome. Thanks also to the Science Fiction and Fantasy Writers of America for their staunch advocacy on behalf of writers— and for being such a great tribe of geeks.

This book wouldn't have received any attention without the reviewers who took the time to read and opine, and the news sites who thought my work worthy of attention. Thank you to John DeNardo and Paul "PrinceJvstin" Weimer of SF Signal, Stefan Raets of Tor.com, Charlie Jane Anders of io9, James Floyd Kelly of GeekDad, Dan Hanks, Abhinav Jain, Sally "Qwill" and Tracy "Trinitytwo" of the Qwillery, Matt Mitrovich, Caleb Flanagan, Joe Frazier, Feliza Casano, Luther M. Siler and so many others I'm probably failing to mention here.

I have fans! That's been mindblowing—and such a wonderful thing. To everyone who reviewed my books on places like Goodreads and Amazon, to the folks who sought me out to say hello at conventions and events, and to those who took the time to write fan mail—it means so very, very much to me.

Finally, there's my amazing daughter Anna, who once again took my author photo and continues to be a source of inspiration and love. She also sat through the World Fantasy Convention in D.C. this past November with good grace and a lot of patience. I'm so proud to be her dad.

And then there's my wife Kate. I don't think this book would even be here without her unflagging support and love over the past year. She continues to make our lives together the best sort of adventure. I love you.

The *Daedalus* trilogy is concluded. I look forward to seeing what happens next.

Michael J. Martinez

The sun shone brightly over manicured lawns and white adobe-style houses and buildings, giving the entire campus a sense of resort-like tranquility. Pathways laid out in concrete and tarmac crisscrossed the grounds. People in white coats and smocks were everywhere, giving the uniformed military officers genial smiles—and wide berths.

"Nice place, this," said the Marine captain with ANDERSON on his name badge. "Get a couple girls, some drinks . . . could be a swell place to spend a few weeks." He walked with the precision of a disciplined military man across the grounds, his eyes scanning for danger the entire time and his prodigious muscles unconsciously flexing.

Next to him, Lieutenant Commander Danny Wallace smirked and shook his head. "Trust me, Andy, you don't want to be here if you don't have to." Danny knew Anderson from their time together in the Pacific, and had pestered Hillenkoetter—still his superior despite the captain's new command—for some help. If all went well, Danny had plans for Anderson. If only the latter man could starting getting a little more comfortable with . . . unusual situations.

A moment later, they watched as several white-coated attendants, all of them big, hulking men, rushed inside one of the low-slung buildings, where screaming could be heard. Not long after, they dragged a man out—one attendant per kicking, thrashing limb—and set him down just outside the building's entrance, where they struggled to get him into a straitjacket. Someone forgot to secure the man's head, though, and with an unexpected twist, the patient managed to sink his teeth into the forearm closest to him, prompting a cry of anger—and a meaty right hook to the screaming man's face.

It was much easier to get him into the straitjacket after that.

"Gentlemen, I'm sorry you had to witness that," came a voice from behind the two officers. They turned to find a bespectacled, bearded man, burly and bow-tied, smiling the weary smile of an overworked doctor. "Agnews State Hospital practices a positive approach to therapy whenever possible, but of course sometimes the health and safety of the hospital's other patients, as well as our staff, must take priority, and we have a handful of patients who simply don't respond well to anything we do."

Danny nodded grimly and extended his hand, which the other fellow took and shook with seeming gratitude. "I'm Lieutenant Commander Dan Wallace. This is Captain Andrew Anderson. I don't know if my message was passed along, but I called yesterday inquiring after one of your patients here."

"Of course, Commander. I'm Dr. Stanley Abrams, director here at the hospital. I'm so glad you came. We would of course be glad to assist the military in any way we can. If you'll follow me?"

Danny and Anderson followed Abrams through the hospital campus as he gave them what felt to Danny like a typical VIP visitor speech. The mental hospital—*insane asylum* was, apparently, no longer a term in use—was the finest serving the San Francisco and San Jose areas. They used traditional "talk therapy," as Abrams put it, but were also experiencing a lot of promising success with hydrotherapy and, more recently, modern "electro-shock" treatment.

If someone strapped me down and shocked me, I'd tell them anything they'd want to hear to make it stop, Danny thought. *No matter how crazy I am.*

"Excuse me, Doc, but maybe we can get on to the part about why we're here?" Anderson eventually interrupted.

The doctor smiled obsequiously. "Of course, Captain. Let me just check my folder here." Abrams shuffled through the papers he carried as they walked, and finally pulled out the right one. "Ah, here we are! Margaret Ann Dubinksy, age twenty-seven, hailing from the Chicago area. Moved here when she was eighteen, before the war. Became an elementary school teacher."

"You have a lot of elementary school teachers here?" Danny asked.

"No, no, it's actually quite unusual," Abrams said. "Saddest thing, actually. She was teaching up in Mill Valley, receiving very high marks, I'm told. There was an incident during a meeting with the parents of one of her students. She had asked for the meeting to discuss the possibility that the child's low marks might have been due to a learning disability."

"A what?" Anderson interjected.

Abrams shot the Marine a look. "A mental issue that keeps someone from understanding the information presented to them in an academic setting, Captain. A minor mental issue, but one we're now recognizing among students who might have simply been considered 'slow.' At any rate, she explained the matter to the parents, who were reportedly dismissive of the whole matter. They believed their boy was simply being lazy. Miss Dubinsky disagreed strenuously, and the meeting became confrontational. Then the father suddenly became violent. He attacked Miss Dubinksy as well as his child and stormed out of the meeting. From there, he acquired a knife from the cafeteria and took several school employees hostage in the main offices. He killed a janitor and a secretary before the police shot him dead."

"Jesus Christ . . ." Anderson muttered. "Was she seriously hurt?"

"She was knocked out before the father got the knife," Abrams replied. "A slight stroke of good luck, if you care to look at it that way. But Miss Dubinksy isn't a patient at Agnews because of any physical condition, as I'm sure you're aware. Following the attack, she became withdrawn and introverted. She apparently blames *herself* for the incident and began experiencing severe depression. Her condition deteriorated to the point where she eventually quit her job. I'm told she'd been living for two months on the streets of San Francisco, avoiding contact with all friends and family. The police picked her up on a loitering charge and soon determined that she would be best served if they brought her here."

"So, she went crazy after the shooting," Anderson said, shaking his head. "Understandable."

Abrams wheeled on Anderson, literally getting in front of him as he walked so that they both came to a halt. "Captain, please understand. We practice serious medicine at Agnews and do *not* use that terminology here," he said with what could be best described as polite urgency. "Nor do we use 'insane' or 'nuts' or anything else like that. We strive to maintain a positive environment. These people are patients, and they are being treated for an illness. I cannot have you using that kind of language around Miss Dubinsky or any other patient!"

Danny moved between the two men and held his hands up in mock surrender. "Our apologies, Doctor. We understand. I'm sure all the captain meant is that it would've been tough for anybody to go through that."

Abrams nodded curtly before turning and resuming his way at a quick pace, leaving the two officers rushing to keep up. "Most days, the patient is nearly catatonic. She bathes and dresses, she eats, she sleeps. The rest of the time, she seems to be just staring off into space. She'll answer our questions, depending on the day, but won't really engage in conversation beyond a few words. She avoids any gatherings of the patients, even though interaction with the other residents here at Agnews is something we actively encourage for anyone staying with us."

Danny thought about this a moment. "I bet it doesn't go well when she attends, does it."

Abrams shot him a look before answering. "This is a mental hospital, Commander, and yes, there are risks of incidents when even the most docile patients are placed together. For example, the man you saw just now has progressed significantly since when he first arrived. But just like us, our patients have bad days now and then. Their bad days are simply far more pronounced."

"Have you seen progress in Miss Dubinsky?" Danny asked.

"Progress is measured differently with each patient, Commander," Abrams began. "It's simply unreasonably to expect just because one our patient shows—"

"She's been here twelve weeks and there hasn't been a single indication that her condition is improving, has there, Doctor?" Danny pressed.

Abrams sighed. "We've tried many different therapies to bring her out of her fugue, from hydro to electric-shock to experimental drug treatments. I admit, we haven't had much success," Abrams said as he came to a stop before a secure wooden door in one of the smaller buildings. "These are the residences. Each patient has a small room of his or her own. Maggie isn't a danger to herself, so it will look familiar to you. Shall we?"

Danny nodded, and Abrams rapped on the door. "Maggie! It's Dr. Abrams. You have some guests here to see you. May we come in?"

There was no response, and Abrams produced the keys to the room. "It's unlikely we would have received a reply. Let's go in."

A few jingling keys and several deadbolts later, the three men entered the sunny room. And to Danny's surprise, Abrams was right—it looked more like a hotel room than an asylum or mental hospital or whatever they were calling it these days. There were a nicely made bed and pillow, along with matching dresser, desk, and chair. There were a small closet and a little bathroom, and the décor was California cheery, with lots of peach and mauve colors. A floral throw rug covered most of the tiled floor.

The woman inside, though, was far less welcoming.

Margaret Ann Dubinksy, in Danny's estimation, was on the plain side of pretty, with a broad, sort of flat face and blue eyes. That was probably unfair, though, given what she'd been through. She kept her blond hair straight and parted right down the middle, with very little effort put into it. No makeup, either, and whereas she might've qualified for "curvy" once, she was looking kind of wan and pale. Her cheeks were a little hollow, her eyes a little unfocused and tired. Her clothes were standard-issue white pajamas, though the closet seemed to be stocked with other, more colorful and ladylike options. She was sitting cross-legged on the bed, no shoes.

She didn't acknowledge her visitors whatsoever, just continued staring off into space while the radio at her bedside played some ballad or another.

"Creepy as hell," Anderson muttered, earning a whack on the arm from Danny and a glare from Abrams, who entered the room slowly and made his way to the girl's bedside.

"Maggie, these gentlemen came from the naval base up in Alameda to see you," Abrams said slowly and clearly. "Can you say hello to them?"

Maggie's head turned slowly in their direction, acknowledging their presence for the first time. Danny's eyes met hers, and he was shocked to find just how detached her gaze was. It was as though the girl saw right into his goddamn soul and found nothing there to remark upon.

"You can go ahead and ask questions if you like," Abrams said after a moment of silence. "Perhaps the new stimulus will be useful to her."

Danny and Anderson exchanged glances. Given that Danny outranked the Marine, and it was his idea to come out there in the first place, there was no question who would be providing the stimulus. Anderson extended his hand in the patient's direction, as if to say, "She's all yours, Commander," and retreated to the other side of the small room with Abrams. Danny took a quick breath and pulled up a chair next to the bed.

"Hello, Miss Dubinsky," he began, speaking quietly and leaning forward with his elbows on his knees. "My name's Dan Wallace. I'm with the Navy. Your case came to our attention through, uh, various channels we . . . keep a watch on."

Danny paused. Maggie simply continued staring forward, unmoving. Her breathing was so measured, she could've used it as a metronome. Danny had never really tried to talk to someone this unresponsive before.

"So, Miss Dubinsky," he continued, "I'd like to talk to you about what happened up in Mill Valley. You know, with that student's father. It seemed really . . . out of character. Can you perhaps tell me a bit about what happened?"

Still nothing. The woman's face was utterly blank, her eyes lacking any spark at all. There were photographs with more life in them than this woman, Danny thought as he leaned in closer to her. Time for plan B.

"I have a theory about what happened. I'd like to tell you about it," Danny whispered. "You see, people don't just up and go mad like that. OK, sure, a few do. But I read that father's file. He was a stand-up guy, real pillar of the community: banker, Methodist, Mason. They say he was a rock. Never so much as spanked the kids."

Maggie blinked a few times. Her breathing hitched momentarily.

Danny couldn't help but smile slightly, feeling as though he was getting somewhere, and an idea began to form in his head. "So, what makes a man angry as all that? Sure, nobody likes it when a teacher tells them they're all wrong as parents, but I don't think you did that. And I took a look at the paperwork you prepared for little Johnny there, about how he might've needed extra help because of . . . what's that word? Dyslexia? Some sort of reading thing. Never heard of it, but figure you're up on that sort of thing."

Danny heard Abrams clear his throat a bit. "I'm not sure, Lieutenant Wallace, how this is supposed to help Maggie," the doctor said, somehow sounding both apologetic and defensive in the same friendly-sounding breath.

"Not sure she needs help, Dr. Abrams. Do you, Maggie?" Danny replied, not taking his eyes off her as she began to shift slightly on the bed. "Your student there, Johnny, he just couldn't read very well. You knew he wasn't being lazy or anything—the boy couldn't help it. But maybe the parents didn't see it that way. Maybe they just ignored you, or maybe they thought you were trying to tell them their boy was sick, somehow, or crazy. Either way, they weren't going to do anything. So, what happened then? What made that father go off like that?"

A single tear trailed down Maggie's face. Her hands clenched. Her breathing grew quicker. And she screwed her eyes shut tight.

"I don't know what happened, and you do, Maggie," Danny said. "You can't hide here forever. If you can tell me what happened, maybe I can help you. Maybe together we can . . . oh . . . oh, God."

Danny stopped and clutched at his chest. His muscles suddenly felt like they were constricting, pulling taut, and there was a brief moment when he thought he was having a heart attack. His heart raced and his head swam and panic began to take hold. But there was something more, too—an emptiness inside him, blossoming from deep inside him, as if anything meaningful in his life was somehow wrenched away. Everything around him struck him as immensely sad, from the vase of flowers on the table that would wither and die in days, to his own once-strong hands now trembling before him like leaves. And this woman, Maggie, was the saddest thing of all, her eyes now full of tears that broke his heart over and over again with each drop.

Eyes that were now intensely focused on Danny. And not just full of life again . . . full of sadness. Longing. Fear.

There was a gasping sob behind him, and Danny turned to see Anderson doubled over, his arms wrapped around himself defensively, weeping. Next to him, Dr. Abrams had one hand on the wall, another over his eyes, and his cheeks were wet with tears as well.

Danny slowly turned back to Maggie. "This is what you wanted," she said quietly, tears running down her cheeks. "This is what happened. Is that what you came to see?"

Danny choked off a sob. "Oh, God, I'm so sorry. Yes, this is exactly what I came to see," he cried. "This is exactly what I wondered if you . . . you could do. *You're* doing this. And, oh God, this is how you feel about what happened, isn't it?"

Maggie's gaze was cold, even as more tears escaped her eyes. "This is *exactly* how I feel. Each and every goddamned day. Morning, noon, and night. That boy, that father, those other people—they're dead because of me."

Danny tried to stand but could only stagger backward. He knew, somewhere inside himself, that what he was feeling wasn't real. It was . . . manufactured. And with that came the sense of being separated from his body—that there was the real Danny, now more aware of his surroundings, and then there was the force that was puppeting him around, making him feel so incredibly, hopelessly bereft. He tried to focus past the sadness but simply wasn't strong enough yet to wrest control back from his own emotions. His chair got away from him and he fell on his ass onto the tiled floor. "Maggie, oh, Maggie . . . I'm sorry. So very, very sorry," he said through clenched teeth. "But I have to ask you now . . . please, I beg you, can you . . . can you rein this in? Can you please stop this?"

She looked at him and slowly shook her head, quickly wiping a tear from her face. "You think I can turn this on and off like a light switch? You think I enjoy what's happening right now?"

Danny got onto his knees and put his arms on the bed next to her, as if he were praying for some kind of divine intervention. His mind flashed from thoughts of his mother, his father, and the horror of war and everything that ever made him miserable to the promise that this intensely sad woman had within her. "Maggie, what if we can find out a way to help you? What if . . . What if we can teach you to control it?" he sobbed.

And then, suddenly, the vise on Danny's heart loosened. It didn't go away, but it definitely stopped squeezing so goddamn hard. He still felt sad, foreboding, lonely . . . but there was something else there. Just a thin sliver of hope, enough to begin staving off the darkness a little bit.

Maggie looked at him intently. "How do you plan to do that, sailor boy?" she asked, menace in her voice. "You didn't even know for sure until now what I could do. How are you gonna pull that off?"

Danny straightened up as best he could from his kneeling position before her, his self-control coming back in tiny bits and pieces that he desperately tried to reassemble. "I . . . I don't know. But I can at least give you some hope. I . . . I think I just did. Maybe that's something right there."

Maggie stared hard, but something in her eyes relented just a tiny bit, and Danny felt like he could finally take a breath without holding back a sob. But she wasn't done with him. "I know what I can do. This goddamn curse I have, I know what it can do to people. People *died* because of me. And you . . . you're from the Navy. And the Marine over there. What do you even know about any of this?"

Danny felt a new stirring inside him . . . anger. He could see where arguing with her could escalate quickly. Even as his sadness waned and his temper rose, he clamped down on everything and focused on his answer. "Right now, Maggie, I can't tell you. I don't know exactly what it is, because I don't know the extent of it yet. But right now, we're the only ones who believe you. The only ones who even have a *chance* of helping you. Please. Come with us."

Maggie regarded him for several long seconds, during which Danny's mind cycled through every emotion in the book. Anger . . . fear . . . and hope. How much of that was hers and how much was genuinely his, he couldn't say.

"Fine," she said finally. "Let's go."

Photo courtesy of Anna Martinez

ABOUT THE AUTHOR

Michael J. Martinez is the author of the Daedalus trilogy and other works of speculative fiction, including the forthcoming MJ-12 series from Night Shade Books. A former journalist for The Associated Press and other outlets, he now works in marketing and communications by day and, like a superhero, comes out at night to craft adventures. (OK, maybe not *exactly* like a superhero. No capes are involved.) He lives on the Jersey side of the New York City area with his wife and daughter. He can be found online at michaeljmartinez.net and on Twitter at @mikemartinez72. Mike is a proud member of the Science Fiction and Fantasy Writers of America.